THE VAMPIRESS

T.K. RICHARDS

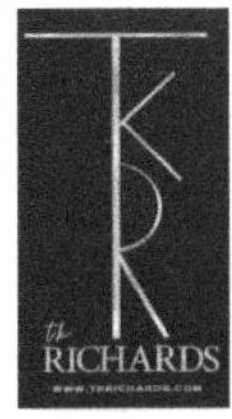
RICHARDS

ISBN: 978-1-959253-09-9
First printing, 2023 LNK Publishing
Copyright © 2023 by T.K. Richards
All rights reserved.
www.tkrichards.com

To Mia & Kiki & every other vampire girl
who draws blood when they are crossed.
This one's for you 🤍

NOTE FROM THE AUTHOR

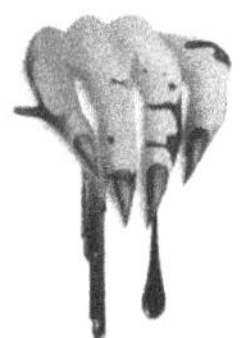

This novel contains mature themes and is intended for Mature Audiences. Warnings of violence, intended abuse, drugging, kidnapping, gore, heavy sexual content, witchcraft, magic, dark themes, and profanity.

Please note this book contains words and dialect from certain characters that DO NOT REFLECT traditional English, and are spelled to reflect how the characters speak.
For example: YOUR=YARE, THAT=DAT, YOU=YA, ME=MI

The only pain in pleasure is the pleasure of the pain.

ANNE RICE

CHAPTER 1

THE TURNING

VANITY

I COULDN'T FEEL my legs. Numb below the waist and hypnotized by the red in his eyes, fear immobilized my body to fight. I held my breath, terrified to exhale, horrified to move a muscle or open my mouth to scream. "You are quite the specimen." He paced back and forth with a proud stride and small steps. His hands unfolded, and he licked his lips. "There's something different about you. I sense it but can't put my finger on it. What are you?" His sharp, coffin-shaped nail pressed below my chin, and I trembled.

He reeked of whiskey sour, overpowering the foul odor of garbage in the bins. His eyes gleamed in the mirror of moonlight sneaking between the tiny gap of brick buildings behind the café where I worked. They danced looking into mine—redder than poinsettias, like a blood moon with flares around the iris. Sinister and evil.

I had survived this city on my own for two years and never encountered one of his kind. A pale one. Creatures the locals told tales of and oddly held in high regard. I considered myself lucky to never have crossed paths with such demons lurking in the night, plaguing this city. Especially since I worked the night shift cleaning hotel rooms to occupy my mind during restless nights to pay for the house I secretly bought. A place of my own. A place to finally call home. Then comes this asshole. A child of the night. A soul lost to the darkness.

The trembling from my chin traveled throughout my body. I shuddered in the face of what I wished had remained a myth, afraid of the way he peered at me and how fast he moved. From my left cheek to my right, he taunted me with quiet chuckles, blurring before my eyes like an image being fast forwarded on film.

My chest heaved, and I closed my eyes, thinking of how I never saw his feet lift from the ground when he rushed forward and attacked me. It happened so fast I thought maybe I blinked longer than normal, but after being closed in with his daring eyes gazing into mine, I realized my mind wasn't playing tricks on me. I was in the presence of danger.

"It's as if I can hear your muffled heartbeat. But then it stops. And not when you exhale. I don't know what or who you are, but I must have you. Speak your name, girl," he ordered.

"Vanity," I mumbled.

"Yes," he purred. "That name suits you. A perfect name for a perfect face. Beautiful topaz skin, sweet honey eyes, tight round ass, and long legs that don't beg, I'm sure." His laugh whirred low and deep. "Something told me I would strike gold tonight."

"Please. I beg you. Don't—"

"Shh." He placed his murderous nail to my lips. "I will have you. I am a king after all, and kings always get what they want. Tell me, Vanity, how does it feel capturing the attention of royalty?"

I kept silent, ignorant of how to answer what felt like a trick question. He chuckled villainously, then placed a strand of my locks against his nose, sniffing the mint scent of my shampoo blowing in the wind. I stood still in his grasp, sensing my death was near.

"Ah yes. There it is. The scent of mint leaves that drew you to me. I promise this won't take long. I already know I won't be able to contain myself."

His razor-blade teeth violently pierced my neck. I shook in his locked arms as he effortlessly fought to hold me against the bricks, grunting below my ears, and moaning of orgasmic delight. My fingers slipped on the back of his greasy, black hair. I tugged on the back of his collar, unable to pull away from the pain of his siphoning. I was outmaneuvered and no match for his power.

Weakened by his torture and lecherous bite, I submitted to his dominance. My eyes focused on the buzzing ivory light above the café door, and my arms fell limp to my sides. Flashes of the past two years flew below the light. My failure to hold a steady job, living in cheap motels until Cason, the owner of the café, took me under his wing and housed me in his spare room.

Cason, the handsome brute with the heart of gold was secretly in love with me. I pretended not to know for some time, but as blood from my neck was being sucked by a fucking vampire, a life with Cason soothed my final moments, nearly depleted. A life somewhere out of this grim city where I would finally act on the impulse of connecting biblically.

The thought of us together suddenly made sense as my life was ending. It would have been nice, giving him what he had given me over the past two years. Love.

The word was foreign to me. I had trouble expressing and understanding it as my heart was stone. It was an emotion buried somewhere deep inside my soul. A feeling I was sure existed every time Cason looked at me, but I couldn't bring myself to say it.

The images of rolling hills, Cason as my devoted husband, and a life beyond the bayou came to an end as the light above the café's back door began to fade, and my body was tossed atop a wet, rocky puddle.

Lifeless and depleted, I lay on the ground, watching my assailant gloat of his gluttonous victory through the crevice of my eyelids. He rid his fingers of my blood like a savory treat. Licking. Smacking. Relishing. His long tongue fully cleansed his hands, tasting the last trickle of my blood from the corner of his mouth with his eyes closed, then he placed his fingers to his nose and inhaled. The imprint of my flavor was filed in his memory as he adjusted his crooked necktie, then waltzed down the alley, cocky and carefree as if he hadn't just taken a life—my life—with a smile graced on his blood-stained lips, humming in a low, monotonous tone.

The buzzing light went silent, the stench of the trash disappeared, and the hardness of the rocks no longer hurt my face. Everything turned black.

"Ahuup!" I gasped, holding my chest.

Then there was light.

CHAPTER 2
THE AWAKENING

VANITY

THE RETURN of my sight was enhanced. Everything was luminous, as if stars fell from the sky to place a radiant glow around every object surrounding me. The horrendous odor from the trash was more repugnant than before. The smell stung my nose alongside a lemon-scented candle burning through the bricks from the lingerie store next door. I could smell the musky scent of rain moving in…and whiskey. The whiskey scent of my killer, begging me to follow him, perfumed a trail strongest of all.

The feeling in my legs returned with a tingling sensation in my feet. I was back alive. How unfortunate for the king who stole my last breath, strolling arrogantly in his steps, turning the corner out of the alley.

I sat up and stretched the crick out of my neck, cracked my knuckles in front of myself, and waved my hands loose. The two open wounds on my neck mended together, sending an itchy, prickling feeling throughout my body. Then I rose from the damp concrete, disgusted that my blouse was covered with muddy water and rock stains.

An anger birthed inside of me like I had never felt before. The thought of how that pale one uprooted my night and tossed me aside like I was nothing filled me with pure hatred.

As I shook the leg of my pants and cracked my back, my feet reacted on impulse. My thoughts rolled images in my head like film on a movie screen, controlling my movements reel by reel. I sped up the alley, stopping short before I reached the end of the passage. There, at the end of the lane, I studied my appearance in the faint reflection from the back window of the cigar shop.

How the hell did I do that? I thought, observing a lustrous haze on my skin.

The sweet smell of rose perfume and pungent oils traveled up my nose. I turned toward the scent, meeting eyes with a group of women standing outside of The Riviera Club.

Join them, then later enjoy them.

"The fuck was that?" I muttered, looking back at my reflection in the window.

You're right. Go after the king.

I shook my head, confused by the invasive thoughts speaking to me internally, as sudden urges of sex, a taste of blood and vengeance, and the smell of whiskey overpowered my will to focus on a single thought. I shot off like a cannon toward the scent driving me insane. The closer I succeeded in reaching the king, now hiding in the shadows, the more I noticed my surroundings had become enhanced. The pine in the trees, the staleness of the air, the minimal sound of a mosquito buzzing all heightened.

I stopped my sprint and paused in the vacant park, perplexed by where my target disappeared to, yet mesmerized at how loud the crickets chirruped, the bullfrogs trilled, and the bats sucked the nectar from the surrounding flowers in the square.

The scent of whiskey grew close. Then closer. I turned around and caught the king charging me by his throat and lifted him in the air.

His eyes bulged in disbelief as he croaked, "I…killed…you."

The sides of my mouth curved, and my hungry eyes narrowed as they stared into his. "Wrong," I laughed. "You thought you killed me."

"But…but…how…is this…possible?"

"You're asking the wrong question. And you call yourself a king." I grinned at his lean, medium frame struggling midair. "Speak your name." I tightened my grip around his throat.

"Carlisle."

"Tell me, Carlisle. Why should I let you keep your pathetic life?" I loosened my fingers to hear him clearly.

"You can't kill me. It is forbidden." He coughed and adjusted his blazer and tie.

"Forbidden by whom?"

"The Bayou Bind. The laws of The Bayou Bind state we shall not kill our own kind. Death of a pale one results in death of self." He smirked.

"And if I were to kill you right now, who would be the one to avenge your death?"

"That would be Rue. The queen."

A wicked laugh flowed from my lips as I turned the tables on him, making him my prey. I circled him with slow steps, then seized him swiftly, clenching his throat tight and firm. His legs swung, and his eyes bulged, forcing me to snicker sinisterly at his failed attempt to escape my attack.

I glared into his blood-colored orbs. "You can't outrun me. I'm faster, and stronger, and smarter than you. A pretentious king. How pathetic. Did this Rue bitch give you the title of king?"

"Yes." He strained.

"Then fuck the queen." I sneered, firmly squeezing his neck to where his slowed heart barely thumped.

The aroma of lilies and vanilla fast approached from the east. The shrilling of the insects silenced, and the wind settled as if I were controlling its direction. *Whoosh.* The scent circled me. *Whoosh.* The figure blurred closer to my face, orbiting around me like a typhoon.

I timed the rhythm of the mysterious presence and studied the pattern of its movements. It zigzagged, circled, then grew cocky, repeating its steps a second, then third time. *YOINK.* I snatched it by the neck.

"Who do we have here?" I grinned, holding her up next to Carlisle. "Of course you'd summon a woman to rescue you." I squeezed my grip around his neck tighter and dug my nails into his blood-filled throat.

Their alabaster skin would have been pink by now, then blue if they weren't already children of the dead.

"Argh," the woman groaned, fidgeting in my other hand. "Who the fuck is this bitch?" she grunted through her teeth.

Carlisle looked at her with disdain. "Just don't piss her off." He gasped.

Villainously, I laughed. "Feisty, this one. What's your name, girl?"

"Remove your hand, and maybe I'll tell you," she mumbled.

Her spirit humored me. She fought as she dangled from my fingers like drapes, while her paramour begged for mercy. My mercy.

"I took a risk coming to your aid at this hour, Carlisle. Do something." She struggled with panic.

"I already tried." He wiggled like a fish out of water.

"How is she stronger than a goddamn king?"

"We'll figure that out later, Billie. The sun's coming up soon."

I grinned and loosened my grip on my second assailant. "Billie, is it? Tell me. How loyal are you?" She cleared her throat. "Right. You thought you were coming to free this weak imbecile. Let's you and I make a deal. You settle down and watch me kill your king, then take me to this queen he speaks of. In exchange, I'll spare your life."

Struggling to free herself, she nodded. I released her from my clutch and threw her against the big oak tree. At my command, the bats sucking the nectar from the nearby roses swarmed around us in a tightknit cyclone. Billie and Carlisle shared a look of panic as she wiped away blood dripping from her eyes.

"Hurry up and get it over with. I'd rather die quickly from wood in my chest, than from the heat of the sun," Carlisle groaned.

"Look at you, still giving orders as if you're in charge." I scoffed.

I stretched my arm behind me with my eyes set on his dead heart. Billie cried out, "No!" interrupting my strike to pull his insides out of him as a metaphor for what he'd done to me moments before. I placed my arm back to my side and studied the care in Billie's eyes. She may have been soulless, but she loved her maker—maybe even in love with him.

She charged me a second time, and the bats flew faster around us. I smacked her with one hand into the tornadic barrier of flying mammals serving me with a perimeter. Carlisle cheated death as my eyes shifted to Billie sneak-attacking me from behind. He kicked his way to freedom and fled through the barrier, leaving his protégé to deal with my wrath alone.

Billie felt the back of my right hand greet her cheek. She fell to the ground for a swift second, using her supernatural speed to lunge forward and scratch my face.

"That better not leave a mark," I warned.

She grinned, proud to have landed at least one successful blow to my dominance, then raised her fists and posed in her fight stance, ready for more action. Her eyes suddenly grew wide, and she dropped her guard. Standing tall and unprotected, she gawked at me in awe.

"The fuck," she muttered.

The scratch on my face glowed yellow and bright as it healed. "Who and what are you?" she asked, searching within the bat barricade for Carlisle.

I exhaled a deep breath. "Call me Vanity, your new ruler if you survive tonight."

"Who made you?"

"That would be the fleeing man who left you to clean up his mess. Typical, don't you think? Men like him have a sense of entitlement. Going around and doing as they please without repercussions. Unfortunately for him, I'm the ramification he didn't see coming."

Billie relaxed her tightly clenched fists and gracefully straightened her shoulders. "I can't believe he left me here to die when I risked my life to save him."

I waved my hands, and the bats flocked back into the trees. The denim sky lightened to a shade above navy. The nervousness in Billie's eyes humored me, while her floral scent became drowned out by the loud smell of her fear of the sun.

"We're both going to die if we don't get inside," she said.

"Speak for yourself." I grinned. "I will set you free, but know this, you now work for me. I want the inside information of everything that weasel, and this queen he speaks of, has planned. You'll find me at Cason's Café when the sun goes down."

She nodded and placed one step in front of the other.

"P.S.... If you choose to kill Carlisle before I do, plan it carefully. As a scorned woman, I'm sure you've thought about it."

Billie scurried off in the same direction as Carlisle.

I slowly strolled out of the park as the sun crept above the side of Cason's building. Unafraid. Unharmed. Unburnt. In search of the rose perfume still calling out to my lips.

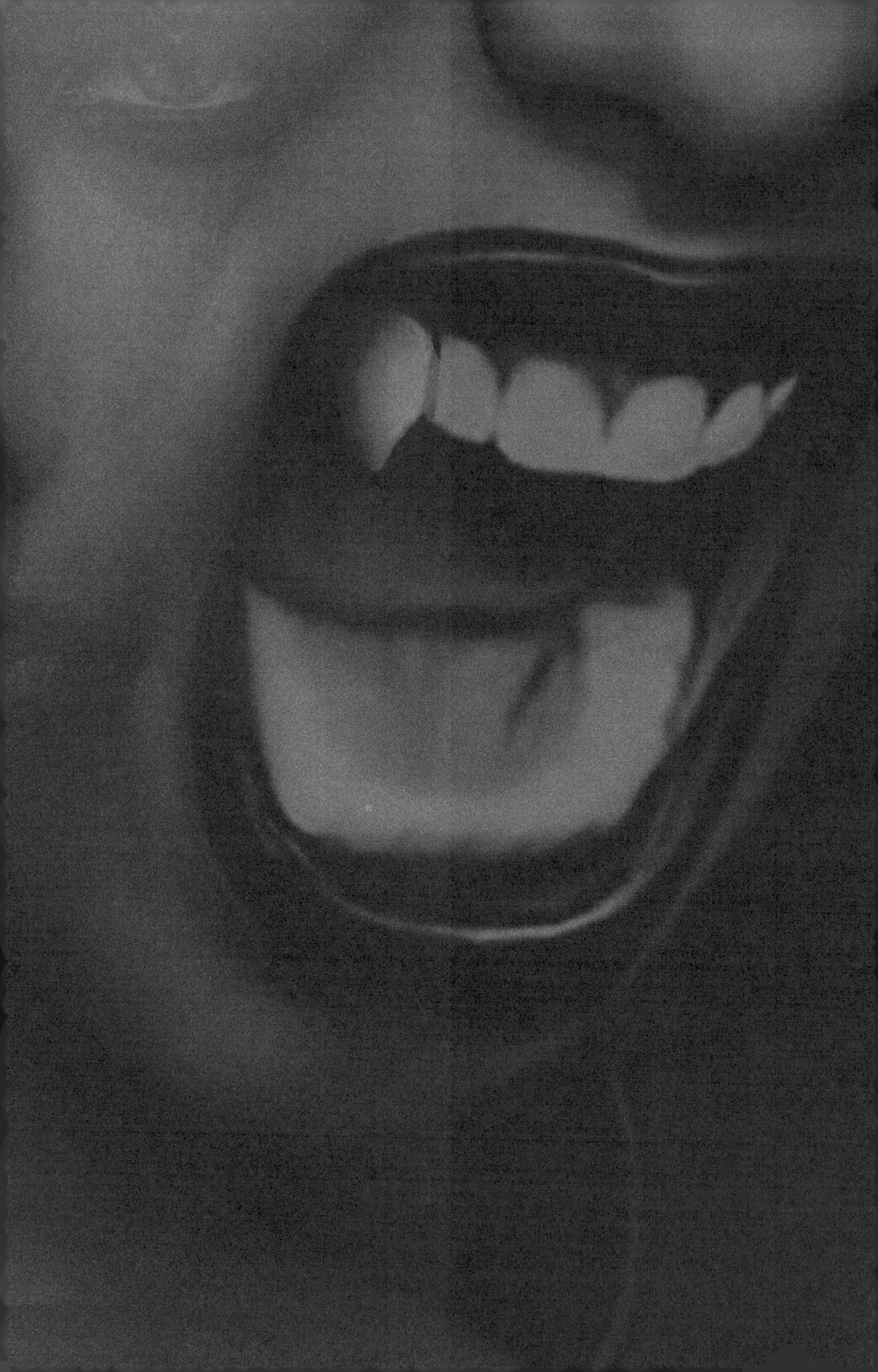

CHAPTER 3
THE KING
CARLISLE

"QUEEN ADELA RUE requests your presence." Boris, her right hand announced outside my door.

I tossed my jacket into the back of my closet and changed my shirt and tie, then hurried to her side.

New servants of freshly turned bloodsuckers, guarded the windows in front of velvet red shades eclipsing the light of the sun. Boris stood beside Rue's golden throne with his hands folded and eyes to the floor.

"Where have you been?" Rue asked.

"Forgive me, my love. A late-night stroll in the VC led to an eventful evening, but here I am, at your beckon call. May I approach and sit with you this lovely morning?"

"You may not. My ears burned with your name as I was about to turn in for the day. What chaos have you created without my permission this time?" Her copper eyes glowed as she glared at me.

"Nothing to worry you, my dear. I'll have it sorted out by nightfall. I assure you, my love."

"Don't!" She slammed her scepter into the ground. "Now look what you've done! Have the blacksmith create a bigger and better one. I expect you to have it when I wake this evening. And sleep in your own chambers."

I nodded and excused myself to the southern wing of her majesty's castle and summoned one of the human servants to tackle Rue's demand.

"Tell the blacksmith the queen needs a staff one hour before the sun rises. Your life depends on it." I flashed my fangs, and he ran off.

As I closed the door, Billie's hand crept between the crack and pushed it open. I dashed forward and choked her against the stone wall. She kneed me in the groin and reversed our position.

"I've had quite enough of being manhandled by the hands of women these past few hours," I said.

"Fuck you very much. I came to help you, and you left me behind to die with that creature," Billie grunted. "How could you do that to me?"

"I had no choice. The sun was coming up." I pushed her off me.

She slid across the room and hissed at me.

"I knew you would escape. That bitch's quarrel was with me. Not you. And here you are." I smiled.

"I ought to tell the queen about the mess you've created. She'll have your head."

"You know I don't take threats lightly, especially from subordinates. I'm your maker. Your allegiance is to me."

"My allegiance is to the queen. Or have you forgotten she only gave you the name king to sit at her side. You have no power." Billie chuckled.

She of all people knew I hated being laughed at. I lunged forward and smacked her giggling mouth with a backhand, then cross-smacked her again with my palm.

She fell to the floor and looked up at me with vengeful eyes. Holding her lip, she said, "You will pay for that."

"By whom? The likes of you?" I scoffed. "Leave my quarters and sleep off your rage. Meet me in the garden when the sun sets."

"Why should I, after what you've done? Maker or not, I'm done taking orders from you." She rose from the floor.

"Billie. Sunset. Get word to Madame Cecil that we'll be paying her a visit tonight. Make sure she clears her schedule. And ugh, lock the door behind you." I clapped my hands twice.

Once Billie left, I gathered the soiled clothing from the back of the closet and inhaled Vanity's scent, intoxicating me into a frenzy, then placed them in a duffel bag.`

"You could possibly be my greatest mistake to date," I whispered, sneering to myself as a smile riddled my lips from the memory of her taste, and the essence of her blood stained into my hands lingered in the air. "Mmm," I moaned. "But the taste of your blood was worth it."

CHAPTER 4
THE MADAME

CARLISLE

THE RUSH of blood pumping through the veins of the servant shivering with Adela's staff in his hand made my mouth water considerably. I fed from his neck for breakfast and tossed him from my room—with just enough life left in him to crawl back to his quarters.

I placed the newly designed gold scepter with a red ruby in the center of the handle at the base of her bedroom as the sun fell west of the city. Once it turned red and traveled its nightly path, I waltzed into the garden, disappointed Billie wasn't there waiting for me.

The last quarter moon was on the rise, and my impatience of her tardiness turned me violent. *I will teach her a lesson for disobeying me.*

Upon my exit out of the Garden District, I carried the bag filled with Vanity's scent against my back. Billie appeared at my side out of nowhere, pouting no less.

"Nice of you to join me." I scowled.

The stomping of her footsteps spoke the contempt she felt for me without words. "You know the silent treatment is the best gift a woman can give a man." I smirked.

"Well, when I meet one, I'll give it to him," she said.

"And why were you late?"

"Who said I was?" She grinned.

"Did you make the arrangements with Madame Cecil?"

"Would it matter if I did or didn't?"

"A question answered with a question. You're still angry with me."

Billie turned up her nose and resumed her silent treatment until we arrived in Vieux Carre. Madame Cecil's glass door was wide open with one patron at the counter, and Madame Cecil herself was absent.

The patron took a good look at me and Billie, then left the shoppe in a hurry. The Madame herself entered the room through colorful jangling beads from a door behind the counter. She looked around for her customer, then exhaled deeply at the sight of us.

"You *gonna* pay for *scarin' me* customer off?" she asked.

I grinned at her sharp tongue, reached into my wallet, then threw a fifty-dollar bill on the counter. She picked it up and held it above her head, then studied it against the dim light.

"I don't have all night, Madame, but I'm sure you knew I was coming."

She scoffed. "I saw darkness in *me* dream. What bring *ya* here?"

I threw the bag on her wooden table in the corner and gestured for her to sit. She grabbed a statue of Jesus from the counter and a bottle labeled holy water from the rack on the wall behind her.

"Close me door," she said, pointing to Billie.

The brass shopkeeper's bell hanging above the door rang as Madame and I faced each other, waiting for the weakest link to blink.

"You're enjoying this, aren't you?" I chuckled.

"For sure. You need something from me, so I *don't needn't* fear your curse of coercion." She smiled.

After our *glare-off*, I unzipped the bag and slid the shirt and tie between us. She held the pieces in her hands and spoke without looking me in the eyes.

"Speak what it is you seek," she ordered with her eyes closed.

"A new kind of vamp drew my blood on these garments. Some of it may not belong to me. What can you tell me about it?"

Madame opened her eyes. "It?"

"You heard correctly." I reclined in my seat.

A low chant repeated from her lips as her hands hovered and formed orchestrated circles over the shirt and tie. "Pour dénicher la vérité." She inhaled a deep breath and closed her eyes once more.

Continuing with the chant, her eyes roamed beneath her lids. "The it is a woman—was a woman. She was happy long time ago. Indifferent to happiness in her most recent life. I see three births, one very recent, tears of water then blood, and now darkness. She holds great power and is close," Madame stuttered. "I feel her eyes upon us."

Madame Cecil opened her eyes and stared past me and Billie. I turned around, and there was Vanity, standing in the window, smugly smiling at us, leaving a blurred trail where she stood.

"Go after her!"

CHAPTER 5

THE RUSE

CARLISLE

I RACED through the glass door and stood at the edge of the entrance of Madame's shoppe, searching for a dark-blue shirt and Vanity's locks. She disappeared into the crowd of drunken townspeople and visitors flooding the street to celebrate age-old tales to fulfill their pathetic lives.

Billie paced behind me while I cleared our path through the horde, containing my thirst as I weaved my way around the pushing and shoving of clueless peasants begging to be tasted.

"To your left," Billie whispered.

My neck snapped as I scanned the scene. Easily, I spotted Vanity standing on the balcony of a saloon, illuminating in the strobe light flashing from across the street. She saluted me with two fingers from her temple and grinned, then backed into the loud, packed club filled with innocents I planned to later feast upon and ravish.

She's toying with me. How cute. And bold.

I didn't fall for her bait. I waited for her outside on the street. The chatter from a group of drunks passing by amused me with talk of how *they* thought they saw vampires inside the party.

I chuckled to myself, knowing Vanity amateurly revealed her identity to the patrons for show, not suspecting her actions would lead me straight to her whereabouts.

Pretty bitch can't help but be seen and watch others marvel at her beauty.

One of the clubbers lit a cigarette and said, "I was on my way over to ask her for a dance, but she disappeared in the blink of an eye. *Poof.* She was gone."

Hearing those words grabbed my attention. I tapped Billie on her shoulder. "Do you see anything?"

"Nothing." She breathed out. "I think we lost her."

"Impossible," I muttered.

"FWEET!"

I looked up to where the whistle came from, atop the stone building parallel to the strobe light. Vanity had slipped past me in a stolen black hooded jacket—a scent not on my radar.

"That bitch," I grunted.

I seethed at her trickery on the outside but secretly enjoyed the cat-and-mouse game she was playing on the inside. In all her marvelousness, she threw me an air kiss and dashed into the night.

The street was jammed to capacity, the music too loud to hear the direction of her footsteps. "Fuck!" I kicked a hole into the souvenir stand on the curb.

"Let her have this one," Billie said, lusting at a woman in cut-off denim shorts and a tank top exposing her meaty cleavage.

"I don't have time to let her have this one. You walk east. Call me when you have something."

Billie placed her tongue back in her mouth and fetched our subject while I returned to Madame Cecil's. She stood in the window of her practice, waiting for me, I presumed. I made my way inside her shoppe and loosened my tie.

"What's your final analysis, Madame?"

"Not good for you from what I saw, Monsieur. I saw a battle of blood, red filling the streets, and the packs of the forest no longer hiding in the bayou. Sides will be chosen. *Ya're* not in alliance with the winning side. But *ya're* responsible for what is to come. Ya must choose wisely." Her voice lingered on the last of her spiel.

"I don't suppose you'll tell me the side I need to choose."

"Free will, Monsieur. I only tell ya what I see."

The vibration from my phone tore my focus from Madame's eyes. "Yeah, Billie," I answered.

"I found the jacket on the fence behind the building. She's long gone if you ask me."

"I'll meet you back on our side." I slammed my phone on the table, then stared back into Madame's eyes. "If you have any visions, you know how to reach me," I said, then headed back to the alley where it all began.

It's time I learn more about this café owner Cason.

CHAPTER 6

THE DIFFERENCE

VANITY

I FOUND the taste of human blood disgusting, but other desires intensified. That streetwalker smelled of roses, but the way her flesh and blood stung my tongue saved her from death.

She escaped as I hurled into the garbage behind Cason's Cafe.

How can these pale creatures crave such a thing, I wondered as I held myself up against the bricks.

Becoming a bloodsucker turned out to be quite the opposite for me. My thirst for nourishment grew stronger by the minute, but the blood of human beings did not excite me. I found my way outside the city limits. Down in the bayou, I roamed and feasted on the sweet-smelling flesh and blood of beavers and cowbirds, leaving a trail of them a mile long until I was satisfied.

When I reached my fill, I wiped the residue from my mouth and breathed in the foul smell of the wetlands. The swamp was filled with cypress trees to offset the stench of decay in the air. Fitting for the change of life transforming inside of me.

A sexual yearning burned inside me once I completed my first feast, and after a night of scourging battle, sex was the perfect way to end my morning.

My attempt to sneak into the house failed. Cason opened his bedroom door when I twisted the knob to my bedroom. Bare-chested and freshly showered, the wild man smelled of cologne-scented soap, cuffed to perfection in navy-blue boxer briefs.

"I've been worried about you all night," he angrily chastised me. "No one saw you come back inside after you took out the garbage last night. I told you to let one of the guys do it. Did you know you dropped your phone between the bins?"

"I didn't know I lost it."

He reached behind himself, then handed it to me. "Was there a party in the bayou last night? You smell like outside." He grimaced.

My eyes struggled to remain above his chest. In my mind, his golden, smooth pecs begged to be licked. A shadow covered half of his beautiful face from long strands of his hair hanging to the side. I watched his full lips as he lectured me, picturing them sucking on my nipples, then my eyes drifted toward the morning wood shying away inside his boxer briefs.

"Something like that," I answered softly. "Do you mind if I hop in the shower and meet you up front for some of your famous buttermilk pancakes?"

A smile replaced the stern look on his face. "Sure. When have I ever said no to you?"

I removed the stench of the marsh from my locks and my body, then followed the smell of buttery syrup and vanilla to the kitchen, wearing an old t-shirt with a hem that stopped mid-thigh. Cason greeted me with another smile. *How should I initiate this?* I questioned myself, staring at his adorable man bun from behind.

He flipped three pancakes on the cast-iron pan, then layered them on his white porcelain plates with the grooved ridges on the edge. As he delicately tapped powder sugar on top of my favorite breakfast I no longer craved, I took one of the strawberries he had sliced in a bowl and placed it in his mouth.

He held onto my finger between his lips as he chewed, then turned to face me with innocent eyes. I placed my lips on his and gave him what he had been wanting for over a year.

"Is this really happening?" he asked.

I took his hand and placed it against my cold, bare ass. His eyes enlarged once he felt the softness of my skin.

"Tell me you have a thong on under there," he whispered.

I shook my head side to side and fervently kissed him again, hearing the blood rush throughout his body and his heartbeat increase.

Cason cradled my face with his hands. His almond eyes gazed into mine. I shied away from the moment when a glitch startled me as I returned his gaze.

Careful not to coerce him. He's been waiting for this. Let's see what I've been missing out on.

The most delicate of kisses lasted seconds before he lifted me onto the soapstone counter. The passion he had been holding back consumed him as he took charge and violently removed my t-shirt. My breasts filled his mouth, better than I had imagined moments earlier.

I moaned of overdue attention to my erogenous zones. It had been years since I felt the touch of a man's hands against my body, and Cason was the perfect choice to end the drought.

The cut on his thumb was rough, sweeping against my hips. The tender caress of his wet tongue brushing up and down my neck ignited my burning heart.

"Take me now," I sighed.

Cason ran his fingers through my hair and rolled my neck around, sending me into a frenzy. I spread my thighs and gripped his shaft with the tips of my fingers. He shook in my embrace and inhaled a deep breath. I slid farther to the edge and rolled his tip around my entrance. He punched inside with the force of a storm hitting the coast—my coast, dripping for him the moment he stretched my abandoned cave.

"Oh yeah," he exhaled. "I knew this pussy was fire."

He has no idea how much.

"It's been so long. Fuck me like a savage," I crooned.

Cason placed his wrists under my thighs and held onto them with a tight grip. Back and forth, he led my pussy to cream on his long, stiff wood, grunting with profound bass in his voice. I held myself up with one hand on the counter and the other around his neck.

"Thank God you came home," he said, then bit his lip.

I looked away and buried my head into his chest. *Don't let him see the difference in me,* I thought. Better to hide the way my eyes constantly turned red from the passionate heat between us, and my fangs wanting to taste him to see if his blood would suffice when I'd need to feed.

Instead, I watched how he orchestrated his moves to please me. Powerful strokes and rolling thrusts to experience every inch of my palace. I grinned to myself when he pulled it all the way out to demonstrate control. His head wobbled of rejection, ready to return to my warmth.

Cason arched his back and slipped my thighs down to the fold of his elbows, my torso leaned back, my shoulders gripped by his fingertips. He dug farther inside, pulling my hair until the top of my head touched the counter. My yonni vibrated and exerted from the applied pressure of his cock knocking around where it pleased.

He called out my name, "Vanity," choppy and weak, then let loose in my juice. I lost sound when I came, hearing nothing but my own slowed heartbeat.

As my orgasm began to settle, sound returned to me slowly. The pounding of his chest pressed against mine while the winded spaces of his breathing warmed the side of my face.

"Please tell me we're going to do that again." He sighed.

"I promise we will as soon as you get home from work."

Kind and soft kisses traveled down my cheekbones to my lips. Cason held me securely in his arms, lifting me from the counter. Our eyes met, and he grinned.

"If I wasn't the boss, I'd call in."

"A double play does sound nice." I nibbled on his lobes, then tugged on fallen loose strands of his hair with my lips.

He grunted. "Vanity, you're making me think irresponsibly."

I giggled. "That's what'll be waiting for you." I traced his head with my fingers. "And there's something you need to know."

CHAPTER 7

THE CHANGE

VANITY

I STOOD in the mirror and examined my reflection closely. There was no scar where I had been bitten, nor on my face where Billie slashed me. But an enhanced version of myself smiled back at me with a certain confidence that somehow felt familiar. No longer was I the meager girl who kept her head down in search of herself.

I laid low until the sun went down, processing the change within. Feeling like my name, I threw on a pair of tight black pants and popped the tag on a revealing blue top hanging in my closet. My locks flowed freely, and my red lips commanded attention as I walked over to the café.

Cason smiled at me with his eyes, then looked away with rosy cheeks and a grin on the side of his mouth.

Oh boy. He's even more in love with me now. It's so cute how my simple existence makes him blush.

Pretending not to notice, I eyed the patrons inside. Auras of glittery dust appeared around some of the customers. Gold for some. Lavender for others. I studied them without staring, landing eyes on Billie sitting at the bar, dust free, with a dark aura surrounding her.

I went behind the counter and wrapped my apron around my waist. Retrieving my pen and pad from the side pocket, I leaned down across from her. "You kill him?" I asked, clicking the pen.

"I tried." She sighed.

"Don't sweat it. You'll get him next time—if I don't."

"I got here as soon as I could. Carlisle should be waiting for me back at the grounds." She checked the time on her phone.

"What's he up to?" I pretended to write on the pad.

"Madame Cecil's Shoppe in thirty minutes." Billie tapped on the bar. "I gotta go."

She threw a twenty-dollar bill on the counter and raised her brows. I watched her exit the café like a normal person, then dash off down the street in the blink of an eye.

I turned my head toward the other end of the counter. There stood Cason, staring at me with the usual adoration, modestly blushing from the hint of lust in his eyes. I lured him over with a smile. He wiped his hands on his pants, then cornered me near the beer tap.

"You have friends now?" He grinned and narrowed his eyes.

"Something like that." I looked away and avoided his gaze. "I have a lot to tell you tonight. Who's on the schedule to close?"

"It was just me, but that could change to us."

I inhaled the smell of dough and malt mixed with his natural scent as the door opened and welcomed a breeze inside. My mouth watered as the image of us having a quickie in his office played in my head.

"I'll tell you everything once we have this place to ourselves." I exhaled. "I was going to ask if it'd be okay for me to step out real quick. Think you can manage the bar without me for a few?" I batted my eyes and sank my teeth into my bottom lip.

Save it for later.

"Anything for you, V." He licked his lips and backed away.

Twenty minutes later, I blended in with the crowd of painted faces on the corner of Madame Cecil's Shoppe. As Billie stated, there she was, alongside Carlisle, walking into the shoppe with a bag swinging free on one of his shoulders.

What's with the backpack? I wondered.

Still learning how to control everything new to me: heightened senses, heavy sexual urges, thirst for beaver blood, visuals of glittery dust around beings, and hearing distant chats that had nothing to do with me, I practiced how to focus on one conversation.

Once Billie closed the door to the shoppe, I eased across the street and listened in on their exchange. The fury raging inside Carlisle excited me, but the puzzling reading Madame gave weighed heavy on my mind.

What did she mean by 'three births'?

Suddenly, I felt a connection between her and me. The hairs on my arm raised, and I approached the window. Her eyes opened, and I was made. Carlisle and Billie turned around with concern, and I waved to my chauvinistic maker and fled the scene.

Toying with his pride and arrogance, time got away from me as I led him on a goose chase, but I remained persistent to watch his every move until Billie and I met up in the alley where he last saw me.

"Take this jacket with you. Tell Carlisle you found it. Let's meet here again tomorrow night," I said, then left her behind to follow his scent.

Carlisle returned to Madame's and left in a haste shortly after Billie called him. I observed the disappointment in his body language. His slumped shoulders exited the shoppe, but seconds later, the cockiness in him returned as he strolled down the street as if he hadn't been defeated.

I entered Madame's and locked the door to the entrance. "We're closed!" she shouted from behind a beaded door. I tapped my foot against the *ungrooved* concrete floor. She rattled her way through the beads and huffed at the sight of me. "You. I knew ya would come to see me. Didn't think it'd be so soon."

I smirked. "I have several questions, and I believe you have the answers. Shall we begin?"

CHAPTER 8
THE READ

VANITY

MADAME CECIL WAS tough mentally and emotionally. Her fearless, stoned face and statuesque figure suited her well for her line of business. She took her time walking from behind the counter and sat with her legs crossed and arms folded at the wooden table she performed her readings.

"And where would ya like to start? *Femme de trois vies.*"

I smiled at her devilishly and sat back in the chair across from her. She smirked at me, then uncrossed her legs and unfolded her arms, placing them in front of her.

"I like you. You don't scare easily," I noted.

Madame lifted her hands and said, "Living here, I *done seen* it all. Until you. *Femme de trois vies.*"

"Then let's start there. I don't speak French. What did you just call me?"

"*Femme de trois vies* – three life woman." She pointed toward me.

"You said something similar to Carlisle. What does it mean?"

"Give me your hand."

I leaned forward and placed my palms against hers. She gently squeezed my hands, then tightened her grip and closed her eyes. The skin on her lids wrinkled, and her eyes rolled beneath.

"*Ya* have three births. I see *ya* born as a baby to a *mudda,* no *fadda.* Then a second birth on a roadside, here in the outskirts of the bayou." She jumped.

33

"What is it?"

She opened her eyes and let go of my hand. "The third birth, the most recent one. So violent. I see what he did to ya. I understand *ya hate fa* him."

As Madame's eyes stared at me with sorrow, I pulled away and zeroed in on the conversation of the couple walking past her shoppe. "Focus," I whispered aloud to myself.

"I beg your pardon?"

I met eyes with her once more and asked, "What do you know of this second birth on the roadside?"

"Deadly car accident," she blurted.

"Was I alone?"

"No. A man was there. He made a deal with a powerful priestess to bring ya back to life. But there was a cost." She raised her brows.

I was very aware of the cost. For the past two years, I was a bartender and a waitress, cleaning up after ungrateful people's shit at a hotel on the weekend.

Quit that job immediately.

The inn was the only place that would hire me without any identification as a favor to the homeless shelter I found myself in after I was released from the hospital. The nurses told me I was in an accident, but I had no recollection of it or who I was. Desperate to remember anything that was real about myself, I stared in the mirror all day and night during my hospitalization, so the staff called me Vanity. And the name stuck.

As I sat and revisited what I remembered about the past twenty-four months, I felt Madame intruding on my thoughts.

"I tried to leave this city. Several times, actually. And each time, something surreal happened. I assume that is the cost you're speaking of?"

"Yes. Ya're bound to the bayou. It was the deal the priestess made for your life. She was trapped here and gave *ya* your life back so she could take it for herself. If you can remember who ya once were, you'll find the one who cursed you to this city. Except…"

"Except I can't leave this place."

Madame Cecil nodded. "A trickster, that one. Must have been in some real trouble here."

I huffed at the news Madame shared with me and looked around her place. My finger rotated as I pointed around the room.

"Can any of this stuff be used to find my true identity?" I asked the omniscient one.

"Come back and see me in a few days. I'll have an answer for ya then, but it won't matter. When your nemesis turned ya, he rebirthed ya for the third time. The power of three flows throughout your body. I've seen many a creature in these here parts, but a cursed one such as yourself has never become one of them. Until now. You, my dear, are an anomaly."

I nodded, vaguely remembering the rule of the power of three. The look in her eyes set in my bones and made me feel like I held some sort of destined responsibility on my shoulders.

"Now tell me what that pale-face asshole knows and what I should know about this queen he adores they call Rue."

"Her name is Adela Rue—undefeated queen of the bayou's under-world. Many have tried and failed to dethrone her. Her mansion and her army reside in the Garden District," Madame shared.

"Should I be afraid?" I asked, picking a piece of lint from beneath my fingernail.

She smiled. "Why ask such a question when *ya'ren't?*"

She was correct. I hadn't felt fear since I was at Carlisle's mercy last night. I rose to my feet. "I'll be in touch," I said and smirked at her on the way out.

One block away from Cason's, I could smell Carlisle's musky ass nearby. My senses heightened on alert, waiting for a sneak attack. My steps increased, and his scent became unrelenting to my nose.

The drowned sound of a band playing within a mile interfered with my ability to zone into conversations close by. The trumpet's solo struck a chord in me, sounding like the anticipating soundtrack to a battle—and for good reason—as I spotted Carlisle standing across the street amongst tourists surveying the café.

I hung back and waited for a group to walk with, heading toward his position. His eyes flickered between red and black when he blinked, forcing the violence within me to rise. The group standing near him had no idea they were in the company of a selfish demon plotting on the inno-cent where they stood.

I trailed behind a pack of smelly college boys, reeking of beer and sex, then eased my way behind Carlisle and his posers.

It's time I kill this bastard.

CHAPTER 9

THE AUDACITY
CARLISLE

"WHAT ARE YOU, a vampire with a death wish?" her voice whispered in my ear.

"I come in peace," I said.

"Imagine that. A demon that doesn't lie." She chuckled. "Let's take a walk, shall we?"

Her rage-filled emotions flowed heavy in her tone, her words sharp and short, her chuckle villainous.

I did as she instructed and walked slowly away from the busy street. Vanity matched my pace, steady on my heels, with her eyes burning into the back of my head. The stomping of her boots reminded me of the marching bands in the HBCU competitions. One two, one two, her heels clanked on the pavement until I led her into a deserted parking lot.

"Can we talk here? It's pretty secluded," I said, turning to face her.

My head hit the old bricks, and my face imprinted between the dull, ashen cracks. Vanity's nails dug into my cranium. She squeezed until the pressure of the pain shot back toward her skinny fingers.

"Is that how you picked me last night?" she asked.

I swallowed big. "May I turn around and state my case?"

"You'll do as I say, when I say. Now answer my fucking question, you prick."

"I'm a vampire. I act on impulse. You surely feel the urge to do as you please," I snarked.

The blinking light from an abandoned lamp post dimmed and brightened, buzzing before it blew completely. Vanity lifted my face from the bricks, then slammed it back against them—harder this time. The sharp point of the heel on her boot cut my back while she pressed it vigorously through my blazer.

"You're ruining a very important designer. I can see your sudden appreciation for fashion by the name of your boots," I teased to ease her hold of me.

Vanity's grasp of my hair softened, then the pressure of her boot released me from the bricks. I turned around. *Wham!* Her fist landed on my mouth. I touched the bottom of my lip and traced the cut with my finger.

"I promise you, I want no trouble. I came looking for you to call a truce. I cannot defeat you, and as a diplomat for my queen's court, I ask to end this row."

She watched the cut heal from my mouth and reopened the wound, striking me with an open hand.

"Truce? We've only been at it for twenty-four hours, and you're alive because you sacrificed your friend. When should I expect her to jump me from behind?"

"I came to see you alone." My voice elevated.

"To apologize?" she assumed.

"Vampires don't apologize. I may have taken your former life from you and discarded you like nothing, but I did say how exquisite I found you. And this look you have going on is quite different from the worker bee café girl. Your ass is spectacular in those pants."

I believe she blushed at the compliment for a quick second. Her eyes narrowed in on me, and I suddenly stopped seeing an enemy but an adversary I pictured spread wide from the Pacific to the Atlantic in my bed.

I closed my eyes, and the imagery took over me. I inhaled the traveling scent of dough being fried in the air as I imagined how our fuck fest would begin. I'd slash everyone in that homely café and make my way over to her behind the counter. She'd whimper at my wrath and beg me not to hurt her. I'd silence her with my finger over her lips and say, "This will hurt. But you'll wish that I never stop." Then I would strip her naked and fondle her perky nipple with my nail until she trembles with desire and begs me to give her the fucking of her life.

"Are you done?" Vanity interrupted, wiping the smile from my face.

"No," I answered honestly.

She smacked me senseless, but I smiled. My response didn't amuse her, so she smacked me again and pressed her boot deep into my stomach, putting brick marks on my back. Her head twisted side to side, her eyes fiery like the torch burning above my legs.

"Can't you tell I'm enjoying this?" I grinned.

"Any last words?" she asked, turning her heel to pierce inside of me.

"Yeah," I said, gazing into her eyes. "Fuck me before you kill me."

CHAPTER 10
THE FIRST

CARLISLE

FROM THE WAY Vanity's eyebrows curved, I felt a butterfly in my chest that she was actually considering my proposal. She would be my most exquisite lay of the century—after the runway model from Egypt whose beauty was unlike any other this world had ever seen, until I took it too far and sucked her dry, in more places than one.

Ah, what a night I shall never forget.

The pressure of Vanity's heels grew numb against my stomach. I stood still and admired the excitement of carnage and fornication in her eyes.

"Me…fuck you? You flatter yourself." She laughed at my request.

"I created you to be what you are after all. The newborn of a king."

"Mere technicality. You're so weak I should be ashamed to have fallen at your hands in my former life."

A cackle vibrated from my throat. "Your arrogance is so…cute."

She blushed.

"Can you say you haven't thought of me since last night?" I pressed my luck.

"I have. Of killing you."

I smirked at her pouty lips secretly imagining how I would taste in her mouth. She fixed them to deliver another witty remark as Boris rushed her from the entrance of the alley.

"Fuck!" she screamed, crashing and cracking the bricks with Boris on top of her.

"Stay down!" Boris shouted.

"Fuck you!" Vanity replied, squirming beneath his monstrous hold.

He slapped her face. *Welp!* "I said stay down," he grunted.

I shook off my torture and approached them, curious why Vanity easily surrendered to him. "What are you doing, following me, Boris?" I asked.

"The queen has had it with your secrets, you fool."

"You stand next to the queen and run her errands. Who are you to call me a fool? But thanks for the save, by the way."

"Don't thank me. I'm sure the queen will denounce your useless title as king at her side when I report that a girl had you by the balls."

"That woman you strong-armed is no girl. Trust me." I clapped the remaining dust from my hands.

A victorious, taunting laugh sounded from his mouth. "Ugggghhhh!" Boris hollered in replace of his chuckle. His shoulders stiffened outright, then slumped before he toppled over the debris. Vanity rose and gently kicked him aside. Her bloody hand dripped of his blood as she tossed his heart amongst the shattered slabs of fallen bricks.

"Humph." She scoffed. "And I thought you would be my first kill," she said.

"You don't really mean that." I slowly backed away.

She kneeled down and wiped her hands on Boris's sordid choice of clothing, then jumped from the rubble. Her flaming eyes turned gold as a glow of the same hue shone from her open wounds, mending back together as she healed before my swollen eyes.

"Magnificent," I muttered, then bolted into the wind.

Vanity was fast on my heels as I led her on a wild goose chase up and down the squares about town until we were lost of one another.

A civil conversation was all I craved from her after our minor exchange of blows. She could have killed me in an instant. I wondered if her hesitation and toying with me was out of affection or for sport. Either way, I was drawn to her and feared her the same.

When she didn't find me drinking in the bar around the corner from her place of work, I took one final pass of Cason's Café. Her big, brooding boss locked the door and closed the blinds.

I stood across the street, waiting for Vanity to sneak behind me and say something clever in my ear or drive a wooden stake through my heart. But no. Instead, I heard the laughs and moans of her being defiled by his hands. The wrong hands.

I sighed. "One day, I'll get my turn."

CHAPTER 11
THE SUMMONS

CARLISLE

ONE FOOT inside the Garden District and I was held captive, chained and roughed up by Adela's men. They beat me with metal until my clothes were torn to shreds, then stripped me bare before throwing me into the trunk.

"Get your hands off of me!" I decreed with authority.

"Take him to the queen," said a nobody.

They threw me into The Great Hall. Adela sat unprotected on her throne with one hand gripping her new scepter and the other on her knee.

She snapped her fingers. "Leave us."

Her guards lifted my chains and attached them to the wrought iron below the steps leading to her stage. My arms were spread wide like an eagle. Not my finest of moments.

Adela knew this punishment terrified me. She had seen it in my dreams, from when I was a warmblood. The terror of watching humans stretched out like that before their death. Yet she chose to treat me the same.

Vile bitch.

The doors of the hall shut, and we were left alone. I stood humiliated before her with my head down. Defeated. Angry. Silent.

"Where is Boris?" she asked.

"Dead, I'm afraid."

"Say that again," she demanded.

"I said he's dead." My head rose, and my eyes finally looked into hers.

She lifted the scepter and slammed the bottom of it on the marble floor at her feet. I heard cracks slowly creeping across the floor from her powerful blow.

"I wonder what it is exactly that you've gotten yourself into. Care to tell me before I lose more men for your mistakes?" she said in the form of a question.

"My queen, I have made a mistake, but as a man, I am taking care of it."

She scoffed. "As a man…"

She rose from her throne and lifted the hem of her black gown. The red-rose decorations sewn into her train flopped down each step. She placed her staff inside one of the grooves of the iron and circled me. I stood fearless, awaiting my death at any moment.

"Do you think I don't know what you are hiding? I have eyes and ears everywhere. My spies are spread wide from this district, to the many wards, the bayou, and the Vieux Carre. I hear you've been running through the streets like a bitch in heat, embarrassing yourself and me. I can't have my name associated with such buffoonery. What I don't know is why, so I'll ask you again. What have you gotten yourself into?"

"Adela," I said.

Her eyes were fiery, but they shred me like blades. "Queen Adela," she corrected me in a thunderous deep tone.

"I accidentally sired another creature. One like I've never seen before. One that is proving to be hard to kill," I confessed.

"Is that all?"

"Yes. I swear to you. That is all, my queen. I promise I can make this right."

She placed her cold fingers on my cheek. The black lace on the palm of her hand felt warm and rough. Her mouth formed a curve on the side of it, and her eyes glinted deep-red specks in the center.

"Yes. You will make this right," she purred and kissed me gently.

I returned her advance, then pulled away. "If you're done humiliating me, can you please remove the chains and let me hold you in my arms?"

A grin crossed Adela's lips. She placed her sharp fingernail on my neck and stuck the gold-painted weapon slightly below the surface of my skin. Bits of my blood filled it, and her mouth parted. She curved her tongue and sucked my blood from her nail and moaned. "Mmm. It's been a while, hasn't it?"

"Yes, it has. Have you missed me, my queen?"

The nail returned to my chest, creating a second incision that traveled down my torso, stopping short of my manhood.

"It never did take much to get you to rise," she teased.

I smirked of shame and chortled as she was turned on from my menacing night. She grabbed my cock and stroked it while looking into my dreary eyes. I sighed at her touch, and my legs jolted in excitement.

"Adela. Free me so I can make up for lost time," I said.

She grinned, then lifted her dress and placed her black lace undergarments in my mouth to shut me up. With speed, she hopped on my cock and straddled herself aboard. Her nails dug into the back of my neck as she rode me with the intensity of a jackhammer, shouting with her head held back.

Her delightful screams weren't the screams I wanted to hear, but my body carried on with the act effortlessly. She released and slowed her strokes, then sighed. "Oh, Carlisle."

I pulled my hips back to thrust forward, but to my surprise, Adela hopped off my rigid cock still at full attention. A wicked chuckle sounded from her mouth.

"Delicious as always," she said. "I knew you were hiding something from me."

"Adela, please. Let me finish you off," I struggled to say coherently, impatiently waiting for her to hop back on.

"I am finished." She laughed.

"Don't leave me like this. Adela, please." Blood tears nearly formed in my eyes.

"You love her. I saw it for myself. You men are so weak. A simple fucking is all it takes to enter your thoughts. And now I know what she looks like," Adela growled and exited the hall.

I am fucked. Literally.

CHAPTER 12

THE DESIRE

VANITY

THAT FOOLISH CARLISLE ran for his life after I pulled the heart out of his sidekick. The adrenaline from my first kill exploded within me. The rush of learning my power…fulfilling. I could feel myself gaining confidence in each passing minute, and the experience increased my thirst. Not for blood. But sex.

I tapped on the back door of the café. One of the busboys let me inside, and I snuck into the ladies room. As I cleansed the traces of blood from the cracks of my fingernails and my blouse, Cason called out the changes in the schedule to the servers. I scrubbed and soaked my blouse, then stopped when he knocked on the door.

"V, come see me in my office when you're done."

I could smell him through the oak. He held the scent of many things, but since I turned, he smelled of the one thing I had lacked for two years—a big, sexy man. The man I craved.

My eyes glimmered a pastel red from the thrill of his voice.

I've got to learn how to control that.

Lust shot throughout my body. My urges pulsed between my thighs, and I could no longer contain myself. Nor did I care if he saw the blood stained on me. I went into his office and closed the door.

"Everyone's gone. You can leave it open," he said.

"You sure about that?" I leaned on the edge of the door until it shut behind me, then placed the deadbolt lock across the panel.

I threw my wet shirt on his desk and sat on his lap, rolling my hips in a circle. His lips brushed the side of my neck while his hands traveled up the side of my waist. I reached back and rubbed his temples with my palms and moaned.

"I told you we would talk tonight." I giggled and opened my legs.

"I've never done this at work," he said.

"First time for everything."

"No," he whispered. "Let's take this home where I can focus solely on you and not worry about my business."

"I can't wait that long. I want you now," I sultrily whined.

A silent cry wailed from his mouth. His hands stopped exploring my body, and he rested his forehead on the back of my shoulder. I slid my bra straps down my arm and placed his hands on my bosom. His fingers stretched, and he sighed.

"I shouldn't," he said.

"You should." I lifted my head and kissed his luscious lips.

He growled in my mouth, and I panted in his, waiting for him to expose my nipples from below the padding.

A voice entered my head and said, "One day, I'll get my turn." I paused our kiss and shot up from his lap. I recognized that annoying voice. A voice I had become too familiar with.

"You're right. Let's finish this at home. How long until you get there?" I threw my wet blouse over my head.

"Thank you for understanding. Maybe an hour?"

"I should be there. But let's talk first. Okay?"

I left Cason inside and followed the direction of Carlisle's voice. The lot was empty across the street except for the vendor closing his kiosk and a few teens out past their curfew. The smell of rain was in the air. I inhaled its earthy scent and embraced the sense of calm being brought in with it. Its fragrance shifted my energy, paralyzing my aggression and hostility.

Nearly in a trance from the aroma playing ownership of my senses, I walked home with the word petrichor on my lips and having my way with Cason on my mind. But this time, I decided to let him be the predator in heat, while I played the gentle prey waiting to be pounced on.

CHAPTER 13

THE RAVISHING

VANITY

STILL IN THE beginning stages of my transition, a lot about the new me needed to be learned. The lesson I needed the most help with—control of my craving of the flesh.

Days without eating hadn't affected me, yet somehow, I was full of energy to be indulged by Cason, and full of ideas on how I would delight him. We would eventually have *"that"* talk, but first, the ravishing.

Dressed in a black silk nightgown, I hid in my room, blending in with the drapes.

"V," he called from the hallway. "You home?" His voice carried disappointment.

His heavy footsteps traveled back to the front of the house. I used my speed to sweep past him and closed the door to his room. He followed the swooshing sound of my increased pace and looked around his room with great suspicion.

The moonlight seeped through the cracks of the shutters in his bedroom. As his eyes shifted around the room, the gray hue of his pupils turned silver, caught by the filtered light creeping in.

Why am I not in love with this beautiful man?

He saw me standing in the shadow of his closet but walked away.

I know he saw me. He's enjoying this cat-and-mouse game.

I waited for him to exit his quarters, then whipped down the hall back to my bedroom. I closed the door and made myself invisible with the drapes again. Cason opened the door within seconds and stepped inside without my permission.

As he breathed quietly through his nose, his heart rate increased. The intensity of its pounding attracted my fangs by nature. I withdrew them easily—the one self-controlled thing I mastered.

The silver in his eyes excited me. My nipples pebbled near the point of pain, aching to be pinched, touched, and sucked. I held my breath the closer he crept toward me, timing the right moment to attack him and pin his tasty ass to my bed.

One foot away from being made, a low growl rumbled from his throat. The heat rose within my body, and the desire of Cason striking his match to set me ablaze called him to my need. "Looking for me?" I whispered.

His silvery eyes glistened, and his growl intensified.

"We can have that talk later," I said, then revealed my thirsty flesh.

I closed the space between us and licked his lips. He licked mine in return, grunting in hunger for my flesh. I removed his soiled clothing slowly while marveling at his smooth, robust chest as I inhaled every scent trapped on him: beer, wine, pastries, steaks, "work."

I rubbed my nose against the grooves of his cut physique and licked every crease. Below those aromas laid his *davana* scent—the scent that sets him apart from everyone. It was heavy on him. Always. And it increased its deliciousness throughout the day.

Purring to feel him inside, I lowered the straps of my gown and dropped to my knees. Looking up at him, I nibbled on his zipper, then gripped his belt with my teeth. My hands slid down his chest to unfasten the caged, savory prize thumping against my chin. I could already taste him as the sweetness of his essence called to me like an addiction.

Cason stood tall and strong like a king. His shoulders squared and stretched wide with his chin up, knowing he deserved what was about to come. I freed him and examined his dick close up. The shades of brown from the base to his tip, to the plumping veins growing impatient to feel the wetness of my tongue to massage them. The *davana* scent was heavier near his manhood: sweet, fresh, rich. My nose rubbed every inch of his manliness, and I lost control.

No wonder I crave him. He satisfies my sweet tooth.

I placed him in my mouth and rolled my tongue around his head. Gripping the shroom tip with a snug tug and pull, Cason groaned and placed his hands behind his neck, watching me turn his dirty thoughts into reality.

"I will not stop you," he whispered.

His deep, sultry voice inspired my creativity to please him. My thumbs traveled between his thighs and massaged his tight, trembling muscles, pressing inward as I slid my mouth down his shaft. His hands cradled my head as he sighed from the pleasure I brought him. They led where he needed it. How he needed it. Fast when he desired. Slow when he demonstrated control of his release.

"Thank the moon I'm not dreaming." He sighed, sticking one thumb in the side of my mouth as he slowly fucked my throat.

My voice hummed on his pipe from the trapped laughter in my chest. Proud laughter of my skill set serving a true king. The vibration shocked him motionless.

"Yes. Do that again," he ordered. I stopped sucking and moaned with him lodged at the top of my throat. He opened his mouth wide and gasped. "Ah, yes. Hold it. Hold it."

I retreated, and he exhaled, quivering in a locked position. The smell of him being pleasured inclined my performance level to rise, and the plumping vein I examined earlier called for my attention. My tongue traced it with a deep stroke, back and forth until my body twisted around his tip and brushed the bottom of my chin as Cason rolled his fingers around my hard nipples and softly pinched them.

My pussy throbbed from the fondling, the sound of chaos inside me, and the sound of ecstasy expelling from his lips. My knees slid forward like I was stealing home base, and my back lowered. Cason couldn't wait to feed me below him, dipping his cock downward into my obedient throat.

Gently, he fucked my throat, shivering when I opened my mouth wide for him to stroke it. I lathered him slick while patting my nub, aching for his entrance.

"Can I cheat you?" His words rattled with intense gratification.

I released his mouth filler and shook my head. "I want to feel your big dick inside of me. And if I don't…" I lowered my voice into whisper. "You'll have hell to pay."

Cason growled with silver eyes beaming into mine. "Then rise."

CHAPTER 14
THE TWINGING
CASON

THE BEAT of my heart matched that of a drum found in villages serenading their gods, or that of a ritual summoning healing, or a harvest.

Heal me and let me be your harvest.

She rose from her knees as commanded, hiding her eyes with her head tilted back. She wanted to be kissed. I wanted to taste the pouty lips on her pretty mouth before I devoured her open, aching flesh with a heartbeat of its own.

I pulled on her locks at the back of her nape and took a whiff of her neck, her hair, and her face. There was something familiar and different about her, but I loved her still the same. She smelled of the earth. I inhaled an aquatic scent mixed with cedar and moss, then tasted her sugary full lips and sniffed the spoor of myself.

Vanity obliged my advance in an animalistic lip lock filled with passion, heavy breathing, and the sound of replicated drums between us. My hands kneaded up and down her back, weakening the fight within her. Her shoulders relaxed, and she rested submissively in my arms. I was in full control, caressing her body and stealing air from her lungs. And she permitted me, resting in my arms like a lifeless doll.

A growl slipped from my lips and wavered into her mouth. My cock was losing control being near her and not between her already.

Vanity reclaimed her power and pressed her hands against my chest.

She flashed her eyes open and closed too quickly for me to gaze into them. From a glimpse, they sparkled a brick-red jasper color, but I believed my eyes deceived me in the dark.

My interest in her eyes lasted for a split second as she reminded me I wasn't in control—yet. She leaned down and circled her wet tongue around the tip of my dick and dashed to the opposite side of her bed. She moaned on all fours, enticing me to chase her like prey. I climbed on the bed, and we circled the four edges in a dance of *catch me if you can.*

She had no idea the way she crawled around the bed on her hands and knees made my dick grow harder, and my need to punish her tight pussy overshadowed my love for her. I wondered if she could hear the drums rumbling too, or were they only beating in my head? Either way, I knew the moment my cock split her slit, it would be ceremonial.

The intensity of the heat between us climaxed to its peak. I cut the chase in half and grabbed her feet, then dragged her hedonistic body next to mine. She spread her legs open for me without a request. I grinned and kissed her forehead, landing tender pecks down to her lips.

"Let me see your eyes," I said, hovering over her.

Show me they're still brown. Show me the red jasper I saw was my mind playing tricks on me.

She opened them at my request. There was no red, but a hint of gold I hadn't noticed before. As I held her eyes with mine, I rubbed my cock against her clit, gazing deep into her need before she closed them fully, weary from the agony my teasing brought upon her desirous body. Then I confessed.

"Last time you told me to fuck you like a savage, I held back. I can't promise I'll have restraint this time. In fact, I know I won't."

"Good," she said, then stole my lips.

I growled into her mouth and placed her supple abandoned breasts in my mouth, rotating between the two with light grazes of my teeth and twinging them between my fingers before ending the sharp pain with a soft kiss to her nipples. Her back arched and lifted from the bed with each nibble, her hands reaching for mine to take control.

I trapped them above her head with one of my hands as restraint, then used the other to flick her clit. *Flip. Flap. Flip.* She panted and squirmed from the flickering while I pulled on her nipple between my closed lips. Her lower body thrusted upward, searching for my sphere, my hips locked above her pussy growing weak of not wrecking her warmth.

My taste of her flesh lost the battle as I raised her hips and swiped her mess with my tongue. My knees sunk down into the bed as the sweet water that escaped her quenched my thirst while my tongue fucked her hard and intense. Her fingers massaged the top of my head, loosening the band holding my hair out of the way. I swept my locks behind my head and dove my tongue farther into her cave, savoring the taste of her honey until her cunt was distended and the heartbeat inside of it blended with the drums banging in my head.

Vanity begged for the visceral attack I helped build in her needy body, yearning from the firm oral thrashing of my mouth. The tongue-fucking ceased, but my need to taste her hadn't yet been satisfied. I took care of her precious palace, tending to it with a delicate brush of my lips, delivering soft sensual licks and *pillowy* kisses to her plump folds and swollen entrance.

She was now prepared for my *slaying.* I lifted one of her legs and glided inside her slippery fortress, then paused as her walls clamped tightly around my dick. She praised me with worship as I pounded her delicate pussy, performing a ritual of my own, sending us both on a journey to a realm of pure passion and ecstasy only she and I would remember.

Her walls swallowed my dick like her throat, clenching on it like a fist as my pipe pinched her pressure points. A simple turn of her waist and she was split wide open, one leg beneath me, the lifted leg now pointed west. Her ass was plump like two perfect peaches, ripe and round, flinching after every stroke.

I pressed down on her lower back and rolled my hips in a circle. My cock carved Cason on her flesh as she buried her face between the sheets and bayed my name.

"Yeah, baby," I answered, massaging her ass with my fingertips.

"I don't want this to end," she whined.

"Neither do I," I admitted, wishing I could carry on until the morning.

She rose to both knees and backed her sexy ass onto my dick. I stood still and watched her work, applying assistance with a sudden hard stroke when I felt her grow weary.

"That's it, baby. Throw it to me. You're not afraid of me anymore."

We groaned together. She squealed, and I howled. The sighs shared between us summoned the animal inside of me to drill her field until she was empty of her black gold. I plowed and worked her tunnel, buried deep between her folds, as I felt the release of my aggression was near. My fists pulled a handful of her hair until her lower back caved in, and her shoulders elevated from the bed. I pounded deep and hard with a sturdy, meticulous stroke as the muscles in my thighs tightened, and my knees locked below. "Owooo!" I yowled, depositing my seed inside her pulsing walls as my true nature emerged from the shadows, no longer hidden, and howling like the Silver Leaf King I am.

CHAPTER 15
THE WOLF

CASON

VANITY WAS a combination of cold and warm in my arms. I pulled the soiled sheets hanging halfway on the floor up onto the bed and covered the lower half of her body. She sighed with gratification and relaxed her head on my chest, then moaned once again as the afterglow settled in her bones.

A low, roaring growl escaped my lips as my racing heart took its time to wind down. My mind was clear for a brief moment, and my cock was on the verge of rising again from listening to her moan.

"Cason," she called. "Now is as good a time as ever to have that conversation."

"You sure about that?" I said. "You don't sound like you want to talk to me. More like you want to pull an all-nighter."

"That's definitely on the table after I say what needs to be said."

She sat up in the bed, topless. Her supple breasts stood at attention as a distraction from her speech. I waited for her to pull the sheet from her thighs to cover herself. Vanity sat next to me, exposed, with her perfect brown nipples teasing me to taste them.

"Something happened to me the other night. It's freaking me out, so I expect your reaction to be brash." She exhaled deeply with a twinkle in her eye. "My goodness, you are a beautiful man in the moonlight. You have a silver aura all around you right now."

"A what?" I rose in the bed, examining my arms and chest for a visual of her words.

"The thing that happened to me has led to some strange, unexplainable changes in me. Like when I arrived to the café earlier today, auras of different shades shrouded the customers. Some were gold, some were lavender. Some black. And now you. A silver glow surrounds you."

"What exactly happened to you the other night?"

"I was bitten by a vampire."

With speed, I threw Vanity to the wall, rose from the bed, and stood in battle position on my side of the room.

"The fuck was that?" She groaned.

I held my hands out to keep her at bay. "I knew something was different. But it can't be. I should have picked up on you being…"

"A vampire. Yes. But something about my transition was different from the norm."

"Explain yourself!" I demanded.

"I turned in a matter of minutes after being bitten. I can walk in sunlight. And I detest the taste of blood."

"Vanity, tell me you haven't fed on a human."

"I tried, but the taste of human blood disgusts me. I could taste my first victim's fears, weaknesses, disease, insecurities, and regrets. It made me sick to my stomach. I let her go and had my fill down in the bayou."

"I knew I smelled the marsh on you the other morning."

"So you believe me, then?" Her eyes felt powerless looking into mine.

"Show me," I snarled, staring into the abyss of her soul.

After a brief pause and an exhale, Vanity flashed her ruby and golden eyes, then buried her head. I charged at Vanity, resting her back against the wall. It was seconds before she looked at me again, standing still as a pole cemented in by concrete. Not a flinch. Not a drop of fear.

My hand wrapped around her throat. I sniffed her neck on both sides, then toured her mouth slowly.

"Humph. I don't smell blood on you."

Her eyes turned back to brown. "And you won't. This change has heightened my sweet tooth craving. Cowbirds and beavers seem to do the trick."

"That was you? Whispers about a trail of dead birds and beavers made it out of the bayou this morning." I sighed. "You are different from the other bloodsuckers I've met. But how? And why?" I asked.

"Don't call me that," her voice sharpened. "I have no desire for human blood. I'm still the same person you've known for two years now—with minor enhancements. Nevertheless, I need your help." Her voice trembled.

The fragile, needy, delicate bud I gardened into a flower appeared to be strong but still desired my help. My fingers slowly lost the anger flowing through them and eased from around her neck.

"What do you need?"

"A few things, actually. First, don't throw me away. You're the only person I have in my life. The only person I trust. And I need you. Second, teach me what you know about the power of three. Third, explain why your eyes have a glowing, platinum ring around them and why you're covered with a silver aura."

"Anything else?"

"Yes, actually." Vanity grinned and slapped me. "Start with the number three, and don't ever choke me out again unless it's when we're fucking."

With a mischievous laugh vibrating from my throat, I placed one foot behind the other and studied Vanity, posed against the wall with her legs slightly apart, her shoulders tilted back, and her brown eyes glazing for punishment. I wished I could pin her flawless, perfect body up high in that very spot like a poster. It'd keep her safe, out of trouble, like what she'd found herself in. And available for me at all times.

As my lips touched the sting from where her blow slid off, I wondered which V I wished stood before me. The amnesiac, normal woman, or the feisty, hypersexual creature. The amnesiac who lost her memory was everything I wanted in a woman, but the latter let me fuck her and couldn't get enough of me.

"First, yes, ma'am. I'll remember to do as you requested." I grinned. "Second, I have a secret of my own. My grandfather was brought here from Japan as the last living male of his kind. When he and his wife felt it was safe to call this place home, they started a family, giving birth to all daughters. It was believed his enemies had cursed him. Then, finally, on the fifth try, my grandmother gave birth to my father. Once he was of age, the burden was placed on him to continue my grandfather's sacred bloodline. And so, my father met and married a woman, but unknowingly, she could not bear him any children. Out of desperation, my father planted his seed where he could. Then I was born to a woman shamed by her people out in New Iberia for giving birth to a mixed-race, bastard child. My mother fled to Houma to live with the one aunt who didn't turn her back on her and raised me under her roof. It wasn't until she was on her death bed that she told me why I was fatherless. She presented the story as if I was some sort of gift to the philandering man leaving his mark wherever he pleased, but it wasn't until I moved to New Orleans that I learned the truth of why I was seen as a gift."

"Explain please." Vanity's eyes beamed red as a coal fire.

"I was the first of many bastard children my father created. When I moved here, I sought him out and found him, but he had been dead for some time. His wife took one look at me and called me his name. Asahi. She invited me in for tea, then shared his secret with me. He was the only son of the last standing General of the Silver Leaf People, believed to be extinct in the Shikoku Islands. What would be the highest-ranking were-wolf pack."

"What became of the others? Your brothers, if any?"

"Three brothers and twin sisters have met with my father's wife. She introduced us during the last blood moon."

"As the eldest brother, did they recognize you as their alpha?"

I nodded, releasing a low growl in my throat.

A sinful curve formed on the side of Vanity's mouth. "So when you do that, it's not because I excite you?"

"You excite me very much, but it's also because of who I am."

"That explains your carnal nature." She dragged out the last of her words.

I grinned. "Believe it or not, I've been holding back on you."

Vanity's skin gave off a golden glow, matching the gold streaks between her fiery eyes. I blinked, and there she was in a flash, standing in my face, purring and moaning as her hardened nipples pressed against my ribs.

"This conversation can be continued after a small intermission of you showing me how you've been holding back," she said, softly kissing my chest.

My eyes lowered past hers to below my waist. "I'm already up for the challenge."

CHAPTER 16
THE MARKING
CASON

"GRRRR," echoed from between my clenched teeth by her request. Vanity slipped from my grasp. "Being hunted gets you going something fierce," I said, creeping down the hall. Her scent was heavy on my lips, her arousal heavy on my nose. She was stretched across the breakfast nook, posed with her head resting on her palms. I pretended not to see her and turned toward the den. "Care to join me?" I grinned.

A slight shift in the room raised the hairs on the back of my neck. I turned and met her speed with my hand catching her by the neck. Her feet dangled loosely as she stared down at me with intrigue blazing in her eyes. With ease, I brought her featherweight body closer to mine and straddled her legs around my waist, promptly inserting my needy cock inside her pink cushion.

To and from, I led her up and down my dick—still choking her, still in control of my promised smashing. Her chin lifted with pride as her eyes disappeared, rolling behind her closed lids, while her lips pressed deep into her teeth. My eyes narrowed while studying the offbeat of her heart and the sharp tips of her breasts begging to be sucked. Grazing them with my teeth, they rippled until they were plump. Vanity's back withered, and her chin sunk lower, resting on my wrist.

I carried her to the window and fucked her senseless on the sill. The condensation squeaked and rattled the case as I drove my dick rough and far up her swollen pussy, mending her slippery back, the print of her ass, and my knuckles with the fogged glass.

The creature inside of me pinned her legs wide above my head. I howled in the night, digging out her dripping pussy as the moon's reflection became unclear from the overcast of the smeared frame. The pressure from this angle served her pleasure she had never known, and the depths I entered felt like I had shot past the stars in the sky.

Trembling in my wrath, Vanity's vibrating moans and throbbing walls fed my ego. I increased the pressure and choked her again when I felt her drip trickle on the bottom of my shaft.

"Hold on," I roared.

"I'm holding," she said, digging her nails into my shoulder.

The smell of my drawn blood caused her eyes to turn red and her fangs to bare. I saw the silver in my eyes flash in the reflection of hers.

"I don't like blood, remember?"

I nodded. "Go ahead and do it anyway. I want to mark you with a bite of my own."

"Mark me," she whispered.

I sunk my teeth into her flesh. Visions of the night she was manhandled and violated flashed in my mind, a car accident near the bridge, her pushing a cart at the old motel, and her radiant smile serving drinks at the bar. I groaned and released her delicate, candied flesh from my mouth.

As I wiped her blood from my lips, she bit me with a quickness and released me before any blood stained her lips.

"How do I taste?" I asked.

"Better above your thighs. And me?"

I grinned. "Like fresh fruit plucked from a tree."

She smiled, and the red in her eyes faded back to brown, and my knot expanded to an extremity.

"The fuck!" she panted, placing her hands against my shoulder.

"I said hold on," I growled.

Her nails dug deeper into my flesh. The pain, sharp and welcoming from the moment, caused me to burst like a broken hydrant on a street corner and Vanity to shriek unlike the two times before.

She blasphemed a god I had never heard her speak of and sighed against my cheek. I released my hold of her neck and gripped my fingers tightly around her ankles as I emptied my clip into her barrel. Naturally she was my enemy, but now I saw her as mine. My coldblooded bronze goddess of the night, and I'd kill anyone if they ever got a piece of her. She was the heaven to my hell. Once pure. Now damaged. But still mine.

Locked inside of her sugar walls, I stared at her tri-colored eyes flashing a different color each time she blinked. Her palms caressed the side of my face as I lifted her overworked body to the sofa. Laying her on her back, my hands massaged her head down to her thighs, endlessly convulsing from the enjoyment she felt from my presence entwined with hers.

"Why can't I move?" she asked.

"Give it a few minutes to release you."

"You say it as if it has a mind of his own." She joked.

"It does."

"Talk about two people with secrets." She giggled. "And this is called?"

"Knotting?"

"Why didn't it do this before?"

"I was in control the other times. This time, my true nature took charge. Consider yourself mated to me."

"Sounds like ownership."

"It is. You belong to me now. Let me hear you say you're mine."

"I disagree. I don't know who I truly am, so I can't belong to another."

"That mark on your neck says otherwise." I turned her head and ran my fingers across her skin, searching for my bite. "Where the fuck is it?"

"When I heal, I heal completely. Unscathed and unmarked."

I didn't know what Vanity was, but I was mesmerized and more in love than ever. Just as the words to say so formed on my lips, she and I both sat up on the sofa.

"Someone's outside," I said, easing my cock from her grip and jumping to my feet. I turned to face her. "And you know who it is."

"How do you know that?"

"When a Silver Leaf leaves his mark, he can read his mates' thoughts. It keeps us in sync."

"Nice time to share that bit of information." She scowled.

"So, who is Billie, and why is he lurking outside our home?"

"He is actually a she, and she's my informant. She must have information to pass."

Vanity zipped past me and went to the window. She signaled to her acquaintance, then flew past me into her bedroom, returning to the den wearing an oversized t-shirt and rain boots.

"Be back in a sec," she said.

"If you think I'm letting you go out there alone, you're mistaken. I protect what's mine."

I raced to my room and threw on a pair of sweats and my work boots. When I returned to the den, Vanity was gone.

A hard head on this one.

CHAPTER 17

THE ALLY

VANITY

I DENIED Cason's claim of me merely seconds ago, yet he stumbled out of the house, portraying that of *my* boss. "I thought I told you to wait," he said, snarling at Billie leaning against the white wooden rail on the porch. His glistening muscles flexed in his arms, and the pecs on his chest tightened. Billie's round eyes shifted from me and ogled Cason.

I cleared my throat, regaining her attention, then turned to face Cason, raging in fight mode. Billie attempted to finish her previous thought, then stopped as I raised my finger for her to pause.

"I told you I can take care of myself," I said in an exclaimed whisper.

Cason ignored me and addressed Billie. "I recognize your face. You were sitting at my bar. How do you know where we live?"

"Good question," I added, turning back toward Billie. "I told you to meet me at the café. Never here."

She dropped her hood. "Your boyfriend wasn't hard to track." Billie smirked.

"And you trust this one?" Cason pointed toward her.

I flashed my reds and pursed my lips for him to get a clue. He needed to learn quickly—I answered to no one, including him.

"Jeesh, his scent is all over you. I don't know why I'm surprised after hearing that beastly racket you two had going on in there, but now that I'm seeing what you look like under those plain work clothes, I can't say I don't get it. Pardon me for interrupting your night. I'm Billie." She offered her hand.

Cason relaxed his fists, then covered one hand with the other. "I'm confident you already know my name."

"The café worker is all I know."

"Owner," he corrected her.

"Billie isn't a threat. I mean, she was, but she's on my team now. We're working together. Go back inside."

"Not until you're done here," he said, looking past me at Billie.

His commanding presence rattled her. She stared back at him, losing the battle of who would blink first, then spoke lighter, with less confidence.

"I wanted to check in and give you the update. Carlisle is being held captive. Adela has him chained and is beating him endlessly. I fled before she figured out my allegiance no longer lies with her. I want no part of her torture."

"What's her grudge with him?" I inquired.

"You. She knows about you and has been on the rampage about Boris."

"How did she find out?"

"The queen has spies everywhere, but she also bit the truth out of poor Carlisle."

"Poor Carlisle?" The peaceful tone of my voice swiftly turned stern.

"I know you and I are plotting to kill him, but after seeing what Adela has done to him, I feel bad for the guy," Billie confessed.

A deep sigh escaped my mouth, and I turned to Cason. His eyes were upon me with a raised brow.

"You hear that? A compassionate vampire."

"A load of crap if you ask me." He grunted.

"Billie, need I remind you that Carlisle left you to die at my hands. And here you stand in my face, proclaiming to feel bad for the man I gave you an order to kill."

"I have my reasons—well, *a* reason for my change of heart," Billie stuttered.

My eyes widened. "Let's hear it."

"He said he's in love with you."

Cason's fists reformed as he took a step closer to Billie. She zipped to the other side of the porch.

"And to think I took you for the chivalrous type," she said.

"If your bitch queen doesn't kill your precious Carlisle, I will. He has to answer for doing what he did to V," Cason barked.

"Well, I doubt he'll get out of Adela's alive."

I eyed Billie from head to toe. "I get the feeling you came here asking for my help to save him."

Billie's mouth twisted to the side.

"You did come here with that hideous idea in mind."

"He's sorry for what he did to you. I believe he does love you."

"But I loathe him. If he survives, you tell him I said that."

Billie's pink face slowly lowered before she bypassed Cason, humming a low, raspy groan, intimidating her on the way down the stairs.

"I take it you have somewhere to stay since fleeing the palace?"

"My family has a wall vault in Lafayette 1. That's where I'm hiding out for now."

"Do me a favor. Stroll past the alley near Fulton. If Boris's body is still rotting, burn it."

"Ten-four." Billie saluted and disappeared.

Cason took me by the hand. "When I marked you, I saw his face. He came by the café, pretending to be an investigator when you were out. He claimed he had information you requested, but he was fishing for answers instead."

"Did you know he was a…?"

"I did. His pale face next to that gray blazer he wore in this heat washed him out completely."

"Yeah, that was him."

"He didn't even have a card to leave behind. I told him we were busy and to come back later when you would be in, but he never showed. I was going to put an end to him then."

"Makes me wonder if he was coming to tell me what Billie said with hopes I'd let him live."

Cason scoffed. "Listen to you. Is my sweet, innocent V in there somewhere?" He stroked my arm. "Calm down, killer. I'll take care of this."

CHAPTER 18
THE WARNING
CARLISLE

THE DOWNSIDE to being dead is the inability to die. Never would I have imagined Adela to be so cruel—and to me of all people. Other than being queen of the Underworld, she was basic. A boring, pretty face with zero sex appeal and a kingdom of psychopaths who worshipped her because of her power—the controlling factor she used to lure me into her world.

From the moment I arrived in New Orleans, I ignored the signs of despair floating in the air. The misery on the faces of the nightwalkers scouting tourists to cure their thirst. The fear surrounding Adela's presence when she proudly showed her face during the Night Twilight Ahsaka La Culte Parade.

The unsuspecting crowd of human flesh had no idea they were in the presence of a true queen of the night, cheering her on as she was carried before them down the crowded narrow streets. Half of them served as snacks to her army that night. The looks on their faces when they realized she wasn't a character covered in makeup for a show, I'll never forget.

Now I'm being discarded like those tourists, shredded by whips and weakened by silver chains heavy enough to bury a witch. Me. The stranger who strolled into the bayou one hundred and fifty years ago and had every woman I desired, until I settled for a silly title of king to sit alongside a basic bitch with a silly scepter at her fingertips.

The memory of my foolishness seems punishment enough. My bare body hung on display from chains for everyone in the palace to see. They pointed, laughed, and stared as I collected the faces of whom I shall off once I broke free. Though my behavior has not shown it, I'm still a man of faith and believed strongly I'd escape the hell hole before the sun rose. For if I didn't, Adela would have slid my chains near the window and watched me burn alive.

Where the fuck is Billie?

'Gone,' a woman's voice responded.

My weary body looked up. Blood dripped from my head into my eyes. No one was present. Not a beating heart or weakened pulse before me.

"Who's there?" I whispered.

'A friend,' the voice replied in my mind. *'We don't have much time.'*

The chains broke an inch from the bands locked around my wrist. I fell to my knees, hunched over and drained.

'I said we don't have much time. Get up and come to the left exit. I'll guide you from there.'

I listened to the voice and limped to the left entrance. I winced as I opened the door, waiting to be struck by the guards.

"I took care of them. Let's go," she said, pulling my hand.

My vision was blurry, but I trusted this woman rescuing me with ease. She hid below a red-caped dress and led me down the hall. *Crack.* A huge flop sounded to the right of me. A bang against the wall surprised me up ahead on my left.

"Who are you?" I asked, clutching her hand.

"Did Adela gouge out your eyes?"

"Close to it."

Snap. Another body brushed my lower leg and fell at my feet.

"Thank you. Whoever you are."

A door creaked open, then closed suddenly. Her soft footsteps traveled away from me and returned within seconds. "Here. Wipe the blood from your eyes and put this on," she said, handing me a clean black t-shirt and sweats. "We have thirty minutes before sunrise. I'll get you past the garden, then after that, you're on your own."

I wiped my eyes clean as she instructed and covered my exposed body.

"Melanie," I whispered.

"So you can see. Good, because we're taking up too much time," she said, then threw a navy-blue bag over her shoulder before tossing me one.

She opened the side door of the pantry next to the cook's hall. Together, we crept below the cameras with our backs pressed against the chilled stone of the house.

"Once we're out of the gate, we part ways. Got it? Do not follow me," she ordered.

"Why are you risking your life for me?"

"I've seen what's coming and don't want to be around for it. I'm using your escape as my one good deed since waking up on the dark side. Good luck out there."

"However I can repay you, please let me know." I held out my hand.

"You'll never see me again after tonight. Now, on my mark. You take out the guard on the right. Goodbye, Carlisle."

She nodded, and we bounced from the corner of the house and snapped the necks of the guards at the gate, then hopped over the black iron spikes. Melanie dashed off to the east without a second look at me, leaving my path to the west a predetermined decision in her planning.

I flew through the streets, backyards, and bushes, racing against the sun. I circled through Lafayette Cemetery No. 1 for Billie's family lot, sure she would forgive me for disturbing their peace with a night's stay. "Hays, Hays," I muttered to myself in a frantic rage, searching for the name carved on the boulder walls. I turned near the corner of a second entrance and followed the sound of scraping stone. "Got room for one more?" I asked Billie on her way inside the tomb.

CHAPTER 19

THE VAULT

BILLIE

"AHHH." I froze. "Did anyone follow you?"

Carlisle stepped forward, shaking his head side to side, helping me remove the heavy stone before the sky turned pink. "I expected you to be a memory of my past. Good for you, I was wrong."

He placed his foot across the threshold of my resting place. Swiftly my reflexes reacted and kicked his leg back. He lost his balance and fell to his knees. I placed my hand around his neck and stuck my wedge-shaped thumb nail below his skin.

As blood trickled down his neck from a reopened wound, Carlisle surrendered at my mercy. He was restless and broken, too tired to fight me and too afraid to be seen. His crimson-covered eyes were caked with dried blood, thick like red clay, and they looked past my chin while his body rendered motionless in my grip.

"Say it," I demanded. "You will not enter until you say it."

"May I sleep here this morning?" His voice trembled.

"And?"

"Please forgive me, for turning my back on you and being a shitty maker."

I stepped inside my family's tomb. "You may enter."

I gave him a once-over as he hopped inside, and we closed the stone covering to protect us from the rising sun. With his hands resting against the cold stone, his shoulders slumped over while the pounding of adrenaline boomed through him.

I couldn't recall a time I saw Carlisle wearing casual clothing. Jeans, never. Sweats, no way in hell.

"That's a new look for you," I said, hoping to lighten the mood.

"Beggars can't be choosy. Especially naked ones being whipped and beaten with his glory on display for an entire coven to mock."

Carlisle sat in the corner on the ground and released a heavy sigh of relief, starved and thirsty. Pensive and brooding. I reached up high on the shelf and sliced a line in the center of my palm, then dripped my blood into a cobwebbed goblet—one of the many priceless family heirlooms buried with what was thought to be the last of important relatives from which I came.

Carlisle gulped down my offering in one swallow, begging me to fill it once more with sorrowed eyes. I obliged and sneered at him. He knew to savor it, for it was the last offering he would receive going into our time of night.

"Thank you, Billie. For everything."

"If I didn't know any better, this maker and child bond we share seems to flow stronger in one direction. If I were anything like you, you'd be ash on Adela's floor in a few minutes."

"*You* sent Melanie. I couldn't figure out why she would help me. I should have known it was you."

He rose to his feet and attempted to place his arms around me. I stopped him short and lowered him back to his spot for the night with a signal of my hands, shaking my head side to side.

"Let's both be glad Melanie pulled it off. Just don't make me regret it."

"I'm indebted to you, Billie."

A silence formed between us that I was thankful for. I hopped on top of my ancestor's coffin and stretched out across the cold stone.

"Let's call it," I said.

Carlisle sighed. "Have you seen her?"

I closed my eyes and crossed my hands on top of my stomach. "I have."

"Do I stand a chance of forgiveness with her, as I have been granted with you?"

"Sadly, her affection resides with another. Goodnight."

"The café owner?"

My silence confirmed what he already knew. The vault grew deafening silent, but I could sense Carlisle was still awake. I lifted my head and peered at him on the ground. His eyes were open with his head tilted back against the filthy stone. His frail body stretched out along the base of the rocks.

"It sucks not getting what you want when you want it. Doesn't it?" I snickered.

Carlisle remained quiet. Internally, it pleased me to see him suffer the way us lower-level vamps had to suffer his and Adela's ruthless reign and tedious tirades. Granting him an easy death would have robbed me of seeing karma find him, and I waited a long time to witness his downfall since he stole my fertile youth.

Such satisfaction took me under, as the hours of cruelty eventually carried Carlisle into a long-awaited peaceful rest. After our enemy in the sky traded places with the moon, the time had arrived for him to embrace a life outside the mansion walls. A life on the run from Adela's army. A life outside of N'awlins perhaps.

"Do you smell that?" he asked, standing over me.

"I do," I said, recognizing the familiar scent lurking about on the grounds.

CHAPTER 20

THE MARK

CASON

VANITY and I had much to discuss, after one more shameless session of sheet sliding wore me out once we got rid of her frenemy. I held her in my arms, daydreaming what we would be like if we had gotten this close before her unfortunate change. Would the sex between us be as explosive, intense, and carnivorous? Unfortunately, there was no way of knowing, but I was glad to finally get the chance at all.

Her thoughts ran rampant while she lay on my chest. I couldn't tell if she wanted me to see her thoughts or forgot my mark allowed me to pry inside her mind.

"Has your mind always been so busy, or are you incapable of relaxing?"

"You can see all of that?" She lifted her head.

I kissed her forehead. "I can only see when I bite you, but the words of your thoughts are talking to me."

"I'll have to remember that in case I want to talk shit about you." She laughed.

Dryly, I chortled.

"I'm kidding—unless you piss me off." She pinched my arm.

"I'm sure I will."

Her mind went calm, then suddenly '*Asshole*' flashed in my head. Vanity chuckled. "I was testing," she said, then pulled on the growing stubble protruding from my chest.

"What are we going to do about your dilemma with Adela? She has more people in her army than there are packs. I'd have to reach out to my brothers and have them call in favors from the other alphas down the coast."

"Thank you, but it shouldn't come to that, unless this so-called queen refuses to battle me one on one."

"This change has made you fearless. Has it made you wiser, I wonder?"

"Maybe I should mark you so I can see your truth," she threatened me.

"It's also made you cocky. Don't get me wrong; I'm loving the sultry, badass goddess persona, but I was quite fond of the sweet girl from before. Is she still in there at all?"

"That bitch is long gone—helplessly wondering who she was, what her real name is, why can't she tell the handsome café owner she loves him too."

I huffed. "What did you say?"

"I know you love me. I've known for a while now."

"Why didn't you say anything?"

"Because I'm incapable of love. It's like the emotion is lost somewhere inside of me, and I don't have the answer as to why. I thought it was because I'm a stranger to myself. I was lost when we met, and I'm even more of a stranger to myself now, but this version I plan to get acquainted with."

Her revelation struck me as a mixture of possibly feeling the same, crossed with her newborn cockiness of being too invincible to be bothered with such an affliction. I was in love with her, but as a king, I would not beg to hear her say the very words. Instead, I reminded her of the question she asked me earlier.

"Why did you ask about the power of three?"

"Madame Cecil said I possess it. I know you're worldly and intelligent, so I thought you could school me on the matter. Give me the Cliff's Notes if you will."

I took a deep sigh, piecing together the fragmented words scrambling through her mind. *'Accident. Priestess. Man. Trade. Deal.'* As none of the words made any sense to me, I pulled a summation out of my ass.

"The number three is known as a powerful triad, but in several different contexts. It can mean continuation—like in man, woman, and child—or the completion of something. Some people call it *The Angel Number* or *The Number of the Divine*. The simplest answer is it means the beginning, the middle, and the end. To those who believe in nature, it represents heaven, earth, and water. For the spiritual, it means spirit, soul, and body. Think of how often things come in threes. There is the past, present, and future. The circle of one's life—birth, marriage, death. It is symbolic throughout history in many countries. Some churches have the holy trinity, pregnancy has three trimesters, and my favorite—there are three sides to a story: his side, her side, and the truth. Those are just a few examples. It goes deeper."

"The three wise men. A genie grants three wishes," Vanity mumbled.

"Yeah. That sort of thing."

"Now my question is why did Madame Cecil tell me I possess it, and what does that mean for me?"

"What exactly did she say?"

"She called me femme de trois vies, a three-life woman. Somehow, I have had three births, once as a baby, a second on the side of a road, and this one as a bloodsucker."

"That's the first time I've ever heard the power of three in that sense. Three births?"

"It's what she said. I also can't leave the bayou. The accident that took my memories was used as a hijacking for a priestess who made a deal with a man I was with. She brought me back to life with no memory and bound me here so she could steal my life."

Now those words in her mind made sense, jumping around searching for a spot to stick. I rolled her to her back and stroked the side of her face.

"We're going to do everything we can to help you find out who you were in your past and get that curse removed—especially if we lose this fight and have to flee N'awlins."

She smirked. "I won't lose, and I hope we can get this hex off of me. I'd love nothing more than to travel the world with you and not be confined here. That island your people come from sounds like a nice place to start."

I kissed her mauve lips. "Sounds like a plan."

Birds chirping outside below the kaleidoscope of blue hues in the sky ended our night of passion. Dawn was upon us. A new day to figure out our next moves and watch our backs. "I need to feed," Vanity whispered, with eyes glowing solid red, staring at the window.

The chill down my spine knew pancakes and strawberries wouldn't satisfy this hunger. I rose from the bed and offered to go with her to the swamps, but she declined.

"I don't care for you to watch me," she said.

"I'll look away. I just want to make sure you're safe. And let my brothers know not to attack you."

"Fine. You drive." *'And cover your sexy ass up,'* her thoughts read.

I grinned.

She scoffed, unamused by the smirk on my face. "Ugh, I have to remember I'm marked." She vanished from the room.

CHAPTER 21
THE KYOUDAI
CASON

I HURRIED to the swamp before the sun fully rose. Driving out of the city limit, V's breasts bounced like a mound of *Jell-O* from the potholes in the road. I watched them and smiled to myself. Vanity smirked. "Only one of us in this car has a hundred percent chance of surviving a deadly car crash. Eyes on the road." The smile on my face grew wider at her smartass mouth and assurance.

Quiet out in the bayou meant one thing. Danger was near. I asked V to stay close as I sniffed for who and what was near. She ignored my request and jetted off near the marsh. A crack and heavy inhalation filled my left ear, and faint taps into the mud filled my right.

I followed the sound of the crack and trekked to my left toward Vanity, kneeling with her legs spread apart, sucking the life out of a beaver. She peered over her shoulder at me, then turned away to face the water.

"We're being watched," I said.

She grunted, then continued to smack and lick her fingers. I turned away, scanning through the mist as the steps became closer. *Swoosh*, the body of the beaver hit the water. "So, let them watch. I'm not afraid. Are you, big boy?" She patted my ass and winked, then strolled farther down the edge. *Swoosh*, she reached down into the water and snatched another beaver hiding just below the summit.

The slicing and cracking of the poor animal unsettled me momentarily, then I thought, *'Better it than a human,'* and shook off my disapproval.

Eyes were now upon us. Six to be exact. I growled and braced myself for the pain of transition as my blood began to surge throughout my body.

"Vanity! We're not alone!"

"I know." She appeared at my side straightaway.

"Vanity?" one of the voices hissed.

"Who dare calls my name?!" Her eyes turned crimson.

The steps slowly approached closer through the smog, and I heard their thoughts. *'Kyoudai.'* I reached up and held Vanity back with my hand.

"Brothers," I grunted.

"Cason." Sana appeared before me.

The boiling blood in my veins began to cool at the sound of his voice. I relaxed my chest and squeezed V on the shoulder. Sana, Junichiro, and Shun glared at me with a thin layer of fog between us, then shifted their eyes to Vanity.

She tossed the flesh of the beaver over her shoulder into the water and wiped the blood residue from the side of her mouth. Her red eyes switched back to brown as she stood on one side with her hands at her sides, wiggling her fingers, slightly on alert.

"Nice to see you again, Sana." Vanity smiled.

"Normally I would say the same, but something's different about you."

"I can explain," I said.

"I don't need you to speak for me, Cason." Vanity rolled her eyes at me.

"Let her speak!" Junichiro voiced.

"I am the eldest!" I punched my chest with my fist.

"Calm down, boys. Why the tension?" Vanity chuckled.

"How could you let this happen?" Sana asked.

Vanity tilted her head and grinned at Sana, picking up on his affection for her. She smiled at him the way she smiled at me the first time we fucked on the kitchen counter, and my blood began to boil again.

"I marked her! She is not a threat!"

"She is a vampire!" Sana's voice cracked as he shouted.

"A vampiress," Vanity corrected him. "I'm not like the rest of those dead walkers. As you can see, the sun has risen, and I am fine."

My brothers stared at her posed with her hands on her hips. Sana barely controlled the look of lust in his eyes as Juni and Shun gasped at the revelation.

"I don't care what you call yourself. A bloodsucker is a bloodsucker." Junichiro clicked his tongue and scrunched his nose at V.

"She doesn't consume human blood," I explained.

"Is that so?" Shun asked.

"Yes," she answered. "I prefer these beavers and…"

"Cowbirds," Sana interrupted. "You are the reason we were called here. You left a trail of your sickness out here the other morning. The people here are worried about what is lurking near their homes."

"I'll clean up behind myself next time," she said in a sardonic tone.

Juni spoke to Sana in his head. *'So what, she eats animals. She is what she is now. Stop being a weak little boy for a girl covered in your brother's scent that is never going to love you back. Stand up for yourself. Stand up for what we believe in.'*

"V, go wait in the car," I said with venom on my tongue.

"We good?" Vanity asked them.

Sana nodded. Juni seethed with veins popping from his neck. Shun lowered his head and looked up at me.

"See you boys around." Vanity snatched another beaver on the edge a few feet away from us and strutted to the car.

We watched her walk away and cringed at the neck snapping of her prey. Sana exhaled deeply from his chest, then spit in the dirt with disgust formed at his brows.

"How the fuck could you let this happen to her? You knew how I felt about her?" He huffed.

"How *we* felt about her. It was no secret we both wanted her."

"And it's obvious she made the wrong choice."

"She was violently attacked a few nights ago. If I was around, I would have protected her like I am now."

"And I would have wifed her by now. With me, she would have been safe."

"Enough!" Juni announced. "Have you told her everything?"

"I have not. It's been a hectic few days, as you can see. This is fresh to all of us."

"The sooner she knows, the better," said Shun.

"All this time, Vanity has been the one the seer warned about." Sana shook his head. "Tell her tonight."

I nodded. "I need a favor in the meantime. Tell the locals they have nothing to worry about and find a way to have the prey she feasts on delivered to the café. I don't want her out here alone. Also, a battle is coming. The pale face that did this to her may or may not be dead. I hope to know more the next time we speak."

Simultaneously, we pounded our chests. "Brothers." I bowed my head and walked away with my head held high.

"Brother," the lot of them said to me in the lowest baritone I'd ever heard them speak.

Shun's mind remained clear as I left them behind, but Juni's and Sana's thoughts troubled me. Juni's more than Sana. I could feel the hurt flowing through Sana as his mind pictured him and V laughing together on a swing. I knew he loved her as much as I did, but as Juni preached earlier, he would have to get over it and accept she chose me.

The anger raging inside Juni stemmed from his resentment of me as the eldest and their alpha. With Vanity becoming one of our natural enemies, he'd use that more than anything to take her away from me as his way of hurting me. He fought to resist his thoughts of hovering over her in wolf form, ripping out her throat, but I saw it deep inside of him and feared I had two battles to prepare myself for.

When I hopped into the car, Vanity sat on the passenger side, cleaning her fingernails. Avoiding eye contact with me, she questioned, "What was with all the secrecy?"

"I'll tell you later tonight. Let's get out of here and head into work."

"Speaking of work, who can run the café for an hour at sunset?"

"Why?" I scowled.

"I need to check out this cemetery Billie mentioned, and I could use some reinforcement." She looked to me with mesmerizing eyes, asking without asking.

I sighed. "I'll arrange it once everyone arrives for their shift. I wouldn't let you go there alone. I'm all yours."

CHAPTER 22

THE CEMETERY

CASON

AFTER THE QUIET ride home from the marsh and a busy opening at the café, I kept my word and chaperoned V down to the money side of town. I was a bit worn out from the high energy of last night, the run-in with my brothers, and the bustle of work with zero hours of sleep, but Vanity's newfound life form kept her from feeling the fatigue settling on me.

She was pensive during the drive—more than her usual. Before her transition, I caught her staring off into space quite often, searching her brain for a memory of her past to cling to. I feared she'd one day remember she didn't belong with me, leave me behind, and go back to her real life. Even though I'd marked her, I still feared losing her.

"We're almost there. Whatcha over there planning?"

"I'm wondering who I'm gonna have to kill." She sucked her teeth. "The homes are really nice on this side of town. Maybe when this is all over, you and I should snag us a spot over here."

"So you're a big spender now?"

"Maybe. I am confined here, so why not have the best?"

"Back to the killing part. Think you can turn it down a notch. Say, kill only if necessary and not go into every situation with death on your mind?" I sighed.

"Don't get me wrong, I like Billie. I think she can teach me a few things, but she is what she is, as Sana said."

"Speaking of Sana, what was that back there?" I cleared my throat.

"Jealous?"

I puckered my lips.

"Ha! You are!" V tapped my forearm, then laughed.

"You acted as if you have a thing for my brother."

"Did I?" She mocked me and chuckled lightly. "I've known Sana had a thing for me for years. He is a cutie and a sweetheart, but a dalliance with him wouldn't be as explosive as it is with his big brother, who also has feelings for me." She stared at me with a side-eye.

"That didn't answer my question."

I paused, waiting for her to give me the answer I wanted. She toyed with my emotions, popping out her perfect bosom with an arched back, running her finger back and forth near the crease formed from her cleavage. I exhaled, thinking to myself, *Can't wait to taste those later.*

"Sana was right. He wouldn't have let this happen to you."

"Too late to think about that now. Not unless you want him to join us on the replay from last night." She smirked. "I wonder, could you share me with your brother?"

"Stop playing with me, V."

"I can see it now. Him serving me while I serve you. Ooh, the noise you two would make might wake the dead." She laughed villainously.

"Stop teasing me," I said, feeling my blood warm in my veins.

"So that's a no," she continued to quip.

"We're here."

I parked the car a half mile away from the cemetery just as the crickets began to buzz and the sun ducked behind a row of trees. I lowered my baseball cap just above my brow. "It's this way." I led V toward the main entrance. Her slowed heart rate increased as she walked beside me. "Take my hand." I reached for hers. She grinned at me and swatted my hand away. "What was that for?"

"What's with the sappy act? You weren't a gentleman last night," she said, twirling her eyes at me.

"I figured we could appear to be on an evening stroll, instead of stomping around the grounds like we're on a mission."

"Good idea. Thought you were getting soft on me."

If only you knew.

"Later we may need to clarify the gender roles in this relationship," I joked.

Vanity belted a loud laugh as she took my hand. A flutter in my chest puzzled me, and I began to question exactly how soft and sappy I had become.

"Damn that smells good. Almost as good as the food on our side of town."

"If this goes well, how about I treat you afterward…" I slowly stopped, my mouth running all on its own. "It slips my mind. Still fresh, you know."

"I understand. It's new to us both. The smell is inviting, but I'm not so sure the taste of it will be. The only food I seem to want are your specialties. To be honest, I don't know if I can stomach it."

We crossed through the iron gate, light on our feet, listening to the quiet. "You got anything? All I'm getting are crickets. How about you?" She placed her finger in the center of my mouth, then paused our steps. One foot slowly slid forward, then turned east. V wrapped her fist around the top of my shirt, then led me down a narrow aisle with a granite angel statue welcoming us forward.

"This would be easier if we knew Billie's last name," I said.

"I know. Don't pretend as if you didn't see how fast she took off before I could ask her last night."

"The list grows longer. We need to discuss gender roles and that smartass mouth of yours," I whispered.

Please. You love it. I read her mind.

"I might."

"Dammit. I don't think I like you doing that." She rolled her eyes at me.

Together we paused and set our eyes on a tomb resting ahead on the right. Her fist released my shirt, and I flattened out the wrinkles.

"There's movement in that one." She pointed.

"Stay here while I check it out."

CHAPTER 23
THE PLEA
CASON

THE SILVER in my eyes radiated in the dark alley as the sun escaped the N'awlins sky. I approached the tomb, alert to rustling and whispers inside. I raised my hand and signaled the number two to Vanity.

She planted into my mind. *I hear them.*

The motion and chatter stopped abruptly. My fingers waved for Vanity to follow me sliding in the shadow of the tomb across from the one in question. I looked where she was standing and found a vacant alley. *Where the fuck did she go?* I turned back toward the tomb as the stone began to scrape. My veins grew plump from adrenaline and worry about V's safety. Like a flash of blurred lightning, Vanity appeared in front of the opened tomb and snatched the ass-vamp who turned her. "Carlisle," I mumbled and ran beside her and placed my hand above hers, clenching his throat.

Vanity spoke. "How is this one not dismembered?"

"Love, please. When you talk like that, it excites me," I groaned. "If that is your wish, it will only take a second, my dear."

Billie exited her family's resting place and stood beside us. Vanity left Carlisle in my grasp and wrapped her hand around Billie's throat, then lifted her in the air.

"I thought I could trust you," she said.

Billie's feet swayed below her. "You can trust me."

"Not with that last name. Punishment for the sins of your forefather will apply to you, Billie Hays."

"I'm nothing like those hicks who came before me." She struggled midair.

"You expect me to believe you when I catch you out here with the enemy." Vanity's voice deepened like that of a baritone.

"He showed up here just before dawn and begged me to take him in before burning in the sun."

"It's true. I had nowhere else to go after I escaped." Carlisle squeezed from between his lips, lifeless in my grip. "I'm on the run from Adela."

"You should have let him burn!" V roared, then faced Carlisle. "Why didn't Adela kill you?"

"Someone on the inside helped free me before she woke. I'm certain she'll have me hunted tonight. I need to leave the city."

"That's impossible. Also, not my concern. Though I do wonder how you have managed to escape a permanent death twice."

"Call it luck. I hope you have more mercy upon me tonight."

"If she does, I don't." My grip tightened around his neck piercing blood from a vein. "You have to pay for your attack. This entire dilemma is your fault."

"I beg for forgiveness—yours and hers." He squirmed. "I pledge my allegiance to Vanity, my vampiress."

"What did your once precious queen do to deserve such a double-crossing piss ant like you? And now you beg to serve me." She scoffed. "You can serve me alright. On your knees."

"Gladly," he said, grinning at me.

I growled as I released him and bared my teeth, preparing to end him against Vanity's wishes. He leaned forward and kissed the back of her hand, then grinned at me once more. V sent a mental message to me.

Not yet. We can use him.

"What can you share of Adela's hunt tonight?" She released Billie from her clutch.

"I know the city won't be safe. Her army is ruthless and will feed on anyone they please. When Adela is angry, she doesn't care about the people of this city as much as she pretends to," Carlisle blabbed.

"Which is why they fear her," Billie added.

"How many will be at the mansion?" Vanity inquired.

"Maybe a dozen, but her best soldiers will be protecting her."

"Coming from you, that makes me think I'm walking into a set-up more than a challenge. And looking at you makes me want to place your face next to 'double-backstabbing prick' in the dictionary," said V.

I read her mind as she glanced in my direction with a menacing look in her eyes.

Cason, I say we go evict the bitch living in our new house.

No. We're not ready.

The three of us can take out twelve men easy.

Billie isn't invincible like you, and neither am I. Patience, my love.

A shrieking scream parted V's lips. I felt her anger cover me as my knees quivered from the screeching sound. She punched the stone, resting her fist between the cracks.

"What's wrong with her?!" Billie shouted.

"She's angry!"

I dragged Carlisle by his throat against the tomb, then knocked his head against the stone. I whispered in Vanity's ear, "You're luring Adela's army straight to us, and we need to get the word out about her attack." The shrieking abruptly stopped, and she removed her dust-covered hand from the stone. A gold light gleamed as the cut on her hand healed. "What the..." I muttered. I had never seen anything like it. Her golden healing trick was captivating and beautiful, and I couldn't see her as a vampire in that moment. I saw her as a goddess. My goddess.

The three of us observed her scar mend until the goldish hue vanished from her skin.

Vanity spoke to me internally. *Send word to your brothers.*

She extended her hand to Billie. "Make sure Madame Cecil is safe during the raid. If you survive the night, meet me at the café before dawn. There's a foreclosed home on my side you can stay in. If you want this fucker to join you, suit yourself. Your choice, not mine."

Billie shook her hand and nodded. "I guess this means you're coming with me." She looked to Carlisle.

Vanity took my hand. "Like I said…your choice."

We raced to the car. Vanity's slowed heart rate increased from the adrenaline pumping throughout her rage-filled bones like an athlete on steroids.

"Does that telekinetic magic work for you and your brothers all the time?"

"Not in the way you're thinking."

"Call Sana and warn them."

"I will as soon as we get to the car. You sure you're ready for this?"

"Doesn't seem like we have a choice."

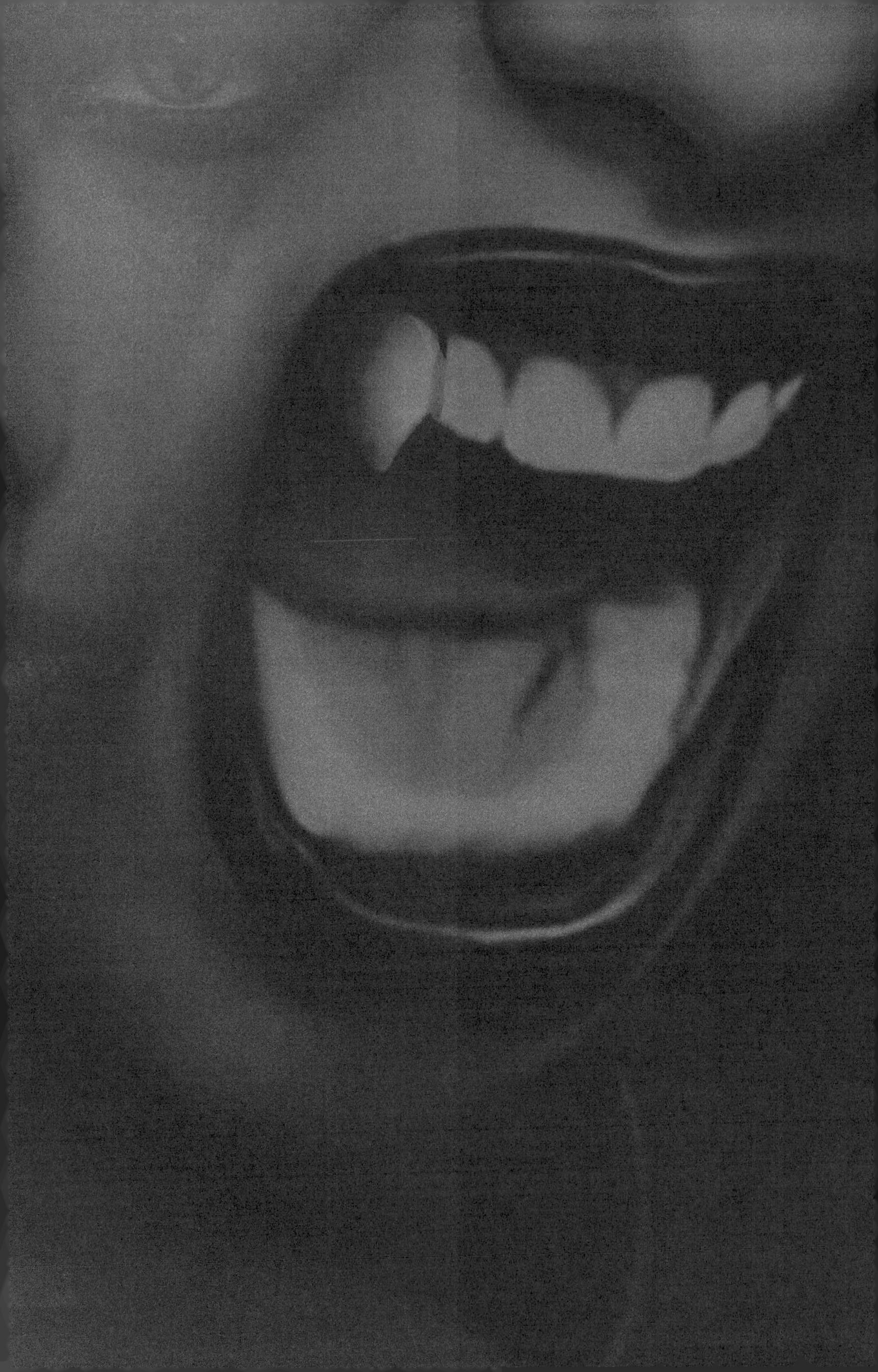

CHAPTER 24

THE CONNECT

VANITY

I HEARD my name sputtered with creative descriptors by Junichiro. His disdain toward me could be heard in his piercing, rage-filled voice through the phone. Juni yelled, "You lay with our enemy! How can you lead us?!"

I rolled my eyes and thought to myself, *Give it a rest.* Cason exhaled from his brother's emotional outburst, then scorned me with his eyes as he read my mental note. *Watch him closely the next time.* I cringed as he talked over Cason, questioned his leadership, and tested his patience until the king inside of him erupted.

"Enough, Juni!" Cason's eyes turned silver as he punched his hand into the wheel. "Brothers, I've received word of an attack happening tonight by Adela's army. Tell everyone in the bayou to be on alert."

"Where will you be?" Sana asked.

"I'm leaving the Garden with V now. We're going to warn as many as we can in the city and fight until the sun comes up. I'll see you then."

"Be safe, brother, and protect her until we figure this out. There's something urgent we need to discuss."

Disturbed by the call, Cason sighed and threw his phone into the seat. He glanced at me in between keeping his eyes on the road and speeding toward the city limit.

"We'll worry about Juni later," I said.

"Sooner than later. I need to smooth things over with him and Sana. He's worried about you and says there is something we need to discuss."

"I'll deal with Sana. I'll let him down easy. Unless…you've reconsidered my suggestion from earlier." I winked.

He growled, shook his head, then ran his hand through his hair. "It saddens me to know you are serious about that." He sighed.

"And?"

"And makes me miss the old Vanity—the sweet and innocent one."

"What if she wasn't…sweet and innocent?"

"I'd still love her, and it's how I'll always remember her."

His adoration for the woman that was part of my past deserved my loyalty. Beyond the unscarred mark where he staked his claim. I lowered the sun visor and circled my neck where I could feel its sting, then reflected on how he took care of the sweet one he missed.

He deserved to hear I loved him, but the words were something I could not fix my mouth to say.

I leaned over and kissed his cheek. "I'll stop teasing you about it."

The dip in his cheek formed, and he smiled on the side of his mouth.

"How do you want me to make it up to you?" I asked him with the image of him fucking me bent like a pretzel flashing in my head.

"That'll do." He joked.

"You got it. Now explain to me how this plan of yours is going to work."

"There is one person all the wards in The Easy respect. With his connections and control, I'm sure he can get the word out that a raid is upon us."

"And people will listen to him and stay inside?" I questioned with doubt.

"I'm certain of it."

"Well, I hope so. I'll hate it if I have to undo any damage she causes when I could have eliminated her tonight at her mansion."

"It's not as easy as you imagine. People aren't telling you the full story about Adela and her powers."

My patient tone turned demanding. "Then enlighten me."

Cason parked the car near the edge of a corner on a one-way street across from a housing project. He turned off the engine and scoped the perimeter from all possible angles. "I will once we get out of here."

"Where exactly are we?"

"The Grove. Third Ward. Home of Keshell Martin."

CHAPTER 25

THE WARDS

VANITY

CASON LOOKED over his shoulder continuously with shifty eyes and concerned brows. We were being watched, but the ward didn't frighten me. I hopped out of the car with my sworn protector grasping at my ass to pull me back inside.

"Vanity, wait!" he exclaimed with a whisper, slapping my seat with his palm. "You can't just jump out here. You wait until you're invited in. Get back in the car please."

I leaned down and raised my brows at him. "Fuck that. We don't have time to wait. And what's with you? You've been casing this place like a lookout boy. Eyes have been on us since we arrived, but I don't get the feeling I'll have to snatch them from their sockets. Let's go."

I closed the door and headed toward the porch where three teens sat on blue crates, watching us watch them. Human eyes hiding behind the curtains on several floors stalked me as I entered their territory. The place felt familiar, like I was no longer far from home, and fear was nowhere on the list of emotions flowing through me as I approached the youth.

Bounce music crept into my veins from one apartment, while a heavy bassline from an old-school hip-hop classic sounded from a car parked on the side of the building. T-shirts, towels, and sheets hung from every other balcony on the top two rows, and lights inside of the apartments turned off like dominoes falling in a chain reaction.

Cason caught up with me on the sidewalk. "You and I need to have a serious talk about planning." He fumed.

I scoffed and nodded, then stopped mid-step when a chill traveled down my spine.

Cason messaged me. *I assume that means you've figured out why I was waiting to be invited in.*

Vamps?

Yup.

Just casually hanging out with humans?

Keshell's orders. I'll explain when we get back in the car.

The young boys grinned perfect white teeth amongst each other, then scowled at us, creating a staring competition of who would break first to speak.

"You dere," said a voice from behind.

Cason kept eyes on the boys while I turned around.

"What a gal like ju wan 'round dese here parts?"

I smiled at the sound of his Haitian/Creole accent. "I'm here to speak with Keshell."

"Mi don know a person by dat dere name." The man stuck a toothpick in the side of his mouth, sizing me up like his next conquest.

"Tell him Silver is here to see him," Cason stated with his back turned.

"Silva? Which one a you is Silva? The brown beauty or ju, big man?"

I pointed to Cason.

"Silva, ju think dat name mean somethin' 'round here?" He sucked his teeth. "Mi don know no Keshell."

"Tell him it's important. He knows I wouldn't have come if it wasn't," Cason persisted.

The man removed the toothpick, observed Cason from head to toe, then smiled at me. "Dis your man?" His eyes gazed into mine.

I nodded.

"I know you're Keshell's right hand," said Cason.

"Mi can't say I've seent ju a day in mi life." His smiled turned into a grin.

"Okay, enough making us sweat. Cason, this man knows who you are."

The man wagged his finger at me. "Sharp gal," he said, then nodded to two bulky gentleman who appeared from the left of the building. "Follow me." He walked in between me and Cason and didn't bat an eye. I turned and followed him with Cason peddling on my heels.

A barricade made of graffiti-covered cinder blocks sat in the middle of the courtyard. Mumbles and mutters whispered from every direction, blended with a bongo drum tune from a distorted radio speaker in the center of the terrace. Two of my kind standing in front of the door of a blue-and-yellow caravan hissed at Cason.

I flashed my crimson eyes in return and stood in front of him. "Not today," I hissed back.

The door of the caravan crept open with flowing tie-dyed pants and suede sandals strolling down the steps. A cloud of ganja smoke preluded the shirtless, earthly creature, and without a doubt, the most beautiful black man I'd ever laid eyes on appeared before me.

Beneath the moonlight, one of his eyes appeared hazel, the other cool brown. His locks were neatly twisted and longer than mine, hanging to the middle of his back, and his shiny skin had to be the inspiration when naming The Black Sea. Smooth, silky, and luminous.

He lifted his hand, and the two men trailing us returned to the barricade, then he opened his mouth, and I shivered at his grill covered in pure gold.

Well shit.

A low grunt in Cason's throat made me chuckle.

I smirked. *That's what you get for reading my thoughts.*

Keshell retracted his fangs, looked at Cason, then slowly turned his head to me. "Silva. Been a long time. Must be important. Who dis goddess whichya?" he asked, never taking his eyes off me.

"Goddess is absolutely right. V meet Keshell. Keshell meet V."

"V is it? You must be the commotion I'm hearin' 'bout from the streets."

"I like reggae music myself," I said.

"It may sound like reggae to ya, but back home we call it compas. And I like flattery. What can I do ya for?"

"We come with a warning."

I interrupted. "To prevent a bloodbath."

"Adela has given her goons the order to wreak havoc on the streets tonight. Can you get the word out to the city?"

"How you come to know dis?" Keshell inhaled the final puff of his joint, then blew it out away from my face.

"The one they call *king* is now her foe. She hunts for him."

"Carlisle?"

"Yes," I added.

Keshell grinned at me and pressed the glowing red ash on his chest, then flicked the roach to the ground. He looked up at me.

"Let me guess. Ya have part in this?"

"I do now."

"Ya know Adela?"

"Never met her."

"I'm betting she knows you." He nodded to the vamp sitting on his right. "Somethin' 'bout ju has set her off. Wha'tis it about ju that has the mad queen seeking blood?"

"I've never met one of your kind like V," Cason interrupted.

"Ya mean prettier than me?" Keshell joked.

Cason chuckled. "I mean different. Show him."

"*You* show him," I snapped, then placed my neck to Cason's mouth.

Cason's eyes turned silver, and the blood pumping through his veins burst with a greatness. My eyes met Keshell's as Cason bit into my neck, fighting the heat growing inside of him. He grunted as he eased off and wiped my blood from his mouth. The two subordinates at Keshell's side hissed, obediently staying in their place.

The golden light within me lit on my neck as the scar healed. Keshell's hazel and brown eyes sparkled into mine.

"The whispers I've heard 'bout ju don do ya justice. Where ya from?"

"I don't know. That's a story for another time."

Keshell pointed to one of his soldiers at the gate. He whizzed to his side. "Get word out to the lieutenants to close up shop tonight, and tell Hesh to warn Bourbon and Frenchman that Adela is on her bullshit tonight." The messenger nodded, then fled in the blink of an eye. "You two may want to camp out here tonight. Adela's army knows all bets are off on dis here side."

"Thank you, but we have other matters to tend to." My eyes flashed from brown to golden to red.

His eyes widened. "Respect. But our bidness not over. Ju and I have much to discuss. Come back'n see me when ya wan' know your root."

"I'll keep that in mind. Nice meeting you."

Keshell blurred and appeared directly in my face. He lifted my hand, kissed the back of it, then said, "The pleasure's been all mine."

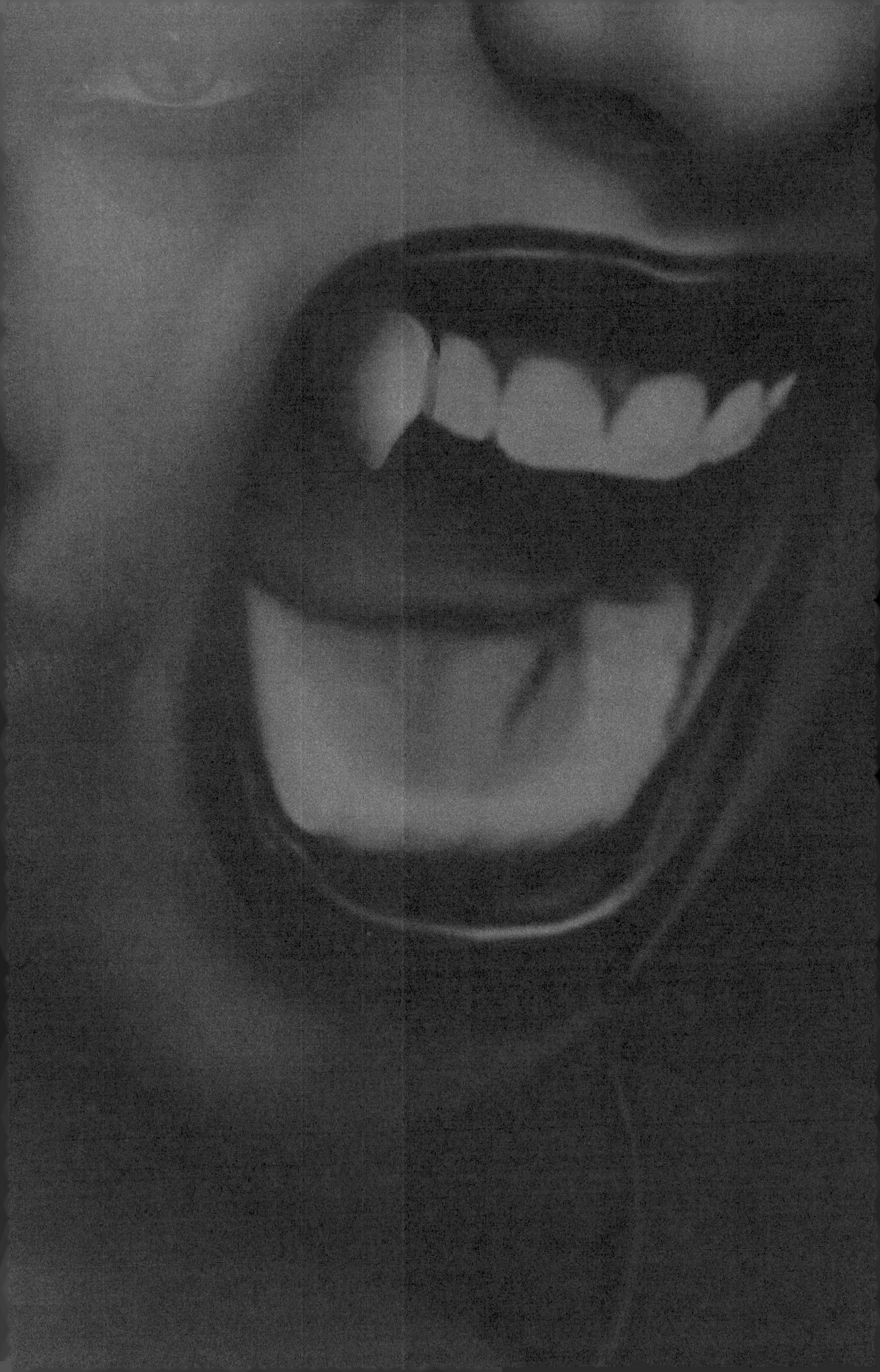

CHAPTER 26
THE WORD
VANITY

I POSED with my back against the car door and waited for Cason to hop inside. "What's the story here? *You*, friends with a vampire? How long were you going to keep that little gem in your pocket?"

"I wouldn't call us friends. Keshell is more like an acquaintance, V."

"An acquaintance with a natural-born enemy. How did that come to pass?"

"He sniffed me out as soon as I arrived into town. It's one of his super-powers—or whatever your kind calls it."

"One of?"

"Yeah." Cason took a big swallow. "Remember when you asked me about the power of three?"

"I do."

"Well, Keshell has been rumored to have powers of his own. He's a visionary of some sort. They also say he can sense powerful creatures who enter the city."

"So when he said he heard about me in the streets..."

"His spies were most likely sent to verify a feeling he had after your transition. It was only a matter of time until he paid you a visit."

"I see. What's his other power?"

"It's been said he can raise the dead."

"That guy's a necromancer?"

"That's the word. As long as the head is not severed, he can bring back anyone or any creature. I haven't seen him do it personally, but I believe it by the way he controls the vampires running the other wards."

"Without having seen it myself, I believe it. There is a mystique about him. I could feel it." My shoulders shivered.

Cason gave me the side-eye as he sped through red lights on our way toward the café. As I processed the new information of my possible ally, a flaw in Cason's explanation stumped me.

"I'm confused. Between Adela and Keshell, who is feared the most of the two?"

Cason puckered his lips and hummed. "Hmm. Hard to say. Adela is feared and hated. Keshell is feared but also respected. He's restored order in The Easy."

"How so?" I sighed.

"Unlike you, your kind consumes blood to survive, but Keshell has a system in place with the other wards. He doesn't condone bloody murder for the sake of hunger and lack of control. Vampires can feed on the locals and the tourists as long as they don't kill them, and they must compel their victims to forget the attack. The vampires that disobey are treated like the humans who commit theft, domestic abuse, and murder within the city. He calls them bandits, and they are rarely seen by the law. They are given to Keshell as offerings by his lieutenants, and that's how he feeds."

"A vampire with systemic morale," I scoffed.

"He's the one true enemy Adela had 'round here—until you. It'll be interesting to see if she violates their truce."

I glared at Cason, perturbed at his tone insinuating I was the cause of Adela's fury. *The fuck did he mean 'until you'?* I rolled my eyes and sighed.

"I didn't mean it like that," he said, having read my thoughts.

I fanned him off. "Earlier you mentioned that I don't know the full story about her powers. What aren't you telling me?"

Cason avoided eye contact with me, shifting his eyes to both sides of the road. His fingers stretched before gripping the wheel tight, and he exhaled so deep I could hear his heart pause for a few seconds.

"Legend has it, she can set you on fire with the snap of her fingers."

"So I'll take her hands off first."

"I said *legend*. What if she can do it from simply looking at you?"

"So I'll take her eyes and her hands off."

He huffed. "Damn, you're confident."

"Is that all?"

"That's enough, shit."

"If that *is* true, why didn't she burn Carlisle when she held him captive?"

"Because she's a sadistic, crazy bitch. She gets off on affliction and takes prisoners captive to torture them."

Fear trembled in Cason's voice. It was the first time I felt distress in his hard body. The first time I sensed he was worried about me. I turned from his troubled face and looked ahead on the road as we turned down the street of the café.

"Is it me, or does it seem like Keshell's people got the word out?"

"The roads are empty," Cason said under his breath. "And it's quiet."

"Too quiet."

Bright lights flashed ahead.

"Ahhhh!"

The sound of a rusty engine and loud muffler quickly drowned out my screams.

CHAPTER 27

THE HAVOC

VANITY

SUDDEN IMPACT from a black truck pushed our car from the road and sent us tumbling onto the sidewalk. My head smashed into the window, but my heightened sense of hearing was affected more by the traveling cracks of glass and the banging of the roof rolling against the concrete. The car settled upside down and rocked side to side, then screeched as it slowly leaned sideways on a patch of grass with steam from the engine whistling below a deep growl from Cason's side of the car.

I opened my eyes and turned my head toward him, meeting silver ones gleaming in my direction.

"So it begins," he said with a deep, raspy voice, then grinned on one side of the top of his lip. "You alright?"

"Surprisingly," I answered, reaching for the seatbelt latch.

"Allow me." He reached over and set me free. "What's that look in your eyes? If you're afraid, stay here while I kill these assholes."

"I'm not afraid. I think I remembered something."

Cason's eyes stretched, and a minor smile flashed across his lips. His hands cradled my cheek. "That's good news. We'll unlock the rest of what's hidden in that gorgeous brain of yours soon, but right now we have a visitor approaching your side of the car."

"How many are out there, you think?"

"Let's go see."

I sat still as polished black boots inched closer to my window. A male voice shouted, "There's no movement inside!" Footsteps charged toward Cason's side of the car. Six sets of matching boots surrounded us, laughing and boasting how easy their mission was. I flashed *'now'* in my thoughts, then punched through the shattered glass and pulled the set of feet closest to me inside the car.

He screamed for a split second as I dragged his full body inside, then twisted his head off his neck. I rolled his head like a bowling ball out of my window as his fellow soldiers flew to my side of the car. Cason kicked his door off the hinges and freed himself with ease through the mangled mess, then hopped across the bottom of the car. I snatched a second set of boots. One of his feet kicked me in my already wounded head as he grappled onto the dash, wriggling from my cobra clutch.

I shrieked in pain and unleashed a vicious bite to his neck. He hollered, pulling at my face with his hands to release him. The tang of his sour blood infuriated me as I drained him, tasting the trace of his victims' blood meshed with his. A new trick presented itself to me as I latched onto the soldier. Visions of a captain dressed in black, with identical boots to the pair he was wearing, giving orders for the attack, and a face I met earlier in the night stood in the background as the order was given to kill Cason and me. Then I saw her.

Adela sat on a gold throne, draped in a black-and-red gown with a braided updo replicated from past centuries. She was far from what I expected. I imagined her old and decrepit with bad fashion sense and a hard face. To my surprise, her features were soft, her skin the shade of silk cocoa, her jaw round and mean, looking down on her army. I looked into her eyes from my victim's memory and saw the evil Carlisle spoke of. She was calculating and cold, cutthroat and callous.

The shivering body in my grasp wobbled in my arms, running dry, and the image of his queen faded. Angered by what I saw, I pulled his heart from his chest, and threw it out the window next to the head of his compadre.

A body hit the chassis as I was lugged out from below my two kills by a fist clinging to my hair. Kicks thudded against my stomach from a punk dressed in all black and a beret turned backward. Hunched over from the blows, I muttered, "Nice to meet you, Captain," then grabbed his steady foot while the other was kicked back. I dragged it forward. He toppled over mid-swing. I pounced on top of him and repeatedly slammed his head into the street, cracking an imprint of his noggin into the black tar.

His long arms reached up, running his fingers across my face while I beat him until he was dazed and confused. I raised my hand to end him as a breeze hit me from the left. I rose to my feet, met with a charge from another member of the army. My back smashed against the brick of one of the businesses on the block, denting my figure into its structure. I gasped for a breath, met with a crippling slap to my face. *This fucker's big.*

Be there in a second, Cason messaged.

I got it.

I smiled at the second blow, sending me to the ground. I swept my feet behind him, then jumped into the air. He rolled from where he tripped as my foot came down with all my power, missing him and crushing the sidewalk instead. The ground trembled and roared below my foot, sending a wave of tremors on the block. He removed his beret, threw it to the ground, then positioned his fists to fight.

"You hit like a—"

He punched me in my mouth before I finished my critique. "Like the man about to take your body back to his queen." He chuckled like a kid fascinated with the villain in superhero movies, then slapped me to the ground once again with the back of his hand. "Or you can surrender and give her the pleasure of killing you herself."

I looked up at him. "Is that what she told you?"

"Shut up and stay down. No one asked you to speak."

I lunged at him with the speed of a cheetah, wrapped my legs around his waist, then bit his right cheek off. "God, you fuckers taste awful."

He slung me off him. "You bitch!"

Cason caught me before I fell to the ground. "Allow me."

The two brutes' fists cracked as they met. I feared Cason's wrists were broken from the forceful connection. He swung with his free hand and landed a blow that stunned the last foe standing to the concrete, then shook off the pain throbbing in his other hand. The fallen soldier charged into Cason's stomach. With high-powered blows to his back, Cason pounded him to his knees.

"Now you stay down," he said, then cracked his body in two.

I cleared my throat. "I said I had it."

"And I said I wouldn't let anything happen to you. Are you alright?"

"I'm fine. How many were there?"

"Including your two, I counted seven."

I scoffed. "He would have been three," I said, pointing to the broken brute at his feet, then whizzed past Cason and stole the dead soldier's heart.

As I scouted the scene for the body count, I pulled the hearts out of the remaining four, removed the jacket from the last kill, and tied the six hearts and decapitated head of the night's first slaughter inside of it.

"Was that necessary?" Cason sighed.

"It is."

"Why?"

"To show that bitch I ain't fuckin' 'round."

Cason dragged the bodies we slaughtered behind the café and burned them in the dumpster. After hurling the blood I consumed from my kill, I swiped a t-shirt from the glass case on the wall, then joined him outside. He stood with his arms folded together, cringing at the odor of flesh melting and decade-old rigor mortis and bones crackling in the fire.

"I haven't been back here since it happened." I sighed.

"When all of this is over, I'm moving the café to the Bywater neighborhood. I could use a fresh start. How about you?"

"Because of the trouble I've brought to your doorstep?" I asked.

"I didn't say that."

"You didn't have to. How's your hand? Or is it your wrist I need to be worried about?"

"It's fine. I'm fine. My body hasn't had to tussle in a long while. Pain doesn't last long with me."

"I guess I have to take your word for it." I stared into his distant eyes.

I could see the stress in his forehead, the pulsing temple on the side of his face, and the constant breaths he exhaled as he collected himself while I tried to read his mind and evade his initial question.

We had more to discuss, and I had personal conflicts to solve before I agreed to something serious. Then it dawned on me that I was already forever tied to him since I had been marked.

I needed to get more clarity of our connection, besides the physical and sharing mental space. There was definitely a pull I felt when I was near him. I was sure it was love, but the powers and changes happening with me derailed the explanation I desperately needed to know why I couldn't say what he had been waiting to hear for two years.

"I'm pretty sure it's against the health code to have dead hearts and a severed head inside the restaurant, V."

"Don't worry. They will be disposed of by morning."

Cason exhaled deeply and rotated his shoulders. "I hope so."

"In the meantime, what are we going to do about a car?"

"Give me a few days. I'll have that sorted out." He glanced at me and turned away. "Has Billie sent word?"

I looked at my phone. "Still nothing."

"We ought to go check on the Madame. It's still a few hours until the sun sends those fuckers hiding to their bat cave."

I grabbed the bag of kills from beside the dumpster and threw it over my shoulder. "Thought you'd never ask."

We set out on foot toward the touristy streets of Bourbon and Frenchman. Not a soul in sight, but eerie eyes stared at us from the owners of hotels, bars, shoppes, and rooftop apartments hiding from Keshell's warning.

Low jazz tunes pacified the fear raining down on the block covered with shiny, reused throws hanging from the posts and abandoned kiosk carts. A window above one of the restaurants opened wide, and the music shut off. "I bet I can tell ya where ya got ya shoes!" a voice yelled from inside the multicolored loft. Cason placed his arm in front of me as we stopped in the middle of the bead-covered street.

"On your feet!" Cason shouted.

"I've been here two years. I knew the answer to that."

"Adela knows you're not from here. She's sending a message that you, my dear, are a tourist."

"Ol' bitch," I muffled below my breath.

A balled-up note fell at my feet from the balcony. I looked at it, then back to the apartment window where the jazz music began playing once again. The tenant turned the volume up louder than the soft tunes heard from the loft when we first arrived, and its shadow watched us like a black silhouette in a red light.

"You keep watch. I'll pick it up." Cason swiftly kneeled and opened the wrinkled sheet, then read aloud. "I will torture the people of this city, then burn it to the ground until your head rests on a spike in my garden for the crows to feed on."

"She sounds lovely, doesn't she?" I quipped.

"What's her beef with you again?" Cason asked without the bass in his voice.

"My presence, my power, and my maker. She's pissed Carlisle fell in love with me and kept me a secret."

"That prick is definitely not worth all this trouble."

"What about me?"

"I'm here, aren't I?"

My nipples pebbled below my shirt. "God I can't wait to get home and have my way with you."

"I can see that." He grinned.

The soles of boots stamped along the sidewalk and into the middle of the street. One by one, Adela's army jumped from rooftops and balconies, surrounding us like the darkness.

"Any chance some of them will switch whose side they're on?" I joked, then dropped the bag of death from my shoulder.

"Ugh. Seriously doubt it. I also doubt the people who live in those apartments are still alive."

My eyes turned red with fury. My hands shook uncontrollably from Cason's morbid—but most likely accurate—assumption. I placed my back against Cason's and lost count of the many soldiers closing in on us. "Since they don't want to play fair, why should I?" I said, then closed my eyes and reached within.

My hands stopped shaking as I regained control of my anger. I placed them at my sides, palms facing outward and opened my eyes. Heaves flooded my chest as the rushing winds picked up, and my allies of the night swarmed in from above. I raised my hands and orchestrated a group of the bats in the shape of a V, then guided them toward the vampires charging toward Cason.

They jumped, screamed, and dodged the swarm as best as they could while their brethren stepping forward on my side of the street watched on in amazement.

"What the fuck is happening right now?" Cason questioned.

"You're welcome. Let's fuck these assholes up."

CHAPTER 28

THE UNCAGING

VANITY

AIR RUSHED me as Cason leapt forward to dismantle the horde escaping the swarm. I dashed forward to the soldiers facing me, took off two heads with ease, and tossed them on the sidewalk below a rusted balcony. The beads hanging from the iron jangled like music to my ears as I spun between the group of brave ones surrounding me. Before they could box me in, I zigzagged my way around the circle and ripped out the hearts of three, sliced the neck of two with my coffin-shaped nails, and snatched the head of one before two warriors held me against my will by my arms and gnawed at my shoulders.

"Aaauughaaaa!" I echoed into the night. The bloodsuckers released me and fell to their knees, holding their ears. Cason eased beside me with scratches on his beautiful face. He cradled his ears with pain in his eyes. My crippling shriek bought us time to catch a breather as a gold light flashed from my arms, healing my wounds.

Internally, we spoke.

You good? I asked.
Yes…but your scream…affects us all.
Get ready to fight.

With my back resting on Cason's, I closed my mouth, and the gang rose to their feet, attacking us simultaneously from both sides. Hit in the face, kicked in the shins, and thrown into the glass door of the tattoo shop in the middle of the block, was far from my idea of being gangbanged.

I jumped to my feet before the approaching stampede rushed me inside. I caught the closest night devil, snapped his neck, and used his body to swing around like a cyclone to clear a path back to Cason.

"There's too many of them, Vanity!"

"No shit! We knew this wouldn't be a fair fight going in!"

"I have no choice!"

"For what?!"

"Move back!" he shrieked.

A howl of grueling agony turned the blood-thirsty eyes of Adela's goons into bloodcurdling fright. I did as he ordered, slowly pacing backward with the mob of bats circling me for protection.

Bones cracking and snapping weakened my back as the screams bursting from Cason tortured my soul. Through gaps of open space, I watched him transform into the innate altered being trapped inside of him. Such a sight was captivating and horrific to my eyes—the elongation of his muscular arms tripling in size, the platinum hair sprouting from his pores materializing a thick, silver mane, and the sweatpants I adored him in, bursting into shreds of gray cotton into the middle of the street.

Cason's legs changed shape before my eyes, and I felt faint. His strong, cut legs were now wider than three versions of himself, and white claws at his feet created a creature of beauty that took my breath away. A roar of arrival echoed from his lips, then he turned to face me. A tiny, feather-like image glistened in the center of his eyes. I grinned at The Silver Leaf King glowing in the moonlight of a blood-filled street, acknowledging his adoration for me after the pain he'd just tolerated on my behalf.

He charged the crowd before him, biting the heads off of fleeing vampires running back to their crazed queen. The brave ones attacked him from the side and behind, climbing on top of him and being thrown into the bricks and balconies with an effortless jerk from his body. While Cason kicked his attackers with his hind legs, sending them down the street, thrashing the fleeing horde to the ground, I pounced and pulled as many hearts from their wounded bodies with the superspeed of a cheetah on steroids.

A duo of death-wishing soldiers that moved as fast as I did tag-teamed an attack during my wrath. I found myself passed between the pair, striking me back and forth like a tennis ball on match point for a championship, neither of them letting up, neither of them willing to lose Adela's prized trophy. I withstood the tortuous game, timing which of the two was the fastest, and which of the two was weaker.

As the blows bruised my skin, and hints of gold light attempted to heal me in the milliseconds I was between them, I grabbed the fist of the weakest vamp and found my footing, then threw him into his partner, immediately charging them both as they clashed. My fangs sunk into the back of the punk on top, while my sharp nail pierced the eye of the one on the bottom.

Being the stronger of the two, he threw me and his partner off him. "That bitch took my eye!" he hollered. I swept past his blind side and stuck my nail into his other eye as Cason's shadow darkened my view from the streetlights. He bit the other vampire in two and pressed forward through the wall of bats picking the others apart.

The numbers of Adela's army decreased heavily by the seconds with wise followers abandoning the battle and brainwashed soldiers fighting Cason and me to the permanent death they believed they would escape. And as the final exchange of blows ensued, I noticed a solo vampire running into a dead-end alleyway.

I looked at the *Dead End* warning sign posted on the bricks.

"It sure is," I snarled.

Let it go. It could be a trap, flashed in Cason's thoughts.

I'll be fine. Just finish them.

CHAPTER 29

THE MESSENGER

VANITY

THE LIGHT from the street faded with every extra step I made toward the acute angle of shadow from the side of the building. Darkness surrounded the smell of old beans, fresh blood, and rotten vegetables, masking the scent of fear from the vamp prolonging its date with death. "The sun will be up soon. May as well get it over with now or fry like an egg in the street," I said.

A cat moved in the garbage, and I sprang to its location, swooping it up with my hands. "You're not who I'm looking for," I whispered, freeing it from my grasp. "You are!" I declared, rushing to the back corner where the buildings conjoined.

By his throat, I lifted the lanky body into the air and pinned him up against the grimy bricks. "Please, don't hurt me. I'm just a kid," he begged with sparing breaths.

I tightened my hold of him. "A kid in an evil bitch's army, no less."

"Not by choice." He trembled. "Please, I came to this city with my parents as a graduation present."

I lowered him to his feet, observing the fear in his eyes. He lacked courage with zero fight in him. No aggression. No nerves.

His lips shivered. "I wanted to see the great jazz musicians play music live, and my mom and dad brought me here. I snuck out of our hotel to enjoy the city without my parents watching my every move and was attacked in the bathroom of a bar. I woke up with this thirst for blood and a burning sensation on my skin. I slid away from the window and stayed hidden in the bar until nightfall, begging people for help and killing them uncontrollably until another vampire knocked me unconscious. When I woke, I was in the presence of Adela's captain. He gave me two choices: pledge my allegiance or die by sunlight."

"And you pledged, of course."

"I didn't want to die. I still don't want to die. I want to be the old me. I want to see my parents." Red tears fell down his brown cheeks.

I cradled his face. "Such a blessing to know your past and a curse to want it back, but you can't like this."

"I beg you. I don't want to fight. I don't want to be like this. I just wanna go home."

"What's your name, boy?"

"Malik."

I took his hand. "Come with me."

Together, we exited the alley. Cason stood at the opening, grunting and flouncing. I messaged his mind.

I'm sparing this one.

Why?

Look at him.

The silver leaf in his eyes gleamed and examined the boy. *He's just a kid.*

I know. Makes me wonder how many kids we've slaughtered tonight.

Vanity, a vampire is a vampire!

Don't use that tone with me!

It's true. His tone simmered down.

I hear you. But this one hasn't drunk the Kool-Aid. He doesn't want to fight. He thinks he can be cured and go back to his human life.

So what are you going to do with him?

I held his hand and led him to the center of the street where the night's battle began. "I have something for you," I said, then rummaged through the stack of death contaminating the street. "Take this," I said, placing the pouch of piled hearts and severed head across his back. "Deliver this to Adela's house as your pledge of allegiance to me. Do what you have to do to stay alive. If I don't see you in the next battle, I'll know she killed you, and I will avenge your death."

A red tear bubbled in the corner of his eye. "Please don't send me back there."

"It's the only way I'll know I can trust you. Because frankly, my boy, vampires can't be trusted. Remember that."

He nodded.

"If I do see you in the next battle and find out you've lied to me, I will come for you first. But if your pledge tonight was honest, I will help you find your way home."

"Like this? I can't go home like this. I want to be cured. Can you help me with that?"

"I'll ask around, but I haven't heard of a cure. Use that optimism to stay alive to see what I've learned the next time we meet. Now go."

Malik opted to walk away slowly instead of escaping with the speed his nature afforded him. Cason whimpered, nudging me from behind. I turned around and touched him as Silver for the first time, running my face against his jaw and brushing his coat with my stained hands.

"Sorry about the mess. I couldn't resist. You're gorgeous."

Which do you like best? Cason or this beast?

I rubbed my nose against his muzzle. *Cason, of course, but this'll do when he's not around.*

He sniffed. *I recognize that smell. That sensation has to be burdening*, he teased me.

Only if I don't get what I want.

Hurry. Let's pile the bodies and get out of here.

Cason and I stacked the stiffs into a mound. A human hiding on one of the balconies tossed a flaming shirt on top of the pile and set it ablaze. As the fire trickled down and the heap began to burn, the tenants and shoppe owners who survived the night opened their windows and cheered as the blue sky turned orange with streaks of red and gold.

"I don't want to hear or see how you transform. Well, maybe the last part after it's done." I grinned. "Meet you at the house."

I would hate to shame these men with my goods. He howled, then pranced away.

I waited for the pile to turn to dust and reached inside to channel what was needed to clear the street. *'Petrichor,'* I repeated to myself with my eyes closed, thinking of the day I smelled the rain coming in. Minutes went by, and the scent failed to land on my nose. I called for it desperately, anguished with the result of a dry, cloudless sky.

The sun tipped over the horizon of The Mississippi as rumbling and distant warnings traveled from the block closest to the port. A stream of water flowed over my boots, swishing the residue of blood and ashes past me and down the drain.

About face I turned, smiling to myself on the heels of Cason, embodied with the second power given to me with my curse. And this power, I knew better than myself. Rain water was not needed in this instance, and a quick flow of water from the river was just what the doctor ordered. And I pondered, *The nature of wind and the nature of water. What's next?*

CHAPTER 30
THE BOARDING
VANITY

THE NIGHT WAS on the cusp of meeting dawn as I approached Madame Cecil's shoppe, and I was not alone. His footsteps squished through the puddle flowing down the street, stopping when I paused and picking up behind my every step.

I ducked into the first alley and high-jumped to the top of the building. Looking down below, the shadow of my stalker appeared before his arrival. I plopped down behind him, aware of his identity from the first whiff of his stench embedded in my brain. *Carlisle.*

"The fuck are you doing following me?"

He spun around. "I was watching your back."

"I don't need you to watch my back. Shouldn't you be worried about the sunrise?"

"I am, so can we hurry this along?"

"Where are you coming from?"

"The same as you."

I scoffed. "What did you do? Watch me in action from a corner?"

"More like took care of the back while you and your boy toy played tag team."

"Really? Look at you, making yourself useful. I suppose you want to be rewarded with shelter?" I raised my brow.

"That'd be lovely."

I sucked my teeth and carried on toward Madame's. Billie stood in the doorway with nervous energy. "How did it go here last night?" I asked, taking a quick glance behind her. She looked over her shoulder and shot Madame a salute.

"I did as you asked. Madame Cecil is still in one piece."

"As am I," I added. "Did any of Adela's goons stop by here?"

Billie hopped from the top step and tapped the garbage cans on the curb in front of the shoppe with her foot. "I put two of them down. I know you said to meet you at the café, but I didn't trust leaving her here alone since they showed up."

Madame exhaled, eyeing me with gratitude that I showed up to collect Billie. "As a thank you, I would have put her up in the back until night-fall." She exhaled with a shaky breath. She and I both knew the last thing she wanted to do was house a vampire in her sanctuary.

I grinned at her. "That won't be necessary. I'll be back to have a word with you soon. But you knew that already, didn't you?" I winked at her, then raced the sun-challenged pair to the abandoned house.

I entered the home and circled the open, vacant living room, talking to the lot standing in the entranceway. Billie cleared her throat. "V, how are you able to go inside?" I turned around and chuckled at their pale, worrisome faces, then stopped them from sweating bullets.

"My apologies. You may enter."

They raced through the door together and slammed it shut.

"Follow me," I said, leading them to the bedroom. "There's only one bed, but this room has blackout curtains."

"I thought you said this place was abandoned?" Billie asked.

"It was when I bought it. You're welcome. Enjoy my place as your refuge in the meantime until you two get sorted out."

"Is it safe to say we have proved our loyalty?" Carlisle asked.

I sighed, then took a long pause. "Perhaps. When I return tonight, I expect to be filled in on what Adela's next move will be. I'm sure you are aware."

He nodded.

"And Billie, you and I have a few things to discuss. 'Til tonight." I signed off.

I strolled beneath the orange sky to Cason's house, unsure of what I was going to find. A deep exhale escaped my lips as I readied myself for the awaiting pleasure my body ached for, rushing toward a low, wounded growl coming from the bathroom. There, I found my courageous warrior, stretched out and covered in an ice bath.

"Come. Join me."

CHAPTER 31

THE REWARD

VANITY

I CRAVED his buff body glistening between the melted ice chips, but I could tell he was sore as his limbs healed from the gruesome shifting.

"What's with you being hesitant? I know your appetite."

"I'm covered in blood and filth," I said, turning the nozzle on the shower to full heat. "You sure you can handle me after what you've been through last night, big fella?"

"I endure pain. Hurry up and get your sexy ass in here."

As the shower bled red down the drain, I studied Cason's moans and aches as his legs swished around the chilled water. His bruises slowly faded one by one as the water dried on his skin.

"I need to see a few people today. What do you have planned besides work?"

"Sana and I have a few things to discuss. Other than that, I'll be around."

He rose from the water, grunting as though he were still transformed. His knuckles cracked, and he stretched his connected hands, then approached me in the shower. "I've been waiting for you to get home." His hungry voice blew against my neck before he raised me in his arms and pinned my dampened back against the checkerboard square tiles.

"Tearing off limbs gets you going too, huh?" I sighed.

"Watching you kick ass had me fighting the biggest hard-on last night."

"That was all the foreplay I needed. Give me what you got."

Cason plowed into me like a fighter jet crashing into the ocean, and my waters welcomed his running engine with a splash. Strong and sturdy his cock grazed my throbbing womb, filling it with extended excitement from the night's victory. I submitted to his leadership and relaxed in his grasp, tightening my walls around his wide girth splitting me in half. Up and down his dick, my pussy rode his rewarding ride.

"That's a good girl. Take this beating," he said, pounding into me so hard the tiles cracked against my back.

"It's the only beating I enjoy, Silvaaaa." I laughed low and feloniously. "I've been wanting to call you that all night. Fuck me, you beautiful, barbaric beast."

"Shhh." He silenced me and stuck his finger in my mouth.

I sucked it and moaned, then spoke with my mouth full between sighs and pants and ecstasy. "Let me know when you want to switch holes," I whispered.

He stuck four fingers in my mouth to gag me, then rolled his hips savagely deeper into my cave. *Crack* went the tiles falling from behind my back down to the sides of his feet. My hands climbed the slick slates above me, sliding without grasp. "Mmm," Cason groaned in my ear, nibbling on my neck and grazing my skin with his sharp teeth. The pain of his sensuous bite electrified my body. My feet rose above the sides of his head, and my knees locked against his shoulders. He howled. "That's it, baby. Squeeze that tight pussy on my dick. Yes. Just like that. I'll fight alongside you until the day I die to come home to this juicy pussy."

I mumbled inaudibly. "And when the fighting stops?"

He removed three fingers. "What's that?"

I exhaled. "And when the fighting stops?" I slurred.

"I'm still gonna fuck you like you want me to."

Cason pulled back, lowered my feet, and turned me around with the water sprinkling between us. His pipe lunged back into my warmth as beads of water splashed between our bodies. His fist gathered my locks in a stronghold as the other hand pressed my torso against the frosted glass. My nipples squeaked against the condensation while my cheek held steady, blowing circles into the steam.

"Ahh," I sighed as the water drizzled into my mouth. Cason lined my lips with wet fingers, tracing their fullness with his tips. I gripped them gently with my teeth before he snatched them away and wrapped his hand around my throat.

With all his strength, he forged forward. I slammed my palms against the glass, forming a thin, cracked line to the door of the shower. Slowly it traveled like a rock hitting a windshield on a busy traveled road. "Cason," I panted.

"Fuck it. We'll replace it later." He lashed out with concentrated strokes. "You feel too good to give a damn about it."

And he felt so manly and strong and commanding that I didn't care. I came as he choked me, and I thought I had inherited the power of flight. My body felt as though it left itself and floated above my immortal existence as I gasped for air.

Cason let go of my throat at the right time and pulled my face to his by my hair, breathing oxygen into me. His choking hand caressed the side of my face as our lips met for a sloppy kiss, while his free hand circled my nipples. He growled in my mouth. "Mine."

"What's yours?"

"Every fiber of your being. Every inch I hold in my hands right now."

He palmed my pussy with a firm hand and placed his other hand back around my neck. A glow of silver flashing in his eyes ended our bout for the morning.

"Make sure you find time to get some rest today."

"Ten-four. But you and I have lots to discuss."

"We do. I'll stop by the café once I'm done running my errands."

"And may I ask where you are off to?"

"If I need you, I'll call you."

I exhaled, and the cracked glass on the shower shattered. Cason gripped my shoulders, then swooped me up with his arms. He carried me across the clutter into my bedroom and tossed me on the bed.

"Was that wise? I heal faster than you, remember?"

"Faster, true. But I rebuild stronger."

"Humph. We do have a lot to discuss."

A knock at the door caused us both to snap back into defense. Cason leapt toward the front room while I threw on a t-shirt, then zipped to join him. As I stood on the opposite side of the door panel as Cason, I didn't sense fear or endangerment.

"Yeah," Cason's voice roared.

"Brother. It's me. Sana."

CHAPTER 32

THE RUMOR

CASON

VANITY and I shared a look before I opened the door. "I circled the block a few times. I thought that would never end," Sana grunted, leaning with one elbow against the sill.

"Sorry to torture you, brother." I grinned. "I was coming to see you. Why are you here?"

I welcomed Sana inside. His eyes shifted toward Vanity like a helpless pup unable to fight the urge to stare. He gave her a look, a cross between admiration and disapproval, then rolled his eyes at me.

"We heard there was indeed a brawl in the city last night. Why didn't you send word you needed the help of your brothers?"

"We took care of it." I pointed to Vanity, then back to myself. "But that's not to say we won't need you for the next one."

"Any idea when that will be?"

"I'll know more at sunset," Vanity slipped in her two cents.

Sana grunted. "Be sure to send word when you do." His eyes danced as they peeked at Vanity's exposed legs. Terribly hiding a smile, he looked at me. "Brother, may we…"

"Nice seeing you as always, Sana. I'm going to go get dressed."

My brother watched V strut out of the room until her silhouette disappeared at the end of the hallway.

"Don't rub my face in it," he said, tossing the throw from the back of the armchair at me.

"What brings you by, brother?" I asked, wrapping the knitted blanket around my waist.

"I bring news of a cure—for V's condition. Father's wife told me of a healer in her old village."

"A cure for vampirism? There is no such thing, brother."

"Oh, but there is. It's just not here."

"Then where?"

"Our homeland. The island father fled from."

"And why would any of us go back there when they have no idea our line survived?"

"To cure the woman we both love."

"I'm not fond of your ease with the word *we*. I've marked her. I've claimed her to be mine."

"That doesn't mean you control her. She's not one of us, and I doubt she has submitted to your claim of ownership. I see how she looks at me."

I paused to mask the anger rising inside of me, playing back my conversations with Vanity. She confessed she had feelings she could not express, but I couldn't recollect a time when she agreed to be solely mine. And Sana was right. She was a vampire with the sexual nature equivalent to a bitch in heat.

"Calm down. I feel your blood boiling. I didn't come here to fight with you but to save our...save Vanity instead."

"Save me from what?" She appeared between us, and we jumped.

"Please, stop doing that," Sana growled.

Vanity laughed. "Seriously. Save me from what?"

"Yourself," he answered. "There is a cure for vampirism. In Japan, our forbidden homeland."

"Well, I appreciate the concern, but I didn't ask for a cure."

"What?" Sana scowled. "You'd prefer to be of the dead and not the living? How could you say such a foolish thing?"

Vanity raised her brows at Sana. "Don't ever speak to me in that tone. And for the record, I didn't say I wouldn't want to escape this state one day, but something worldly is going on with me, and I intend to find out exactly what I am before I give up this power."

"That is what I was afraid of. You're enjoying this transformation when it is beneath the woman you were before. A pure goddess."

"That pure goddess you speak of couldn't do this."

Vanity held her hands to the side and summoned forceful winds to tap the windows of the house. She blurred and appeared next to them, lifted them, and allowed the strong breeze to blow inside, then closed them once the trinkets on the glass end table rattled uncontrollably.

"I get it. You have tricks and newfound power. But is it necessary?"

"I'm not interested in your offer, but I would still like to have a sample —for the day I change my mind."

"Then I will go for you," Sana emphasized. "I think you'll change your mind sooner than you think."

"Brother, it's too dangerous."

"I won't advertise who I am. I'll pose as a tourist."

"I can't let you go alone. As your pack leader, I forbid it."

"Then come with me."

"And who will protect V?" my voice heightened.

"She'll need to lay low until we return."

"You two speak as if I'm not standing here. I'll be fine. I promise." She clicked her teeth. "I'm gonna get going."

"You're being vague about where?" I questioned.

"I told you. I'll call you if I need you." She opened the door. "Sana."

Vanity flashed off, sending a trail of freshly spritzed perfume toward us. I closed the door and looked at my brother.

"So when do we leave?" I sighed with worry.

"Midnight."

CHAPTER 33

THE FINDING

VANITY

I WAS proud of myself for hiding the heated images of Sana and Cason sharing my body and pillaging my hidden forest like two muscular mountain men on a hunt. Cason delivered a powerful punch, but seeing the two of them stand side by side, oozing wild testosterone and authority, brought out more of an animal in me, when the carnal nature lived within them.

I hurried out of the house before Cason saw the visuals of him and Sana spearing me at the same time, but when I cut the corner a ways away, I entertained myself with the thought of Sana feeding his cock to my hungry mouth, forcing my pussy to slam into Cason's perfect pipe as he jabbed forward. My body ravaged to a timed rhythm, back and forth with precision like two trains entering a tunnel at the same time.

How I wished Cason could love me and allow me the pleasure of the two men who love me enough to protect me when I'm their blood-born enemy. There was fun to be had, but for the time being, it was only in my head—and when Cason wasn't within telepathic range.

I wasn't sure how long I could protect his feelings and hide my desires, and I had to decide if such a craving was worth losing him. The visions and the dilemma pleasured and plagued me as I strolled to Madame Cecil's shoppe. She sat behind her counter, puffy-eyed and calm.

"I wasn't sure you would be open so early after staying up all night."

"Sleep is no friend of mine when ya surrounded and visited by creatures wit'out an invitation." She grinned. "And ya said it yareself. I knew ya were coming to see me."

I pulled up a chair at her reading table. "Whatdya think of Billie?"

"The descendant of the confederate soldier?" Madame raised her brow and scoffed. "I'm thankful ya sent me a guard, but what grows in the blood, flows in the blood."

"Hmmm."

"Have you seen the news dis morning?"

"Didn't have time."

She turned up the volume on her television, then sat with me at her table. The fire pile of dead ones burned down to three-fourths its original height. The tenants formed a circle around it, preventing the fire department from stopping the inferno, understanding the importance of the blaze. The reporter announced numerous calls were made to law enforcement of dead relatives found in the lofts and apartments throughout that block, and I remembered fearing that would be the case before our riot began.

I watched the chaos ensuing in the background closely. If I didn't know any better, the firemen and the law weren't forcing their way beyond the border of citizens.

"Is it a stretch to assume city hall knows creatures exist around these parts and have been complicit with Adela out of fear?" I asked her.

Madame turned off the television. "Normally a person becomes an ass when they assume. Dis is not one of those times."

"Anyone down there worth wasting my time?"

"I'll find out when the next town hall meeting is held. Ya be sure an attend."

"Will do. So, before you tell me what you know, I have a question. Why do I feel love but can't verbally say it to the one who deserves to hear it?"

Madame chuckled. "I'm not an expert on creature relationships, and not knowing exactly what ya are, I can only attest to what I know of pale ones."

"Which is?"

"They are only loyal to their maker. And I know who yares is. You would be the first of that kind to despise the one who made ya, which already complicates ya matter. Ya want him dead, right?"

"I will see to that."

"Pale ones always put themselves first. Ya love is for yaself. Only."

"But I feel it."

"Ya still feel from ya human side, but ya dead side is in control. Ya may feel it, but ya more powerful side won't allow ya to be weak for love."

"I see. So what news do you have for me?"

"I've narrowed down known high priestesses that have disappeared or have been quiet. There are two names that possess the knowledge and power to do what they did to ya that night. Domini Caroux and Ria Lucia."

"Only two?"

"The two most powerful. Ria was last seen three years ago and rumored to have double-crossed a few higher ups that wanted her head. And Domini was said to have not shown up to a meeting with an associate of mine a little over two years ago. Both Ria and Domini would have sensed a hidden power inside of you. I'm guessing the one who bound ya here saw something in you that ya didn't know ya possessed."

"Like what?"

"Lineage perhaps. Power of some kind. Yare survival is detrimental to the priestess who stole yare identity as a cover. The people looking for both Ria and Domini have spells to track them, and if ya die, yare stolen cover will be unveiled, and whichever priestess cursed ya...her location will be revealed."

Vanity grunted. "Well, I don't plan on dying—I mean, any further than I already have."

Madame grinned. "Good one."

"So how do I investigate which one cursed me?"

"There is a way, but it will require blood."

"Whose?"

"Yares."

I glared at Madame. "No one is getting my blood. And why is that the only way?"

"It's for the seer. With yare blood, she can see into yare memories."

"But I don't remember anything about that night."

"She can access even those you've suppressed. One drop of yare blood and she can see the woman ya were before, the woman who cursed ya, and the man who was fooled by her trickery."

"No. There has to be another way."

"If there is, I haven't found it yet."

"How about a strand of my hair?"

Madame scrunched her lips and shook her head side to side.
"What about this three-life-woman, power-of-three business?"
"I'm afraid only you have access to that knowledge."
"Then what do you think it means?"
"I think it means you have a purpose."

CHAPTER 34
THE BYWATER

VANITY

CASON SPOKE SO HIGHLY of the Bywater area, I taxied over to that side of town to see what fascinated him so. As I strolled through the neighborhoods and saw its appeal, a library on Alvar Street called to me.

With hours until nightfall and time to kill before the deadly visit I had to make when the sky turned Aegean weighing on my shoulders, I researched what I could find on the history of the city versus creatures. The articles I stumbled across cleverly alluded to "unknown circumstances" when referring to unexplained violent deaths around the bayou, but my bones knew Adela and her menacing followers had those victims' blood on their hands.

A friendly clerk suggested I visit the Cita Dennis Hubbell Branch in Algiers Point. "It's the city's oldest public library. You may find more of what you're looking for." She shifted her eyes away from my search on the computer screen.

"Do you know if they have a microfiche machine?"

"I haven't heard that word thrown around in a long time." The clerk chuckled. "The public library on Loyola had one. I'd have to make a call to see if they still do. Most of those records have been transferred to digital, I believe."

"That won't be necessary." I cleared my throat and turned back toward the screen.

"Sorry I couldn't help. Good luck with your search."

When she walked away, I turned back toward her. She peeked at me over her shoulder, then hurried off when her eyes met mine.

I will remember your face.

I changed my search and pulled books on the power of three. As I skimmed through my second book on the theory, Cason called.

"I was thinking you'd have made it back by now. Where are you?"

"Interestingly enough, at the library in the Bywater."

"You see its appeal?"

"I do. What's up?"

"Sana and I are leaving for Japan tonight."

"So soon?"

"Afraid so. We'll be back in four days. Sana and I both agree the sooner the better. I need to see you before our flight."

"Come over here."

"I'm on my way."

The clerk watched my every step until I marched past her and flashed my red eyes at her nosey ass. Her face turned flush, and her heartbeat increased. She dropped the books in her hand and dove to the floor, then I saw her sneaking peeks at me through the blinds as I left to meet Cason for lunch on Louisa Street.

"If you see a petite, fairly attractive, light-skinned woman with dirty-blonde hair spying on us, let me know."

"Not how I expected to be greeted, but okay. Another to add to the list?"

"Not sure. She's human as far as I could tell. I'm supposed to save the people of this city, not kill them, right?"

"That heart of yours is how I know the human in you is still fighting. Sana and I are doing right by getting you that cure."

"My heart? What do you know of my heart besides it beats slow?"

"That you still have one. I saw compassion in you with regards to that Malik kid. Any other vampire would have killed him—I would have killed him if you hadn't taken a shine to him."

I scoffed. "Never thought I'd hear you say such a thing, especially when you're fucking one."

"You got me there, but you aren't just any old vampire. You're the woman I—well, you know."

"What's this?" I narrowed my eyes at him. "You can't say it now?"

"I could. But I haven't heard you say it. Not once."

"I talked to Madame Cecil about that earlier."

"And?"

It's not an easy fix. But you know I feel it. I just can't say it."

"So you've said. Any word if the kid is still alive?" Cason sniffed, then mumbled. "I seriously doubt it."

"I won't know until tonight. I'm having the two liars held up at the abandoned house do recon work tonight."

"How did you know about that house, by the way?"

"Shit, Cason, I feel like I'm on trial here. But I don't mind telling you. I bought it after it was foreclosed on, in case you got tired of me one day. Once you've been on the street, you kind of don't want to return to it."

"For the record, I would never tire of you or put you out on the street. We share a home. Should we go pick one out while we're on this side?"

"I don't know. Are you done giving me the third degree?"

He leaned back and looked at the time. The waitress brought our order to the table, then lingered close by, pretending to wipe empty booths so she could stare at Cason. I wasn't sure if he noticed, so I told him to leave her a large tip when he paid the check.

Maybe I do have a heart.

While we waited for a taxi to pick us up, Cason questioned why I had been at the library. *So the interrogation isn't over?*

I wanted to ask him if he trusted me, with all the questions being thrown at me, but I resisted the impulse, forgetting our telepathic connection.

"Was that on purpose, or are you toying with me?" He raised his brow.

I shrugged my shoulders. "I was reading up on the history of violence in this city and learning more about this power of three. I have a connection to the wind and water. Just waiting for the third to reveal itself."

"You're definitely strong, but it can't be that."

"And I learned nothing new from the books I read today except identifying your purpose blah-blah-blah to achieve blah-blah-blah something about adversity. None of which applies to killing a psychotic bitch."

Cason interrogated me with his eyes, searching my mind for a flash of truth, but it was clouded with words from the books I'd read.

"If I ask you one more question, do you promise not to spazz?"

"What is it?"

"What did you remember last night?"

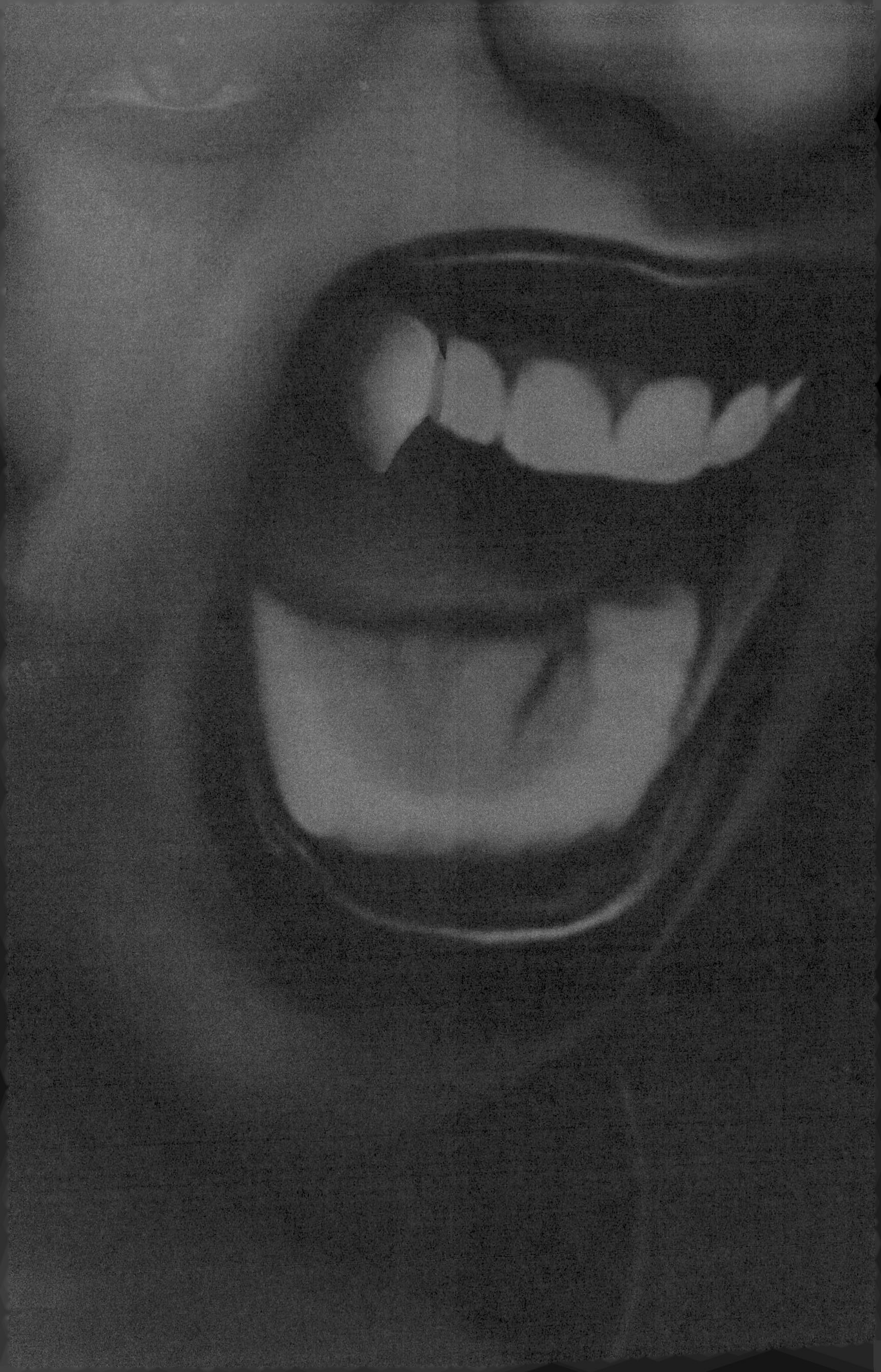

CHAPTER 35
THE HIDDEN

VANITY

"YOU'VE QUESTIONED me so much tonight. I was waiting for this one. And I'm not spazzing. I'm touched that you care so much."

"When you said you remembered something, I thought, great, we're one step closer to getting the answers you've been searching for."

"Maybe." I sighed. "I didn't remember anything in particular, but I saw a face as the car was tumbling. A face that felt familiar."

"Can you describe it?"

"Male, copper-bronze skin, clean-shaven, bald, chiseled cheekbones."

"Anything else?"

"His arm was draped across me, and his eyes were full and shaken. And I saw bright lights. That's all I remember."

"Déjà vu perhaps?"

My bottom lip turned upward. "I'd rather it be that than a premonition."

Cason grunted, and I knew why. If it were a forewarning, the thought of me in the company of another man pissed him off. He took that marking business seriously.

The taxi pulled in front of the restaurant. Cason opened my door, being the gentleman he is, and kissed me on the lips. "You sure that last round is enough to hold you until you come back?" I said, then hopped inside.

He slid inside next to me and gazed into my eyes. "It better be enough to hold you."

"Who did you leave in charge while you're gone?"

"Kyle volunteered. Can you make sure I made the right choice?"

"Of course. It'll keep me busy while you're gone."

"And hopefully out of trouble." He sniffed. "On your eight. Is that the woman you were worried about?"

I leaned forward and checked my peripheral view and moaned. "Mmm-hmm."

"Promise me you won't do anything until I get back."

My stoned face looked straight ahead.

"Vanity?" He caressed my chin, raised a brow, and curved the side of his mouth.

"I promise I won't do anything foolish while you're gone."

"Where to?" the driver asked.

"The library on Loyola," I said.

"And you, sir?"

"Royal Street, after the lady."

I stole a baseball cap from a corner stand and entered the moldy building. An older woman with her hair pulled back stared at me over the rim of cat-eye glasses.

I tapped on the desk. "Where are the microfiche machines?"

Suddenly too busy to turn away from her computer screen, she answered, "We only have one. I'll be done here in a sec, then I'll show you where it is." Her silver-haired bob bounced as she covered her hands with blue latex gloves as she loaded the card below the lens. "When you're ready for the next film, tap the bell, and I'll load it for you."

"Can you bring them all now? I'm in a bit of a time crunch."

Her eyes chastised me from behind her glasses. "History is not to be left in the hands of anyone outside of personnel. Consider yourself lucky to see these files. I'm sure they will be classified one day."

"You seem to know about this subject matter. Is there something you'd like to share?"

The clerk paused and exhaled deeply. "I'm no spring chicken. I've seen a lot in this melting pot of wonder, and I don't care to revisit the things I've put behind me. If you'll excuse me, I'll be at my station—watching carefully." She stepped back. "A bit of advice. Hit the green button to print before those articles magically disappear."

As my chaperone sorted books and shifted paper two tables down, I took her advice after scanning and skimming through the images. She was right. These documents were somehow overlooked during an inventory and should have been classified.

It made me wonder why they hadn't been as I read articles of power being taken from prominent families by unknown diseases categorized as hematology loss, featuring a photograph of a pale man and his family standing proudly on the steps of the governor's house. Not a single one of them was smiling. "Vampires," I muttered to myself.

I hit the print button on that image and another of a man standing in front of a mirror, baring his fangs with a horrified audience in the background. *No wonder the residents of New Orleans are a strong and unafraid people. They've had to endure our kind for centuries.*

I collected my stack of findings and asked my overseer for a folder. She reached below her desk and handed one to me, still refusing to look me in the eyes. *She knows.*

The light was about to die when I exited the library. I sped to the café, hoping to catch Cason before his flight and show him what I had found.

"You just missed him. He's been in and out all day. I'll be surprised if he actually gets on the plane," Kyle joked.

"Did he tell you I'll be in and out of here for the next few days?"

"Something like that. I don't know why he is worried. I've got this. I'll call you if we get slammed."

When Kyle wasn't looking, I snuck into Cason's office and taped the file in the vent above the filter. I stopped by the house and could tell Cason was gone, so I made my way over to my second stop for the night—the abandoned house.

"How'd you sleep?" I announced my presence in the room as Billie and Carlisle stretched.

"How long have you been standing there?" Billie hopped from the bed.

"Just got here." I peeped out the window.

"Thanks for this place," said Carlisle. "And thank you, Billie, for sharing the bed. So much better than a stone floor."

"Sucks not being a king anymore, doesn't it?"

"I'm pretty sure I've upgraded." He parted his lips, looking at me with lust in his eyes.

"Sure. Billie, let's take a walk. "You"—I pointed to Carlisle—"be ready to tell me what I need to do when we get back."

"Yes, milady."

"Yeah, don't call me that. V will do."

Billie followed me outside and inhaled the night air. We strolled the neighborhood to put some distance between us and the house when I asked her a burning question heavy on my mind.

"Tell me everything I need to know about vampires."

A car passing by blasting Soulja Slim's *"Slow Motion"* honked the horn at us. Billie stopped walking and waved to the driver.

I slapped her hand down. "What are you doing?"

"Finding me a regular feed in this neighborhood. I won't kill him. Just love on him a little bit." She licked her lips.

"Have you and the traitor ever hooked up?"

"Once. Long time ago. The night he turned me."

"That's kind of fucked up, don't you think? You give him the goods, he murders you, and then you're stuck being loyal to him because he's your maker."

She chewed on her lower lip and turned back toward the car, seeking attention. The way she studied it until it turned the corner told me she was serious about feeding on the driver. I broke her gaze and repeated my question.

"Tell me everything you know about vampires."

"What's there to know? We're cursed and damned."

"I need to know about powers. How and who and why some have certain abilities."

"Like your little bat trick?"

"Little?" I raised my brows.

"What I meant was, are you asking me what my special ability is?"

"Yes, and others."

"Mine isn't so special. I'm faster than other vamps."

"As in running?"

"As in everything."

"And Carlisle?"

"If he touches you, he can read your thoughts. If he touches two people at once, he can show the other person what the other is thinking."

"Is that all he can do?"

"I'm not sure if this was from his life before, but he plays the hell out of a violin."

I sighed. "Billie, seriously. The fucking violin? What's he gonna do? Hypnotize people with the help of a string quartet? I need to know the skills I'm up against. Is there anyone in Adela's army I should be leery of?"

"Adela can set you on fire with the snap of a finger, I'm told. One of her bodyguards has the strength of the Hulk—if he were real. They call him Bruno."

"I think I met him." I pointed to the healed bruise on my ribcage.

"She has a lieutenant they call The Fly—not that I've seen him do it, but it's rumored he can. Then there's The Singer. He compels his victims through song."

"So we have a firestarter, a singer, and a flight risk."

"Don't forget Bruno."

"I think I've taken care of him already."

Billie's eyes widened, staring at me as if my assumption couldn't be true. We turned around and headed back toward the house. Carlisle stood out front, waiting for us.

"Not all blood suckers have a special ability. Sucking blood is all most of them can do. Think of it like superior human beings. There's usually one star on a team. The same with vampires."

I turned to Billie. "You left off this one's supreme hearing."

Carlisle gloated. "It is superior compared to others."

"Any more I need to be aware of?"

"Quite a few, but they are nameless in my head, and not all are in alliance with Adela. There's an old one we call The Claw—use your imagination. The Re-birther and The Inhaler. I'm not a fan of any of them."

"I'll keep that in mind. I need you to be incognito tonight. Think you can handle that?"

"I'm at your service. What do you need from me?" he asked.

"I'm going to let you look into my head for a second. There's a boy I need you to rescue from Adela's. Bring him back here and keep him safe. Billie, I need you to keep your ear to the ground. If anything pops off, call me."

They both nodded.

"No news is good news. Got it?" I clicked my tongue and hopped from the porch.

"Got it," they answered, and we jetted off for the night's mission.

CHAPTER 36
THE SNITCH
VANITY

A FEW BLOCKS away from the house, I cornered an innocent older woman getting out of her car. Startled at my flashing red eyes, she whimpered.

"Don't hurt me, please."

"I would never," I said, then felt a rumble burst inside of me.

Looking into her eyes I channeled the power traveling fast to my brain and gave her an order. "You're going to give me your car keys and go inside of your house, then forget I was ever here."

"These are for you," she said, handing me a key ring with a lucky rabbit's foot on the chain, then walked inside her house and closed the door.

As I cruised the streets and unpaved roads, I geeked at my first time placing someone under compulsion while checking for suspicious activity. The city appeared tame in its early hours, so I headed over to the third ward for my final errand.

My welcome into The Grove was honorable this time, though what I was about to do filled me with a great sadness. I bypassed the entrance to Keshell's without an invitation, taken aback how I was greeted upon my arrival. His watchmen dropped to their knees as I approached. I paused my steps and looked at the tops of their heads bowing, waiting for them to stand. They remained kneeled with each step I took to pass them, and I grinned to myself. *This ought to be good.*

For shits and giggles, I said to them, "Rise." They stood tall, avoiding eye contact with me, then relaxed at ease once I continued on the path beside the cinder blocks. As I entered the center of the courtyard where Keshell's caravan rested beyond the stones, one of the subs standing guard the last time I was there curtsied and rose.

"He's been waitin' for ya. Follow me," he said, then walked away from the door of the van.

"He's not inside?" I hesitated and took a step back.

"Not since he knew you were coming. This way."

I was led to the top floor of the housing unit by a stairwell. The beige tiled floor of the hallway paraded my reflection to a glossed black door. "Come," Keshell shouted from the other side before his subordinate knocked. He opened the door for me, then closed it once I entered. I skimmed the place quickly, then opened with a warmer.

"Let me guess. You knocked down a wall and made two apartments your personal palace."

Keshell sat with his feet up on the far edge of his sofa, looking at the news. The center line of his dark-brown chest shone between his unbuttoned shirt. My eyes lingered longer than they should have, and my nipples told him hello through the flimsy fabric of my top. He glanced at them, then huffed from the cigar of marijuana between his fingers. "Like I said to ya the first time we met. Smart gal."

"Your people said you were expecting me."

"And here ya are." He exhaled a cloud of smoke and tapped the bottom of the cigar into an ashtray built into the armrest. "Come sit. I've been wanting to see ya before the vision come to me of ya gracin' me wit' ya beauty."

"Tell me about this vision." I sat two feet away from him on the couch.

He leaned forward, resting his elbows on his knees, and flashed his gold fangs at me. "Ju, those black leather shorts ya wearin', teasin' me wit' those long legs walking through dat door." He pointed. "Ya come'ere and tell me sumtin not so good wit' ya legs crossed sittin' in dat very spot."

I crossed one of my legs over the other, and he chortled low in his throat. We exchanged smiles, then I took a deep exhale, erasing the smile from my lips. "Then I'll get right to it. You have a traitor in your camp."

"Nah. No one is foolish to cross me."

"I wouldn't be so sure if I were you."

"Mi people know what I do to traitors."

"I heard what you do to people who violate in the other wards. Do I wanna know what you'll do to someone from your very own?"

Keshell ignored my question and peered over at me. "Who was it?"

"One of the young ones at your gate. I unfortunately had to put a few creatures down the last time we saw each other. I bit one of Adela's men and saw him at the scene when she gave the orders to ambush me."

"I heard about what you did downtown. I never got the call to send in some of my soldiers."

"I hope they are still on standby."

"I keep my word. I got you. So, a kid you say?"

I nodded. "I'm no kid killer. In fact I'm trying to save one. I may need your help with that if my plan goes to shit."

"So ya come to me to be a kid killa while ya be a savior. Saint Vanity." He chuckled. "Come closa and show me what ya saw."

"How so?"

"Ya blood. I promise to be gentle."

I wouldn't give my blood to anyone. Not Madame Cecil and not her friend, the seer. Cason was the only one I trusted pricking my skin, yet I raised my wrist and let Keshell get a taste.

He kept his word, piercing my vein for a trickle of blood with a gentle bite, sucking it slow and moaning as he swallowed with his eyes closed. Heat traveled through me watching him sensuously sampling my blood, humming while he sucked from my vein like it was a fresh piece of fruit. Flashes of me being pleasured by a faceless lover played in my mind. I uncrossed my leg, giving my throbbing pussy some air, then placed the other leg on top.

Restrained and disciplined, Keshell licked the wound dry, then flashed his half-and-half eyes at me. I pulled my arm away and wiped it dry against my blouse, waiting for him to confirm he would handle the problem.

"Ya sho me da truth. I'm grateful for the information. Can't have a snitch in my unit."

"Sorry I had to be the one to tell you."

Keshell drew another pre-rolled spliff from the pocket of his shirt. "No need for ya to be sorry." He lit the joint and sat back. "I saw more than the snitch in ya blood. I saw confirmation. Wish I saw more."

"Confirmation of what?"

"You as queen of N'awlins—for a short while."

"Short while?" I frowned.

"You will rule, but you'll also leave this city."

I slid closer to him, hopeful he saw the curse of me being confined to the city lifted. "Do you need more of my blood to tell me how?"

"Ya blood is sweet on my tongue. And not good for me to taste again so soon."

"Why?"

His eyes narrowed as he puffed and withdrew a mouthful of smoke. He lifted his head toward the spackled ceiling, and smolder formed a cloud bridge between us sitting a foot apart.

"It's addictive," he exclaimed in a whisper. "And I think ju already know I want more of ya."

I smirked. "I do know that."

"And it will happen. I've seen it. As a vision and a wish. After tasting ya, I hope I can help myself."

I laughed. "You won't have a choice." Keshell licked his lips, and I rose from the sofa. "I should probably leave to prevent whatever you saw happening in that dream."

He stood in front of me, and his teeth glistened from the flashing lights on the television. "There's something you should see." He whistled, and the sub opened the front door. "Pull the car 'round."

CHAPTER 37
THE BELIEF
VANITY

WE ARRIVED at a neighborhood in Algiers Point. Slim crowds hanging out in small groups stood in front of a bar on the corner next to what Keshell called shotgun houses. "You've never been on this side, have ya?" I shook my head no. "Do ya know why they call these homes shotgun houses?"

"Enlighten me." I curled my lips at him.

"Look at them closely. What do ya see?"

I was clueless how to answer his question, but I continued to observe the shape of the houses on the block, then blurted, "I'm sure my answer is wrong, but what I see are homes a large family could never survive in, but I don't see how that relates to it being called a shotgun house."

"Ya are wrong." He lowered his window. "Large families were happy in these homes, and many survived. I came from one of them. And had to watch them all die while they thought my curse was a gift. Generations of my people occupied that house right there." He pointed to a narrow, tube-shaped gray home with blue shutters. "My papa and I built it with our bare hands."

I watched him smile to himself and assumed memories of his century-old life had come to him at that moment. He snapped out of his own mind and continued to teach me. "My people are the original architects of shotgun houses. We brought this style with us from Haiti. If there was a vacant one, I'd give you a tour of the inside so you can see they are made like the barrel of a gun. There's an old saying that's been around for decades. If ya shoot a gun inside one, rest assured the bullet will leave out the front door, and the shell will go out the back." He chuckled.

"How old is that saying?"

"Are ya asking my age, Vanity?"

"You just said you and your father built that house, so yes, I am."

He scoffed, then grinned. "One hundred and thirty. But who's counting?"

"Well, you look good for your age." I smiled.

"I could never tire of dat sense of humor ya got."

Keshell's driver parked the car, and he stepped out. The crowds on the corner thinned out within seconds. "Tough crowd," I joked. He extended his hand and pulled me to my feet. "Did you bring me here for a history lesson?" I asked, removing my hand from his grip. It appeared I offended him.

"I promise not to bite—until you beg me to."

I raised my brow at him. "That cocky shit might get you somewhere, but not tonight."

He grinned, and his left gold fang shone faintly below his top lip. "We're here because I want to show ya somethin'," he said, guiding me past the ferry landing.

We strolled along the levee, passing the Louis Armstrong statue. Keshell saluted the jazz great and continued to lead me farther down the path, saluting every jazz legend stamped on the lampposts until the pavement turned into a gravel path.

"You could have provided a girl with sneakers for this walk."

Keshell stopped a few feet ahead. "We're here."

"Where exactly?" I looked around, surrounded by darkness, tiny rocks, and an open, midnight-colored sky with stars visible few and far between.

"This is where we'll meet if my place—or yours—is ever compromised."

"Really? Because I was thinking this would be the place you murdered me if I wasn't already dead."

"You aren't exactly dead—not like the rest of us." He sniffed.

"What do you mean?"

"I see auras around the living and the dead," he shares.

"So do I."

"What colors do ya see?" He gazed at me with a smile.

"So far, lavender, silver, gold, and black. All vampires have been outlined with black."

"Except you. Your aura is deep purple and red."

"How is that possible? It has to be one or the other."

"It is fa everyone else. The night I met ju it was a deep red. Magenta I think dey call it. Today, it's bright purple. I believe it changes with ya mood."

"Is that so?"

"It's the only explanation I can muster. You were wired the night we met. Fired up and feisty, hence the red cloud shroudin' ya. Tonight ya relaxed, giving off the color of royalty, which ya are." He looked into my eyes.

I didn't fight our connection. "You flatter me." I blushed.

"There's another place ya need to see."

It was quiet between us on the walk back toward the landing. I studied the New Orleans skyline across the calm river as the rippling of its bed caught my attention. I slowed the pace of my steps, putting a small space between Keshell and myself, then turned toward the river and summoned it to rise slightly above the wall.

The top of the river bubbled, and the lights flickered in the lampposts lined beside the sidewalk. Drops of river water trickled from the rush pushing forward. An urgency compelled me to withdraw the summons. I cooled the bubbling sensation building within me, exhaled deep from within my chest, then whizzed up to Keshell a yard ahead of me.

The residents peeped from behind their curtains as we trekked back through his old neighborhood. One by one, I witnessed a few of them step onto their porch as the car drove away. Keshell wasn't put off by their fear of him. He held his head high as we left his stomping grounds, still thinking of the past I assumed. I used the moment to quiz him further.

"Why does Adela respect you so much that she honors a truce?"

He rubbed the hairs on his chin. "She has her weapons, and I have mine. Not that she didn't try me early on. But I refused to bow down to her. I come from a strong people. She had no choice but to respect my muscle and waved her white flag. Ever since then, it's been peace between our camps."

"And you'd end this truce for me?"

"I will. It's time fa a change. And I know what ya are. Ju chosen to free the people from our kind. My troops know how I feel about the people of this city and respect my law. I only feed on those who go against it."

"You'll have to explain this chosen business," I said.

"Allow me," he said as the driver stopped the car and let us out in front of the entrance to Congo Square."

Keshell took my hand and led me over to a tree resting in the center of the courtyard and kissed the back of my hand. "We call this the Eggun Tree. Are you familiar?"

"No. I've only been here two years, and as you know, a lot has happened."

"Meaning?"

"My accident. The amnesia. Have you not seen any of what I'm saying to you in your visions?"

"None of what you speak. I've seen you blooming flowers with the touch of a finger, throwing wind to put out fires, floating above the ocean, and controlling the water like you did at the levee."

"You saw that, did you?"

"I did. I took you there on purpose. Mi saw it in a vision."

"Sneaky," I purred.

"With a purpose." He released my hand and dug in his pocket, then placed a beet at the base of the tree. "We the children of pure light, what some call voodoo, continue to practice our customs away from our homeland. This tree connects us with those who walked before us, and it is where we come to pay our respects to the gods and goddesses slavery tried to force our ancestors to abandon. Are you familiar with the ancestors, the Orishas?"

I shrugged. "I don't know. The old version of me may have been familiar, but when I lost myself, I lost my mind. I have no idea who I was or what I knew."

"The night we met I saw Yemaya in you. You looked divine in that blue top. But tonight, you've been tempting me with your glazed brown skin glowing against the yellow gold shade of your blouse."

"And whom does that shade represent?" I asked.

"Oshun."

"Yemaya and Oshun," I said, repeating their names for confirmation of their pronunciation.

"Daughters of the Great Orisha Oya. The purplish glow that shrouds ya is her flowing through yare divine connection to the gods. It is she who empowers you." He reached in his other pocket and pulled out a packet of honey. "Here. Give her this as an offering to show thanks. But ya must taste it first."

"Why?" I scowled at him. "This feels like some sort of test. Haven't I trusted you enough this evening? I let you taste my blood, remember."

"A taste so divine I'm fighting every ounce of desire to not steal more. But the honey mwen renmen anpil, is not a test fa me. It's to prove ya offering is not tainted."

"Then I should have selected something on my own."

"Very well." He retrieved his hand.

"What else is in your pocket?"

"Nothing."

"Is there a rule you can't taste it first?"

"Not that I'm aware of."

Keshell split the packet open with his teeth. He placed a drop on his finger and hummed as he swallowed. "Sweet, but incomparable to yares I presume." I scoffed at his candor as he handed me the packet, then tasted a sample. "Now pour for the goddesses."

As I kneeled to pour the honey around the tree, I felt the earth vibrate below my feet. Torn pieces of paper, old and shiny new pennies, cornmeal, and candles crowded the bottom of it as Keshell continued to educate me.

"Where we are right now is where the slaves used to come together. This tree has seen three centuries of chaos in N'awlins. It was only right fa ya to pay a visit and feel the connection to our past and ancestors on the other side with what is coming to this city."

I rose from studying the offerings and reading a note requesting prayer tucked below a candle. "Hearing you talk of the city's history and reflecting on your homeland explains why you are the kind of vampire you are."

"How so?"

"I think you were kind before you turned, so you aren't as ruthless as the others like us. It gives me an inkling of hope that I, too, was a good person before becoming whatever it is I am."

Our eyes met as instinct told us we were not alone. We placed our backs together and surveyed the square. Worshippers of the ancestors surrounded us. "The goddesses are with you. The goddesses are with you," they whispered with bowed heads.

Keshell and I slowly exited through their barricade. And when we made it to the car, I looked back and witnessed a triad of colors glowing from the tree. Luminescent hues of maroon, royal blue, and orange gold highlighted from the center of the trunk, outward on its branches. The worshippers dropped to their knees, bowed their heads, and shouted prayer requests while others thanked the goddesses.

Keshell eased closer to me and grabbed my hand. "Ya believe me now?"

CHAPTER 38
THE SEER
CASON

Hours earlier the same day

MADAME CECIL GRINNED when the chimes above her door tapped a soft melody upon my entry. "Didn't see you coming by. That's not good. You were in mi blind spot. Have a seat ova dey." She pointed to her reading table.

"I prefer to stand."

"What brings ya by?"

"Where can I find this seer Vanity refused to meet with?"

"Wha ya wan' wit' her?"

"Answers."

"Like I told V, she will need her blood. Without it she can't see nuttin'."

"Will this work?" I lifted the ripped, bloodied blouse Vanity left at the café.

Madame's eyes flickered, and she held her chest. "Humph. I'll give you the address, but I warn you. You will regret this."

"Ever heard of a fool in love?"

A chuckle rolled off her lips as she nodded.

"This fool is taking a chance."

The hours before my flight with Sana sped past, but I took my chance

181

to meet with the seer. I knocked on the door of the address Madame wrote on the back of one of her business cards. The house was secluded, close to Venetian Isles, not far from where my brothers formed their community.

Sitting in the middle of underdeveloped land, the house had a nice strong foundation and enough land for a garden to grow fresh vegetables to trade with the locals and serve farm-to-table at the café. Minus the potential for heavy flooding, I fancied the open area on the property, expecting a man to open the door.

"You," I said when the door opened.

"You!" she shrieked, then closed the door in my face.

"I don't have time to play games!" I pounded on the door. "I have about ten minutes to spare before I…"

"Need to leave for your flight!" she shouted through the door.

"So you are the seer?" I confirmed.

The door opened as the woman who had stood across the street, watching Vanity and me earlier at lunch, welcomed me inside with a wooden candle holder raised in her hand.

"No need for that," I assured her.

"I'm not so sure. I know what I saw."

Confused by her statement, I held up my hands. "I don't know what vision you've had of me, but I would never hurt a woman. I'm here to protect one."

"The one you worry about needs no protection. You, on the other hand…"

"Yeah, I know. The Madame told me I would regret this, but I'll worry about that later."

She placed the candle holder on a glass table near the front door and sighed. Her eyes gazed into mine, and I felt exposed. I didn't like being studied, especially not by her kind. "Look, Madame Cecil told me where to find you. I have something I need your help with." I handed her Vanity's blouse. "Can you see from dried blood?"

"I can."

She traced the crusted patches with her finger and shivered. Her eyes closed as she inhaled a deep breath and held it in. I observed her taking in visions while her eyes rolled beneath her light-brown lids. They were the only body part moving on her frail frame as she remained still as if frozen in time. Not a movement from her chest, nor a twitch of her hand.

Nearly a full minute later, she exhaled a deep breath, gasping and holding her chest. Vanity's blouse fell to the floor. The seer lost her balance, and I stepped forward to catch her before she knocked her head on the wooden end table behind her. "Is this reaction normal?" I asked. She nodded, still catching her breath and clinging to my shirt. "I'm Cason, by the way."

"Neveah," she respired, smiling at me with her eyes. "Don't go on your trip."

I lifted her with ease and carried her over to the sofa. When I laid her down, her grip on my shirt strengthened. For a second I felt as though my act of betrayal went beyond having Vanity's blood read. In some sort of weird way, I felt treacherous for finding Neveah attractive, lying weak and needy in my arms, looking up at me the way women look when they want affection, doughy-eyed with heat blazing into me, yearning to be touched as passion filled the space between us.

"What did you see?" I asked, removing her hand, then making myself comfortable on the chair across from her.

Her eyes continued to stare into mine like a woman yearning for my touch. "Before or just now?" she asked.

"Both, if you don't mind."

"Just now I saw chaos. The Mississippi flooding the streets, fire in several wards, and Mother Nature on a warpath. Bodies everywhere. Human and creature. An innocent boy smiling, and those who survive chanting your friend's name. Vanity. That is her name, correct?"

"Yes."

"There was also an accident, your friend's blood on the side of the road, and a familiar face staring back at me, warning me to close my eyes."

"Who did you see?"

"A high priestess by the name of Ria Lucia, but that isn't all. A man was there. I saw him twice, talking with Ria, but also in a bar downtown sometime in the future."

"Which bar?"

"It was unclear. So were his intentions, but he poses no threat to your friend."

"Did you see anything about her past? Before the night of the accident?"

"Yes. Your friend looked happy. I believe she was in love with the man who was speaking with Ria."

"You said *was*. So, no more?"

She shrugged. "I do not know her heart, only what I see. And I saw them together, but he didn't call her Vanity."

I rose to my feet and knelt beside her. "What name did he call her? You saw them together how?"

"He called her Lauren."

"Lauren," I whispered, then smiled.

"And I saw them walking somewhere, then she bit a man, but the face of her victim is not clear."

"She doesn't consume human blood. How can I trust your visions are correct when I know she only feeds on animals."

"I saw her biting a man. I've never been wrong."

"Then why were you surprised I was at your door?"

"Because of what I saw in a vision earlier today. Don't go on your trip."

"Why not?" my voice raised, and she trembled.

"Don't be angry with me for telling you the truth. I know you love her. I saw how you looked at her."

I reached in my pocket and gave her two hundred dollars. She sat up and crossed her hands.

"No charge."

"Take it," I insisted. "Hire someone in Jackson Square to draw the faces of the man in your visions and Ria Lucia. When I return, I'll bring you more cash for your trouble. You can tell me then why I shouldn't have gone on my trip."

"Doesn't sound like I can say no."

"One more thing. Why did you have your weapon raised at me when you opened the door?"

"I saw you carrying me in a vision. Like you did a second ago. I thought you were here to hurt me." She exhaled. "The visions don't explain themselves."

"Well, as you can see, I would never hurt a woman. See you when I return."

CHAPTER 39
THE MISTAKE
CASON

THE DRIVER of the cab left dust flying in Neveah's yard as I was cutting it close to leaving with Sana. We made it out to the woods in time, traveling faster than the speed limit and swerving around cars along the way. For his trouble, I slipped him a hefty tip, then made my way inside my brother's cabin.

A combination of bliss and curiosity overwhelmed me as I staggered from the family reunion waiting for me inside. All the remaining silver leaf wolves stared at me, each with a different expression on their faces.

Junishiro was glum as always. He sighed the moment my feet crossed the threshold and smirked at Shun who had the worst poker face of us all. According to his roaming eyes unable to lock onto mine, I knew I was the topic of conversation. "You three were right. He's smitten with a bitten." The eldest of the twins, Homare, joked as she took me by the arm and wrestled me to the ground.

"Little sister," I grunted while I rose back to my feet. "It's good to see you too."

"Look at our leader. Pussy whipped by a vampire bitch. Papa would be so disappointed."

"Papa was an asshole." I wrapped my arms around her and squeezed her tight. "Pussy whipped or not, I could break your little ass in half. How have you been?"

"I was doing good until these guys called us down here to explain the shitstorm of commotion you've gotten yourself mixed up in. Word about a silver wolf fighting in the middle of the street has traveled all the way to New Iberia." Homare pushed me off her.

"Well, I think it's good you've found love, big brother," Akina chimed in. "But why did it have to be with a vampire? Several of my friends would have been happy to give you a try." She laughed.

I extended my arms to the gentler, kinder soul of the twins. "Akina, my favorite sister." I hugged her with a grin directed at Homare. Homare scrunched her face and gave me the middle finger. "Be happy for me, is all I ask," I said to Akina.

Homare cleared her throat. "Enough, you two, with the bonding already. We're not supposed to be in the same place long, remember? Sana, get on with it."

"Homare's right. I asked everyone to meet as a security measure." Sana paced the room. "If Cason and I run into trouble on the homeland, it'll be useless to send word. We'll be days away and outnumbered, which is why we must keep a low profile. We'll reach our destination by sea, which will take longer, but it's safer."

"If it's so safe, then why call this meeting?"

"Because if something happens to the two oldest in our line, one of you becomes the new Silver Leaf King."

"Or queen," Homare added.

"Yes. Or queen." Sana nodded. "In case your votes end up in a tie, father's wife will have to choose, and you must all agree to honor whomever she deems worthy."

Mumbles and indistinct expletives grumbled from Juni. His hate had doubled for me since the last time we saw each other. I could feel it in my bones.

While my siblings argued amongst themselves, I excused myself and rambled through Sana's desk. I took to pen and paper, while the deliberations in the other room grew loud and intense, and wrote a note for Vanity.

I returned to the front room and slipped my letter to Shun. "Deliver this to my house tonight. If anything happens to V while I'm gone, act as the only sane wolf in this family and get as far away from here as possible. Adela has no mercy."

Shun nodded, then slid my letter in his pocket. "Don't worry, brother, you'll return. And hopefully with the cure so you can be in love with the woman of your dreams and not a dead one—with all due respect."

I grunted. "Just do what I said. Protect your sisters from the chaos of this place."

"Ten-four. Operation Get the Fuck Out of Dodge is a go."

Sana and I set forth on our quest to the Shikoku Islands. When our plane ascended into the dreary sky, I looked down at the city I was proud to call home and began counting the minutes I'd return to it with a potion to make the love of my life human again.

CHAPTER 40

THE TEMPTATION
VANITY

KESHELL and I spoke with our eyes as his driver took the scenic route back to The Grove. Cason was on my mind, but the sexy, smoldering black Prince of Night was in my presence, stirring heat between my legs with a wicked, vicious glare from the corner of his eye.

Two years of a clueless, sexless life had me worshipping the good boy with the feral ability to fuck me senseless. But the bad boy gazing at me in his absence woke the sex-craved inhibitions suppressed deep within my body.

"Right here is fine," I said, breaking Keshell's spell.

"So, no nightcap?"

I scoffed. "Like you said, it's not happening tonight."

"Why ya can't change dat? Ya fraid Silva will be heartbroken when I make his woman mine?" His tongue clicked his gold fang.

"Goodnight, Keshell Martin, vampire playa."

He laughed. "It will happen."

"We'll see." I tapped on the door.

The driver pulled the car over, then helped me escape a night of self-betrayal and treachery. As I strolled toward the car I stole, Keshell lowered his window and whistled at me. I laughed and kept my eyes forward. "It will happen! Call me when you need me, goddess!" he shouted as the car sped up, then turned the corner.

I swung by the café and parked across the street, watching Kyle lock up for the night. There were no reports of action carrying on, so I moseyed over to the old woman's house, placed her car keys above the sun visor, then made my way over to the refugee house where Carlisle horribly hid in a shadow on the porch.

"No luck with the kid tonight," he said. "It would help if you'd let me look inside your head for longer than a second."

I huffed. "And be vulnerable at your hands? Not going to happen. I showed you his face. That should be enough."

"There are at least two dozen kids hanging out over there. Some are blood servants. The others are new turns."

"The boy I'm looking for is a new turn. Dark-brown, slim, timid in the eyes with full lips and a narrow nose. I sent him back to Adela's with a bag of hearts and a severed head."

"That information would have been helpful before you sent me on a death mission."

"Yeah, well I didn't think there would be dozens of kids in a vamp zone. The fuck is wrong with you people? Turning kids and shit."

Carlisle laughed. "You're so cute sometimes."

"Whatever. Do you have anything to report? It's been quiet most of the night."

"Too quiet, though I wouldn't expect Adela to strike tonight. She knows you're waiting for it. My advice: prepare for a sneak attack."

"Where do you think she'll strike first?"

"Wherever she thinks you are is my guess."

Billie casually walked up on us with blood dripping from her fingertips as she sucked them clean. Carlisle grew fidgety, watching her savor the illicit deed.

"Who was it?" I inquired with a balled fist.

Billie smirked. "As if you have to ask." She smacked her lips.

"Is he still alive?" I alluded to the gentleman in the car, blasting his music earlier in the night.

"Of course he is. I told you. He'll be my regular feed."

I sighed and shook my head at the two of them. "Well, kids. Let's try this again tomorrow night. Silence from a villain is never a good thing."

"You don't have to leave." Carlisle grinned devilishly. "Stay here with us. I'm sure we can find a few things to keep us occupied until the next sunset. You reek of arousal, my vampiress."

"Only in your dreams."

"And dammit, I wish that one will come true," he purred, rubbing his hands across his manhood.

Billie and I glanced at each other and chortled before I dashed off into the dusky night. Since Cason wasn't home waiting for me, I took one final look over the French Quarter, hopping from the top of one building to the next. The travelers appeared to be fine, enjoying themselves as tourists of the city should be, frolicking in the streets, tossing beads, and marching alongside unauthorized parades of locals in costumes.

With Adela giving her raids a rest, I called it a night and headed home, catching a shadowy figure leaning on the handrail of the steps. "Shit!" He jumped as I appeared in his face. "It's me. Shun," he announced, slightly rattled.

"The fuck are you doing here this time of night?"

"Cason asked me to look out for you." He reached in his back pocket. "And give you this."

I smiled. "Your brother is the sweetest. I'll be glad when he's back."

"Same."

Conversation was never Shun's strong suit. We stood in silence, avoiding eye contact, for so long it became unbearable to be in his presence. I had to put an end to the awkwardness.

"Well, thanks for checking on me. You don't have to do that. I know how to reach you guys if I need anything."

"Yeah," he said, leaving me on the porch, muttering below his breath.

Shun was always quiet, but something was off with him. I assumed it was because Cason chose him to babysit. Putting the guessing game aside, I kicked up my heels in the living room and opened the letter, ready to devour the sweet nothings Cason cleverly orchestrated to fill my ear until his return.

V,

I already hate being apart from you, but I'll go to the ends of this earth for you. I think you know that already and hope you'll keep that in mind as I ask for your forgiveness. Before I confess my deceitful actions, I should mention, after reflecting on the night we were ambushed leaving The Grove, I believe your third power is connected to the earth. Do you remember how you attempted to stomp one of the hitmen, but he rolled from underneath you, and your foot crashed into the ground instead? The ground trembled around us.

I paused reading his words and recalled the incident, remembering it play by play as the memories of our first battle scrambled rampantly in my mind. I didn't notice it at the time as I was deep into the moment of killing my assailant. Cason's theory led me to recall the events of that night and how, hours before, I had felt the earth rumble below my feet at the Eggun Tree.

I think he's right.

My eyes shifted back to the page.

Of the four elements, you have a connection to water and air. The earth has to be the third. I'm guessing, but you should test this theory while I'm away. Forgive me, my love, for going against your wishes. I acted on my own recognizance and found an answer you've been searching for. Does the name Lauren mean anything to you? I believe it to be your true name before the accident. The woman that was tailing us in the Bywater is the seer Madame referred you to. I've given her instructions to have an artist draw the face of the high priestess Ria Lucia and the man you were with the night your life was stolen from you. We are a few steps closer to the truth. I love you.
Cason

I folded the note and laid my head back on the sofa, confused by Cason's confession. My knees jittered, and the heel of my boot tapped against the coffee table. I jumped up and paced the house as my mind wandered restlessly about how Cason gathered this sudden knowledge. Stumped and mildly irritated, I looked at the time, and my blood boiled. I would have to wait for Madame Cecil to open her shop to get the answers I sought, and those were hours I didn't have the patience to wait.

CHAPTER 41
THE ANSWERS
VANITY

MADAME'S NOSTRILS FLARED, and her eyes narrowed. She huffed. "I won't invite you in." Her arm left the side of the door and tucked beneath the other hanging at her side.

"Did you see me coming?"

"At this hour? No. Wha ya want dat couldn't wait for me to open shoppe?"

"How do I find the seer?"

"Ya gon' give her the blood?"

"No need." My eyes flashed red.

Madame sucked her teeth. "I warned him not to. Told him he was making a mistake. Called him a fool even."

"Did you really?"

She nodded, then sighed. "Said he was a fool in love."

I breathed out a bit of my rage. "It appears he is. About this seer, I know she works at the library. I thought she was a witch of some sort. Maybe she is. Where can I find her now?"

"Venetian Isles. Green house. I'll give you the address."

"Thank you. Do you know about the high priestess?"

"No."

"It was Ria Lucia."

"Then you are in for a fight, Ms. V."

Swiping a car was easy with compulsion. I arrived at the house of Neveah calmer than I should have been and was sure it was because Madame Cecil relayed Cason's profession of love I already knew was real.

The house sat in the middle of nowhere, dark throughout. But I could hear the seer's heart beating inside. I dimmed the headlights, and the front door unlocked and slowly crept open. A black silhouette formed in the doorway as I slammed the car door shut. "I take it Madame told you I was coming?" Her voice sounded exactly as I remembered, annoying and low-toned like she read sex stories for a living.

"I was expecting you before she called!" she bellowed.

"Is that supposed to convince me you're the real deal?"

"You're here, aren't you?"

I walked the dirt path leading to her front door and stood with my foot on the bottom step. "You can come out from the dark. I'm not here to hurt you."

The top half of her face appeared in a circular light.

"So we meet again," I said.

"He loves you," she blurted.

"Excuse me?"

"Cason, the man you inquire about, loves you. He asked me to do something for him, something to help you. I hope to have what he wants tomorrow."

"The drawings?"

"Yes."

"Were you planning to give them to me or Cason?"

She didn't answer.

"I asked you a question."

"I heard you."

"Then why the long pause?"

I knew the answer to that question. Her heartbeat skipped the first time she said Cason's name, and when I asked who she intended to give the drawings to, her heart rate tripled. She was in love with Cason but afraid to admit it—especially to me.

I grinned. "I have my answer."

"Do you?"

"Neveah, if what you've told Cason is true, how do I contact this Ria Lucia?"

"When I get the sketches, I will know more. But there's something you need to know."

"What?"

"I told Cason not to go on his trip."

"Why is that?"

"I didn't see him coming back."

My eyes flashed red and gold. My slowed heart sped up equivalent to her racing human heart, beating faster than a car on a racetrack. "Come again?" I asked, inching closer to the threshold of her door. Her eyes widened, and her hands gripped an object in the shade surrounding her.

"Cason's not coming back." Her voice trembled.

I pulled out my phone and dialed him. "Call me," I said to his voice-mail. I dialed him a second time. "Call me, you son of a bitch. You went behind my back and met with this woman who is obviously in love with you. Don't you dare leave me like this."

Neveah gasped and dropped the object in her hand. "I...I..."

"You are. You don't have to deny it." I stepped backward toward the car.

She swallowed hard. "I mean no harm."

Facing her, I continued to step backward, listening to her blood flow swiftly in her veins and her breath hitch. "Neither do I—as long as you stay away from him when he returns."

"But he's..."

I paused my steps and locked eyes with her. "Don't finish that sentence."

CHAPTER 42
THE ORDER

VANITY

A TRAIL of dust filled my rearview from Neveah's house as I fled down her dirt road. I had hours until Madame unlocked her doors with no way to release the fury bubbling over inside of me, all the while fighting my natural sexual need to be bent over a couch and ravished for hours.

As the city was still quiet and there was no word of violence in the streets, I ditched the car I had compelled from some unlucky schmuck on the side of the road the closer I drove into the city and popped up at my house. "Knock, knock." I barged inside, still raging with Neveah's premonition of Cason and his betrayal, quickly becoming amused at the moans and grunts of passion. I leaned against the door. "Why am I not surprised? Don't stop on my account."

Carlisle groaned, thrusting his ass forward, and looked back at me with a proud grin while Billie covered her face. "You want to join us. I can smell it on you." He purred his words, calling me over to them, still stroking, still grinning.

"The offer is tempting, but I'm not here on a social call." I tapped the back of my feet against the floorboards.

"Well, if you aren't going to join—but how I wish you would—allow me to…"

Billie tossed Carlisle to the floor. "You came back. Must be important." She hopped to her feet and scrambled for her jeans.

"Precisely. I need you two to go on a trip."

Carlisle zipped up his trousers and rushed to my side. "Where? The sun will be coming up any minute now."

"You've lived centuries, and you're not from these parts, so you know how to get around."

"Where are we headed?" Billie's eyes lit up.

"Japan."

"Can't be done." Carlisle shook his head. "It takes days to get there. The sun will burn us alive."

"Not if you travel below the sea."

"By boat? That could take a week. Weeks?" Carlisle bitched.

"But you won't die."

Billie sat on the arm of the chair in the corner. "What's in Japan?"

"Cason."

"Fuck that. I'm not spending a week below deck for your boy toy. What kind of trouble has he gotten himself into?"

"That's what you're going to find out for me."

"I'm in," said Billie.

"I'm not." Carlisle huffed. "So, your bodyguard isn't here. That explains the stench of desire running in your veins. I can take care of that for you."

I sighed. "You have to be the horniest vampire of all time."

"You did interrupt me at my finest. I still need to finish. And so do you."

Billie cut him off. "When do we leave?"

"Tonight."

Carlisle paced the floor, running his fingers through his hair. "Say we do go on this recon mission of yours…who is going to be here to help you when Adela goes off the rails? And she will. We're sitting ducks right now."

"I have backup."

"Who?"

"Keshell Martin."

"You've met The Rebirther?"

"Is that what you call him?"

"He's the necromancer."

"Have you seen him do it?"

"No."

"Just like you haven't seen Adela set anyone on fire, correct?"

Carlisle mumbled. "Let's hope you won't personally find out."

"What's that? Smartass." I dashed into his space and smacked him. "I'm not in the mood for your disrespect. Get some rest. You leave tonight."

They followed me onto the porch for a final breath of the night air before turning in for the day. *Zip.* A dagger hit Billie in the neck. *Bloop.* A second one took out Carlisle. The heat rose in my veins as I scanned the movement lurking in the darkness. The smell of murky water, dogs, and muddy pastures closed in. I dropped low to strike from the ground. As I squeezed my thighs to pounce on who or whatever was approaching me on the steps, "Aah!" I screamed.

A metal cloak weighed me down. My knees buckled, and I keeled forward to my stomach as a dart pierced the back of my shoulder. "Get the fuck off of me!" I yelled, feeling a sting flow through my arteries. Then... nothing.

CHAPTER 43
THE HEALER
CASON

I HATED LEAVING VANITY, but what must be done, must be done. Sana and I traveled east to Biloxi, eliminating the chance of being seen leaving N'awlins. One short flight to Hartsfield International and an eighteen-hour excursion to Osaka, I set myself up thinking we were close to our destination.

Upon leaving the airport, it was clear we were on foreign land. Cajun cuisine no longer filled the air, and my nose turned unfaithful to the scent of The Big Easy, craving the taste of soy fried rice and seafood ramen veiling the neon-lit streets.

Along our search for our lodge, we crossed paths with street performers engaging crowds with their rendition of hip hop, what appeared to be a modern version and less acrobatic form of break dancing with assistance from a guitarist, and young girls in school uniforms cheering them on.

Everything was big. It was as if the city was alive in 3D with various forms of music blasting from different corners. Clean streets, curious faces, some hidden behind masks, some not, and all on very different missions—including us.

We passed a restaurant with heavy foot traffic one block away from the hotel, dropped our belongings, and padded back in that direction to grab a bite to settle the rumbles in our stomachs. Still reeling from the jet lag, we selected a restaurant with a minimal crowd hanging outside its doors.

Sana suggested, "Let's place our order at the bar and eat in the room."

"No, brother. We've come all this way, finally seeing our homeland. The least we can do is enjoy our dinner before another four hours of travel in the morning."

"If you insist."

Between the two of us, dish after dish a la carte style filled our bellies. The fish was seasoned, but not overly done to hide the freshness of it being pulled a few hours ago from the local port. I couldn't help but compare it to the city I had come to know as home. Different flavors, different tastes, both delicious.

"You boys here to *kuidaore*?" Our waitress snickered, testing us.

Briefly, Sana and I met eyes.

He replied, "Why not? Bring all the house favorites."

"Will do, but make sure you save room for our famous Inunaki pork dish."

My taste buds adapted to *Japan's Kitchen* as if they had been waiting to experience it my entire life. A part of me felt complete, like something I didn't know was missing suddenly gave me a sense of fulfillment and belonging.

To finish off the experience, the waitress laid the pork dish in the center of the table. She was correct in that it was the best thing I'd ever tasted, but also the worst dish Sana and I chose to indulge in, as we paid for it hours later, taking turns keeled over the toilet.

"We could have easily said no," Sana grumbled.

"I haven't had pork in fifteen years," I confessed.

"Ten for me." Sana ran back into the bathroom and croaked. "I'm never going near it again."

I stretched across the bed, waiting for room service to deliver a bottle of the pink stuff to end the suffering. A few swigs and a bottle of ginger ale soothed us into the night as the running bright lights of the city flashed through the drapes. I counted violet flashes blinking at the bottom of the curtain until I fell asleep, waking up to Sana standing over me hours later.

"We need to get moving." His stern face glared down at me.

After clearing the crust from my eyes, I tied my hiking boots and threw my bag over my shoulder. A taxi delivered Sana and me to Osaka's southern port. There, we boarded a ferry to Kochi of The Shikoku Island, our final destination. During the four-hour ride, my brother and I barely spoke. The rolling of the waves taunted his upset stomach from the night before. While he stretched out on a hard wooden row inside the ferry, I captured the beauty of the Pacific Ocean, inhaling the scent of seaweed and kelp mixed with the saltiness of the tepid water tapping the side of the boat.

Once in Kochi, we hopped on the tram to the Niyodo River and trekked upstream along its clear, cobalt-blue water until we reached an edgeless bridge leading us into the territory of the healer. Falling red leaves decorated the backdrop of cilantro green trees half covered with veils of fog descending from the sky.

"Look for statues, brother," said Sana, staring at a map of the forest.

"Of what exactly?"

"How am I supposed to know? The person I spoke with said we are close once we reach a waterfall and encounter statues of some sort," he argued.

I picked up a pebble and threw it at him. "Calm down. We have to be close. I hear a waterfall nearby." I pointed east. "It's this way."

We crossed another bridge, this one half the size of the first and wide enough for two hikers to cross at a time. I spotted two statues hiding amongst the shrubs as the waterfall crashing against the rocks grew closer.

"We're not alone," I warned, looking over my shoulder.

"We're definitely being watched." Sana retrieved a flashlight from his bag and turned it to the blink setting.

A man appeared from the bushes. "Follow me," he called from across the stream.

Behind the waterfall was civilization. A carved entrance into the cave home of Hinata the Healer. Two black steel doors opened, and an elderly woman chanted as we entered with rolled herbs burning from each hand. We bowed to her and were allowed to pass, arriving inside a glazed auburn temple with high, edgy ceilings. "Remove your shoes." Our guide pointed to our feet. We stepped out of our boots and followed him behind a white sheer curtain beside the temple.

"I can feel the presence of royalty." Hinata smiled. "The ancestors are happy you are here."

Sana and I remained quiet, taking in her regal presence. Her aura was large for a small woman. Her blue silk gown covered her feet, dragging against the floor, and her nut-brown, smooth skin was radiant against the candles providing all of the light in the room. The wrinkles on her hands told her age, whereas her face could fool someone she was younger. She was still young in spirit and in her appearance, but old in wisdom and gifts of nature.

"Nervous royalty? My, the times have changed." Hinata lifted my chin. "Know that you are missed in these parts."

I straightened my shoulders and stuck out my chest. "It's good to be home."

"Much better. A king has no reason to be humble in my presence." Her warm hands cradled my face. "I couldn't believe your kind still walked this earth. Imagine my surprise when I learned your highness wants to save a demon."

Sana cleared his throat. "I'm the one who requested your help, ma'am."

The pounding in my chest stunned Hinata. She took a step backward and grinned, then sharply turned her head to Sana. "I see. You both love this vampire." She clicked her teeth before releasing my cheek. "The plot thickens."

CHAPTER 44

THE PROMISE

CASON

HINATA'S ASSISTANT returned to her sanctuary with a tiny glass bottle. A long, black braid stopped short above her raised nipple piercing through a sheer white gown. She smelled of lavender soap. Her big dark eyes glanced in my direction from her bowed head, then she and Hinata shared a quick smile before she ran behind a curtain, where other girls could be heard whispering and giggling.

Hinata examined the bottle against the candlelight near her station. She held it near her bosom, then closed her eyes, reciting a quiet prayer and raising the bottle above her head. Her lips stopped moving when she opened her eyes, then held the bottle above the flame on her mantel and smiled. "The fire doesn't lie. Give this potion to your vampiress, and she will be human once again." Hinata called me forward and placed the bottle in my hand and rolled my fingers to form a fist around it. She wrapped her palms around mine and whispered, "Birth, death, rebirth."

"Is that your power of three?" My voice rattled.

She nodded. "You are familiar?"

"Just a smidge."

"Promise you will bring your vampiress to visit with me."

"Before or after?"

"After, preferably." She released my hand. "Her current form won't be allowed to enter my temple."

"I'll do my best."

"As a king, you have much to learn of your homeland and the people your grandfather left behind."

"I promise. We shall see each other soon, Hinata."

Sana spoke. "We have what we've come for, brother. We must be on our way."

"Thank you for your help." I reached for Hinata's hand and kissed the back of it. "I'm grateful my brother found you."

"What is written is law. Our paths were meant to cross."

Hinata and her two guards escorted us out of the sacred cavern and sealed the black steel doors. Sana led the hike down a trail alongside the river filled with colorful stones. "I don't remember coming in this way, brother!" I shouted ahead. Sana kept trekking, leading us across an overpass without rails during a magical moment where the blue waters turned green.

"We're almost there," Sana finally responded.

"Where?"

"I shouldn't have to tell you we can't stay in the same place twice."

I didn't appreciate the condescending tone but always gave Sana a pass because he couldn't control the chip on his shoulder. With his map in hand, he dragged us through the field of a tea plantation. The smell of mint, green tea, and a medley of flowers blowing in the gusts permeated the air, calming the agitation rising in my blood toward my brother's behavior.

Past the fields and up a hill, we climbed a rock path ending with a container house overlooking a stream from the river.

"We will lodge here tonight and travel by train to Kobe before dawn," Sana announced, checking the power of our unit.

"It's a beautiful place. This country. Too bad we can't enjoy it. I feel a connection to this land. Do you?"

He grunted. "This unit was supposed to be fully equipped," he griped and stepped outside.

I treaded on his heels. "What's wrong with you? You've been acting strange since we landed."

"You are what's wrong with me!" His voice echoed across the stream. "I'm the one who knew about the cure! I'm the one who found the healer, and she wouldn't even acknowledge me!"

"I did not ask to be born the eldest. I did not ask to be a part of this clan. We are dealt the cards we're dealt. How many times do we have to have this argument? Huh?"

Sana kicked the outdoor grill sitting on a stone slab in front of the unit. Waiting for a response I would not get, I returned inside to our lodging for the night, stretched across the bed, and studied Sana standing on the edge of the deck outside, then closed my eyes.

With the past few days running long and eventful, I drifted off with a hiccup, unsure if it had been minutes or hours when I heard the front door open to the house.

"Cason?"

"Yeah, brother?"

"I'm sorry," he said.

"Crrrr!" was the last sound I heard, then darkness embraced me.

CHAPTER 45
THE BLACK
VANITY

MY HEIGHTENED SENSES FELT ORDINARY. I couldn't make out if I was in a steam room or if whatever drug was pulsating through my veins blurred my vision. The smell of blood, death, and mold perfumed my nose as I sat chained, swallowing regurgitation of the poison my captors had infused into my body.

Lift your head, I said to myself, weaker than I've ever felt, missing the power and ruthlessness I was recently afforded. My feet failed me, refusing to lift or spread wide to break the chain anchoring me motionless.

"She's awake!" His voice rattled my bones.

"Put her back to sleep! Dart her again!"

Draped in chains bound to a cemented wall fit for a prisoner, my fingers struggled to wiggle, and my wrists felt lifeless above my head. I jerked my neck to lift my head when the two cracks that looked like worms at my feet became clear, then *splaa*, I was sent back into the darkness.

Hours, days, possibly weeks I'd lost, depleted from famine, drugged near my end, and dubious of my way out, but sure of three things: I craved the taste for blood, I was somewhere near the swamps, and my captors were Junichiro and Shun.

I recognized their voices before they sent me back to the black, and the rage of realizing my lover's kin had me hanging like strange fruit more than tripled when I woke the second time.

This time, I was covered by a hefty, silver net, like the one tossed over me when I was captured. The weight of it would bury me above ground if my hands weren't pinned up high. Dangling like windchimes, I listened for footsteps and rapid heartbeats before I opened my eyes this time. My legs and feet had lost their brown color, resembling that of an actual pale face. Muted gray and ash. If set free, I wasn't sure I could move a muscle in my body, but hope never left my will to seek revenge on the blood of my dear Cason.

Why haven't you come for me? I called out to him. *Can you hear me? Do you not feel the treachery in your brothers? I need you. Rescue me, my love,* I said to myself in hopes my hero could hear me.

Feeling as though I was alone, I pushed and pushed until my head lifted upright to view my cell. To my left, spiderwebs, rot, and decay covered the walls and ceilings of my hellhole. To my right, an empty, drab wall. Facing me was a thick steel door with bars in the center where the poisonous dart shot me.

The smell of blood nearby gave me a light boost. I sniffed and followed the scent to the corner of the wall nearest to my left. Billie's eyes stared into mine. Her head, detached from her body, sat one foot away from my very own.

"They beat me to it, friend. I'm not certain I would have changed my mind to kill you myself," I whispered. "Thank you for your service."

The floorboards creaked upstairs, and the faint pitter-patter of mud boots grew closer, blended with deep voices talking over each other. I lowered my head and stunted my breaths. A feud between the brothers ensued as I listened for Cason's voice to tell them to free me.

"We are not naming you king," Junichiro fumed.

"I am the new king of our clan as the second-born," Sana argued.

"Father's wife should be the one to decide."

"Why? Have you threatened her to choose you?"

"You speak nonsense. At least I took action and put a stop to a threat and violence in the city."

I felt their eyes turn toward me.

Sana stood before me, encouraging me with a smile behind his concern. "And you have yet to explain your actions, Juni. Why did you capture V when she was protecting the city? She is no threat and looks to have been tortured."

"To answer your questions, she has not been tortured," Juni replied with an eerie cheerfulness in his voice. "She's just starved. And I captured her as a part of a truce with Adela. She wanted her head. I lied that I set her on fire, and voilá, peace has been restored to the city."

"If Cason were still alive, we'd be at war with each other. That is not what father would want. Open her chamber now. I'm giving her this cure."

Keys rattled, and the lock clicked, then a slap echoed on the other side of the door.

"We don't know if it will work, Sana. She's better off dead like her little friend," said Juni.

"You've never liked her," Sana's voice heightened. "Or is it that you do want her, and she's never paid you any attention."

"You mean the way she's ignored you and pranced behind Cason these past two years?"

Sana growled.

Juni grunted. "Face it, brother, you were born number two and will always come in second. Giving her that cure won't make her want you."

"Just open the door."

"She's awake!" Shun peered at me through the bars.

"She can't do anything beneath that net," Juni assured his brother.

The door crept open, and two of them approached. Each of their heartbeats differed, but Shun's pumped the fastest from the hallway. He was terrified of me—bullied into doing this by Juni. I was sure of it.

"V," Sana softly called my name. "I'm here. Everything's going to be okay. Forgive my idiot brothers for their treachery."

"Where's Cason?" I croaked.

Juni's eyes sliced me in half. "You don't ask the questions."

"Where is he? Does he know what you've done to me?"

"Listen to me, V. I need you to drink this potion, then we will have a talk about Cason." Sana's heart rate increased tenfold.

I lifted my head and looked Sana in the eyes. He was keeping secrets, and so was Shun, hiding his face below the bars behind the steel door.

"Shun, come here please."

He hung back by the door, refusing to look at me.

"Shun, where is Cason? What aren't these two telling me."

He opened his mouth to speak, then Junichiro warned him. "Don't answer her."

"I demand to know. I overheard you two big-dicking about being the new Silver Leaf King. Where the fuck is my Cason?"

"Dead," Sana answered with dark snake eyes and not an ounce of emotion in his tone.

"I don't believe you." I sighed, feeling heat inside of me for the first time in weeks.

"We were ambushed after the witch doctor gave us the potion. Cason didn't survive the attack. He died for us both."

I challenged the lack of remorse in Sana's eyes. "Died for us both?" I asked, heaving of fury and denial.

"Cason died a hero. He gave me the potion with orders to leave him behind and get the cure to you." Sana's warm hands soothed my sunken cheeks. "I told you. I'm here for you. Please drink this, Vanity."

"If I no longer have Cason, I no longer have a reason to change back," I cried as a burst of power jolted my body against the wall.

CHAPTER 46
THE KEY

VANITY

A SCREECHING cry silenced Sana's plea, and the brothers held their ears to stop the piercing echo from dropping them to their knees. Junichiro's mouth moved, but his brothers were deafened by my cry stifling the room. I read his lips. "Dart her, Shun." His lips quivered.

Strong wind gusts hit the house, and dust fell from the ceiling as a shattering vibration from the floor shook the room above and below. Sana crawled on his knees toward me and raised his hand at me. My left hand broke the chain sealed to the wall and came down at him aiming for my mouth, but I would not be silenced.

Sana flew into the molded wall with the cobwebs hanging from the ceiling. My fists struggled no more, tugging on the loose chain, swinging it toward Junichiro. Full force and disdain went into that hit, clocking him harder than the blow that sent Sana flying to the other side of the room.

Juni curled into a ball. His yellow eyes inflamed with the hatred he'd felt for me all along. He screamed, and I screamed louder, shrilling of pain in my chest and anger in my cold veins.

Sana held onto the wall for aid to stand. He stared at Shun, obviously communicating telepathically. I didn't want to hurt Shun, but he reached in his front pocket while struggling to stand to his feet. Before he blinked, I stood behind him, wrapped the broken chain around his neck, and killed my cry.

"I don't want to hurt you, Shun, but I will if you force my hand. Who has the key?" My grip loosened to hear his reply.

"Juni," his voice rasped.

I shoved him toward Junichiro. "Out of respect for Cason, I will forgive you for what you've done, but if I have to grovel for the key to take this iron off my wrists, I won't be so kind. We can all get out of here alive if you hand it over right now."

"There are three of us and one of you." Juni spat blood on the gravelly floor.

"How's that working out for you?"

"Fuck you, Vanity!" Juni bent over and charged at my waist.

I spun around him, laughing maniacally, fueling from his rage. Sana approached me from behind. I spun the chain, knocking Juni to the floor with a lash to the back of his knees, then aimed the chain at Sana. He caught it and pulled the chain inward. I fought back against his strength, then gave way, returning his own force. The chain slapped his face, then I pounced to the back of him as he took cover.

In his ear, I whispered, "I'm only going to let you live because I want all the details on how my love was murdered. I will avenge him, and those people must pay. Now tell your brothers to stand down and give me the key."

"Juni. She doesn't want to hurt us. Throw me the key please, brother."

"This is why I should be our pack leader. All of you are too weak and too trusting—for a vamp, no less."

"Give Sana the key, or I will make him choose which one of you dies today!"

The key floated in the air before Sana caught it with one hand. I stretched my arm out in front of him, controlling the dangling chain as his hands trembled figuring out the lock. *Click.* The first one unlocked and fell to the floor. I exhaled. *Click.* The second chain dropped, creating a vibration against the first one.

A smile graced my face for a brief second until my eyes landed on Juni cursing himself for a failed plan. "Which one of you killed her?" I asked, pointing to Billie's severed head staring at me from the back wall. The brothers shared a look and kept silent. "Fine, don't tell me. I was wondering if your creativity matched mine." I chuckled. "I considered several methods," I added, then snatched the potion from the inner pocket of Sana's jacket and fled through the steel doors of the basement, escaping my prison with unexpected enemies on my heels.

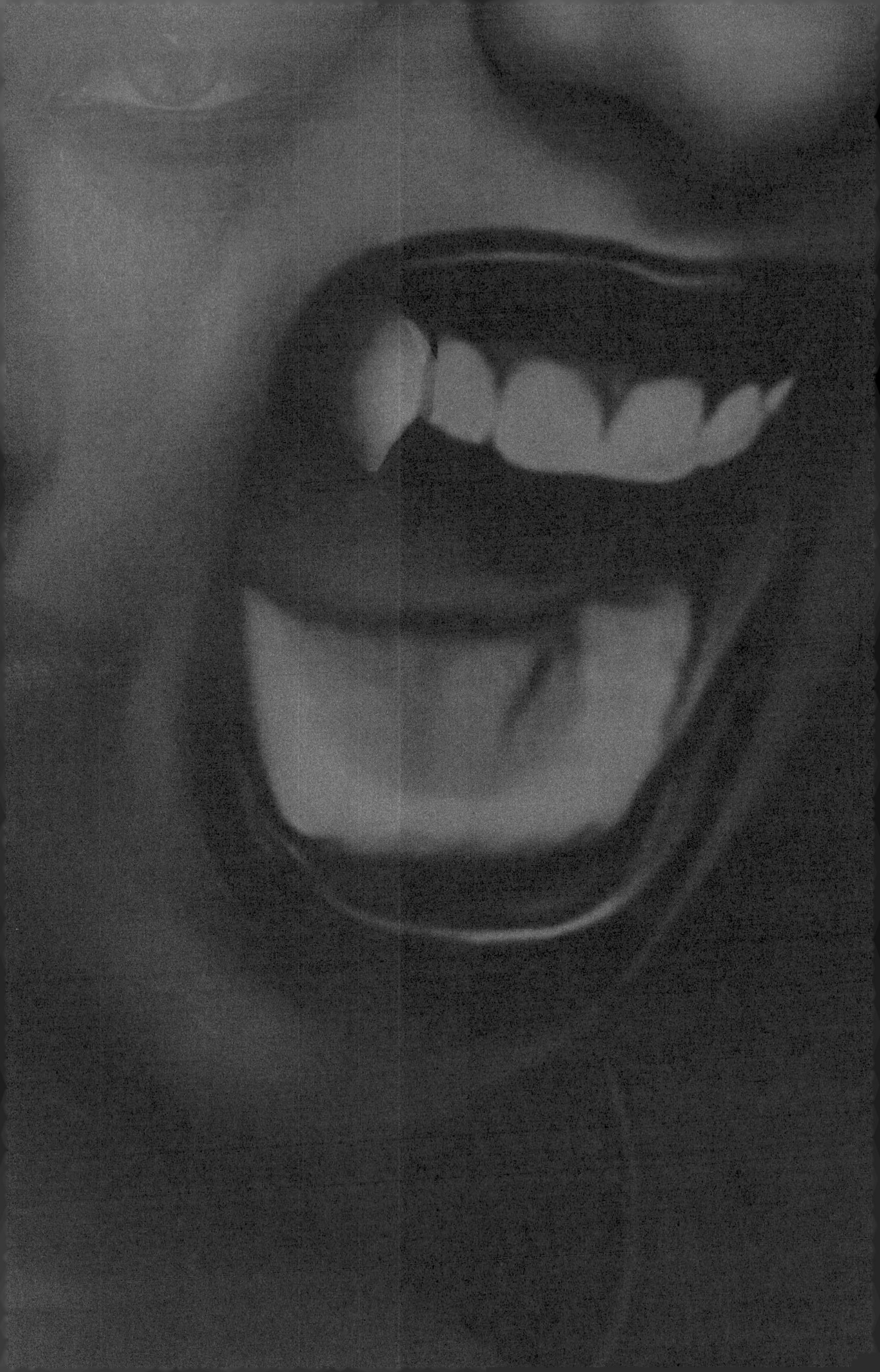

CHAPTER 47
THE HUNGER

VANITY

THE WHOOSHING WINDS hailed outside when I burst through the doors of the cabin. The twins led the pack, trailing close on my ass, transformed into their feral form. They were beautiful in the dawn's light. Their silver fur shone with white streaks for brows. Their growls were less intimidating than Cason's, but aggressive enough that I zipped past a beaver sitting at the edge of the bank when I was near death from hunger.

The scent of the cowbirds and beavers tempted me as I led the pursuit through the woods. I leapt high into the tallest tree to scope the land, the twins, and now the brothers gaining close behind. I needed to feed, and the sudden interest in human blood angered me. I knew it was because I hadn't been fed in days. I needed to end that thirst before entering the city.

Akina and Homare jumped effortlessly but not high enough to reach me. Junichiro climbed a few feet, determined to claim his revenge. As the winds howled around us, I warned him to climb down, and when he ignored me, I formed a patch of high winds and blew him from the tree. Controlling the element, I centered the six of us between a cyclone of orange, red, and brown leaves.

"I am not the enemy!" I shouted.

"You are our enemy!" he yelled at me, lying on his back.

"Twins, I love your brother! I will not harm you. I don't want to fight! Ask Shun!"

Shun lowered his head. "She can kill us if she wants to! I believe her!"

"Traitor!" Juni fumed.

"He is not the traitor! You are! I have done nothing wrong, and you made a deal with a she-devil for my head for what?"

"For peace!" Juni screamed at the top of his lungs.

"She will not keep that promise for long! And you, Sana! You're lying about Cason! I know it! I can feel it." Blood fell from my eyes.

The twins hollered at the mention of their big brother's name. Agonizing cries expelled from their mouths while their bodies malformed from she-wolves into women. Bones crackling like wood burning in a fire, they clung to the ground beneath them, jutting and jolting until the transformation was complete.

Sana and Shun covered their naked bodies with their flannel button-downs. The twins held their shirts together by the buttons, then rose from the dirt. Like robots in sync, the five of them looked up at me with dense silver eyes.

"She's crying blood for our brother," Akina whimpered.

"I loved him." My eyes shifted to Sana. "I want to know why Sana returned without his body."

Unlike the rest, his eyes weren't seething with anger toward me.

"We were ambushed!" Sana yelled. "I'm lucky to be alive!"

"So you've said!" I turned my head to Junichiro, forever ogling me with disdain. "When I'm done cleaning up your brother's mess, you will take me to where this ambush occurred!"

The siblings looked at one another, and their heartbeats slowed—except for Sana's. His heartbeat was steadfast and solid. He was lying about something.

A few branches above me sat a half-woven nest and two cowbirds inches apart. My starvation entertained my audience, cringing when I snatched both birds and twisted their necks. I skinned the first of its feathers. They fell from the tree before being swept into the winds circling us. I bit into its chest and argued with Juni. "Why did you starve me? I told you I don't consume human blood. You have a cruel heart about you," I said.

"Turn off this magic show and be on your way."

I grinned. "Full of insults, I see." I turned to the others. "I've already forgiven you for what you've done to me these past few weeks."

Shun mumbled from a distance. "What Juni did to you."

"Traitor," Juni spit at his brother.

"Enough!" I swallowed the second bird whole. "There will be a battle for the city. After I win that battle, I plan on fleeing for good and give the people control of their city. Will you help me with my fight as your brother did?"

Homare stepped forward. "Because you loved my brother, you are not my enemy. I will speak for this family and declare peace between us, but we will not stand with you. This is between the misfit pale faces running around. Not our kind. We wish you good luck."

I respected Homare for her bravery and candor. We exchanged a thin smile and a nod as the winds died down around us, and the cyclone evaporated into the sky. I jumped down from the tree, landed in front of the twins, then glared at Sana. "I'll be in touch when this is over."

CHAPTER 48

THE STRANGER

VANITY

THE PACE at which I fled the woods was no match for the Kyoudai to keep up with me—if they had tried. Once clear of the swamplands, I came to an open road. The walk into the city could be managed if I were nourished. Being bloodied and ungroomed hindered my sex appeal to hitch a ride, and having been starved for weeks I assumed, with two birds to wet my appetite as a teaser, the hike would be insufferable.

All I could think of was my curse as I trekked alongside the road, stopping at an old-timey gas station with a hillbilly broken down truck with flat tires on the side of the garage. If I were free to leave the vicinity of the bayou, I would have jumped on a skiff and escaped this parish without ever looking back.

Life in N'awlins wasn't worth living with the news of Cason's death heavy on my tortured heart.

I slid back into the woods. Patience was not the virtue flowing through my veins while in search of a ride. What was left of my humanity kept me from jumping an elderly woman with a hump on her back I pitied. As I waited for the next patron to arrive, I had my fill of moss-covered wild berries hanging low from a twisted vine. I didn't know which was worse—the sour taste of the berry or the tang from the moss.

A blond fella in a blue hoodie pulled up to the gas pump, bobbing his head to the loud tunes from the trunk of a black restored Chevette. I took him wearing my color as a sign.

The surprise in his eyes humored me when I flashed before him, enticing him with the gold flecks sprinkled around the red in my eyes.

"Fill the tank, get back in the car, and drive me to the city."

"Yes." He nodded.

Guiding him into the city turned out to be a task. He was under total mind control from my compulsion, more so than the others. "Give me your sweatshirt and wait here," I ordered him, sitting on the corner of Conti Street as a brass band honored a fallen one with a jazz funeral.

The drums from the band made me reflect on the beating of hearts that night Cason and I had lost control like the wild animals we are—we were. A smile graced my face, thinking about the way he controlled my body with power and precision. The apex of my thighs convulsed from the lack of his touch and the yearning for sexual pleasure that had been starved of attention for far too long.

With the hood raised over my head, I blended in with the second line and swiped an obituary from a woman dancing so hard her wig hung onto her head by a thread, then I stopped walking once I read the date printed at the top.

That fool kept me captive for two and a half weeks.

Skipping back to my driver with the engine running a few blocks back, I wandered into a saloon for a shot of gin by way of compulsion.

"Nice trick you got there," a man's voice moaned.

"I'm not in the mood."

"The Lauren I knew wouldn't drink gin without orange juice—nor this early in the day."

I turned to him. "My name's not Lauren," I said, then glared at him with tight-pressed lips.

The bartender placed a square napkin in front of me and poured a shot worth of Sapphire into my glass. The man continued to stare at me and yap. "I come here every year with hopes of running into you. And you just waltz in here looking like...well not as I had hoped to find you." His excited eyes gave me a onceover.

I studied his face in return, searching for familiarity, and got lost in the sexy way his lips formed when he said the word *you*. They puckered like a kiss in action. Plump, smooth, and mauve.

"Mister, I don't know who you are looking for, but I'm not her. So if you will allow me to enjoy my drink in peace, I'd appreciate it."

"Lauren."

I sighed. "Someone is hard of hearing." I slammed my glass on the wood bartop.

"No, I heard you. I was just hoping if I kept saying it, you'd remember who you are."

The muddled weeks led me to forget the information Cason had relayed in his letter, but this stranger obviously knew the woman I used to be.

'Does the name Lauren mean anything to you? The seer will have sketches of the man in the vehicle with you at the time of your accident,' Cason's letter said.

I turned to the boyish, good-looking gentleman incapable of taking his eyes off me. "So, tell me about this Lauren."

CHAPTER 49

THE PAST

VANITY

UNFAMILIAR with the eyes gazing at me from the stranger uttering the name I once carried as my own, I grinned as I stared at his silky lips proudly telling me of the life he claims we shared before our accident.

"Pardon my staring. I'm in disbelief that I finally found you. I've been here four times now in two years, walked alongside parades during Mardi Gras, showed your picture to the police who barely glanced at your photo."

"May I see it? The photo?"

The burn of the gin soothed my aches and burned my chest in a delightful way as he retrieved a white envelope from the inside pocket of his jacket. "You were quite a beauty in this one." His finger slid the picture in front of me. The woman smiling in the photo pressed between my fingers was as much a stranger as the man sitting in my company. His arms wrapped around her waist, and his face was half covered and buried in the back of her neck. "Beauty. Brains. Body. And brilliance."

"I feel like I'm at an alliteration conference."

"Funny." He grinned. "I forgot about that."

"This woman is not me. People have doppelgangers."

"Lauren, I loved…love you. I could pick you out of a thousand doppel-gangers. That is you." He pointed to the picture. "That is us."

"My name is Vanity, not Lauren. I didn't catch yours, by the way."

"Dell. Short for…"

He hesitated with hope in his eyes that I would call out his forename. I tapped on the bar for a second shot with my brows raised. This Dell person lowered his head, letting out a deep sigh of breath.

"Short for what?" I raised my glass.

"Lindell." He paused. "Does my name not ring a bell to you at all?"

"'*Fraid* not." I stared at him, fascinated with the way those lips of his formed when he said *you* again, and the smoothness of his copper-bronzed skin and bald head. A sadness crippled the little joy he had in his face. "Dell, normally I'm not in the business of holding conversations with strange men in bars, and I had a pretty rough night as you can see." I pointed to the empty shot glass.

"May I ask you to tell me something about yourself? In particular, something within the past two years," he asked me.

"What's so important about the past two years?"

"That's how long I've had to live without you." He sighed.

"Tell me about this life."

He smiled. "It's heartbreaking you don't remember. We were to be married about a year ago. I fought hard to get in the good graces of your father, but he eventually saw I was a good man and that I would be devoted to you. I still spend time with him even after…well…since you…I mean, since Lauren disappeared."

"How did she disappear?"

"She actually didn't. I was forced to leave her here."

"So why did you lie?"

"Because I made a mistake the last time she and I were together."

I slid the empty glass away. "Mistake?"

"I think I made a deal with the devil to keep her alive."

"That doesn't seem like a bad deal if you ask me."

"In theory, it wasn't at the time. I didn't want to see her die. But in cheating death, I haven't known peace. I imagined Lauren suffered from the same as I did. Not knowing peace. Left here all alone without a memory of who she was. Her name, her family, her life back in Jacksonville. A selfish choice I made. The wrong choice," his voice whirred. "Her parents don't have closure, and I have to remember my lies every time I'm around them."

"So you're a weaver of lies, then? You told one lie, and now you're stuck telling lies on top of lies to cover your first one."

"I won't have to tell another one if I bring you home."

I cleared my throat. "Did Lauren's parents ever come here looking for answers?"

"More times than I can count."

"And what lie did you tell them?"

Dell paused his story and ordered a vodka on the rocks. Thirst burst within me as I watched his throat expand and retract when he swallowed, envisioning what it used to be like lying below him as I listened to his heart beat at the pace of a ticking clock. *Was he charismatic in bed? I wondered. Tender or rough? Attentive or selfish like the choice he made when he left me here an amnesiac ward of the state of Louisiana?*

"I'm not proud of the chaos I have caused, or the lies I've fed your folks, or leaving you here—I mean, leaving Lauren here," he interrupted. "It pained me to tell Mr. and Mrs. Stuart their little girl burned to bones and then ash on the side of a dark road. At least they were spared the true details of her lying in pain, near death, staring up into an open, starless sky, shivering and murmuring for me to help her. For a while, they accused me of foul play, but then your father's detectives supplied them with proof that I was hospitalized with head trauma and checked into the psych ward after telling the doctors what I had done." He scoffed. "I was speaking of witchcraft and a priestess with gray eyes. It's been pure hell since that horrific night."

"Hell? You don't say." I chuckled, then glanced at the wooden clock above the row of liquors at the bar. "Dell, your story is fascinating, but I need to pay the meter of my driver outside."

His body jolted before he hopped to his feet. "I can take you where you want to go. I will never forgive myself if I lose you after I've finally found you."

"You can't go where I'm going, but I can spare a few more hours with you."

With the burn flaming inside my chest, I exited the bar with a hunger for pleasure and my past. Lindell reached for my hand as he strolled at my side. I snickered and placed my hands inside the cubby of my hood until we reached the blond boy under my spell. "Wait here," I told him.

He nodded.

I leaned down to my kidnapped lad. "You will forget my face, the last two hours, and proceed with your day as planned."

"Yes." His eyes slowly withdrew from dilation as he shook his head freely.

I eased back over to Lindell. "Where are you parked?"

The biggest smile formed across his lips as his eyes held mine. "Right this way."

CHAPTER 50

THE ACCEPTANCE

VANITY

LINDELL PULLED out of the lot where I guided him past Madame's and toward the café. His incessant staring annoyed me more than his choice of music on the radio. "You mind?" I asked, turning the channel before he answered. He scoffed with a curve on his lip, then tapped his fingers to the fast tempo of a local bounce tune for the duration of our short drive. "Park here for just a second." I motioned for him to pull into a vacant spot in front of a parking meter on the corner.

He wheeled in smoothly and searched for change in the cup holder near the dash. I lowered my hood and reached for the latch. "What's this place?" he asked, rumbling through pennies in search of silver coins.

"This is going to sound rude, but I need you to stop doing that and sit still. Please."

The stunned look on Lindell's face was priceless and comical. He sat back and bit his lip while I held in my laughter and listened in on Kyle giving orders to the staff.

I couldn't bring myself to go inside and say the words out loud to Kyle, "Cason is no longer with us." I still didn't believe Sana's declaration to be true.

As Lindell breathed harder with every passing second, I sat immobilized with visions of Cason smiling at me when he thought I wasn't looking, the brush of his hand when I passed him the tally slips from the bar at closing, and the smell of his cologne that drove my endorphins wild.

Customers came and went while I daydreamed of the past, then a smile graced my face. *The place hadn't skipped a beat. Cason would be proud of Kyle for stepping up and continuing the success of what was now a part of his legacy.*

A city cop tapped on the window, breaking my gaze of a life I could not bear to return to. Lindell cranked the car as I let the window down.

"We were just leaving." I smiled, then turned to Lindell. "I've seen enough. Make a U-turn, then take the next right."

"Yes, ma'am." Lindell smirked.

"Where are you staying?"

"Mid-City."

"Is that where you and Lauren stayed together?"

"Lucky guess." He glanced my way.

"Your visit is sentimental. It wasn't that hard of a guess. And you've got to chill on the staring."

"I can't help it. You look the same but also different in a strange way. I'm trying to figure it out."

"If you'd just accept that you picked up a complete stranger and stop making me out to be this Lauren character, I'd greatly appreciate it."

"I don't know how, but I'm going to find a way to get you to remember. I don't give a damn what that priestess said."

"Tell me more about the deal with the priestess. What exactly did she say? Why was she there?"

Lindell took a long pause. "Honestly, she spooked the shit outta me. We were approaching a bridge when a truck slammed into us. The car was smoking when I came to, and I carried you to the side of the road, yelling for the driver who hit us to call 911. He pulled off and left us there when this woman appeared from out of nowhere. She said she could save you, but it would come at a price. Your memory and my love. You wouldn't be able to ever leave the city, and I would have to go on living without you knowing me. You were in so much pain that I agreed. She spoke some sort of incantation, and the wind picked up. Moments later, your cry for help subsided, the woman vanished, and you looked up at me and asked who I was. The ambulance arrived, and we were hospitalized in the same room for a short while. Again, you asked my name, and I immediately regretted my decision."

"You can park here. I won't be long."

"Do you need me to come with you?"

"Sorry, the owner wouldn't like a strange man walking inside his home. Sit tight."

As I entered Cason's house, a drop of blood fell from my eyes into my hand. Him not being there created an overwhelming sadness that chilled my bones and caused my slowed heart to increase. Him not being there made Sana's account of his death true.

Before I hit the shower, where the broken glass hadn't yet been replaced, the pain of a deferred cry pounded in my chest. With my emotions in chaos, the built-up rage from my broken heart and frustration foiled my need for a good cry. A few blood tears were all I was afforded to release while the knot surrounding my heart felt as if it could burst through my chest.

Naked and wet, I wandered into Cason's room. One of his soiled shirts was draped across the edge of his closet door. I held it to my nose. In closing my eyes, I could feel his presence lingering in the room as the scent of my warrior soothed my soulless body, helping the pain of his absence taper off.

I carried his shirt with me into my room, sniffing it as I dressed for every season in a pair of black leather shorts; a thin, vinyl, low-cut blouse with an attached hood; and thigh-high leather boots.

Before embarking on what the evening would bring, I peeped through the blinds at Lindell patiently sitting where I left him, glaring toward the house, mumbling indistinctly to himself.

I approached the car, and his eyes shone like amber rhinestones. "So you just happened to have that outfit lying around in there?"

My cheeks matched my red eyes hidden from my bowed head as I closed the door. "Thanks for being patient. I have a few hours to spare. Let's finish this conversation at your hotel."

"Lauren. You look…"

I huffed. "If I agree to let you call me Lauren, will you put your tongue back in your mouth?"

"I can't make any promises. It's been two years after all."

CHAPTER 51

THE CONFESSION

VANITY

WE HAD nothing more to discuss when we arrived at the quiet side of town. Dell opened the door to his hotel room and welcomed me inside. I made myself comfortable on the bed, spread my arms across the satin comforter like a snow angel, then patted the bed.

"Come." I curled my finger.

He poured a glass of bourbon from the minibar, then swallowed big. "Care to join me? I didn't want to overdo it at the bar and risk getting a DUI around these parts. This place hasn't been too kind to me over the years."

"I'm good for now." I smirked. "Dell, we don't have any further business. You've told me everything."

"Have I?" He scowled.

I nodded. "I suggested we come here because I now have a story to tell you."

"I'm all ears."

"There's something I want you to do for me first."

"What's that?"

"Kiss me."

His lips held the rim of the glass, taking in a swig of his libation. He sat next to me on the bed. The excitement of my request lauded my ears as a bead of sweat formed above his brow. I found his nervousness cute and could see why I would have been with him in the past. Then I leaned forward to sample him in the present.

As our lips touched, I saw a flash of us near the bridge. I heard my voice calling out to him for help, then a flash of us dancing outside somewhere in a crowded venue. His hand touched my face, and I opened my eyes. His were closed. Each lid had one curled, gray lash twitching as my tongue drew his into my mouth.

I lowered my back to the bed, familiar with the taste of his lips, and the scent of bergamot stimulating my mind to moments of our past—me coiling his chest hairs with my fingers, my body lying across his, smiling up at him in a teal bedroom with black furniture. Then, a still image of me, stretched out below him on the ground near the bridge, looking into his eyes until darkness covered his face, felt like more than a memory.

I gasped softly. "Dell."

"Yes, Lauren."

"I need to tell you something."

"It can wait." He kissed me hard, then gazed into my eyes.

"Your heart is beating way too fast."

"Two years I've dreamt of this moment. Only you can slow it down."

Our eyes met as he hovered over me. I saw the need in his dilated pupils, felt the rush of blood flowing in his veins against my fingertips touring his toned chest below his shirt while telling myself, *Ignore the plumped vein throbbing against my thigh.*

It was difficult not to look at it as he rose to drop his pants and the tip of his cock slipped through the slit of his briefs. He stretched the elastic of his boxers, and his dick sprung downward and to the left. The vein pumped vigorously, like a swollen worm caught in the hot sun, searching for water after it rains. I couldn't focus on any other part of him.

"Look familiar?" Dell lifted his shirt above his head, then tugged on the leather shorts stuck to my skin.

I pursed my lips, assisting his effort with a leg lift. "I have a confession."

"I can see you're not wearing panties." He grinned, dropped to his knees, then swirled his tongue across my wet skin. "You didn't need my help it seems," he said, then spread my vulva open with his fingers, driving his tongue in and out of my pussy.

He was familiar with the territory, tracing the curves of my folds in waves that sent me spiraling. I crowned his head between my thighs, thrusting my head upward. Dell withstood the pressure and didn't fold, swallowing my drip as if his throat were a drain to a fountain.

The moans I expelled aroused him. He licked and flicked and flipped my slick, moaning and tasting my juice like a caffeine addict finally getting a hit of Pepsi to satisfy a craving.

I throbbed in his mouth. "You're good."

"And you are more than ready for me." He climbed to mount me. "Leave the boots on."

My blouse glided above my head. His mouth wrapped around my needy breasts, pulling from my nipples like a cigarette. His dick split me open, and my body felt electrified that the neglected, hypersexual desire within me was finally being appeased.

He rocked, and I rolled. I squeezed, and he stroked. Memories of us laughing flashed in my head like clear photographs on a memory card playing on a slideshow. With every intense motion of his pipe drilling my walls, I saw us. I saw myself. Me in my past life. Happy. Normal. Human. No red and gold eyes. No blood craving.

A surge of imagery of us posing for pictures, screaming on a roller-coaster, and fucking on a balcony intensified the slow strokes he applied.

"More." I sighed.

"More what?"

I threw him to his back. My knees lined with his hips. The slow grind was romantic and kind, but I liked it rough, with fire-burning passion that could melt glaciers in the Arctic. The more I desired wasn't just physical, but mental as well, as I had a taste of the old me, and he had the pieces of the puzzle I could not solve.

The decline on his dick felt nice at a faster pace while I skimmed through the visions for moments of myself. His increased heart rate, and the throbbing of his vein inside my walls and on his neck tempted my hidden nature. I lowered my breasts to his smooth chest, closer to the pounding of his gratified soul near exertion.

My fangs protruded. "Dell."

"Lauren."

"I'm sorry."

"Sorry for what?"

"For this." I latched onto his neck.

He jittered. "Lauren," his voice heightened.

I fucked him harder and faster while sucking his sweet, warm blood, hoping to see more of the life I'd lost from consumption. Dell fought to push me off him, but his strong body was no match for my power. His legs kicked, and his voice screeched while the panic in his blood flowed on my tongue like acid. Then, hot cream heated my pussy. I let go.

His eyes were bug-eyed, his lips parted slightly with a curve on the side. His chest jumped with acceleration, his body immobile of delight.

Blood dripped from my lips as I swallowed my heave. "I have a confession." My teeth retracted.

His narrowed eyes judged me. "What did you do to me?"

"Dell, I remember some parts of who I was, but I'm no longer the woman you left behind. And I don't love you anymore."

"Lauren," he said with a ragged breath.

I wiped my mouth. "Lauren is dead. My name is Vanity, the vampiress."

CHAPTER 52
THE FAVOR

VANITY

THE FEAR in his eyes matched the increasing beat of his heart as he looked up at me with contempt. Hours prior, he adored me with glistening eyes and love in his heart, and I stole the joy from him with one simple bite, emasculating him with the strength of a bull as his body fidgeted below me, and muffled screams from his mouth blew into my hands.

He shook, and his breath hitched. "Is that the change I see in you?"

"Unfortunately, yes. I can only think if you hadn't left me here, this wouldn't have happened to me. But I forgive you."

"Are you going to kill me?"

"I could have, but no." I hopped off him. "My bite allowed me to see if what you've been feeding me these past few hours is true. You'll heal."

He sat up on the bed and held his neck. "Thank you."

"For what?"

"For sparing my life. For forgiving me for what I've done to you. For giving me the chance to explore pleasure with you again after all this time." He smiled and looked at the blood on his fingers. "Since you're not going to kill me, I hope I'm safe in saying that was fucking incredible."

"Oh yeah?"

"Whatever you did to me felt like a double climax all over my body." He grinned to himself. "What do we do now?"

"We? We don't do anything. There is no *we*. Get dressed. There's someone I need you to meet."

His face turned glum. "Damn. I was hoping for seconds."

I zipped to the middle of the room and threw him his shirt. His eyes followed me into the bathroom where I steamed a few towels to clean the blood from his neck. The sound of buttons being pressed sounded over the flow of the water. He jumped when I appeared next to him sitting half-dressed at the foot of the bed.

"Who are you calling?" I snatched the phone from his grip.

He stuttered. "Y…Y…"

The name on the I.D. read *The Stuarts*. I locked the phone and slid it between the band of my bra. "I'll hold on to this." I clicked my teeth.

He wiped his neck and threw his shirt over his head. "Where exactly are we going? And who and what is so important I need to meet them at this moment when we could be making up for lost time?"

I chortled. "So the part about me being a vampire doesn't bother you at all because of one intense orgasm?"

His eyes closed, and he huffed. "I was freaked out at first. I'd still be freaked out if my life was in danger."

I've gotta get him out of this city—fast.

"Let's go."

Lindell smiled nonstop during the drive back into the city. I chuckled to myself. *That must have been one hell of an orgasm. It seems the old me could not compete.*

"How did this happen to you?"

"I'd rather not relive it."

"It sounds awful without knowing the details. I was hoping if I heard your account, it would ease what I'm imagining."

"It was pretty gruesome. A vamp jumped me in an alley, and now I'm like this."

"What happened to it?"

I scoffed. "You know, I've been wondering that myself."

The chimes above Madame's door brought a smile to my face. Lindell trailed behind me with wonder in his eyes, looking at all the trinkets on the shelves, afraid to touch the figurines on the counter.

"You hang out in places like this?"

"Something like that. The person I want you to meet runs this place."

"I'm not sure I want to meet this friend of yours."

The beads jangled behind the counter. "I take it no one saw you come in?" Madame walked over to the door, locked it, then flipped the blinds closed.

"I was careful." I lowered my hood.

"Should I be afraid right now?" Lindell's face turned ghostly.

"Not with me around." I turned to Madame. "Miss me?"

She grinned on one side of her mouth. "It's good to see you, V. I didn't doubt for one second the rumors were true."

"I hear it turned into the Wild Wild West for a few days. Anyone give you any trouble?"

She smirked and pointed to her eyes. "I had intel, chaos was coming."

She and I snickered.

"Neveah invited me to sit with her for a few days. She gave me something to give you." Madame unlocked a drawer behind her reading table. "We both knew you'd turn up sooner or later."

Lindell interrupted. "What am I missing here? I feel as though you two are speaking in code."

Madame shared a look with me, turned to him, then back to me. "I see the missing piece to your puzzle has turned up." She handed me two rolls of sketch paper.

I skimmed the drawings. Lindell stood behind me and gasped lightly under his breath, breathing down my neck with his heart beating like it was on steroids.

"Why does this woman have a drawing of me?" His finger traced the lines on the other sketch. "And that's the woman I made the deal with." He looked up at Madame. "Why do you have these?"

"Don't question her. She's a harmless messenger. I requested these." I looked up at Madame. "Thank Neveah for me." I frowned. "I'm getting more than I came for this visit."

"What can I help you with today?"

"Excuse us for a second," I said to Dell.

Madame and I stepped behind her curtain of beads. She peeked at Dell freaking out at the drawings and grinned.

She whispered, "Handsome boy. Very different from the wolf. But handsome still. How is Cason?"

My voice trembled, "His brother says he's dead."

"What?"

"I can't believe it either. It doesn't feel real. But if he were alive, I wouldn't have been held hostage for two weeks."

A sadness crossed Madame's face.

"Listen, you and I can sort out my fucked-up emotions and theories on my fallen beloved when this ordeal is over, but first I need your advice—or your help, whichever is best."

"With what?"

I nodded my head toward Lindell. "Is it better if I compel him to forget he found me, or if you do some sort of incantation?"

Madame sighed. "How much does he need to forget?"

"A fucking lot. Me. What he knows about me. Knowing I'm alive. He will tell my parents—who will come looking for me. The last thing I want is for them to see me like this."

"But wouldn't them knowing you're alive relieve their suffering?"

"It would. But until I settle this curse with Ria Lucia, how do I explain why I'm trapped here? I also don't need my parents here with this chaos. I'd be hand delivering a way for Adela to hurt me by hurting them."

"Point made. Compulsion has left humans confused before. The images become blurry in their heads, and they believe it was all a bad dream."

"But the images are there? Right?"

"Sometimes." She stared into my eyes and read the desperation in them. "I'll put a spell on him."

"Thank you, Madame. Does he need to be conscience?"

"Get him to join us at the table."

Lindell sat next to me with shivering legs and child-like eyes. I placed my hand on top of his in his lap, then kissed his cheek. He turned to me, and we shared a delicate kiss.

"Give her your other hand. Trust me," I said.

His lips pursed as he pulled away and followed my request. Madame took his hand and exhaled a sharp breath. She closed her eyes and sang a chant of French words, Patois, and broken English. Lindell squeezed my hand and looked deep into my eyes. A tear formed in the inner corners of his as our hands turned wet with nervous sweat. I kissed his lips as the memory of me faded in his mind, placed his phone in front of him on the table, and disappeared from Madame's shoppe at top speed, releasing my past love back into the wild, stripped of occult information, knowledge of magic, and the living dead.

CHAPTER 53
THE SAFEHOUSE
VANITY

TWENTY MINUTES in a cab ride landed me on the block of the ward. I posted up across the street with my eye on the top floor. Moments later, Keshell grinned at me from the side of his curtain.

I strutted past the guards lowering to their knees as two escorts walked me through the courtyard, then stood at each side of the elevator ride to Keshell's floor.

"I got it from here, boys."

"I'm sure, but we have rules." His top man cleared his throat.

The two guards walked ahead of me, then positioned themselves on each side of the open door. Keshell stood with his back against the wall near the window. The orange light of his spliff and a thin stream of smoke hung from the side of his silhouette as I crossed the threshold of his home.

"A sight fa sore eyes." He whistled.

The door closed behind me.

"My eyes and ears failed me on ya whereabouts. It's been a long time since I was handed a cold case."

"You want the long or the short of it?"

He shrugged his shoulders. "Dat's on you."

"I was darted, kidnapped, held hostage, freed myself, and now I'm here. I need shelter for a few days."

"Whatever ya need is yares."

"I need some comfortable clothes and shoes, toiletries, and the 411 on everything you know."

"Anything else, goddess?"

"Yeah. Let me hit that."

Keshell swaggered over to me and placed the spliff in my mouth. He held it in place as I inhaled, staring at me with his devilish, enticing eyes. My lips let loose of it, and I blew the smoke in his face.

He bared his gold fangs and grunted. "Ya comere dressed like dat fa me?"

I smiled. "After weeks of being covered in filth, shot up, and starved, I was desperate to look like myself. You like it, I see."

"Me love it, goddess." He placed the joint in his mouth, hiding a grin on the side.

"What's that look for?"

"I'll tell ya in the mornin'. Allow me to loan ya a t-shirt for tonight—or not." He licked his lips. "One of me people will run ya errands."

"Thanks. So, how bad was it?"

"Bad enough I'm ready to make moves with ya. Maybe a thousand innocents died fa her obsession with ya. But not in any of my sets."

"So tourists, then?"

"Mostly. Adela has to be put down. This city can't survive another one of her tantrums.

"And the media?"

"In her pocket and too 'fraid to mention what g'wan here."

I sighed. "Give me a few days to regroup."

"I'll give ya two. There's a town hall meeting in a few days. We should attend to hear what the people have to say."

"You sure Adela won't have spies there?"

"I'd bet money she will."

"Then I'll be ready. Can you gather intel on what that bitch has going on in The Garden in the meantime?"

He looked at me with turned-up lips. It was a foolish question, but I had to ask. The silence from his refusal to answer created a moment of laughter between us.

"Have you decided on dat t-shirt or not?"

"I believe I know which one you prefer."

He grunted. "I can smell the need on you, Vanity."

"Then you shouldn't trust your senses. I've already been taken care of."

"But not properly."

Keshell lowered the hood of my blouse. His fingers lingered near my neck before cupping both sides of my face. He pulled me in until his nose touched mine, breathing in my air, receiving my approval to proceed by gazing deep into my eyes and listening to my stunted breaths wait for his lips to press against mine.

I had been kissed softly earlier in the evening, but Keshell had other plans, finally doing to me as he had dreamed.

His hands lowered to my neck, and he grinned. "I hear two pulses in ya body." He poked my chest gently above my heart, then palmed my pussy with aggression. "I will capture one and punish the other."

"Show, don't tell." I bit his bottom lip.

A sharp fingernail slashed a hole in the seam of my shorts. His fingers protruded my slit with force. The bone of his thumb pressed hard against my clit while his fingers wandered from side to side of my wet flesh contracting around his fingers. I grunted as he sighed, ready for his dick to switch places with his fingers, but the enjoyment of my moans prolonged his finger play to verbally fulfill his ego.

I squirmed and wiggled midair, holding onto his broad shoulders with my head tilted back in ecstasy. The ceiling appeared to be closing in on me before I realized his fingers were so far up my pussy, my feet were no longer on the floor but swinging inches above it.

I squealed as I came on Keshell's hand, refusing to cease the thrusting of his hand stretching my garden wide, filling it with a full fist.

"Fuck!" I screamed, shivering in the air.

Keshell carried me to his bedroom and threw me on the bed. "Soon." He groaned. "But not yet."

Both of his hands reached between my legs. His sharp nails shredded the lining holding my shorts together. As they were ripped, he grinned. "A *panty-less* pussy pleadin' for punishment."

His fangs grazed the five o'clock shadow above my folds. I shuddered with excitement, reaching above my head. The feel of his hard pressed lips rubbing side to side on my made me think of his claim of me. So far, he was very convincing it might be a wise move to consider.

When his lips sputtered against my saturated skin, my legs opened up for him like the code on a gate had been keyed in for entry. Hands free.

His mouth slid between my slit as his sturdy, long tongue shoved inside of my pink. The strong strokes and waves delivered inside of my throbbing walls, forced my body to jostle him on and off when my back arched with the feeble attempt to swallow his face to feel his skillset at the top of my pussy.

He tasted me, then pulled away. I wriggled when air touched my orifice. He planted his lips where they belonged for a few swirls, then pulled away again. I trembled when a nail traced the oval curves of my entrance. When I jumped from the sharpness, he flicked my clit with one of his nails and rubbed the bottom of my entrance on the nerve.

"Mmm," I moaned.

He slapped my pussy gently. My hole throbbed, and he did it again and again, grousing at the sight of my hole spreading wide open for more attention. Then his lips returned to catch the drip falling onto the sheets. His nails dragged up to my chest and ripped my fucking blouse open. His sharp nail sliced the front of my bra and freed my breasts, pinching my nipples while his face rode me, hard pressed with his nose surged inside the interior of my folds, and his tongue curved on the track of my perineum.

The tip of his tongue tapped against my asshole, and I sliced his sheets with my grip, sucking in my stomach and moaning his name.

"Keshell. Fuck you for this, Keshell. You…are not…playing fair."

His chest pushed forward, and my ass rose off the bed. He released my nipples from his fingertips and pressed his hands against my ass cheeks. His tongue dragged up and down with sturdy strides. My body wriggled but didn't move from the stronghold he had on my ass. They squeezed my cheeks as my pussy slingshot cream in his mouth.

He moaned as he swallowed it. "I told ya…yare mine, goddess."

"Not that easy," I whined.

"Ooooh. I love a challenge."

His dick split me open, and he rammed himself inside. One stroke pushed me to the top of the bed where my head slammed into the headboard. "Yes! I love to be fucked rough." My head banged against the cushion panel, making a rhythm as it tapped against the wall, while my nails dug into his shoulders.

"I knew a good girl like you could handle me." He traced the outside of my asshole with one finger.

I gasped. "You gotta put in work to enter the black."

"In time, goddess." He placed one of my fingers in his mouth and dug deeper.

I panted, "Uuuug," taking the lashing as he gave it.

His hips moved at superspeed, fucking me with the swiftness in which we run. I flipped him over and banged his head against the board as I rode him with the same speed to prove I would not submit or be outdone. With me still on top of him, he lifted us from the bed and hurdled to the wall. The coolness of the sheetrock chilled my back as he thrusted forward inside of me with slower, deeper prods, kissing my mouth with gentle pecks.

"Say ya mine," he mumbled in my mouth.

"No."

"Say it." His dick motioned in circles with a harder thrust.

"Make me."

In a flash, I was flipped around, and his face motorboated my asshole. His tongue ran up and down from my ass to my pussy while his fingers tapped my clit disrespectfully, sounding like a butcher rotating a slab of meat being prepped. My nails screeched on the wall, and his nepenthes plunged back inside of me with determination to fuck the words he wanted to hear flow from my mouth. My cheeks burned as my face slid upward on the wall from the forceful strokes, and my fangs indented lines in the paint.

I squeezed my walls when his cock hit the top of my cavern. He fucked me with the force of a man with zero regard for my pussy, honoring me with the thrashing a goddess deserved and the overdue fucking his vampiress yearned. If I were still human, Keshell would have had me cosigning a car lease or an apartment from the way he worked me over.

Up close against me, his chest pressed into my back. He groaned and grunted, servicing me without an inch between us with hopes his dick magic would gain him a declaration of submission.

I held my own and resisted becoming *addickted* as the pounding prolonged until he came inside my dripping warmth, praising names of gods unfamiliar to me.

"Bondye. Loa. You will say it," he called out, kissing my neck and my cheek.

"Maybe. One day."

His fingers felt between my cheeks. "I made ya leak from the black. Does dat grant me access?"

"You wish." I threw him off me.

He flung to the other side of the room. "Still wan' dat t-shirt?"

"Maybe in the morning." I lay on top of the shifted covers.

Keshell flew next to me, kissing my naked body from my feet to my breasts. He hovered over me in silence with a half-smile on his lips and pensive eyes.

"What is it?" I asked.

"My vision was better than it was presented to me."

"If you were human, this would be the part where you flake on me after getting what you longed for." I nudged his forehead.

He opened his mouth to respond, then closed it shut.

"Exactly. You know I speak the truth. The chase is over, so the thrill is gone."

"Actually, I was gon' say I'm surprised Silva didn't take care of ya before sending ya over here unattended to."

I shoved him off me. "Cason is dead."

He kissed the center of my palm, then the back of my hand. "I hadn't heard. I'm sorry, goddess."

"I haven't had the chance to announce it."

"I was fond of Silva, but now I know I must claim ya as mine. To protect you as he did."

"I belong to no one."

"You can tell ya self whateva ya want. But you know what truth lies between us. I, Keshell Martin, would die fa my goddess, fa she is mine, and I am hers."

CHAPTER 54
THE MADDENING

VANITY

KESHELL EXCUSED himself from the room. To know I had his trust and allegiance was comforting, but it was going to take me some time to see him in the same light.

Cason was a hard act to follow. Incomparable and true. I doubted there would be anyone I'd ever cross again with such a pure heart, and as the loss of him began to settle in, I was honest with myself. He was my greatest love.

As the moonlight began to fade, the singing of a nightingale appeared near the window. Keshell returned with the items I requested, then hit a switch on the wall to close the shutters and curtains in the bedroom.

"How often do you have pillow talk?" I snickered.

He grinned. "Mi conquests don't make it past the van in the courtyard."

"Oooh. Guess I am special, then." I covered up in one of his t-shirts and laid the sweatsuit on the arm of the lounge chair in the corner. "Hideous, but it'll do for now."

"Ya look sexy in anything, goddess."

"You know, you're right." I clicked my teeth. "I promise not to watch you while you sleep."

"How could you?"

The wall behind the chair whirred. The painting above the chair slid to the right revealing a white control button. Keshell pressed it, and the connecting corners of the walls opened to a dark, hidden bedchamber.

"Ya welcome to join me," he said, waving his hand.

A dim sensory light shrouded him.

"Do you actually sleep?" I stepped inside the cavern.

"I rest. Not sleep like when we were in our human form, as ya well know."

I exhaled deeply. "I do. Do you miss it…sleep?"

He shrugged. "It's a faint memory. But it's nice to have the time to meditate…reflect…regroup."

"A vampire with a conscience. Where have I heard that before?"

"We can be complex beings."

"You're telling me," I said, observing the black-and-white granite on the walls. "Hey, whatever happened to that kid who snitched?"

"No longer a problem." He walked deeper into the hole inside the wall.

I huffed. "Elaborate, please."

"Mi can't have subs I don't trust. He posed a problem, and as promised, I took care of it."

"Personally?"

Keshell stopped walking. "Why ya ask?"

"I remember hearing something about how you get your fix."

He turned around and glared at me. It was the first time I saw suspense in his eyes—a copper, reddish hue, different from the cool brown and hazel color they normally were that set him apart from the rest of our kind. Seeing him glower at me like that reminded me of the night we met in the courtyard, and I realized I had become too comfortable with him—and too fast.

They didn't change at all when I allowed him to sample my blood. Why now?

From the moment we met, Keshell looked at me with ardor and intrigue. But my question exposed the darkness trapped inside of him, the vampiristic nature flowing through his veins that he could not rebel against—not even if he tried.

"You no need to beat 'round the bush. Say what on ya mind."

The kindness in his voice disappeared. He and I had never butted heads, and this was the first time I challenged him. And he didn't like it.

"Okay, I will. I heard you feed on those who break the rules of your ward and on those brought to you from other wards who break the law. True or false?"

"All true."

"Even children?"

"The boy was a traitor."

"But he was human."

"A spy is a spy. He knew the rules, and he chose not to obey."

"Was his death…painless?"

Keshell raised his arm to the button on the wall. "It's time for me to regroup."

I scoffed. "See you tonight."

The walls closed with me on the other side. Keshell's lack of an answer gave me one. One that sealed what I already knew. His devotion and loyalty was admirable, but he was not for me. Not my equal. And he could never be my partner.

Cason would have never harmed that boy. But Keshell…Keshell couldn't see that his bloodsucking thirst lost compassion. The boy may have rebelled, but he could have been banished, or punished—or worse, turned. He didn't have to die.

Regret fell upon me for telling Keshell what I knew and allowing him to taste my blood to see which kid had double-crossed us. My nails dug into my thighs as the anger inside of me amplified, and I imagined the brutal way his life was taken.

As my blood trickled onto the spread, it dawned on me that the men left in my life were shit. Keshell, a hundred-year-old vampire who meant well but would fail to do so to satisfy his natural need for blood. Sana, the jealous brother of my lover who I would have taken up with if I trusted him. Junichiro, the hateful brother who wanted me dead. And Shun, the brother with zero leadership in his bones.

The gold light healing my self-inflicted wounds brought me back to reality. As my skin mended back together, my anger transitioned into rage from the realization that no one would ever come close to what I shared with Cason. And the thought of never having that with anyone made me madder.

CHAPTER 55

THE HOUSEGUEST
KESHELL

I AROSE from an immersive morning of meditation, and a sense of calmness surrounded me as I slid the chamber door open.

"I apologize for my tone last night."

"No need." Vanity grinned, standing fully dressed near the painting as it glided back into place.

My eyes widened as I took a step back. "What did you…"

She interrupted me while tousling her hair as if she were in a shampoo commercial. "Perks of being able to walk around in daylight."

I hid my arousal and intrigue of her new look. "But your locks suited you," I said, admiring the black and brown curls.

"And yours suit you." Her finger twirled the coils around the ends. "But it was time. Things have changed, and I'm changing with them."

"I must admit, your hair was not in focus when I saw you take claim of the city. You look beautiful."

"That's all you had to say the first time."

God I love her reckless mouth. Her fearlessness. Her sexiness.

"You are correct. Again, I apologize. Should I be concerned about anything else you've gotten yourself into today?"

"I wasn't made, if that's what you're asking."

I nodded. "Well, goddess, the night is young. Can I trust you to lay low for a few hours while I attend to some business?"

"Sure. My feet will be kicked up on your bed until it's time to hear the testimony tomorrow night."

"Kicked up is one way to think of it." I grinned.

She greeted me in a t-shirt when I returned. One night in my place and I found myself complete and content to have her staying with me. She was a sight to come home to, though undomesticated. Her status reigned above mine, but I didn't care. I felt my existence was to worship her.

I stuck my head out of the door and had a word with my subs. "Take a hike. Go play hunger games. But you know the rules."

They replied in unison. "Feed the need, let their life proceed."

"Return to your posts before the next sunrise," I ordered them.

They secured the hall and left us on my floor alone—the way it should have been last night.

Vanity stood in the living room. "What was that about?"

"That was me giving them the night off. So if you want to scream, you can—without listening ears."

She scoffed. "You wish you could make me scream."

"I accept the invitation to try."

My hands ravished her supple ass hanging below the hem of my t-shirt. It was soft and cool on my fingertips. She stared into my eyes, hiding thoughts I could not read. One could only hope it was desire I saw in them. Her hands pressed against my chest, and my dick turned harder than the cinder blocks out back. The new smell of lavender and mint in her hair filled me with the energy of a newborn to fuck her into oblivion.

"We are in for an all-nighter," I said to her.

"Good. I hate to be bored." She pulled my cock out. "Try and keep up."

I was thrown to the wall. Pieces of plaster fell from the ceiling, and lines cracked in the sheetrock. At high speed, she crashed into me and smacked her lips against mine with a sinister laugh rumbling into my mouth. I was turned on and rushed into the foreplay, lifting her above me with her legs parted wide.

Her sweet center coated my mouth, and I moaned. I longed to bite it, to taste the nectar spilling from her cup alongside the rare sweetness of her blood. It tasted like no other. The purest of human blood with a honeyed tinge that became addictive. It was a wonder I was able to let go from the sample she granted me before.

A rush of adrenaline burst throughout my body. My stomach tightened as I restrained myself. My teeth retracted as I nibbled on her brown beauty. I stared at it. It was too pretty. Too perfect. Too ripe. Too comely.

I inhaled her wet pussy, then placed her down on my dick, bouncing her sexy ass up and down so fast her curls began to swell. She smiled at the ride, exciting me even more. I admired her while her head was tilted back, knowing she was and would forever be my greatest conquest. My one. My queen. But I took pleasure in dethroning her pussy with vigorous intent, enjoying the look of pain on her face as it came with delight.

"You're keeping up, old man," she teased me. "But is this the best you got?"

Her challenge took a full night. We fucked like rabbits, as the humans would say. From the wall to my bed, I saw she kept her word from earlier, pillaging her with her feet kicked up high above her head, stroking her as she never tired of the beatdown from my dick.

By the third round against the dresser, she challenged me with taunts and wild positions to get her off. I lost control and broke one of the metal legs, causing it to tilt over to the floor. When we were done, the sun was less than thirty minutes away from rising, and my place was in shambles with broken furniture turned over, and holes stared back at me from the walls, bigger than the one I drilled between V's legs.

"Mind if I play some music while you go night-night?"

"Who ya have in mind? Coltrane? Davis?"

"Did I scream?" she asked.

"Ya squealed."

"But did I scream?"

"No."

She laughed. "Then it's only right I play Lil' Kim since I rode yo' ass to sleep. See you when the moon is nigh."

I had no idea what she was talking about, but when I woke up that night, I heard the Lil' Kim song.

She can't be for real. The way she came on my dick...she couldn't possibly think last night was subpar. She's such a ball busta. I'll show her.

I turned off the racket and found her in the kitchen, snapping the neck of a live bird my subs delivered for her.

"Care to explain?"

She chuckled. "The lyrics, you mean?"

I stared at her.

"You really are old at heart. What time do we leave?"

Two days with her and she mocked me, changing the subject when she didn't want to answer my question. I was amused and impressed. Also annoyed to have my actions turned against me. But I swallowed my pride and smiled at her cunningness.

"Allow me to get changed, and we'll be on our way."

CHAPTER 56

THE GRAB
VANITY

KESHELL MADE a compelling case that my outfit was not appropriate for the Town Hall meeting. He convinced me to change into the hideous, black, bargain-bin sweatsuit his subs bought for me.

"Blend in with the locals," he preached. "We're not ready to go into battle tonight if you're made. Adela thinks you're dead, remember?"

His argument was convincing enough that I swapped out my leather goods for cotton, and when we arrived downtown, I gave him his due credit.

"Your decision was wise," I said, sitting on the trunk of the car one block away from the hall.

He smiled. "When I serve, I serve. I will never steer you wrong."

"You ain't steering shit over here but that D, Mr. Martin," I joked.

Keshell laughed to himself, then flashed his gold fangs my way. "We can fight about this later."

"Look over there." I pointed to a vampy crew walking inside the building. "I need you to bring that kid in the yellow shirt with the arrow on the back to the courtyard. Think you can swing that?"

"Should be easy enough. What for?"

"Just do it. I'm going to hang out here while you go inside. Do what you do best and convince the lovely people that control of this city belongs to them."

"They would believe that if they knew you were still alive, but I'll do my best."

"As long as we find out who's on Adela's payroll, tonight won't be a total loss."

"Try not to get into trouble while I'm gone."

I gave him a soldier's salute and sat at a table below a balcony. The paranoia of being made had me on edge whenever a passerby looked at me twice. The square was crawling with spies and creatures lurking in the shadows, and the setting felt staged.

I texted Keshell.

Vanity: Something's off.

Ya sense it too? :Keshell

Vanity: Are you sure you're respected by most? Because this place feels like it's surrounded with Adela supporters.

And the leaders I made the deal wit' are not present.: Keshell

Vanity: Grab that kid and get out.

Screams shrieked from inside the building, and a rush of bodies fell through the window, then the words, "Come with me," rang in my ear.

I grinned and turned toward Sana. "I'll take a raincheck. Now get lost before you blow my cover."

"Cason would want me to get you out of here."

My blood boiled hearing Cason's name coming out of his mouth. "I get the feeling you know what's going on."

"I don't, and I don't want to find out. Akina spotted you." He pointed behind us at the end of the block. "Come on. Let me get you to safety."

I waved to Akina.

"Got'em!" Keshell shouted, appearing out of nowhere, throwing the kid in the backseat.

Sana's nostrils flared. "You're with…"

"I'll be in touch!" I said, hopping in next to the kid.

Keshell's sub stepped on the gas.

"Hey, kid. Remember me?" I winked at him and smiled.

"You?" He exhaled a deep sigh of relief. "Does this mean I'm free?"

"That depends. What can you tell me?"

"Whatever you wanna know."

I clicked my tongue. "Everything you've been privy to."

"Not much." He took my hand. "Queen was meaner than Satan until she heard you were dead—which you're not...but she thinks so. She sent us to make sure the people who have pledged their loyalty to her kept their word tonight."

"So she can't trust them?"

He shrugged his shoulders. "I heard one of her guards say some of the leaders were supposed to make a deal to overthrow her and make you queen, so I guess she doesn't. Please tell me I don't have to go back. Please?" he begged.

"Don't worry, kid. You're on the winning side now."

CHAPTER 57

THE MEASUREMENTS

VANITY

"VANITY, WHAT'S WIT' ya and the kid?" Keshell barked.

"I owe him, is what, and I'm a woman of my word."

Keshell stared at Malik, shifted his eyes over to me, then back to Malik. "Ya're some lucky kid."

Malik lowered his head, pressing his fingers into his knees.

"Ya snitched too easy fa me," Keshell picked at him. "I only snatched ya 'cause she asked me to. Ya better be worth it." He clicked his tongue on his gold fangs.

"We're being followed. Three cars back. Black sedan," the driver griped.

"It's that dog ya were talking to," Keshell snapped at me.

I raised a brow at him. "Watch your mouth."

He grumbled, "Looks like he's got a bitch wit 'em."

"Bitch?" my voice deepened. "You men have run that one into the ground. Evolve for God's sake." I snapped my fingers. "Pull over."

"Keep drivin'," Keshell insisted.

"I said pull over. I'll get them off our tail."

Akina pulled behind us on the side of the road and dimmed the headlights. I shot out of the car and met Sana stepping out of the passenger side.

He grabbed my arm. "We need to talk."

"I told you I would be in touch. What the fuck is the urgency?"

"You fled with the cure, but you haven't taken it. What gives?"

"A score that needs settling, for one. For two, that's my prerogative if and when I take it."

"But, V…"

"Why are you following us?"

Sana gritted his teeth with burning yellow eyes staring at Keshell studying us from the car. "Are you with him?"

"Keshell?"

"Yes. Keshell Martin, of all people? You would trust him? A ruthless vampire ward lord and not me?"

"I trust no one. And no, I'm not with him like that. Cason introduced us. He's protecting me is all."

"You'd be safer with me."

I sucked my teeth. "Try selling that story to your obsessed brother."

"Don't worry about Juni. I'm back now, and he's in line."

"Only you think that. Look, I gotta go. Don't follow us. And I promise, I'll be in touch. Soon."

He grabbed my face and planted a hard, passionate kiss on my lips. The smell of his blood and clan scent electrified my blood pumping swiftly in my veins. The softness of his lips reminded me of Cason, and the taste of his saliva was almost as sweet.

I pushed him into the door. "Sana!"

"In our culture, it is customary for a brother to marry his brother's widow. You and Cason may not have been married, but you know the both of us were in love with you. The real you. You should not be running around with the dead. Come back to the living. Take the damn serum, Vanity."

"Sana, I am flattered, but even in death, I still love Cason. Kissing you reminded me of him. I cannot love you the way I still love him. It wouldn't be fair to you." I took his hand. "Don't worry about me. I can take care of myself, and if I can't, I know who to call." I bent down. "Good seeing you again, Akina. Get your brother out of here for me, will ya?"

Akina threw up two fingers. "It's good to see you too. Sana, we need to get going."

Sana's hand reached for my cheek. "I won't give up."

Keshell snuck up on us. "What's the hold-up?"

Sana's yellow eyes turned gray in the iris with flashes of silver in the center. A low growl echoed from his throat, and a thick vein pierced the side of his neck.

Akina jumped out of the car. "Sana. Let's go."

I stood between him and Keshell.

"Yeah, Sana. Listen to ya're bitch and go."

"Bitch?" Akina reached behind her back.

I pushed Keshell with a light shove to his chest. "Keshell! What did I say earlier?" I turned to Akina and nodded toward Sana. "Get your brother out of here."

"Sana!" Akina called.

He grinned. "One bite and you'll suffer for your last days," Sana growled with a villainous chuckle rolling from his lips. "Oooh, I'd like to see that." His knuckles cracked like embers fleeing a fire.

"No one is biting anyone." I placed my hand on Sana's chest. "You'll hear from me tomorrow." Then, I looked Akina in her glowing silver-and-white eyes. "I give you my word."

Akina nodded.

"Keshell, let's go." I nudged him along back to the car.

CHAPTER 58
THE POTION

VANITY

I COULDN'T GET that kiss with Sana out of my head, and my pebbled nipples hiding below my hoodie begged me to jump out of the car and run Sana down to stick them in his mouth.

Everything about our lips touching reminded me of Cason, minus the taste—buttery, semi-sweet, and hot.

I lied when I said I didn't want him. How could I not? He had always been good-looking, neat, stylish, and open about his attraction for me. My many mentions of having a ménage with him and Cason were true desires I masked as jokes, but the curiosity of which brother could outperform the other was a mystery I yearned to solve.

Since Cason wouldn't consent and reeked of jealousy whenever I brought up conquering a wild night of sharing them, I denied it to spare his feelings, but now that he'd been taken from me, Sana was fair game. I could finally answer my burning question without the guilt: which brother fucked the best?

To experience what magic we could make, I'd have to ignore my gut telling me he lied about what happened in Japan.

Could I learn to love him with a dark secret between us? I wondered.

Not a word was spoken once we were back in the car. The gates opened up at Keshell's ward, and the tenants stared as usual as we pulled up to the caravan in the courtyard.

"Take him inside. I'll be right back."

Keshell grabbed my arm. "Where ya off to?"

"Upstairs to your place." I ordered him to remove his hold of me with narrowed eyes.

"I'm coming witcha. Ju two..." He pointed to his top two men. "Keep the boy inside, and tell the frontline that no one else gets in or out until I say." He sped to my side. "Mind telling me why ya suddenly calling the shots, and the real reason ya brought that kid here?"

"No one is stepping on your toes, Shellie."

"Shellie?" He laughed. "Ya tryna to charm me, sexy gal?"

"Is it working?"

He grinned. "What was that back there?"

"I don't know what you're talking about?"

"I believe ya do." He pinched my nipples.

I stepped out of the elevator on his floor, looked back at him, and waited for him to blink. He huffed and took a long stride to stand next to me.

"You kissed a dog."

"I kissed a Silver Clan friend. It was nothing."

"It didn't look like nuttin'."

"Is that why you rolled up on us?"

Keshell sighed and took my hand. "Vanity, ya one of us. The better of us. A true queen amongst the lost souls of this city. The one I pledged to honor and protect and place on the throne. And through me, my subs have pledged their allegiance to you. You have an army because of me. It'd be nice if ya showed some gratitude."

The side of my mouth curved downward on one side. "Does gratitude mean monogamy?"

"It means don't lie with dogs."

I threw his hand away from mine. "Is that what you thought of Cason? A dog? I thought you two had a friendship?"

"We had an alliance. A mutual respect for one 'nother, but that didn't change him being what he was."

I scoffed. "Well, I guess you're gonna have to accept that I do what I want, and those dogs you speak of are Cason's family. Don't let me hear you call them that again." I left him in the hallway.

He mumbled, seething through his teeth, "Let's table this fa now."

I raced inside and retrieved the potion from the pocket of my torn shorts mixed in the pile of clothing Keshell bought. A white speck of moonlight put a sparkle in the contents of the bottle.

Keshell entered. "What is that?"

"We're about to find out." I sped past him to the elevator.

Together, we trekked across the courtyard and entered the caravan. Malik sat balled up in the corner.

"Hey, kid, remember that promise I made you?"

He nodded.

I held up the bottle. "Come here."

Malik stood before me, dirty and ashy with curious, big eyes of hope and fear fighting inside them.

"Open up," I ordered him.

His lips parted, and I poured the potion down his throat.

"Wha' the fuck did ya just give him?"

"An answer to a burning question I've had since I escaped. Either poison…or a cure."

Malik's eyes widened. "Poison?"

"It could be, kid. I was told it was a cure, but it could very well be poison."

"Vanity!" Keshell's voice boomed. "Ju should have mentioned this to me. If it is a cure, we could have duplicated the formula!"

"Perhaps. But the ingredients don't grow here. Ironically, the very species you keep addressing as a dog knows where to get it, so if it works and you learn how to play your cards right, you'll get your hands on your very own bottle. Sound good?"

Malik began to shake. His dingy red eyes turned pinkish before rolling to the back of his head. Blank, ruddy eyes stared back at me zombie-like. His body jittered, then his arms raised, bent at the elbow. "Hey, kid." I reached for his shoulder. He fell backward into the sink, then keeled over with his hand clutching for his heart through his t-shirt.

The van shook to the rhythm of his spasms. Keshell's top man opened the door to the van as protocol.

He barged in. "Boss?"

"Me fine," Keshell assured him.

His man's eyes shifted to me. I knew that look. The distrust in his eyes spoke volumes of his displeasure of having me run amuck and influence Keshell's leadership. He didn't have to say the words. He thought I had done something to his maker but was too proud to admit he was wrong before being ordered to go back outside and guard the door.

Keshell shielded me with a hand across my bosom. "Looks like ya precious dog—pardon me, Silva's bruda—was gonna poison ya."

"Give it a second. This could be a part of the transformation."

"And if it isn't?"

"Then I have another enemy on my hands."

Malik's body lurched with huge lumps forming in the center of his chest, bubbling sporadically below his t-shirt. As the convulsions tapered off into mini jolts, a white foam oozed from the side of his mouth. Suddenly, he stopped shaking. His bugged eyes opened and locked with mine. No longer red in the center. Void of life, fear, and pain.

My heart felt full as the rage in my bones began to burst into flames. I stared at his lifeless body lying as still as the night of a quiet, small town, fuming I had failed him. I was now no different, no better than Keshell himself. I killed a kid.

Keshell murmured, "I was hoping I was wrong about that dog."

I peered over at him with my fists balled. "I didn't take you for a liar."

"Why ya say?"

"You wanted that potion to be poison so Sana would be out of your way. You reeked of envy earlier."

"I only liked one of those brothers anyhow."

Hearing Keshell talk about Cason in the past tense made me dizzy. I became off balance and leaned against the linoleum-covered table.

"That didn't come out right, but I meant what I said."

"It's fine," I lied. "Not speaking of him in the present just makes it real." I sucked my teeth. "And now I have to deal with his brother. I was hoping the contents of that bottle could redeem him."

"Redeem him of what?"

"It doesn't matter now. I see him for what he truly is."

"Ya keep a lot of secrets, Vanity."

"They're mine to keep."

Keshell scoffed. "Since the kid is dead, ya mind telling me why ya were hellbent on helping him?"

"Not that I owe you any answers, but the kid did me a favor. And now I have another person to kill for doing this to him."

Malik's body rocked the caravan as it quaked on the floor. He gasped for air with labored breaths holding his chest, then coughed up a thick, black, syrupy film of old blood.

Slowly, he rose to his feet and looked me in the eyes. For the first time, his eyes were white, and his irises a chestnut brown.

I smiled at him. "How do you feel?"

"Free," he answered in a low tone muffled by his hand covering his mouth. "Ready to go home and never set foot in this place again."

"Trust me. I know what you mean. I'll make sure you get there safe and sound."

The ash color of his skin turned richer with color as his blood restored to its natural state. Keshell handed him a bottle of water and flashed his gold fangs. Malik jumped back and looked at me.

"What are you doing?" I stood in front of the boy.

"Nothing. Just admiring the youthful glow returning to his face." Keshell sniffed. "Fresh blood," his voice deepened in a whisper.

"I will fight you if I have to, to protect this kid, Keshell."

"No need for the drama, V. I just have a request."

My eyes narrowed at him.

"A sample of his blood to study the potion."

I swiped Malik's arm with the nail on my middle finger. "Make it quick. I'm getting him out of here."

Keshell pulled a mason jar from the cupboard, trembling with cherry-red eyes. He sniffed a second time the closer his steps approached Malik.

I snatched the glass from his hands. "Let me do that." I rolled my eyes at him. "Go tell your driver I need the keys. I'm getting this kid out of here."

"Yare bound. Rememba?"

"I don't need the reminder. I know what I'm doing."

Keshell opened the door and whistled to his cronies scattered in the courtyard. Malik squeezed my hand and smiled at me while I wiped the dot of blood dry from the cut.

"Aren't you gonna taste it?"

I shook my head side to side.

"Really?"

I scrunched my nose. "Nope. Not my thing, kid."

He wrapped his arms around me. "Thank you. I never thought I would say that to one of your kind."

I snickered. "They're some vile creatures, aren't they?"

"I wish you had the power to erase my memory of the things I've seen."

"I know someone who may be able to help with that, but sadly, she's not on the way to where I'm taking you."

Keshell cleared his throat and jingled the keys in his hand. "You two ready?"

"We are." I took the keys from his hands and handed him the jar of Malik's blood sample. "I'll be back. This here is a solo trip."

CHAPTER 59
THE INEVITABLE
VANITY

HOMARE AND AKINA stepped onto the porch before I hopped out of the car. Malik's heartbeat intensified when the silver in their eyes lit up like cats roaming in the dark.

"It's a little early for a booty call," Homare greeted me.

"I beg your pardon."

"You've got my brothers in a trance, don't you?"

I scoffed. "Your brothers were on me before I could do that. You should be proud. They have great taste."

"What are you doing here, Vanity?"

"I need a favor."

Homare laughed below her breath. "Be fuckin' for real."

"I've got a kid in the car."

She leaned to her side for a look.

"I promised I would help him get home, but I'm still bound to this place, and you lot are the only bunch I trust to see that my promise is met."

"Must suck being friends with a bunch of shady-ass vamps." Akina snickered.

"It does. I preferred being in the company of wolves—one in particular."

Akina and Homare looked at each other, then back to me. Homare jumped off the porch and walked over to the car. She inhaled sharply, then knocked on the roof. Malik's eyes met mine for approval. I nodded, and he lowered the window.

"You're a strange one. I can't quite make out the scent on you." She leaned against the door. "What are you?"

"A reborn," I answered.

"Reborn?" Her voice vibrated.

"He drank the potion your brother brought back from your homeland."

"Homeland? This is my home."

"Homare, I didn't come here to debate irrelevant bullshit. You know exactly what I'm saying."

"Why'd you bring him here?"

"Because I need one of you to take him home. I would, but…"

"Yeah, yeah. Your whole bound thing." She moved her fingers like jazz hands.

I huffed. "So can one of you do it or not?"

"Send Shun. It'll give him a reason to stop moping around," Akina suggested.

"What's wrong with Shun?"

"The unbalance around us is stressing him. He doesn't like chaos."

"Who does?"

"You seem to love it." Sana approached us from the shadows on the side of the house. "I brought that potion back for you to take."

"Took you long enough to show yourself. Have you no shame, eavesdropping on women?"

"I'm serious, V. I gave it to you."

"And I told you I would not be coerced into taking it. It could have been poison in that bottle."

Sana raised his voice, and his eyes flashed a silver light for a quick second. "So you don't trust me!"

"You and I need to have a talk…after I've got the kid settled."

"Homare." Sana nudged his head toward the main house. "Give Shun the order."

"We don't even know where this kid lives," Homare fussed.

Malik chimed in. "Jackson."

The siblings shared a look.

"That's a hop and a skip." Akina sighed and mumbled, "Three hours there, three hours back."

Homare pointed toward me. "I'll take the kid if this one can promise not to start some shit tonight."

"I'll do you one better." I cracked my knuckles. "I'll stay here until you get back so we can work out the hostility you've been spitting at me."

She unsheathed her sword from the baldric on her back. "Can you yield a sword?"

I chortled. "Depends on what kind of sword you're talking about."

Sana groaned. "Enough, you two. There will be no fighting amongst us." He muttered to Homare, "Put that away."

"Yeah, Homare, put that away and fight me with your bare hands," I said.

"Vanity, just say goodbye to the kid so we can end this."

Sana taking the lead ignited a rush of heat inside of me. I ended my stare-down with Homare and walked past her to the car. She gave her brother the evil eye and went inside to grab Shun.

As I comforted Malik getting into the Kyoudai's car, he held my hand.

"Kid, it's been nice knowing you. I hope to be like you one day and leave this place behind me. I would say call me if you need me, but I don't know where I'll be or what my outcome is, so you be careful when you get home."

"I will."

"If that friend of mine can help you out with that memory erasure request, I'll get the address from these guys and send her to you. How does that sound?"

"Like a dream."

"I hope you have sweet ones from here on out."

Shun and Homare hopped in the front seats. Malik mouthed the words, "Thank you," as the car kicked up dirt along the path leading off the property, obscuring my view of the car's red taillights.

Sana stood at my side. "Let's you and I take a walk."

I followed his lead into the woods. "Where does this path take us?"

"To a peaceful spot where I go to be alone."

"Where's your bad-blooded brother?"

He chuckled. "Is that what you think of Juni?"

"That's what I know of Juni."

"He's really not that bad. You bring out that side of him."

"It's pure hatred in that one."

"I think it's the opposite."

I sucked my teeth. "Please."

"I don't want to talk about my brother." He eased between bushes hiding a pleasant, rocky creek behind a cabin. "That's my house." He pointed over his shoulder to the low-lit cabin resting above the creek grass sprouting up a cattail-covered hill. "You're welcome anytime."

"Am I?"

"Do I need to give you a key to prove it?"

A curve formed on the side of my mouth. "I believe you."

He sighed. "What you did for that boy was noble. It shows you still have a beating heart in there." His hands brushed against my bosom.

"So you're not mad about my decision anymore?"

"Mad is an understatement. I'm pissed. I wanted you back—the real you." He stared into my flaming eyes and kissed me. "Have I ever told you I saw you first?"

"No. Never."

"I kick myself for dragging my feet. But I'm not doing that anymore." He pulled me in close and kissed me softly. "Stop fighting it, V. You and I make sense. And I know you want to explore this just as much as I do."

The fireworks between us sparked an unholy revolution in the woods. With nature surrounding us and the waters of the creek rustling against the rocks, I gave in to my curiosity and natural desire, heavily turned on as I watched him drop his rapier belt and step out of his pants.

I kicked off my boots, pulled off my bottoms, and yanked my sweatshirt over my head, swiftly placing his lips on my neck. As I mounted Sana, he slowed down my tempo.

"I know you possess all the power in the world right now, but I'm a man, and I lead."

I felt powerless by his words, melting in front of him as I let him take control and lower me to my back with a careful hand placed at the nape of my neck. Hovered above me, he unbuttoned his shirt, then lowered his slim, cut chest onto mine. If a kiss was a thousand words, this lip lock showcased he was hell-bent on proving to me how long he had waited for this moment.

His fingers lined the sides of my waist as the grass tickled my bum. *Snap.* The petal of a wildflower aroused my nipples as Sana's silver eyes stared into mine. I panted, writhing below him, anxious from the indulgent foreplay budding within me. He teased me, tracing every zone of my body with his floral tool until my body locked of stimulation, kissing my face and my neck longer than I ever experienced from any of my past lovers.

As his lips became one with my body, I trembled with euphoric, mind-numbing passion and yearning. I moaned into the cool breeze sweeping by, picturing him and his brother both pleasing me simultaneously. Embracing the new. Remembering the old. Adapting to his methods while missing the dominance of the alpha.

But this was nice and surprisingly satiating for a girl like me who liked it rough. I found the sensual delivery of wet kisses and Sana's gentle caress profound and gratifying. I'd wanted to sample him for a while, and he was rewarding me extensively for giving him the opportunity.

The mood he created hid the animal inside of him. I listened close for a growl and a light howl below the moon as he conquered my need to be manhandled, but only heard the sighs of urgency between us to finally connect.

Once his lips were done tasting my skin, his fingers slid between my shivering legs.

He placed his finger in his mouth and smacked his lips. "That won't fill my appetite."

My legs spread apart, and his fingers entered my pussy while his lips softly pecked on my clit. In and out, his fingers fucked me, driving my head into the dirt as my back arched upward toward the moss hanging from the trees. I ran my fingers over my breast and down to the sides of his shaved head, then gripped the lock of hair he kept in a top bun, guiding his lips where I wanted them to go.

I bellowed into the wilderness, sensing we were being watched. But I didn't care. I was so turned on I would have invited them to join us as I couldn't get enough.

The faster his fingers stroked in my walls, the softer his tongue licked my swollen clit. I moaned and shrieked at the chilling touch of the wolf head charm on his necklace tapping against the crack of my ass for extra pizazz.

He rose to the occasion and dipped his short but wide cock inside my walls, and I gasped at the shock his width made up for in length. He lifted my hands above my head and trapped my wrists with a firm grip, stroking me slow, hard, and precise, kissing me passionately wherever he pleased.

From my mouth, to my cheeks, to my neck, to my chest, Sana left his mark on me without a bite. But he requested.

"May I, my love?" He stroked deep to convince me to say yes.

"On the first date?" I grinned.

"Say yes." He gently bit my bottom lip and held onto it until I nodded.

"Only if I go first."

As I was still bound from his authority, he lifted his head and placed my mouth to his neck. I grazed him gently and licked the trickle of blood leaking from the prick.

"Sweet. Of course you would be," I whispered, tasting the saccharine flavor of their bloodline.

His face crumpled. "Is that all?"

"Hmm. I told you before. I don't like human blood. But you Silver Leaf men…" I sighed above a moan. "Mmm."

Sana nibbled on my face, thrusting me intricately from side to side. He released his grip from around my wrists, groaning as the circumference of his head scraped the smoothness of my throbbing pussy.

Then, in return, he nipped my neck. His palms lifted my knees and pressed against the backs of my thighs as the speed of his hips pulverized my pussy upon the soil with intensity. I latched on, wrapped my legs around him, and motioned my warm embrace in a slow wind to match his rhythm. He punctured my skin, released his hold, then faced me. Shining his silver eyes into mine, he smiled, waiting for the bond between us to form.

A gold flash of light shone from the piercing of his mark. Mixed with his eyes, a citron color illuminated between us. Sana lowered his lips to mine and snogged me, then nibbled on my neck and my ear.

As my pussy pulsed around him, he released my hands and restricted my neck, gnawing on my cheek as he unloaded inside my warmth. Asphyxiated in ecstasy, I closed my eyes and listened to his sighs and shrieking scoffs escape his muffled mouth pressed against my chest, vibrating into my body.

The beauty in the moment exceeded my expectations, satisfying my thirst for him and connecting us in a way I hadn't planned. I caressed his face, coiling my tongue with his, embracing the notion he could be my shot at love again.

Glued together as one, his fingers brushed my cheeks until our lip lock ended with sweet smooches and chuckles.

"That was everything I hoped it would be."

"I'm glad I lived up to the hype. But next time, I'll lead."

Sana sighed with a smile on his face and rolled over onto his back. "I hope that next time is in a few minutes. You're like an addiction."

"We do have a few hours until your bossy sister gets back, and I know she won't approve of this."

"She's not the boss of me."

"I beg to differ." I chortled. "Which one of us is gonna tell her I got wielded by your sword?"

Sana snickered with his response. "You're a menace."

"She probably knows already because we were being watched."

His fingers linked on top of his chest. "Yeah, that was Akina. I could smell her nearby."

"And you didn't stop?"

"I couldn't if I tried."

For hours we mated, bathed on the edge of the cold creek, and lived out a night of lust in the moonlight. I was revered with the gentlest care until the sun began to rise above the trees at the threshold of the woods.

Lying in his arms, we watched the dark hues of blue transform to a lighter shade. Steam from the creek covered us like a blanket, and the birds chirped and hopped from tree to tree.

"I have a confession." Sana played with my fingers.

"Don't expect me to play along."

"You have to. I've given you my mark, so I should be able to hear your thoughts. I've been trying for a few hours now and nothing."

"Last night was great, Sana, but it could be that I haven't submitted to you...completely."

"What do you mean, 'completely'?"

"I like you. And I'm on board with the idea of us. Just not this instant."

"Why?"

"You know why."

"Don't say..."

My eyes flashed red at him, then narrowed. "Time is time."

"And you think I'm supposed to sit here and wonder what you're doing at that old man's gated fortress when you belong here with me?"

"You have nothing to worry about there. He's helping me solve the city's biggest problem."

"As if I can't."

"Actually, we are gonna need to come together as one unit to take out Adela. Then we can have a discussion about you and me. I might even agree to go to Japan and drink that potion now that I know it works."

Sana rose from the ground and searched through the fog for our clothes. His pulse thumped louder and faster. His demeanor shifted from the kind soul who made love to me all night to an anxious stranger riddled with guilt.

As I watched him, I wondered if the reason his mark didn't work on me was because I was still holding onto Cason. My thoughts gave him life after death, and until I accepted his fate, I would not be able to connect with another living soul.

Sana looked at me with disdain, and a surge shocked my head. I could feel the tension in his body and see his thoughts in flashes. His unsettled mind showed me a beautiful hillside of red and yellow leaves, a shack on top of a rock, footsteps of a woman in wooden shoes, a troubling vision of Cason trekking across of field of tall grass, fluorescent lights in a crowded city, scattered blood on a boulder, and a vision of Cason's final moments saying, "Yeah, brother," before the ghastly image of Sana striking him.

CHAPTER 60
THE WATCHER

VANITY

MY SUSPICION of Sana was accurate all along. His account of the events in Japan was a completely fabricated fairy tale, and I was beyond pissed that I allowed a deceptive kiss to dupe me into believing his temperate manner was honorable.

In learning the truth of my fallen Cason, guilt descended on me, creating a hateful vengeance in my soulless body, overshadowing the beauty of the night's union. The fire in my eyes matched the ball rising above us.

Sana felt the heat raging from them and turned to me. "Vanity," he whispered. "Your eyes tell me you know we are not alone, and this time, it is not Akina." His neck jerked, and his shoulders slumped.

I lowered my voice. "My eyes should tell you I am—"

I choked on my words as the grass pressed against my knees felt cold then absent. Gurgling for air, my body became motionless. As I tried to move, my chest pounded of rigorous pain with what felt like a truck crash landed directly into me. My blood burned inside my veins at a standstill, searching for an artery to tear through.

Sana stepped toward me, and his bones cracked. He howled loud enough to scare away the animals as my eyes locked on him, frozen solid in his stance with his arms reaching toward me. His bottom lip was stuck folded below the top as his mouth formed to call my name. "Va…" was the last sound I heard.

The creek turned stationary, the air was still, and the birds evacuated the trees. My naked body rose in the air when the chanting of a woman's voice crept from the bushes.

"Bond be not broken, bond be sealed.
May this *subplantar* power yield.
May her strength be mine,
Her powers fold.
Unto me I am ready to hold."

Locked immobile midair, I couldn't breathe. I wasn't invincible to the witch's spell linking us. Powerless for the first time in weeks, I was confused by my inability to override her incantation as she repeated it from the bushes, louder each time she chanted the binding verse.

I struggled to utter the words, "Show yourself," as I coughed with an open mouth. Sun rays leaked between the branches, and I felt the binding grow weaker. Without seeing her face, I assumed she thought she would have help from the sun to destroy me as she stole my power. I uttered with a shaky breath, "The sun favors me, witch."

Her chant intensified.

"Give what is mine, give what I seek.
Transfer the gifts of those not warranted for the weak.
Bond be broken, bond be sealed.
Shift the divine right into me and not yield."

Wham! The sound of a chain swept inside the bushes. *Wham!* A spiked flail cut through the shrubs a second time and dragged out with blood on it. I fell to the ground, clutching at my throat, gasping for air.

Sana completed his steps and fell next to me. "V." He reached for my hand. "Are you alright?" his voice cracked, raspy and monotone.

I coughed, staring up at the sky. "I will be," I said, then jumped to my feet.

Sana tossed my sweatshirt into my hands as Akina dragged the witch near the creek with her blade drawn at her throat. I hopped into my sweats, then placed the helm of my boot on her chest.

My face crumpled. "Ria Lucia, I imagine."

I was staring into a mirror. She had taken everything from me. My face.

My happiness. My freedom. My life. She groaned as I pressed down harder into her chest.

"You would know this freak." Akina sucked her teeth. "Who is this witch?"

"The woman who bound me here to N'awlins. We need rope and duct tape. By chance, does your brother have more of the drug he used on me? Or chloroform perhaps?"

"Go ask him." Akina nudged her head at Sana.

He grunted, "I'll be right back."

I leaned downward and flashed my eyes into hers. "So stealing everything from me wasn't enough the first time? Greed consumes you."

Ria's eyes grew big.

"It was rhetorical," I hissed, baring my fangs. "I don't ever want to hear your voice again. And I won't have to for long."

Sana returned with rope, tape, and the rest of the clan. They circled the witch and looked down at her.

Homare growled, then glared at me. "What did I tell you before I ran off to do you a favor?!"

I grinned. "Homare, you and I are going to be great friends someday."

"Well, it isn't today. Just what the fuck happened out here?"

Juni sniffed Sana, then locked eyes with me. "One of those things need not be explained."

Homare glanced at Juni, shifted her eyes toward me, then landed on Sana. "Men. You have no control over those things. Spare us the details." Homare sighed, shaking her head. "Why is there a second thorn in my side that looks like you on our property?"

I tested my telepathy connection with Sana.

Give her the chloroform.

He didn't budge, so I said it aloud. "Sana, hit her with the chloroform, tie her up, and throw her in the trunk." I snatched the tape out of Sana's hands. "I need to have a word with your leader." My eyes shifted to his sister. "Homare. A word," I said, placing the tape across Ria's mouth.

CHAPTER 61
THE RELEASE

VANITY

"SO, explain the tethered witch my brothers are throwing in the trunk." Homare sighed.

"I can't explain her presence, but think of her as a gift. You've been wanting to get rid of me. Well, once I find out how to undo her handiwork, I can finally be unbound to the bayou."

"And my brothers?"

"I'm sorry?"

"I don't hate you, V, but I'm not a fan that my brothers can't see past what you are."

"I wasn't always like this. Sana and Cason had a thing for me before I was turned. What about that don't you understand?"

Homare sucked her teeth. "Look, your kind is our natural enemy, so let's make a deal. I'll agree to come to your aid—within reason—if you'll agree to end relations with my brother."

I scoffed. "Trust me. After tonight, you don't have to worry about me anymore. And thanks for taking the kid home for me."

"Like I said, whatever I can do to help—within reason." She extended her hand.

We shook on our promises.

I looked at Juni, then turned to Sana with narrowed eyes. "Tell them I said thanks."

While Keshell slept, I asked the day guards to keep Ria tied up and knocked out in the caravan. I escaped onto my side of town, parked a few blocks away from the old house, and snuck inside. Deeply, I inhaled the scent of what was once home to me. The scent of Cason fading away and the staleness of the walls settling in from being abandoned streamed a river of blood down my cheeks. I missed him. I betrayed him.

After stacking the pile of bills spread at the foot of the door, I cleaned the mess we left in the bathroom before soaking in a warm bubble bath of milk and honey. Echoes of our laughter, shrieks, and moans lured me into a daze of the good times as I soaked the guilt off me. My conscience wouldn't let go of the pleasure my lover's murderer delivered to my body, burdening my thoughts with flashes of Sana bringing me to unbridled pleasure.

I sprang out of the tub and roamed around Cason's room. Unable to put the guilt to rest, I dressed in one of his old sweat suits, pulled it tight at the waist with rubber bands, and set out into the city.

Covered in oversized gear, I moseyed over to the café. Kyle caught me entering through the back entrance and looked at me as if he had seen a ghost.

"Where the fuck have you been? We've been swamped. Tell me Cason is back." His voice trembled.

A sharp exhale blew from my chest. "Can we talk in the office?"

He wiped the sweat from his forehead. "You get two minutes, and it better not be that you quit."

I followed his lead to the back.

"What's your business?" he asked.

I pushed the chair in the corner below the filter.

"V, what are you doing?"

I removed the file I hid in Cason's office. "Kyle, a lot of shit is going on around here."

"That's all the time. What'd ya got there?"

"Something that will soon concern you. Look, sometime in the future, you may get a note with instructions to close up the café, or not open for a while. I need you to take that warning seriously. Do you understand?"

"I guess." He scratched his head. "What's this all about?"

"It's about life. Survival. And doing what the fuck I tell you to do."

"Whoa, whoa, whoa. I didn't mean to step on any toes."

"Just promise me, you'll take heed when the time comes?"

He clicked his tongue. "I promise."

"As I get more details, I'll keep you in the loop, but as of right now, it appears Cason isn't coming back. I know he would want you to have this place, so hold tight. I'll see to it that his family does right by you."

"Why isn't he coming back?"

"He's no longer with us."

"What?" Kyle sat down behind the desk. "What happened?"

"He and his brother were attacked in a village on their trip. That's all I know. Don't tell the staff just yet. We're still trying to locate his remains."

His head bowed. "Damn."

"Thanks for keeping his place up and running. He'd be pleased."

Kyle placed his hand over his heart.

"I'll be in touch."

I flashed through the back alleys over to Madame's shoppe and knocked on the back window. Her mysterious eyes met with mine as she lifted the bottom half.

"You not coming in?"

"No time. I need you to bring that other powerful witch you mentioned over to Keshell's ward tonight."

"Domini Caroux? I can get a message sent to her, but I want no part of that place."

"Unfortunately, I don't trust the others like I trust you. Of course you'll be under my protection."

Madame shivered, and her lips quivered as she shook her head. "No. That place reeks of darkness."

I hummed as the lightbulb lit inside my head. "That's it. I couldn't put my finger on it, but you've nailed it right on the head. A place of darkness."

"Then you understand why I decline. I'll get word to Domini and make sure she's there."

I shook my head side to side. "Not good enough. I'll be expecting you two at midnight." I backed away from the window, then turned to break off before the sky turned dusk.

"Vanity!"

I paused with one step forward.

"What is this about?"

With my back turned, I answered, "My freedom," then dashed back to the car.

CHAPTER 62

THE WITCHES

VANITY

KESHELL STOOD outside of the caravan when I arrived back to the ward. Without hearing him speak, the cross look on his face screamed he wanted to debate the decisions I'd made without him, my movements, and more importantly…my whereabouts.

"Tell the guards at the gate we have two visitors arriving at midnight." I tossed the keys to his driver.

Keshell's face crumpled. "Again, I say, who's in charge around here?"

I grinned. "Did they fill you in?"

Keshell's voice heightened with sarcasm. "On what? You mean the woman from the sketch tied up and drugged in my caravan? I'm gon' hafta burn it before long."

"You know this means your prophecy is true, right?"

He huffed, sticking out his chest.

I rubbed his shoulder. "Don't worry. I'll come back to check on you."

"How did you know where to find her?"

"She found me, actually. Tracked me with the wolves."

"Nothing good can come from being in cahoots with them. I've warned you many times."

"You may be right about some of them—but not all of them," I muttered.

He grunted. "I get the feeling you are withholding something big."

At midnight, the guards escorted Madame Cecil and Domini Caroux past the gate. Domini withdrew from shaking my hand.

Madame nodded. "She's alright, that one."

"Nice to make your acquaintance, Ms. Caroux."

"Umph." She scowled. "Why ya need me here?"

"Bring her out!" I shouted to the guards.

Ria was lugged from the caravan, half awake and slumped over with her feet dragging through the dirt and her mouth gagged.

Madame's eyes grew big as she clutched above her chest. "Is that who I think it is? As I live and breathe," she mumbled. "How did you find her?"

"Not important." I turned to Domini. "Can you help me?"

She looked at Madame. "What am I missing here? Who is the tethered woman?"

"That's Ria Lucia," Madame whispered.

"Ria?" Domini gasped.

"It's her, alright. She stole my life and bound me here. If I kill her, will the curse be broken?"

"If you kill her, you could die being tied to her, and her curse will forever be upon your soul."

"Well, I brought you here to fix that. Madame speaks of you with the highest regard."

"Thanks for that." Domini rolled her eyes at Madame. "The ceremony you seek should be done on sacred ground. I feel nothing but death here." She glared at Keshell and his men standing beside me.

"This vile witch is too evil to be dealt with on sacred grounds. Right here will have to suffice."

"Here?" Domini sighed. "I'm gonna need salt. Lots of it."

While Keshell's men ran the errand, Madame and Domini drew a circle in the grass and ordered the men to stand guard with Ria in the center.

"She needs to be conscious when I perform the rite," said Domini, speaking over Ria moaning on her knees. "No need for that, Ria. I can't help you now. You've gone too far this time."

"Vanity," Madame called me over. "Super Sunday is in two days. Second lines will take over the streets for six Sundays to follow."

"And?"

Domini cut in. "By doing you this favor in this land of death, where I can sense nothing but evil lurks, I ask one favor in return."

I grinned at her as if her request was any of my concern. She was clueless that she had no choice in the matter at hand. I would be free of Ria Lucia, and she had better succeed.

"What's the favor?" I humored myself.

"Allow our people the peace they deserve during Lent."

My brows furrowed. "Meaning?"

Madame chimed in. "Hold off any plans of violence."

I curved the side of my mouth with shared sentiments as Keshell. "Do I need to wear purple as well?"

Madame grinned. "So you've learned a little of our culture 'round here?"

"Two years stuck here, why wouldn't I? And if you are successful with untying this bond, I give you my word. I won't partake in any violence."

"Merci." Domini nodded.

"The crazy bitch thinks I'm dead anyway, hence the reason I'm in hiding and covered in these baggy clothes—at least for six more weeks."

"Ya sexy in whateva ya got on." Keshell pulled at my waist.

Madame's eyes met mine. "Half dead or alive, men are still liars and full of shit." I snickered.

She and Domini chuckled, quickly killing their laughter when Keshell flared his nostrils, then the mood shifted as the errand boys returned with boxes of kosher salt.

I stepped inside the barrier as Domini lined the circle she and Madame drew in the ground with the sodium, chanting a humming tune until she closed the loop.

"Please don't do this," Ria mumbled.

I hissed. "Get on with it."

Domini closed her eyes, waving her hands in a circle as a light smoke began to rise from the salted sphere. Windows from the building shut, curtains closed, and lights shut off on every floor. Ria cried and muttered at the top of her lungs from her stuffed mouth as the smoke rose high above us.

<u>Domini</u>
Séparez-vous - brisez votre lien
Rompre cette union – De ceux ci-dessous

Libère tes liens non destinés à lier

<u>Translation</u>
Separate thee — shatter thy link
Break this union – From those below
Free thy ties not meant to bind

The rising smoke swirled around us, opaque and thick. Ria's body rose in the air, wriggling, trying to break free, moaning and pleading for Domini to stop summoning the darkness she used to pilfer my existence.

Defying gravity, I rose from the ground seconds later with my eyes on Madame, Keshell, and his squad backing away farther from the circle.

<u>Domini</u>
Les esprits désavouent la vengeance de votre serviteur
Rendre justice et sanctionner les abus de pouvoir
Dénouez ce lien à cette heure.

<u>Translation</u>
Spirits disavow the vengefulness of your servant
Deliver justice and punishment for misuse of power
Untie this bond at this hour.

Ria screamed as her body suspended in the air straight as an arrow with her arms behind her back and head facing the sky. A black, transparent, ghostly figure rose from the center of the circle, screaming a deathly shriek. It stepped toward me, and my eyes turned bloodshot red. It paused its steps, then eerily turned to Ria.

When the wraithlike demon moved toward her, it sounded like *the kraken*, whooshing around her like a coiled snake on a tree branch. It touched the scarf gagged in her mouth, and it broke into tiny particles, vanishing into thin air.

<u>Domini</u>
Avant l'heure des sorcières, l'esprit soit fait
Enlève ta cravate et retourne sur ton trône
Va dans ton monde souterrain avec ton pouvoir qui t'appartient
Sacrée est cette terre à laquelle tu n'appartiens pas
Soulage et libère ton lien.
<u>Translation</u>
Before the witching hour, spirit be done
Remove thy tie and return to your throne
Go to your underworld with thy power that is yours
Sacred is this land you don't belong
Relieve and release thee bond.

My body jerked, then stiffened in the air. My arms hung wide open, frozen in place. A strong sensation stirred within my veins as Ria's body spun around in the apparition's embrace.

"Aaaaahhhh!" Ria screamed.

<u>Domini</u>
Libère ton lien, prends ta malédiction
Retour aux enfers dans votre corbillard
Quitter ce monde, quitter cet endroit
Supprimez ce lien qui lie l'âme - EFFACER !
<u>Translation</u>
Free thy bind, take thy curse
Back to the underworld in your hearse
Leave this world, leave this place
*Remove this soul-tying bind — **ERASE!***

Counterclockwise, our bodies spun above the ground as the spirit covered Ria. A faint black cloud bridged between us as Domini fell to her knees. I stopped spinning as a vibrant violet light encased me, blinding me to my surroundings. Instead, I saw my past playing like a movie on the backdrop of the violet light.

Lindell and I were dancing on St. Charles Avenue, covered in Thoth medallion beads as a float playing *"Choppa Style"* drove by, throwing out teddy bears for the kids reaching behind the barricade.

Beneath streamers hanging from the trees above us, he looked into my eyes and asked, "What would you say if I suggested we move here after we get married?"

I kissed him. "I would love that."

"Let's start looking at places before we leave."

I wrapped my arms around him. "I love those two-story homes we passed on the way here today."

"Then that's where we'll start. I love you, Lauren."

"I love you more, Dell."

I was happy. About to be someone's wife. I was pure. Warm-blooded and human. In love with the city Ria bound me to, turning it into a place I had come to loath.

An image of us riding on the back of a pedicab headed toward the quarter flashed in seconds as I rested my head on his shoulder until the bike crossed over a train track in the middle of the road.

Purple, green, and gold covered the streets. Dropped parade tokens of crown pillows, sequined change purses, *Krewe of Bacchus* paraphernalia, and masks lined the streets as our driver suggested places we should pay a visit and informed us of tourist attractions that were a waste of money.

"If one of those houses you like so much doesn't work out, we could start out small in one of these condos." Dell pointed up at a second-story home overlooking the street with a wrought-iron balcony.

"A condo sounds lovely to me."

"A couple like you would be better off in Metarie," the driver chimed in.

"We'll keep that in mind," Dell brushed her off.

I shook my head side to side.

Dell kissed the side of my face and whispered in my ear, "I know, sweetheart. It's the city you're in love with."

Slowly, I descended to the ground as the violet light disappeared. Ria's body was lifeless on the ground. Her breathing stunted. Her face still a distorted image of mine.

The smoke surrounding us began to dissipate into a translucent off-black hue, sizzling and cracking over distant, muffled shouts from Domini and Madame.

I marched toward Ria with my nails spread wide apart like claws. She moaned as her limp body curled into a fetal position.

"Enough. No more. No more," she whined.

"Vanity!" Madame shouted. "How do you feel?"

I placed my boot on Ria's chest and shoved her. "You ruined my life. I was happy. I had everything."

"I saved your life," she muttered through a cough.

"You call wiping my memory and stealing my identity *'saving my life'*?!"

"You're still here, aren't you, vampiress?" she managed to croak over a throaty laugh. "Isn't that what they call you?" She coughed. "The boy is to blame. All he had to say was no, and you would have died. Humans are selfish. They don't know when to let go."

"And neither do vampires."

The smoke cleared as I jammed my sharpest fingernail into the side of her throat. Her weak hand grabbed a hold of my wrist as a low-pitched wheeze spasmed from her lungs. Gasps from beyond the salted cipher filled the courtyard, and with her last breath, Ria stayed true to form and said, "I'd do it again if I could. I know what you're made of."

A horrid scream blew from my mouth, rumbling the courtyard and sounding the alarm as if a tremor was roaring below the city. Keshell protected his ears and stepped in front of Madame, Domini, and his unit, struggling with each step he took toward me.

The higher my scream elevated, they all fell to their knees, except the dark prince, bravely fighting the siren compelling a bowed audience. Blood dripped from my eyes, and my body bent over as Keshell stood before me, mouthing an inaudible plea to calm my mind and close my mouth. I screamed him down to his knees and released the beginning of my rage upon him, curling him into a ball at the edge of the hexed ring.

The shrilling sound ceased when I inhaled to take a breath. Babies cried in the distance. Every present being and creature in the courtyard uncovered their ears and glared at me with fear in their eyes.

"Was that necessary?!" Domini's voice trembled as she rose to her feet.

I turned toward Domini with flaming red eyes. "Yes, it was! Ria was never going to stop! And I don't owe you any further explanation of my actions."

"Vanity! The fuck was that!" Keshell screamed over her shaky voice.

I lifted Ria's arm and dragged her past the drawn perimeter. Black weeds sprung from the soil, hissing and crackling, tying their sprouts into knots until they formed into a woven design of fruitless bare branches without a base. The pattern shone a fluorescent red light, then the black weeds turned into black stone, sealing the drawn circle in the center of the yard.

Keshell stepped forward and held me in his arms. "I've seen things but have never felt unsure 'bout anything as I have tonight. I was terrified for ya. Are ya alright?"

I dropped Ria's arm and backed away from him. "I'm…something."

"Vanity," Madame called me.

I eyed everyone staring at me. "My name is Lauren."

The look on each of their faces differed—Madame pleased, Domini smug, Keshell confused, and his men indifferent.

"So my work here is done," Domini confirmed.

"Thank you. You've given me what I wanted. Ria is my last kill—for a while."

She widened her eyes to Madame Cecil.

I extended my hand to Madame. "Thank you for bringing her tonight. As always, I owe you one. And I will keep my word, for you."

She smiled. "Ms. V—I mean, Lauren. You solved one part of your puzzle. Next time I see you, I hope it's over a drink that what remains has been solved."

"I'd like that. Then maybe we can laissez les bon temps rouler *(lay-zeh leh bawn taw roo-leh)*."

"Let the good times roll we shall." She smiled. "You've become one of us."

"And I don't want to leave."

Madame placed her hand on my shoulder and gently squeezed it. "Then don't."

"Will you see them out?" I asked Keshell.

He nodded. "Meet ya upstairs."

I stood near the window looking out into the darkness of night when Keshell entered his place. His heart was beating faster than normal, and his eyes burned through me like a laser.

"V, the visions that come to me was nothing like what I witnessed tonight. Are ya sure ya okay?"

"I will be. The bits and pieces that came back to me are tough to process, seeing how my life was ripped away from me."

"I'm here if ya need help with…"

"I'll be fine. I'll continue to lay low, but I need to get out of here."

"Outta where? N'awlins? Or my set?"

"Both, actually. But how do I do that? My parents think I'm dead, I haven't freed the city from Adela, and I'm still a…"

"Vampire."

"Yes."

"Don't torture yaself for giving the cure to the kid. I have his blood. Remember? I will find someone to duplicate what he took."

I pressed my lips together and exhaled sharply. "I have faith you will."

He blurred in front of me and grabbed my face. "Anything for the half beating heart of my vampiress." He leaned down and pecked my lips.

When the sun was on the cusp of putting my frightful night of transformation behind us, I kissed Keshell good night. But it was more than that. It was a kiss goodbye as I left his fort once the glowing orb in the sky was in full spectrum. No note. And no intention of returning.

CHAPTER 63
THE OUTSKIRTS
VANITY

HOMARE OPENED THE DOOR, shook her head, and sighed. "I know opposites attract, but this is becoming stalker-ish at this point."

"You wish." I laughed. "The deed is done. And so am I for a while."

"Done how?"

"I gave the woman who helped me my word. No violence for six weeks, but that doesn't mean I have to sit by the marsh, twiddling my fingers."

"Which means you're on my doorstep with a proposal." Homare huffed. "What do you want now? I'm running out of brothers."

"You're so cute, Homare." I scrunched my face. "I need you to teach me how to wield a sword."

Homare laughed. "In six weeks?"

"Yeah. I need to lay low, so…"

Homare cut me off. "You are *not* staying here."

"Then where would you be willing to meet me for lessons? Cabin on the other side of the lake perhaps?"

"No. That's still too close. But I do have something in mind."

I braced myself for the car to hiccup as we approached the county line. All of my former attempts of leaving the city resulted in me being knocked into a deep sleep for a few hours and waking with a raging headache. But this being the first time I tried to leave as a vampire, and unbound, eased my anxiety on the attempt.

We crossed over without a hitch, but Homare noticed I flinched when the nose of the car drove past the final green-and-white exit sign passing Lake Pontchartrain.

"Selfish bitch."

"I beg your pardon?"

"If the curse was still on you, what would have happened just now?"

"The car would have crashed into a force field."

She gritted her teeth. "With me in it."

The tires on the car drew black streaks on the asphalt until smoke blew from behind. Homare veered the car into the grass, forcing us to jerk forward.

"Get out," she said.

"I know you're a bad bitch, Homare, but I am not getting out. I've been through literal hell tonight and came to you because we're friends."

Homare burst into laughter. "Friends! Since when?"

"Since the day you stepped forward and took over the pack."

"You're crazy."

"Of course I am, but stop denying you like me. Even with me fucking your brothers against your will. We're friends."

Homare exhaled deeply and tapped her fingers on her knee. "I swear you know how to push my buttons."

"Because you like me. Just admit it, get it over with, and take me wherever we're going."

"Why should I?"

"Are you going to take care of the Adela problem, or am I?"

Her eyebrows raised to her hairline as she held her breath.

"That's what I thought. You like me, and you need me."

The engine turned over, and we ensued a quiet drive into the swamplands of Laplace, Louisiana. Driving through the rural community where debris from storms and buildings were still damaged from hurricane winds, I sensed Homare's irritation with me had simmered down to her cool-like temperance. I smiled on the inside, recognizing she was the female version of Cason. A true leader. Calm-natured, authoritative, and an alpha when necessary.

"You like it here," I said.

"I do. How can you tell?"

"A certain peace graced you when we drove into town."

"Yua, my stepmother, is very dear to me. I don't even know why I call her stepmother. She's more than that. I love her with every fiber in my being."

"Well, you've convinced me to move her up on the list of my protection."

"I'm sure she'll let you stay with her. She may even make you a better person while you're here."

"You'd like that, wouldn't you?"

A petite silhouette stepped below a dim porch light wearing a long peach gown. Homare turned off the car and hopped out before I could remove my belt.

"What are you doing up at this hour?"

Yua's light voice replied, "I could ask you the same."

The two of them hugged, then the stepmother crossed the threshold of her front door. I stepped onto her porch, bowing my head to avoid looking into her eyes.

"Okaasan, I come to you for a favor—one I never imagined would spill from my lips."

"Is this the one who loved our dear Cason?"

"Still love," I corrected her.

"Okaasan, this is Vanity."

"It's Lauren, actually. But everyone calls me V."

Homare glared at me and scoffed. "Whatever happened last night definitely worked."

I fanned her off. "Homare tells me your name is Yua. Lovely to meet you. I'm in a bit of a bind and need a place to lay low for a few weeks while Homare trains me."

"Trains you for what?"

"The elimination of vampires in the city."

"I see." Yua turned to Homare. "Homare, I would give you anything you ask for, but this…I am not comfortable with."

"It was a long shot," I added.

"Okaasan, I didn't expect you to invite her into the main house." Homare pointed to her right.

"A shed?" I scowled.

"A she shed," Yua corrected me. "And it's yours if you'd like."

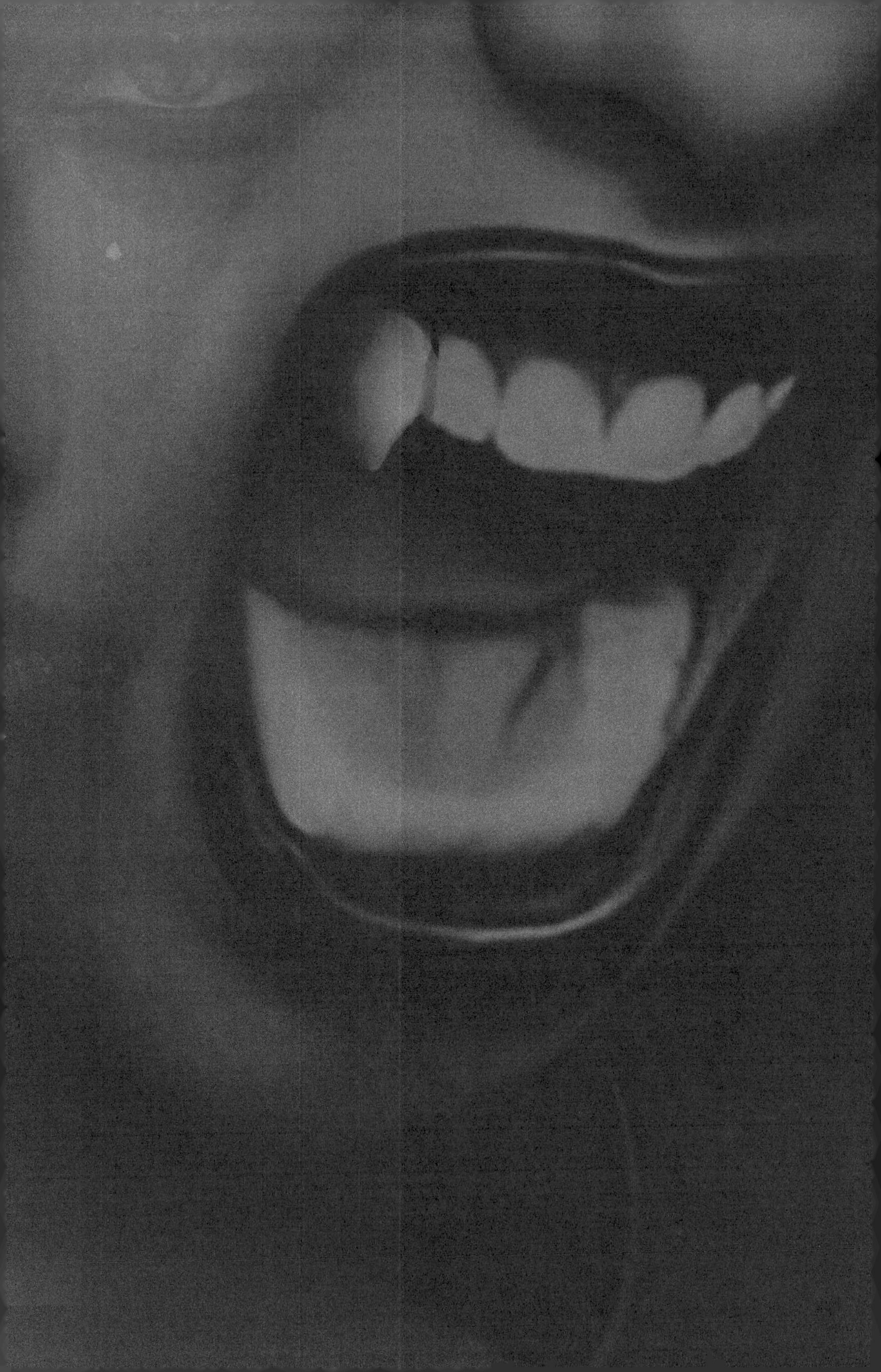

CHAPTER 64
THE SPAR

VANITY

YUA and I kept our distance—me in the quaint, comfy shed and her in the main house. Some mornings, I'd catch her watching me snap a bird's neck without as much as a flinch. She was a tough old broad. Not easily swayed. And heavily guarded.

The little conversation we shared through the window from her deck told me all I needed to know about her, and I saw why Homare loved her as her own mother. She had an innocence about her. A kindness that extended from a distance. And her presence made me think of my own mother now that my memory was back. The mother who hadn't given up searching for me. The mother I was too ashamed to return to as a half-dead vampiress, reduced to living in a shed and in hiding. A bloodsucking deviant.

I used that aggression in my moonlight katana arts lessons with Homare. A patient teacher, that one. A fierce warrior too.

"Posture!" she fussed. "Back straight, feet shoulder width apart. Keep your knees bent. Never locked."

"Yes, sensei."

"That wasn't cute weeks ago, and it's still not cute today. Reset. Head still. Balance."

I wiped the grin from my face and gripped my sword with my right hand on top and my left near the pommel. Homare struck, and our blades slid midpoint. *Ding.* I reset and held my sword upright in front of me.

Homare opened her body to a forty-five-degree angle with her left foot in front of the right. "Come at me."

I cheated and used my supernatural speed.

She huffed, slipping out of the way with ease, then growled at me. "I knew you were going to do that." She swung her blade at me mid-sentence.

"Ow. You got me on the arm."

A gold light lit between us when the wound sealed.

"You were paying attention to my words and not my blade. I could have cut you worse."

"Or not at all." I sighed.

"You'll heal."

"You've gotten used to that, haven't you?"

"Not in the way you think." Her voice softened from her normal straightforward delivery. "Though I am fascinated with the gold light."

"I was hoping Yua would have an explanation for it. You know…since she is the one who told Sana about the cure."

Homare lunged forward. "She hasn't said anything?"

I spun out of the way and blocked her strike with my back turned and blade down the middle of my back. "No, she hasn't."

"Don't get crafty. You're still new at this, but nice move." Her blade scraped down to my point as her hips maneuvered into the Ochs stance.

I stepped away. "I speak when spoken to. That's how much respect I have for her."

Homare's arms were crossed, her sword positioned at the top of her head. I waved her forward, and she pounced at me, cut across my body, and leaned forward with a jab to my chest. I hopped back as she continued to step forward, and parried her stab, pushing her sword to the left.

Her grip was never weak, stopping my plan to knock her sword from her hands. She counter cut, and our swords locked between us at our feet.

Ting.

"Good," she said. "Much better on the defense without cheating. We'll practice footwork next."

"Footwork? No one can keep up with me if I don't want them to."

Homare tricked me and struck at me with a fake jab, knocking my sword from my hands. The tip of her blade punctured between my breasts as my eyes roamed over to my weapon shining in the dirt.

I blurred from the point and picked it up as Homare charged on my heels. Tipping on my toes backward, she pushed me with strike after strike until I blocked her swing coming at me from the side. We both stood back in an open stance and smiled at one another.

"How about that footwork?" I bragged.

"How about I had you a second ago," she gloated.

For weeks we trained under two new moons with Yua admiring from the upper deck. Then, one night, she hollered, ran into the house, and shut the door. Homare and I stopped sparring and listened closely to the woods.

"Vampires," she hissed.

"I count three of them," I said, dropping my sword. "I don't need this for what I'm about to do."

I soared between the trees after a female vamp to the left of me, racing like the fourth leg on a track team. Her black trench sailed behind her short legs, creating a cool breeze as she cut through the wind. Impressed with her speed, I turned it up to full blast and grabbed her sandy-blonde, wavy hair, dragging her in the dirt before flinging her into a tree.

A draft above me blocked the moonlight for a few seconds. "The flyer," I muttered, hopping from tree to tree and pouncing from branch to branch, slicing through the leaves a few feet below the *motherfucka* gliding above the crown of the forest.

He looked down when he heard me rustling my way to the canopy. Our eyes met as I leaped upward and caught his foot. *Snap. Blip. Crack.* We descended through the debris and tumbled in an entangled position as the ground broke our fall.

"We finally meet," I said, jumping to my feet.

"Ohhh." He slowly rose from the dirt, adjusting his cuffs. "You've heard of me. I'm flattered. So how do you want to die? Fast? Slow?"

I cracked my knuckles. "I would ask you the same, but I don't care much about your demise…as long as you do it."

The pale face flyer's dark eyes and red lips flew toward me in a spiraling motion with his fist leading the charge. Underestimating my speed, I sidestepped out of the way, mimicking Homare's effortless motion when I first began my training.

With my hands cuffed at my sides, I spun around on the tip of my toes and waited for him to circle back. "Ugh," I sighed, falling to my knees.

The fast vamp caught her second wind and sideswiped me as I shifted away from the flyer's next attempt to thrash me. We tussled, the two of us, blow for blow, scratch for scratch, cut for cut, until the flyer tag-teamed with her.

I was thrown off guard. I hadn't had to fight anyone as fast as myself or encountered an opponent with the swift gift of flight, and this duo was more advanced than Billie and Carlisle. Those two I took on with ease, but my new assailants fought like a wrestling duo with rehearsed choreography.

The flyer carried me into the air by the back of my hood. His companion pulled my hair as I lodged my nails into her throat while she kicked continuously for me to free her. But I held onto her bony throat, looking down at the pinecones as they turned into brown dots with every second.

"Vanity!" Homare shouted.

I twisted my neck to her location behind me on the ground. Homare tossed her rapier into the air. The sharp point of the blade glistened a bright silver streak as it twirled facing the moon. I twisted the speedy one's back toward the blade. *Gump.* She swallowed in disbelief, then took her last breath, releasing her clenched fist tugging on my hair as I snatched out the blade from her back and separated her head from her shoulders.

Her body dropped to the ground. I retrieved my nails from her neck and let her head fall behind it. I grinned as the flyer glanced down at the sudden shift in weight of his load. His eyes widened as I cocked the blade back, preparing to slice him in half. He released my hood from his claws, and I descended to the ground, landing on my feet and one palm with Homare's blade glued to my hand in blood.

The sweet harmony of a children's hymn traveled a few yards behind me on the path to Yua's house. "Homare," I muttered in a hasty push toward the melodic tune ringing in my ears in a soft monotone.

The blood in my veins began to shatter at the sound of his vocals growing closer. Disturbed like troubled water, I could feel my blood dispersing in clots, searching for a way to exit my body.

My pace decelerated within three feet of him. Homare was in a bug-eyed daze, fallen to her knees, with a pocket knife positioned at her throat. The demon's maroon eyes glared at me from the corner, belting his song louder and more forceful with every step I took to reach him. I was immobile in my tracks, as if hurricane force winds stunted me from moving forward.

With my hand on Homare's blade, my arms hung out wide and still. My eyes locked with the tenor's. He raised his hand in Homare's direction with a sinister grin on his lips. I rolled my eyes toward her as the blade pierced a dot of blood from her neck. "Iiiihhhhhhhhh!" I screamed in horror. Homare's eyes closed, and the knife dropped to her side. The singer became rattled. His monotone verse warbled as the singer's song skipped a beat.

From the heels of my feet, I sprang forward with two leaps. *Swish.* Homare's blade sliced his head clean off his body.

I rushed to her side. "Speak to me! Get that singing ass fool out of your head!"

"What happened?"

"You were hypnotized. A few minutes more and you would have slit your own throat."

"Did you catch the other two?"

"One out of two isn't bad. That flying fucker got away. Come on. We gotta check on Yua."

Trekking back to the house, motion above the chimney caught my eye. The flyer stood on the roof with his feet crossed and hands behind his back. I placed my palm in front of Homare, and we stopped running.

The flyer waved. "See you soon." He revealed a lit match from behind his back, dropped it on the shingles, and flew into the darkness.

Homare ran inside to Yua. I closed my eyes and slowed my racing heart, summoning clouds above the house. Connecting with the mist in the air and the smog from the lake, drops of rain formed into a light shower. The flames fizzled out before spreading into a full-blown fire, but the message was loud and clear.

I knocked on the window of the upstairs balcony and pointed to Yua. "She can't stay here alone."

Homare placed her hand on her chest. "I'll stay here with her. Where do you plan on going?"

"Back to Keshell. The war is here. You two need to be with the rest of your pack."

Akina, Sana, Shun, and Juni stood in the yard as Homare raised the dirt on the road at high speed. She jumped out of the car before me and Yua.

"What happened?" Akina unfolded her arms.

"How do you know something happened?" I scowled.

"I felt it," said Akina, hugging her sister.

Together they turned around and said at the same time, "Twin sense."

As she explained to the pack what she endured by way of song, Yua touched me for the first time. Her soft, wrinkled hands smelled of mink oil and lavender.

She grabbed my face. "Thank you."

My cheeks turned warm. "So you're no longer afraid of me?" I chortled.

"I was never afraid." She pointed to the lapel of her jacket.

"What's that?"

"Sen coins." She reached in her bag. "Four wards off evil. I made this for you." She placed a woven belt in my hands. "Four sen coins are sewn inside just for you. Wear this so you may continue your journey of self."

"Arigatou."

Yua gently pinched my cheeks. "He'd be proud."

I fastened the belt around my waist and stared at the pack lined up on the porch of the main house. One step at a time, I made my way closer to the trees when the ghost of Cason stood behind them. A wistful smile upturned on my lips as I saluted the clan.

"Get that look off your face! This isn't goodbye!" Homare shouted.

Sana's eyes glowed silver as he hopped from the porch to approach me.

"I know!" I yelled back, shaking my head at him, then dashed into the woods.

CHAPTER 65

THE THREAT

KESHELL

I ROSE FROM A DEEP SLEEP, greeted with reports of chaos spreading across the parishes. Malice spread like wildfire according to word from all the wards, and Adela's army was given orders to seek and destroy until Vanity was brought before her.

A messenger delivered a gram written in blood addressed to me.

You've been keeping secrets.

You have one chance to redeem yourself.

Bring her to me.

After being bossed around by my Vanity, I found Adela's threat laughable. I tossed the note in my fireplace, pacing the floor as it crackled into a shriveled burnt ball, wracking my brain on where the hell Vanity had disappeared to.

My captain guarding the door to my chambers knocked.

"Come."

"Sir, a huge fire has been lit in Jackson Square."

"Switch the brigade and gather six men from the courtyard. I'll be down in a sec."

Big, bright, and blazing was the flame on the square. Dead bodies set ablaze like dominos as the flame traveled across the lit backdrop of cathedrals, statues, and dark-blue sky above the French Quarter into a pink-and-orange hue below a snow moon.

Standing at the edge of the park, I felt heat from the flames dance across my face as I watched Adela's men post up near the iron fence. "Rrr-rrr!" I whistled to my men to bring Ria's frozen body out of the trunk.

They laid her in the lot, then we sped off to assess the damage of The Easy. Judging from the reins of two wards, Bourbon and Lafayette, Adela needed to be put down like a rabid dog, and her men needed to burn like Jackson.

I sent one man to check out the café.

"The café was closed, sir."

A second man to check out Vanity's secluded home.

"The house was dark, sir. No movement or heartbeat inside."

"Fuck," I muttered.

My driver asked, "Any other places we need to check, sir?"

I ran my palms across my face and wiped away the moisture from the sides of my mouth. "Take us home." I sighed. "We have preparations to make."

Close to midnight, a warmblood strolled into the courtyard. His aloof eyes were puffy, staring off into nothingness. The tenants cat-called him while my vamps followed him with their tongues out, waiting for me to give the okay that he could be taken.

One of the escorts pushed him forward. "He says he has a message, sir."

I waved my hand. "You all let dis man waltz into ya home! No wan pat 'em down! It coulda blown us to bits! We at war! Don' be fooled by fresh blood! Now fuck off!"

The warm-blooded *opp* opened his mouth. "For Keshell Martin's eyes only."

I gave the okay to my driver.

He retrieved the paper from its hands and read aloud. "You think of me as a fool, I see. A friend of my enemy is my enemy. When the city burns, remember it's your fault when you burn with it."

I pointed to the bonfire.

My driver tossed the note into the flames. "What about the messenger?"

"Drop him off to mi cousin on Frenchmen who lives above the jazz bistro. Have him remove the compulsion."

"Sir, you know he's gonna…"

"And when ya deliver him, tell him I said, "*Rasanble twoup yo* (Rally the troops)."

Waiting on the return of my men, the guards whistled and opened the gate. Her silhouette could be picked out of a lineup in the darkest of night when the moonlight hit her curves.

"Look who decided to join us amidst all the chaos," I snarked at Vanity strolling across the courtyard, smelling of damp woods and dogs.

"The chaos was brought to me tonight, and I'd like to know how my hideaway was found." Her brows raised with venom in her eyes.

"Don't you dare. I've been setting things in motion for your return. Who was it that found you?"

"A fast bitch, the lullaby leech, and the flying fucker."

"So it's true what they say?"

"Yeah, it's true. That fucker really can fly."

I scoffed. "Glad you made it out alright. Wha' ya know?"

"Nothing, minus being ambushed," she barked.

"Well, I didn't ruin ya little vacation. You can pipe down at me. I had no idea where ya were."

My eyes narrowed, and her breathing pattern remained stagnant. Deep down, she knew I wouldn't have given her up had I known her whereabouts.

She mumbled, "Could Juni be behind…? Nah, he wouldn't. He wouldn't dare put Yua or Homare in harm's way. Would he?"

"Whatcha goin' on 'bout?"

"Your men searched me before letting me inside. What's up? You don't trust me now?"

Vanity and I shared a grin, pretending to read each other's minds. My men stood idly by, watching us stare each other down until we grew tired of the silence.

"Of course I trust you," I said.

We shared a laugh to bring down the wall between us.

"What's this chaos you speak of?" Vanity tossed her hair over her shoulder.

"Nonstop violence, a massive fire in Jackson Square, and a broken truce. Adela threatened to end our agreement if I didn't deliver your body to her. I sent the tethered witch's corpse instead." I cleared my throat. "That didn't go over well of course."

"Fuck that truce. This bitch is going down, and the city can be yours."

"Why not ours?"

"As enticing as that sounds, I have plans when this is done. But I may return…one day. What have your visions told you?"

"Besides how this will end?" I paused longer than she liked. "That I would see ya again."

"Then let's get to it. How much of Adela's army do you suspect is at her mansion right now?"

"Not many. She knows I'm coming for her after what she's done today." I signaled my driver.

"So how do we find her?"

"We follow the trail of innocent bodies left in the street or send word where to settle this once and for all."

"I've been thinking about that while I was gone. Draw her away from the city to Scout Island."

I nodded. "There's somethin' you have to see first."

"Do I have time to get outta these rags?"

I chuckled. "And a quick shower."

I studied her crumpled brows and pensive demeanor along the ride, strategizing ways to hit Adela where it hurt. Biting on her bottom lip, she pulled her hair off her face and braided it down the center. My heart thumped in my chest each time one of her biceps flexed as she twisted her locks into shape, and the sight of her toned brown thighs kept my mind occupied in between visions of the evil things to come in a few hours.

"Ya dress sexy to go into battle? Or is that for me?"

"It's for me." She grinned.

"Shall I test its durability? One good tug and I could have ya naked within seconds." I snickered.

"You'd like that, wouldn't you?"

"I missed ju." My hand found its way to her tempting thighs. "It's good to have ya back."

"It'll be good once I end this lunatic's brutality."

The car stopped at Congo Square.

"Why are we here again? And where are the worshippers tonight?"

"The war has begun, darling. Everyone has sought shelter."

I zipped out of the car and over to her side to open her door. She raised the hood on her blouse, then placed her hand in mine, strutting beside me to the Eggun Tree.

"When I was searching for ya, I came here for a vision but found this instead." I pointed to a dark-red rose sprouting from the middle of the tree. "In all my years, I've never seen a rose not grow from a bush, nor have I seen one as deep and rich in color."

"A rose did grow from concrete once."

I looked at her in confusion. "I beg ya pardon."

She laughed. "Tupac…Shakur." Her lips pressed together. "Never mind. An old man like you wouldn't get it." She waved her hand. "How can a rose bloom from within a tree?"

"It shouldn't, but it has. There's one more thing. It won't allow anyone to pluck it."

I reached forward to touch the stem. A vibrant wine barrier formed to shield the rose. I continued to attempt to touch the petals. *Zap.*

"Did you see that?"

Vanity nodded.

"This rose sprouted for you."

"How do you know?"

"Trust me. Touch it."

Gracefully she leaned forward like a ballerina in arabesque form. The closer her fingers drew into the petal, a thin merlot light outlined her body, connecting her with the rose. She inhaled from its center with her eyes closed, then plucked a petal from the outer ring. Shielded in the wine-colored light, she placed the petal on her tongue and swallowed.

"What'd ya taste? How do ya feel?"

Vanity's brown eyes flashed red, gold, then matched the shade of merlot orbiting around her body. She looked past me as if I wasn't there, entranced deeper than in a daze, and beyond stuck in a dream.

CHAPTER 66
THE MOTHER

VANITY

I WAS SUBMERGED UNDER WATER. Waves crashing around me like a typhoon trapped beneath a cargo ship passing through the gulf. Higher, I rose to its brim where a cloud snatched me and spun me around while heavy winds dried my soaked body. Then, I was thrown into the sands of a golden desert surrounded by farmland.

A soft voice echoed down upon me. "Lauren."

I shielded my eyes from the bright-yellow light surrounding a deity figure, hovering above in a star-filled plum sky.

"Daughter of my daughters. Blood of my blood. You've lost your way."

"Do I kneel or something?"

"You're already on your knees," her voice trembled in amusement. "You may rise."

"How do I find my way?"

"With what's inside of you. You feel it. You've used it. Now control it."

"You called me daughter… How? Who are you?"

"Who am I?" She tittered. "Allow me to show you."

The yellow, glowing light illuminating behind her dimmed into a violet orb. The starry, plum sky turned dark gray with raging clouds swarming from every direction. Lightning lit around tornadoes dropping from the rolling clouds as the sand below me vibrated violently, just as forceful winds lifted me above a cracked line drawn in the sand.

"I am Oya. Goddess of the Winds of Change, Mother of Chaos."

Her thin frame ran circles around the tornadoes, slicing through them with a sword in her right hand. "I clear the way for growth, enforce change, and protect those who call upon me. I am transformation, the first and last breath of death. The mother of your mothers." She settled in front of me and smiled.

While she guided us both to our feet, I was mesmerized by her beauty. Her supple, deep-brown skin glowed just as bright as the stars she wiped away minutes before. Braids draped down her back from below a deep currant-and-gold abstract scarf wrapped around her head in the shape of a crown with horn-shaped spikes.

My eyes bowed along with my head. "You're the gold light when I heal."

She took me by the hand. "I am. My blood is the reason your dark side is failing to control you."

"Why didn't my mother, or grandmother, tell me any of this?"

"The history of our lineage was forced to be hidden because of those that oppose you."

"The pale ones?"

"Mmm hmm—demons. Centuries ago, their creator wanted to birth a queen mixed with the purity of our blood."

"Like what I've become?"

"Yes. He fancied us but also envied us. And if he had been granted to mate with one of my daughters, a new breed superior to all creatures would have been born and sworn to serve him."

"So I'm an abomination."

"You could have been, but your mother married a Lacks, and the Lacks blood mixed with my blood made you. A supreme being. A goddess who walked the earth with a heart of gold. Literally. You had no idea who you were, and neither did the demon who turned you into this…"

"Vampiress."

Oya coughed. "A goddess in danger of losing her light."

"I don't want to lose my light."

"I don't think you could if you tried. Think of what you did for that boy. Was it because you're addicted to the power or because you wanted him to return to the life stolen from him?"

A sharp exhale traveled from the depths of my chest. "Because he deserved to live his life."

Oya's eyes gleefully glistened into mine. "There's still good in you, despite the demon seed searching for a cell to plant inside of you. Our blood and the Lacks will continue to fight it off of your soul, for you were a queen before the dark ones shadowed your light. That witch sensed it in you. Stalked it. And tried to steal it. But only we, the chosen ones, can wield the power of earth, wind, water, and fire."

"Fire? I haven't felt any connection to fire. I've only been given the power of three. Earth, water, and wind manipulation. Never fire."

"Because you've had no need for it…yet. You will soon. I know you feel the fire in you, but it will remain buried until it's necessary for you to unleash it. The first three control the last."

"The first three control the last," I whispered, solving the riddle as best as I could. "How will I know when I need it after everything I've experienced thus far?"

Oya tapped the sides of my temple. "You'll know. Just like you knew to swallow the rose petal to get to me." Her warm fingers traveled down the sides of my face to cup my cheeks. "The warrior in me resides in you, Lauren."

Oya's hands dropped from my face. She sashayed the long hem of her dress that matched the gold-and-garnet print of her headdress, creating a breeze to make it flow in the air. Her physical form fell on top of the sand, wisping around before me as a dust vortex, then transcended into a bright maroon water buffalo with glowing white horns bigger than an elephant's tusk.

Clearer than my own voice in my head was hers. "Change is a necessity on the path to being whole."

I repeated her words, "Change is a necessity on the path to being whole," and was embraced by darkness.

When I came to, Keshell was pacing back and forth with me in his arms. I gasped with the taste of dry, sweet petals marinating on my tongue with a hint of green apples.

"Goddess, what happened?" he asked.

Our heads turned toward the tree. The rose retracted inside of the trunk, leaving a single petal between layers of the bark.

I hopped from Keshell's arms onto my feet. "Everything." I coughed.

"Sun's coming up. So, you're ready, then?"

"I was born ready."

While Keshell slept, I took phase one into my own hands with a trip to the Garden District before the first-shift workers crowded the streets. Standing on the top of a bell tower, I witnessed the quiet of the town and woke everyone up with a windstorm, blowing the roof off Adela's mansion.

Keshell was right. At least thirty vamps fled the unsheltered home, shrieking like jackals seeking shade. Into the sunlight they ran, bursting into flares like neighborhood fireworks on New Year's Eve.

The sparks from their combustion sizzled and torched the lawn up to the footsteps of the entrance. *Poof.* The mansion went up in flames.

I watched that hellhole burn to the ground with a smug grin on my face. The smoke bonding with the sky signaled a change was on the horizon, and by the time I made it back to the city to warn Madame Cecil, most of the businesses on her block had already boarded their windows.

I sighed at the beads jingling above the door. "I'm glad I caught you," I said to Madame, turning the key in her register with her purse on her shoulder.

"I take it that's your doing in the Garden District?"

I nodded. "Tonight's the night. Thought I'd eliminate as many of her men as I could, seeing as I'll be outnumbered."

"Humph." She scowled.

"Any knowledge of Adela's other hiding places?"

"You need Neveah for that kind of insight."

"Do me a favor. Hang out at her place until this is over. She lives far enough from the city where I can trust you'll be safe. Plus, you can call me and tell me what she knows."

"You askin' or tellin' me?"

Rocking left to right, I pursed my lips with a smile on the side of my mouth. "Asking. And I'll feel better knowing you're out of harm's way."

Madame set the alarm on the shoppe. "I'll do it for you."

CHAPTER 67
THE UNINVITED
NEVEAH

THE HAIRS on the back of my neck prickled from the news of the ruin going on in the city. Visions of innocent people screaming in horror, dead bodies piled between side streets, and carnivorous creatures committing savagery blinded me until goosebumps covered my arms.

Hives formed on my neck as I channel-surfed and found the same report was on repeat like a broken record. The city was under attack and evil was back on the rise.

I found my way into the kitchen for some chamomile tea to settle my nerves on this sleepless night. Inside the pantry, I grabbed two bags from the container and filled the kettle with tap water half full, then stood on my tiptoes to reach the handle of my favorite mug with the words *Seeing is Believing* painted in gold on the sides.

Waiting for the burner to reach high heat and the kettle to whistle, I leaned against the counter while my eyes got lost in the wood stacked at least five feet high in the backyard. Each piece chopped equally in increments—solid, thick, and long enough to build a perfect log cabin farther out back.

The sound of the water burbling on the stove soothed my racing mind, and restlessness crept up on me. White mist spouted from the nose of the kettle as it began to shrill. I jolted from the sudden whistling as another disturbing vision flashed into my thoughts, forcing my mug to fall from my fingers, breaking into tiny pieces on the floor.

Retrieving the broom and dustpan from the pantry, I cleaned up the mess while the tint of the curtains lightened to a shade of pink, with a hint of marmalade sneaking in at the bottom. "Thank God," I said to myself, then exhaled a deep sigh of relief that night was ending.

I turned off the stove and fetched another mug from the cupboard. As I sipped my tea in front of the television, the astounding number of casualties reported and graphic images became unbearable to watch.

Soon after the tea's effect settled in, I retired to the bedroom. Just as I kicked off my slippers, a knock sounded at the front door.

"I saw you coming but didn't think it would be this soon," I said.

"Sorry for the intrusion. We're here under Vanity's orders. She requests I inform her of any significant visions you may have had, and she thinks we'll be safe this far out." Madame Cecil and Domini Caroux looked at each other and sighed. "May we impose on you, or is this a bad time?"

I opened the door fully. "Please, do come in. I was up all night looking at the news, and now I'm sluggish from chamomile tea. I was just about to turn in, so I'm afraid I won't be good company."

"I could use a nap myself." Madame's face wrinkled, looking around the room. "What's that noise?"

"I don't hear anything," I said.

Domini scowled at Madame. "It's faint, but it sounds like wood work."

"Oh, that. That's just a friend keeping himself occupied."

"So, we *are* intruding." Madame smirked. "We can travel farther north and find somewhere else to go since you have company."

Domini grinned. "Yeah, nothing will kick off while the sun is out. We'll be fine."

"I promise you're not intruding. I'll put on a pot of coffee and let you two get settled in." I showed Madame and Domini into the den. "Make yourself at home, I guess."

While the pot brewed a vanilla blend, I cracked a few eggs, seasoned them with salt, pepper, and cheese, and scrambled the yokes until they were golden. I divided them between three plates and carried one outside.

"I've been up all night and am about to turn in. Here's a little something to get your day started." I handed him the plate.

"I heard a car pull up. Is everything alright?"

"Yeah. Everything's fine. A few friends from town will be staying with us for a short while."

"How long is a short while?"

"'Til the massacre in the city comes to an end...I suppose."

The back door of my house flung open.

Madame stopped on the top step and yelled, "Neveah, you must have a death wish!"

I turned around. "I beg your pardon!"

"She'll kill you over him!"

Cason smiled. "Madame, is that you?"

"Aye! She thinks you're dead!" Madame walked back inside, leaving the door wide open.

A swift flash of a silver leaf glimmered in Cason's eyes. "I think I'll eat inside this morning."

Drawn to the crushed mint and rosemary sweating from his robust arms drifting up my nose, I held onto his strong, overworked biceps, knowing it'd be the last time I'd have the chance.

"What will you tell them?" My fingers lightly pressed on the muscle exposing itself below the hem of the arm of his t-shirt.

"The truth," he said. "Don't worry. I'll protect you. I owe you that much."

Sadly, I had fallen in love with the king of the Silver Leaf Clan, knowing his broken heart belonged to someone else. As he walked ahead of me into the house, I followed him inside, slowly inhaling the scent of cedar wood draped across his shoulders, bracing myself for the blow I saw that very morning to hit me in the face—missing him before he told me goodbye.

CHAPTER 68

THE COMEBACK

CASON

MADAME ENCLOSED my hand with hers. "Yare the living embodiment of a sight for sore eyes." Her clammy palms tapped the back of my hand like an old grandmother happy to see one of her own. "How long ya been hiding out here? And why?"

I sighed. "I've been back for a few weeks now. The why is a story you wouldn't believe, because I still don't believe it myself."

"After seeing the bond ya had with Ms. V, I have to know. Tell me everything."

I slid my hand from between hers and gestured we sit. Neveah stood in the opening of the kitchen entrance, biting her nails with her eyes dead set on the back of my head. The hairs on my neck erected from the nervous energy I could feel from her and the disappointing glare Madame gave her.

"My brother and I completed what we set out to do in Japan, then on the final night, I was wounded. Knocked from behind and left for dead. Some men following us took me to a healer who saved my life. I was down for at least two weeks. Blurred vision. Excruciating pain. Headaches from direct sunlight. But the miracle worker managed to nurse me back to full consciousness. Once my surroundings became clear and I could walk without falling to my knees with a migraine, I insisted I make it back home. I was so worried about everyone. My sisters. My brothers. My staff. My V."

"You and I both know the latter is capable of taking care of herself. She was distraught when she received word of ya death, ya know."

"That's what concerned me the most."

"What's dat?"

"The messenger delivering the news."

Madame scowled. "I don't follow."

"My brother was my attacker. My own flesh and blood betrayed me… attempted to kill me and left me for dead in an overnight camp. If it weren't for the spies following us, I would be a ghost talking to you right now. Anyhow, the healer patched me as best she could, prayed over me day and night in a candlelit room until the light from the sun coming through the windows no longer tortured my eyes. She filled me with herbs and concoctions to make me healthy enough for the journey back here. But when I finally returned, I was met with great disappointment."

"Do tell."

"I wasn't sure who I could trust in my clan, so I kept my return quiet until I was ready to confront the Cain to my Abel. Then, I sought out Vanity. The streets said she was being protected by my liaison, Keshell Martin."

Madame adjusted herself in her seat as her friend began singing French words in a fast-paced rhythm, chanting as she waved her hands and throwing around finger symbols like she was casting a spell.

"Is your friend alright?" I asked.

"Cason, meet Domini. *Thee* very skilled witch dat broke the link between Ms. V and Ria Lucia."

I nodded. "Nice to meet you."

"Enchanté."

My voice slightly raised of excitement. "You broke the link?"

Domini lifted her chin with a smug grin across her lips.

"So, she's free?"

"Oui."

"So much has happened. What were you saying just now? Casting a spell, or…"

"I curse that evil name you speak."

"Keshell?"

Domini repeated the chant faster this time.

Madame informed me. "She thinks of Mr. Martin and his fortress as a place of pure darkness."

"The dark prince!" Domini shouted.

I huffed. "To come home and find my love had taken up with him made me wish my brother's attempt on my life was successful. He and I had a sort of friendship."

"Friends with a vampire?" Domini spit into her fingers and threw the words in the air."

"Well, an understanding. I introduced him to Vanity as a connect for backup in taking out Adela. But when I showed up to his place, he refused to tell me where I could find her, then said to me, "Tings have changed since ju left, Silva. She now belongs to me, and I will make her my bride. Ju two were never a good match. I knew it the moment ju brought her to me."

"I disagree. I've been around ya two. He's dead wrong," said Madame.

"Dead, alright," Domini muttered.

Neveah sighed behind me, then stormed off into the kitchen. Madame's eyes narrowed at her fading footsteps. "So ya came here?"

I dropped my head. "I had nowhere else to turn. I needed to lay low, properly heal, and gather all the information I could on who was with me —or against me. So I came here. Neveah welcomed me with open arms and took excellent care of me."

She crept back to the room at the mention of her name.

"I'm sure she did," Domini whispered to Madame.

"Madame, outside, you said Vanity would cause harm to Neveah. Does that mean she's resurfaced?"

"Saw her for the first time in a month *dis* morning. She sent us out here for shelter for whatever she's planning tonight and for Neveah's insight. Though, I'm sure she wasn't expecting I'd report she was holding *you* up out here." Madame looked at me cross. "The battle has begun, as I'm sure yare aware."

"Where?"

"Scout Island."

I turned to Neveah. "Have you anything to share about what's going to happen tonight?"

"Besides massive bloodshed? No. All I see is death, blackness, and storms."

I grabbed Madame's hands. "Let me be the one to warn her."

CHAPTER 69
THE GIFT
NEVEAH

WHEN I HEARD Cason say he was ready to reunite with Vanity, my heart fluttered, and the night his handsome face appeared on my doorstep all those weeks ago resurfaced.

I took it as a sign he was a gift from God. A gift for me.

"Come." I waved him inside.

I couldn't believe he was standing in front of me. Big, strong, handsome, and vulnerable. Sadness crippled the light in him, buried deep within the manly exterior pacing my floors in search of comfort.

I turned on the lamp in the front room. "Please, have a seat."

A deep exhale sighed from his mouth. "Thank you for letting me inside."

"How long were you out there?"

"A few hours. I was camped out behind your shed, contemplating how to present myself when I look like this." He pointed to his dirty boots with spots of blood splattered on the toe and in the laces. "I'll pay for any mess I've tracked inside…once I'm able to safely return to my house."

"Don't worry about that. What's going on, Cason? My vision showed me that you would be attacked while in Japan."

"Your vision was correct. Did you see who my attacker was?"

"Unfortunately, I didn't see a face. But how are you here?"

"Grace, mercy, prayer, and it must not have been my time."

"I'm glad it wasn't. I've been beside myself for not telling you I saw you lying in a pool of blood near a creek. Every night, I've wondered if I had gone against the rules and told you what I saw, if you'd have changed your mind about going."

"I've been in N'awlins long enough to know there are rules to what you do. I wouldn't want to be the reason you lose your gift." He smiled.

I lowered my head to hide the rosy color blooming in my cheeks and inquired about his injury. "I saw you limping when you walked in, so I won't ask if you're okay. How can I help?"

He struggled to raise his arm, winding it around in a circle. "I would say find me a healer, but I don't know who I can trust. I'm hoping I can trust you."

"You can. I won't tell anyone you're here. I'll do research while I'm at work and get what you need."

"Does that mean I can stay out in the shed?"

"I wouldn't put you out there when you're not well. You can stay in the spare room."

"Are you sure? I would be grateful to not have to sleep under the stars."

"I'd love the company. While I enjoy the peace of staying far out of the city, it gets lonely out here."

"I promise I'll repay you whatever I owe as soon as..."

"You won't owe me anything. It's my pleasure. Let me show you to the guest room."

Cason limped behind me to the other side of the house with the stench of marsh mud, smoke, and wood soaked into his pores. But I still couldn't find anything wrong with him. He was perfect, clean or dirty, in my eyes.

"You're the first guest I've had to stay in this room. I hope it's to your liking. The shower is just through here." I guided him to the corner beside the window. "This knob is tricky," I said, turning on the water to the tub. Once the temperature felt warm enough, I backed toward the door. "Stop it when you're ready. It's easier to turn off than it is to turn on. I'll be in my room looking for the biggest t-shirt and pair of sweats I have. Tomorrow, I'll pick you up some clothes while I'm out doing research for your wounds."

He grabbed my hand. "I appreciate it. All of it."

I melted from his touch. The way I tingled from head to toe walking out of his room, words could never do it justice. If I were to say I was floating, I'd be lying because I was flying higher than the atmosphere in the sky where the blue fades to black. And if I were to say I felt aroused, I'd be lying again because I felt more than awakened. I could practically feel him inside of me. His soul. His heart. His body.

When I returned with the garments, I caught him struggling to lift his left arm.

"Let me help you," I offered, stretching the shirt over his bruised chest.

He groaned at the slight movement.

My hand followed its own mind and massaged the fading burgundy discoloration below his tempting pec. Cason didn't see my mouth salivating over his muscular chest in my grasp.

"Does that help?" I asked, pressing the sore spot delicately with my two longest fingers.

"It does," he groaned once more.

"Come. Get in the water."

His pants fell to the floor, his boxers right after, and the beauty of his nude body led me to quietly gasp in my mouth. I swallowed it, holding my breath while marveling at the most gorgeous man, in all his glory, lower his tight, ripped physique into a tub in my house. I held his hand as he eased down into the water, lathered a washcloth, and rubbed the suds across his shoulders, down his back, then up, down, and around his pounding chest.

He moaned and sighed with his eyes closed as if my hands were removing the trauma and pain from within. His head fell back as his muscles relaxed to the intense scrub of the cloth separating his tempting flesh from mine.

I reached for the bottle of shampoo from the shelf, cleaning his long locks and scraping my nails gently against his scalp. I was wet with desire as a low howl escaped his lips, and his dick hardened, peeking above the pool of water his body heat kept from turning cool.

My arm shivered at the sight of his blossomed tip creating ripples in the water around it. Cason felt the vibration transcend on his head. He opened his eyes, looked at his engorged cock begging for my caress, then leaned back in the tub with a flushed face and modest grin.

"I should apologize. Your hands have stirred an eruption it seems." He stared into my eyes.

I froze. Conversing with myself in my head, fighting with the devil and an angel advising me on my next move.

"Touch it. He wants you to touch it. He needs you to touch it. Look at him. You know you want to feel the sturdiness of it in your hands." The devil winked at me.

"Yes, I do."

The angel smiled at me. "Neveah, think before you act. It's his first night in your home. You could make him feel unwelcome being forward and weak to lust. Breathe in. Breathe out."

"Breathe on it," the devil cut the angel off. "Take his manliness and suck on it. He'll choose you if you make him feel like a man. Suck. Suck. Suck," the devil whispered.

The angel knocked the devil off my shoulder. "Be a lady. He'll respect you more."

"But what if he invites me to, you know, touch it?"

The devil climbed back up and stabbed my shoulder with his pitchfork and whispered, "Do it."

Finally, I responded, "No need to apologize. I'm happy I could help you relax. How do you feel?"

"Better." He closed his eyes and raised both of his knees against the sides of the tub. "Much better," he said, sitting cocked and wide with his member dancing back down into the water.

I don't think that's an invitation to play out my desires.

"Good." I smiled. "I'll leave you now so you can relax while the water is warm. Just call my name if you need anything."

Please call my name and take me in your arms.

He grunted with his eyes still closed. "Neveah. Thank you."

For weeks I waited for the invitation as we took care of each other's needs. Him tending to the upkeep of the grounds, and me his health. The most we shared were dinners and furtive smiles across the table while my mind ran wild and wished he would toss the plates and wine glasses to the floor, mount me on his cock, and defile me on my dining room table. But my wish never happened. Cason never once stopped being a respectful gentleman while, in the heat of the night, I craved he would give in to his carnal nature and make beastly love to me.

After the many nights I tossed and turned with his face as the first and last image on my mind, I feared being rejected by him. For my lack of gumption and fear of unreciprocated feelings would forever stain my heart.

I wondered if I had kissed him on the first night he allowed me to bathe him and confessed that I loved him, would he reconsider leaving? It was my fault I woke up mere feet away from the man I considered a gift from the heavens every morning and not once said what I had hoped he would figure out for himself. But when he announced he wanted to be by that vampire's side and return to battle, regret consumed me. Regret for not telling him how grateful I was to the moon and stars that he chose me as refuge. Regret I never said those three little words.

He had no idea how grateful I was to love someone again, and that someone was him, Cason, the alpha wolf, set to reclaim his title as the Silver Leaf King. I'd rescind my gift to live with him as mine throughout my days, if only he were mine to have.

As he set out on his journey to battle the darkness plaguing our city, we shared one final private moment on my doorstep.

"I'll be here, waiting for good news," I said, shying away from the rehearsed phrase *return to me.*

Gently, his strong hand raised my chin, and he kissed my thirsty lips under the moonlight. "Thank you for everything," he said, gazing into my eyes.

I knew then that he was aware of my feelings. For a quick moment, I grasped onto hope that he would say he would come back to me when the violence was over.

"I'd do it again," I said, dropping a tear from the corner of my eye.

Cason wiped it away, ran his thumbs across my cheeks, kissed me once more on my forehead, then disappeared into the night.

CHAPTER 70
THE NIGHT
VANITY

KESHELL'S ARMS STRETCHED WIDE. The cracking of his old bones brought a chuckle I hid below a grin.

"Is *Sleeping Beauty* fully rested and ready to fight?"

"Uh-oh. I recognize that look in your eyes. What have you done?"

"Nothing major. Just sounded the alarm, burned down Adela's mansion, took out a handful of pale fuckers with the assistance of the sun. You know. Queen shit."

A sinister snicker echoed from where he rose. "So, we don't have much time."

"We do not."

I blinked, and he was in my face, stroking my cheek and holding my gaze with a mix of emotions pouring from his eyes into mine.

"Stay close to me tonight." He kissed my lips with his eyes open. "I won't risk losing the woman I love."

I stood there silent, processing the moment.

Boom. Boom. Boom. His guard beat on the door. "Sir, they're here."

"Who's here?" I asked.

He smiled, leading me to the door. "You'll see."

A small troop lined up in rows outside in the courtyard. The leader stepped forward, and the company relaxed at ease.

"Cousin." Keshell shook his hand.

"This must be her."

"Yes, meet our vampiress, Vanity."

"Vanity tonight. Lauren in the morning. Nice to meet you."

"Colman." He reached for my hand. "Happy to assist you tonight." He turned to Keshell. "My army is spread out in the woods. No word from my lookout on Adela's arrival."

"She has a flyer who will snitch on their location," I told him.

"Then we better get moving," Colman urged Keshell.

He whistled, and vampires hopped from the rooftop and out of the shadows in numbers I had never seen before in the ward.

"Where did they come from?" I inquired.

"They've always been here—protecting me, protecting us."

Colman led the parade with his agents in step behind him. Keshell and I marched on the third line with his ward of vamps covering us from the rear. He led us into the woods from a back road where one of his lookouts waited for us to arrive.

"Report."

"They began trickling in the main entrance, setting up on the west field. I received word that they started a fire in the center and set a border."

I scurried next to Colman's side. "That I *will* cross."

"She's had a run-in with the flyer. Seen him around?" Colman looked back at Keshell.

"It's a clear night. No sight of him." The lookout puckered his lips.

"Yet," I added.

"Tap in if you do." Colman signaled for the troop to trail ahead.

Half a mile of trekking through moss-covered mud and weeds toiling around crooked vines the color of butternut squash, Colman's fist raised. The troop stopped marching in unison.

"How many?" Keshell asked.

"At least ten on the right."

"Another ten on the left. Any way of knowing if they're yours before I lose my shit?"

Colman's chiding voice answered, "They're not mine."

Keshell laid his hand on my shoulder and flinched at Colman. "We'll take out the spies. Wait here."

"You've got five minutes. Then I'm coming in after ya."

"Be back in three."

I tiptoed behind Keshell to see what he could do besides present himself as some stone-cold killer. One man taking on twenty vamps…this I had to see.

He waltzed into the woods bare-handed like a lost animal looking to find its way home. "I know you're there," he said.

A branch cracked three yards away on the left. Keshell remained in his position. Three pale ones positioned above him in the trees, and waited for him to move to attack him from behind. Keshell surprised them with a move to the right and disappeared in the thicket of the overlapping branches hanging low near the ground. Two headless bodies crunched the dead leaves, and the three vamps I spotted in the tree jumped down.

Keshell landed on his feet behind them. "Looking for me?"

The big-eyed surprise on their faces was comical as they slid on the turf and attempted to turn around. Keshell rushed at them as their pointed toes were twisting to about face, and he snatched out the hearts of the two on the outer edge while biting the neck of the vamp in the middle.

His blood-soaked hands released the beating hearts ticking their final pump and dropped the vamp screaming from his bite to his knees.

"I didn't want to," it begged as the other five closed in on him between his 9 and 3 o'clock.

"I am not of mercy." He detached his head from its shoulders.

"The dark prince, all alone in the woods without his bodyguards. *Tut, Tut, Tut*. What are the odds?" spoke one of the approaching vamps forming a circle around him.

"I still like my chances." Keshell leaped above the trees in flight.

"Motherfucker," I mumbled erroneously, not low enough, bringing attention upon myself.

The vamps' eyes shifted in my direction.

I waved. "Which one of you were talking shit just now?"

The ringleader clothed in a long charcoal coat in the middle lunged at me with the other four on his coattails. All I saw were pasty alabaster faces rushing toward me with hunger in their eyes—the hunger to please their master and rise in the ranks with the delivery of my head.

With a grin on my face, I threw the first assailant into his comrade on his right and cleared an opening to slide between the other three. Swiftly, they changed their trajectory toward me, centering myself in their cypher. Their eyes lit up with the assumption I'd positioned myself in error—

moving too fast for their own good. Too fast to notice my hand reaching over my back.

Schling! I pulled my sword from the sheath, cut through the night air, and sliced off one, two, three heads as I swirled around once, dusting up leaves from the surface between us.

As their bodies thudded one by one, the other two stopped in their tracks. *Thump!* A body fell between me and the two vamps rethinking their approach. Their necks lowered to view the slain victim, and Keshell appeared behind them, then shoved his fists through their backs.

"I told you to wait with the others."

I stepped over the body he dropped between us. "Just thank me so we can go."

"Thank you for what?" His hands clenched onto their hearts.

I placed my hands on their shoulders and detached their bodies from the dying hearts in Keshell's hands. "You obviously needed my help, *Keshell Kent.* You didn't tell me you could fly. What other secrets are you keeping from me?"

The last of the ten dropped next to the slain body.

"Recognize that one?" Keshell redirected my attention with a question to avoid answering mine.

My boot flipped his body over. "Was he shocked he wasn't the only flyer in the sky?"

"I'll never forget the look on his face when I cut him off."

"This is good." I shook my head. "Adela may have us outnumbered, but now she doesn't have the advantage of the sky over us."

"I do what I do for you, my vampiress."

I scoffed through a grin. "Let's get back. Colman might need our help."

Keshell raised his chin. "I doubt that."

Colman exclaimed in a whisper behind me, "Are you two having a lover's quarrel over here or something? We're clear to enter."

I rolled my eyes at Keshell wiping blood on his black trousers. "You expect me to believe he took out ten pale ones all by himself when it took the two of us together to take out this lot?"

Keshell nudged his head at the flyer stretched out, turning misty gray in the face. "You mean eleven. And I didn't need your help."

CHAPTER 71
THE COMMENCEMENT

VANITY

KESHELL TOOK me by the hand as we followed Colman's lead. The crust of dried blood flaking on his fingertips tickled my knuckles along the route, picking up the remaining members of his followers and his cousin's army, ready to fight in my honor.

The farther north we marched, the larger our army grew, tripling in size, if not more. The burnt stench of grass, mud, and death filled the air the closer we approached the end of the woods. Spies fled across the field, warning of our arrival, and a faint chant became clear once we exited the brush and stepped out in the open.

"Bow, bow, bow," they chanted like a zombie choir.

The drawn border between us spelled Adela's name in fire. Above it, a massive army stood cheek by jowl behind her red-velvet cape draped around her shoulders with the hood lowered to showcase her crown-shaped hair braided below a ruby-and-gold tiara.

A staff with fire burning at the peak occupied her hand. She stood too far away to see her face, but as the chanting came to a halt, her regal, raspy voice roared across the field.

"You're outnumbered. You've seen the damage I've caused downtown. Luckily for them, I've re-routed my army here tonight. But for how long depends on the submission of the one calling herself *the vampiress*." A sinister laugh croaked between her lips. "Show yourself!"

Keshell and his top two guardsmen, alongside Colman and his second line unit, stood on the front line. Clanging chains and buzzing whispers traveled across the turf like a swarm of bees.

"Show yourself!" The humiliation of repeating her demand echoed in her voice.

I remained hidden below my hoodie amongst the third line of a blended mix of Keshell's and Colman's men.

"She will soon enough!" Keshell shouted.

"You! The traitor! Truce breaker! I'll begin with your submission! Kneel!"

Keshell stepped forward. "You first!"

Her gasp sent a waft of death toward our camp like a warm breeze. "The pleasure I'm going to have placing your head on my mantel! Allow me to give you a preview, you vile vermin! Bring him out!"

The clanging chains rattled behind her. Soldiers stomped forward from the rear and threw her prisoner of war to the ground. A grunting wail bellowed from it as it rolled, struggling to lift its head. Then, a soldier gripped his hair, lifting his face towards us.

A gasp of my own traveled back across the field. "Carlisle," I muttered below my breath.

"I've waited long enough for this moment!" Adela screamed. "Keshell Martin, meet the first wretched to betray me for that wench!"

Carlisle groaned. He'd been tortured, maimed, beaten, and burnt. Kept alive to appease Adela's sick nature. Used as a lesson to induce fear to her flock.

She snapped her fingers, and his body burst into flames. "To think I allowed you to call yourself a king," she said with an evil smile on her face shifting in the reflection of the blaze.

Carlisle was my enemy, the reason I walked the earth half dead, half alive. But he was also the reason my inner goddess awakened within me. As much as I hated and dreamed of punishing him for what he'd done to me, I took zero pleasure in seeing the public display of cruelty Adela afflicted upon him.

I would have given him an easy death, but he was in the hands of the torture queen he once worshipped. A sadistic, power-hungry bitch. Pure evil and unconscionable.

Carlisle's screams sent a chill down my spine. From where I stood, I exhaled a deep breath, forming it into an invisible twister of wind. It traveled across the field toward him, blowing out the fires lighting Adela's name that separated us and the flames burning Carlisle like a birthday candle.

"Give me his head!" she yelled.

The soldier pulled out his blade, quickly ending his suffering with an anger-filled blow to the back of his neck, then hurled his head across the field.

A faint whistling in the wind approached Adela's first line—this time not as invisible to the eye. Disguised as a second gust, I ran the fastest I ever had since my turning as the sharpness of my blade glistened in the moonlight.

"Protect your queen!" Adela shouted.

Gold and red iron shields formed a barrier around her. They screeched when my blade scratched their surface as I flashed by her first line. *Schwing!* The brief sound echoed for a few seconds as I returned to my side of the field.

My footing landed me at Keshell's side. "Well, I tried to end this without anyone getting hurt," I said, casing my sword after I lowered my hood.

"When I told you to stay by my side, did I say it in my native tongue where you couldn't understand me, or did I say it clearly in English, and you chose to ignore me like you always do?"

"We can fight about this later."

"Oh, shit." Colman pointed to the front line of Adela's army.

Like drops of rain hitting a windshield, one by one her front line fell apart. Heads rolled from their bodies like dominos.

"You did that?" Colman pointed to me.

"As I was saying, if her guards hadn't shielded her, we wouldn't have to fight tonight. But blood has been drawn. Let's get this over with, shall we?"

CHAPTER 72

THE STRATEGY

VANITY

COLMAN'S FIST held steady above his head. The movement of his troops behind us settled, and the indistinct chatter roared into heightened screams of rage. His fingers spread half an inch wide, and his unit grunted with the taste of violence on their tongues. He pointed forward, and they charged past us like a rolling bullet train.

Keshell's militia filled in the empty spaces behind us, growling with anticipation to receive the order.

I huffed. "What are you waiting on?"

"Colman is assessing her play. Adela's done this for years. We need to know if she's stuck on her old tactics. Just wait for his signal."

I blinked, and in a flash, the line that arrived with Colman retreated and headed back toward us.

"Now!" Keshell yelled.

The vamps huddled behind us spread out, and the pale ones in the middle leaped high above the battleground. Flamed arrows met a few of them midair. As those that were hit fell short of the line, the rest landed into the midst of Adela's army waiting to enter the madness. Blasts from grenades reduced the number of our foes to our advantage.

A gracious smile curved on the side of my lips as Keshell flicked his tongue behind his teeth.

"Don't get too excited," he said.

"I'm not. But I can't hide the joy it brings me to see those black auras cascading that side of the field like a black cloud thinning across the sky. My odds of getting to the gnarled one hiding behind her broken shields are looking pretty good."

"Vanity, this is a portion of her army."

"You think I don't see the ones hiding in the trees?"

"Good eye." Keshell whistled to his top hitter. "Lead half of the team to the right side of those trees." He signaled for Colman's first line leader to step forward. "You, lead the rest of my men to the left. Go out the gate and hit those trees from behind."

"Yes, sir." Both of their eyes turned redder than marinara.

Keshell laced his hands around me. "You and I will attack another way. Hold on."

We flew above our troop racing out of the gate, then shot up into the sky. My breath was taken away by the clashing of bodies and blood-stained field darkening the green of the land on one side, and the low-lit city on the other.

"Amazing how peaceful the city looks at night from this view." Keshell nodded toward Bourbon.

"At least the people took heed to the warning and stayed inside."

"They are counting on us to end the nightmare." He glided through the clouds toward the crown of enemy territory. "Listen."

"To what?"

"The silence comin' to an end."

Keshell dove down at full speed like a black *Superman* into the fold, puncturing the unsuspecting mob as he soared through the debris while our gang attacked them from each end. As the branches scratched my bare legs, I let go of Keshell and swung around the bark with my feet, landing on the chest of a tree mongerer in flight on his ass.

Grasping at the falling leaves like straws, he fell to the ground. *Crack.* My boot pierced through his neck as I descended on top of him.

Slashing my way through the horde of chaos that arose in the swampy woodlands, I fought my way toward Adela, drawing blood with my bare fingernails with the hunger for bringing her down increasing by the second.

With one goal in mind, I reached the edge of the moss-covered towering oaks, met with more of Adela's army reacting to the surprise attack. Swiftly, I unsheathed my sword, chopping men draped in black and red in half, covering them with their own worthlessness until I backed myself into a corner against a patchouli-scented wide bark soaked in guts.

I squirmed at the slime slathering on my skin, calculating the numbers surrounding me, carefully stepping forward as a bat swooped low in my peripheral.

"Attack," I muttered.

Swarms of bats shrieked as they sloped in flocks, picking apart the bandits closing in on me. I slid forward on my knees, whipping my blade like a lasso, sailing past the severed limbs falling at my backside. The bats prolonged their feast from my order, plucking at the remaining soldiers in the forest battling Keshell.

I pushed forward toward the red-velvet cape, looking forward at the action on the field. Soldiers spotted me on the move and encased her with their armor.

I put my sword away. "So you're not gonna fight me fair after all this time? We're long overdue for a one-on-one, don't you think? Let me get a good look at you."

"Silly girl," Adela's voice echoed from behind the steel protecting her. "This isn't the Wild Wild West. I am a queen. I do not duel with peasants. You, on the other hand, have been busy running around like the low-born you are, fighting like a belligerent animal." A snarky laugh resounded from her lips. "Calling yourself the vampiress."

"Wow. You said a lot just now that should have offended me. If I didn't know any better, I'd say you were trying to hurt my feelings. Too bad I know who I am."

"An abomination is what you are!"

"Wrong again. I am the end of you." I charged forward.

The soldiers closed the gap from which she spoke.

"Fight me!" I screamed, kicking the shields.

Lost in my fury, I pursued Adela's defense, neglecting my offense. Her soldiers fleeing the coppice surged me from behind and the side. I kicked the one closest to me backward into the lot approaching me on the ground just as more stacked on top of me like a quarterback with the ball on the one-yard line.

Below the pile up, I could hear Adela shouting, "Show her who you serve!"

Through broken spots, I could see her for the first time and understood the appeal of her beauty versus her character. It pained me to be so close and not get my hands on the crown braided on her head, so I stretched forward, wishfully thinking my reach would pull her closer.

Then, I saw the unhinged glare in her eyes up close. She snapped her fingers. The mound on top of me burst into flames, screaming like raging pigs.

I shouted up at them, "That is what you serve!"

I wiggled below the weight pinning me to the ground as the black from the spreading fire and their auras melded together with the smoke. Then, buried below the heat-brazen bodies, the load turned lighter, and I could see the navy in the sky.

Hang tight my love, his voice spoke to me from the grave.

Cling. "Huah," a grunt moaned, throwing the bodies into the steel of Adela's armor, pushing her toward the field.

A chill overwhelmed me from head to toe. *Cason. I hear you reaching out to me from the other side. I promise you, this is not my end.*

I know it's not, he said through our telepathic connection. *Did he tell you I came looking for you?*

I kicked and threw the remaining pale ones covering me into the air and met the most beautiful, silver glowing eyes I'd ever seen.

"Cason?" My voice fluttered.

"Where have you been hiding, my love?"

CHAPTER 73

THE BADASS

VANITY

UNABLE TO HURDLE into his arms, resentment ached and pounded in my chest. My back brushed against his, and I became weak from being near him, nearly losing focus of the task at hand as Adela's men surged at us like waves in Waimea Bay.

Together, we tag-teamed to free ourselves, speaking to each other through our linked thoughts.

Hurry up and finish these fuckers off. I have to hold you in my arms to know this is real—that you are real, I streamed into his mind.

Baby, I'm real. I went through hell to get back to you, Cason growled, taking off the heads of two vampires with one swing of his hand, while the other ripped another's chest clean. *Is that increased heartbeat for me or this battle?*

You. I missed you like crazy.

Keshell said you belong to him now.

He said what?!

The rage in me grew tenfold as I heard those words. I turned up the heat, retrieved my blade once more, and cleared a path for Cason and me to escape the oncoming foot traffic. "Follow me," I said, leading him to the hillside past the forest slowing down with violence as the enemy was being taken out.

I brushed his heavy brows with my fingers and inhaled the woodsy scent seeping from his pores.

"You came back to me."

Cason stroked my face with a delicate touch. "My Vanity. I can't wait to get you home and make up for lost time."

"I didn't believe you were dead. But then I had a vision of Sana hitting you on the head. I was going to kill him, but Ria Lucia showed up out of nowhere, and I had to put my vengeance on hold."

"I'm glad you didn't. He's my brother. And I forgive him."

I sighed, staring into his eyes. "Well, I don't, but I will respect your wish since you survived somehow."

"I need to tell you about your power of three."

"I'm in tune with the wind, the earth, and water."

"They all have one thing in common." He raised one brow. "They can put out fire."

I exclaimed in a whisper, "Adela's fires!"

He nodded.

"We have so much to catch up on."

He lifted me in his arms and pressed his buttery lips against mine, satisfying the craving my taste buds thought they'd never savor again.

His tongue stretched into my mouth as mine coiled around his. "Mmm," he moaned. In that moment I couldn't feel the cold-blooded part of me. I was equally warm, exploding inside from that of my lover's return.

"Vanity," he whispered.

"Yes, Cason."

"There's fire in your eyes."

I held onto his lips, swallowing his words. "You've seen them turn red."

"No, my love, your eyes have two small red fires burning in them." Cason stepped back.

Keshell approached from the west side of the forest.

"How are we looking, Keshell?"

Cason's eyes turned silver, growling at him creeping on us in the dark.

"My goddess, it seems we've leveled the playing field."

Cason's growl deepened to a low roar.

I placed my hand on Cason's chest, and Keshell's eyes turned to blood. "Do we have any more of those explosives?"

Keshell nodded, then lowered his stance. "Shh. Someone's lurking about."

A twig snapped yards away, and he dashed into the trees with Cason on his heels. He hissed, and Cason groused, pulling him backward into his stone-pecked chest, and they tumbled to the ground.

"The fuck are ya doin', Silvaaaaaa?" Keshell hissed.

"That's my sister." Cason roughed him up by his collar.

"Brother?" Homare lowered her sword. "It is you." She ran to Cason and helped him up from the ground. "I felt a familial presence and couldn't make sense of it. But it really is you."

Cason hugged his sister. "We don't have time for a family reunion right now. We've got evil to kill."

"We took out a few lurking along the route here." Homare pointed behind her.

"The pack is with you?"

Sana, Shun, Juni, and Akina stepped forward from the shadows. All but Sana ran to greet Cason. His siblings patted his back and warmed up to him, then looked back at Sana.

"Brother," said Cason.

"Brother," Sana replied, then leered in my direction.

Homare twisted her nose. "What's going on with you two?"

Cason exhaled. "No time to get into it right now. We're surrounded by the enemy."

"There's at least a thousand more planning a sneak attack."

"Are they ours?" I asked Keshell.

"Hers." His head nudged toward the field. "We must warn the others."

Cason barked, "Vanity is not leaving my side."

"Vanity can speak up for herself."

I shot off toward the action while they beat their chests in search of the gold armor. Adela was surrounded by rows of her men protecting her in the center, drawing our squadron into a trap.

Keshell ran on my heels. "Your commitment to not listen is a turn-on." He shot up in the air.

Behind me, Cason connected with my mind. *Don't do that again. And be careful, my love.*

I smiled at his doting affection and increased my speed to that of a Dracula ant outpacing a cheetah, then clashed into the commotion as Keshell swooped down from the sky. He picked pieces of the armor apart. Adela's troops tightened their barricade as fire arrows shot at him from the center.

I hung low, crawling between gore-saddened and wounded legs, digging my nails in the dirt, becoming one with the earth. The ground rumbled. All the men on the battlefield whooed in confusion, and Adela's barrier shifted out of sync.

"Earthquake!" a few shouted over the crackling of the rocks.

"Keep fighting!" Colman ordered the troops.

Hollers and riots resounded from the rear.

Was that you? Cason asked.

Yes.

Careful not to cause a flood. We've seen enough of that.

Noted.

They're closing in on us.

I drew my blade, slicing the ankles of my foes holding Adela's line. "Aaarrrrrgggghhh!" Cason rose above the mass, transitioning into his feral form, howling as he shook off bloodthirsty vampires leaching onto him like flies. His statuesque build and silver coat gleamed for a brief moment just as a cloud rolled over the moon.

Cutting down the enemy gnawing and tugging at me, I cleared a path toward Homare.

"Stick close to Cason for me."

Homare wound her Katana sword curved sharp blade backward, trapping a pale one on the point. "Where will you be?"

"Pulling that bitch from behind those shields. She'll try to flee when the sun comes up."

"Got it."

"I'll get you close to him, but I'm gonna need you to trust me."

Homare slashed the face of a vamp approaching us, shifted her blade to the other hand, and separated a head from another.

"Do your thing," I said, holding her from the back.

I rushed the surprise attack closing in on us from the rear, my blade sticking out to the left, Homare's to the right. We divided the onslaught in half, creating a splattered bloody road leading up to the woods.

"You good?" I asked her.

"Better than good. Let's go again."

We ambushed two more rows, divvying up the numbers aiming to surround the chaos from the inside and out. Cason could be seen bobbing and weaving, staining his coat with blood dripping from his poisonous bites. Beside him stood Akina throwing punches, Sana pulling out throats, and Shun collecting blood on his staff as they pummeled the dead ones as their own separate unit.

Junichiro cleared a section, grumbling as he turned. His silver-and-white coat was speckled with maroon flecks, and mud covered his tail. His stature was inches smaller than Cason, and his build was less robust.

Homare and I landed near Juni and joined in with the brawl covering them at every angle. Back to back, we took on the invasion with timed rhythmic slices and dices, meeting swords as we severed the sides of a parasite's head clawing at Cason's back.

His eyes shone at me, and I felt the heat within me rise to a higher temperature.

I'll be right back, I messaged him.

He squealed with blood dripping from his muzzle. *You're glowing.*

As I examined the electric violet current worming around me, my intuition amplified. I could sense those around me growing feeble and the angst of the battle wearing thin on the pack.

Keshell appeared, wiping blood from his lips. "My goddess, your aura is shining the most vibrant I've ever seen," he said in a softer tone than normal.

"I don't think it's my aura. Cason can see it."

He grunted. "The sun will rise soon."

"I have a plan"—I turned to Akina—"if you trust me."

"I trust you." She nodded.

Akina mounted Junichiro. He hopped around the horde, crushing both teams along his path. Akina lassoed her spike and thrashed it into the shields protecting Adela. *Boom.* She knocked, shifting the armor. *Boom.* The armor shattered on the east wing.

Swoosh.

Keshell swooped down and grabbed Adela from the center.

"Our queen!" her men shouted.

Colman's men threw fire bombs inside.

Bang. Bang. Bang. The barricade exploded into pieces, blowing Adela's top men to bits.

Keshell rose in the air with Adela hooked to his claws, then burst into flames. It was the first time I heard his deep voice rise as the cries of his inflamed existence lit above the massacre.

Adela descended to the ground.

Ploof.

Keshell fell within inches from her, calling to me in distress.

Wooh.

I blew a cold wind around him rolling on the grass, then raced to a vulnerable Adela scrambling from her fall.

She glared at me like an inferior futile feline, reeking of cooled charcoal and diesel fumes. A ball of fire shot at me like bullets from her fingers.

I sashayed to the side. "You missed."

She threw a second ball.

I caught it with my left hand and shuffled it with my right. "In all your years of terror on this land, have you ever thought how you want to die?" I pitched the ball of fire back at her.

"Iiiiyyy," she groused, then rose to her feet. "You can't kill me."

Keshell sighed behind me, tending to his injuries. "Don't trust a word she says."

I scoffed. "Thanks. Experience has already taught me that lesson."

His eyes narrowed toward me.

A fierce gaze between Adela and me locked as the unmistakable tension reached its height. Her fangs grew long and sharp. Her nails cracked as they stretched from her tips like winding vines coiling around a lichen-covered root. The youthful appearance of her face transitioned to a wide-mouth goblin.

I sneered. "I knew you were a gnarled one."

She lunged at me, swift and deadly, swinging her loose claws at me from both sides. I dodged her strike by attacking her low with a lightning-fast blow to her waist with my sharpest nail. Her arms swung back, slicing the end of my locks. My senses were so heightened I could feel them detach from me.

I turned around and cast flames to the broken pieces of hair. "Someone believes in Voudon." Adela grinned.

"As do you." I leaped forward.

We exchanged quick, sneaky jabs, testing each other's power and skill.

"Stop playing with her!" Keshell shouted.

"You'll regret the side you chose!" Adela spat at Keshell, refusing to back down.

I reached for my sword. Her long claw wrapped around my fist, forbidding it to unsheathe. A flurry of kicks, punches, slaps, and scratches ensued between us when I saw my chance and took it. She reached back to whip me like a thunderclap. Her claws flailed out wide to do me in.

I sidestepped and countered by running into her at top speed, placing my nail to her neck, applying pressure so she could bleed out.

"Son of a bitch!" I cursed, struck with a fiery arrow to my thigh.

Adela pointed to the mass, snapped her fingers, and set Junichiro on fire. "They say you can't trust a vampire. Apparently, I couldn't trust a traitorous wolf."

She plunged her lethal fangs into my neck. Her thirst for my blood resembled that of Carlisle's. She was hooked on the taste of me, draining the life force from my veins.

CHAPTER 74

THE VAMPIRESS

VANITY

THE SOUND of flying fists meeting flesh in the background, Juni yowling in agony, and Adela's slurping moans upset my core. I focused on the gray cloud covering the moon and summoned a storm to wash over us.

As the rain put out the wildfires and flames consuming Junichiro, whom I should have let burn, I reached down, pulled out the dagger stuck in my leg, then jammed it into her chest.

Her fangs released their hold of me. Her bloodthirsty groans dispelled into anguish. With a power punch, my fist entered her chest. My fingers clawed for a grip of her heart. Adela backed up before I could hold it in my hand and yank it out.

She attempted to run, stumbling on one leg with her hands tugging on the arrow. A wail from the battlefield entered my soul. I knew that yowl. I could feel that howl burning around my heart as if I had been wounded. Cason had been hurt.

"Aaaaaaahhhhhhhhh!" The piercing notes of my scream paused the commotion surrounding me like a telepath that could control movement. Everyone and everything became still. The rain drops turned to drizzle. The creatures dwelled in fighting positions. The pack fell to their knees.

Cason. Are you okay?

Yes. His voice shrilled. *You'll kill all of us if you hold it any longer.*

After unleashing my siren, the violet light casing my silhouette shone in its vibrancy, forming a thick shield around me. Adela threw fire directly at my coating. The flames dissipated into thin specks of ember as they bounced off the glowing orb's protection. A gold light glowed from my neck, healing my punctured neck and thigh.

"What kind of sorcery is this?"

I approached her slowly. "Sorcery…no. That of a goddess…yes," I said.

Limping away, she curated a fire between us, then formed a ball of fire with both hands and blasted it toward me. I raised the dirt below the fire and covered it, creating a trail of smoke, putting out the blaze before shifting that same dirt in her direction, causing her ball of fire to fall flat.

Energy engulfed me. I was hot with fire but cool with water, air, and the earth simultaneously. My hands motioned in circles as the elements forced themselves to the surface. Streams of fire mixed with swirling water formed with sand particles on the outer edge, that of a brown dust, and wind in the center in the image of a forming tornado united in my hands.

One with the elements, my body whooshed side to side like starlings. "Your reign of terror ends now." I drew my blade, chopped off her head, then set her body on fire, emerging victorious.

Her army dropped to their knees and burst into flames along with her. Keshell retrieved her head rolling near the burnt pits that once spelled her name. He lifted it by the braided hair, then handed it to me. I held the dripping crown up high. The unfallen troops clamored, surging toward us.

"Do ya see how evil she was?" Keshell stared at it. "She bound her army to her fate." He kneeled. "The city will be honored to serve you as its vampiress."

I set the fallen queen's dome on fire and tossed it next to her scorched body, crackling and popping. "It's your job to protect the people of this city, Keshell. It belongs to you now."

He reached for my hands. "Ya mean to us."

I looked him in the eyes. "Keshell."

"So the bond we share means nothing to ya?"

"What we shared is what we shared. And it has run its course."

Cason nudged his muzzle on my back.

Keshell's eyes flamed red at him. "Ya expect me to just let ya go without a fight?"

I brushed Cason's coat and rubbed my face against his fur. "He came back to me from the dead. There is no bigger fight than that. Get your troops home. The sun is coming up. I'll see you around."

The look he gave me felt like a promise I made on his behalf, and something in my bones told me I *would* be seeing him again, and it wouldn't be on sweet terms.

Colman staggered forward. "Vampiress." He curtsied.

"There will be none of that. Keshell will explain. Thank you for assisting me with this win." I shook his hand.

"Cousin, we need to be goin'." Keshell whistled, and their militia stormed out of the park like zombies on speed.

The pack marched over, covered in carnage. Cason whined, nuzzling on me as I rubbed his coat with a gentle stroke. I stretched my arms around him as wide as I could, holding him to ease the pain as he transitioned back to his human form in my arms.

Shun threw him a dirty jacket and butchery-soaked pants from a fallen one laid out in the field to cover himself.

"It's good to have you back, brother." He patted his shoulder.

"Good to be back." Cason leered at Shun.

Once he dressed, I draped my arms across his shoulder. "We have so much to catch up on."

"Yes, we do. I have something for you. It was buried where I was forced to find lodging."

Junichiro interrupted. "What do you mean, *'forced to find lodging'*? Did you not return tonight?"

"No, brother. I had to lay low for a while. We'll talk about it as a family tomorrow."

"Why not now?" Homare stuck her sword in the mud.

Cason and I locked eyes.

"Never mind." She rolled her eyes. "So, what's to come of the blood suckers that just ran out of here?"

"Cason, Homare became leader of the pack in your absence. I think both of you should go to meet with Keshell to discuss the details."

Akina draped her spike over Juni's back. "Wasn't all of this for *you* to be in charge?"

"And I am—temporarily. But I need to leave this place for a while. Tend to some personal business. Get reacquainted with Lauren."

Akina scowled. "Who is Lauren?"

"I am."

Cason gazed into my eyes. *I'd like to get to know Lauren myself. Soon. Real soon. Let's go home.* He took the first step to lead the pack.

I chuckled. "Any chance we can pick up with this conversation later?"

Homare plucked her sword from the mud and wiped it clean on her pants. "I'll let it slide for now…under one condition."

I raised my brows.

"Make it rain, please. I've never craved a bath the way I do now."

Light drops of rain lingered over us until we split down our separate paths. Cason and I entered the home we shared for the first time together in what felt like an eternity. We stripped naked at the door and tossed the soiled clothes off our backs in the fireplace. He ignited a small blaze while I turned on the shower and filled the tub with suds to the brim.

Joining me under the nozzle cleansing the bloodshed off my skin, he sighed. "I can't believe I'm stepping foot in this place again."

My nipples pressed against his chest. "I can't believe you're back in my arms. I drew you a bath. Thought you'd like to soak after tonight."

"We can get in there after we get dirty."

His finger lifted my chin to steal the air from my lips. I covered him with soap and rinsed away the gore from the cords of his taut muscles, massaging his scalp as his dick hardened against my stomach, tracing the cuts and bruises on his strong body.

He winced when I touched the blemish below his pec. I kissed it with an open mouth, then gazed in his eyes as the shower carried the muck down the drain.

"Sometimes you have to lose something to realize what it means to you. I love you, Cason. This time, you don't have to say it first."

He raised my body as if I weighed an ounce and inserted his pipe in my pussy. I exhaled as he grunted, steadying his legs with glowing silver eyes.

"It's senseless how we're mortal enemies but feel this good when we come together."

"Yes." I sighed. "We were made for each other."

He worked me around his cock nice and slow to savor our union for a longer ride, to which I had no complaints. It was everything I missed and longed for in his absence, and I graciously took every jab, happy I was given a second chance.

I laid my head on his shoulder and latched to the nape of his neck. "Tell me, Cason, what's this thing you have for me?"

He grunted. "The cure." His hips glued to mine, stretching his dick deeper inside of my warmth. "Will you take it this time?"

The power I felt from becoming the vampiress was still flowing strong in my veins. Mixed with the heightened sense of the pleasure he returned to me, it felt like the ultimate high.

Encompassed with such enhanced emotions and unmatched dominance, my eyes flashed red, and a curve lifted one side of my mouth. My fangs gently grazed his shoulder, dragging toward his neck. I licked the plump vein pulsing like a drum, then kissed Cason softly on the lips.

While holding the gaze of the silver leaf gleaming in his eyes, I pierced his bottom lip with a gentle graze of my teeth, licked the dot of blood clean and answered him, "In time."

YES! A SEQUEL IS IN THE WORKS!

REVIEWS ENCOURAGE VORACIOUS INTEREST EVERY WHERE TO SUPPORT

ME, THE AUTHOR

I GREATLY APPRECIATE IT

AN AFFAIR ABROAD
T.K. RICHARDS

A TASTE OF THE FORBIDDEN
T.K. RICHARDS

BLEND
T.K. RICHARDS

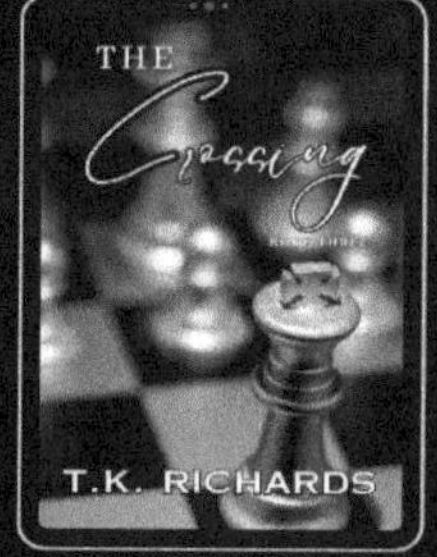
STRAIGHT LINE
BOOK ONE
T.K. RICHARDS

Derailed
BOOK TWO
T.K. RICHARDS

THE Crossing
T.K. RICHARDS

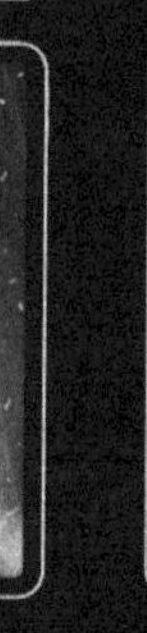

JUKE
INTIMATE EROTIC ADDICTION
T.K. RICHARDS

Lowcountry Legends
T.K. RICHARDS & ALANA KIRKWOOD

THE Vampiress
T.K. RICHARDS

HEAR ME OUT
T.K. RICHARDS

Nikki & Mason
T.K. RICHARDS

EN ROUTE Emery
A NOVEL
T.K. RICHARDS

MY GIFT TO You
TK RICHARDS

CAN'T QUIT you
T.K. RICHARDS

SINS OF THE MOTHER
TK RICHARDS

T.K. RICHARDS is a multi-genre author with popular novels and novellas in several genres of romance including Black, Interracial/Multicultural & Paranormal Romance, Speculative Fiction, Women's Fiction, and Domestic Thrillers.

A graduate of Limestone University, T.K. has honors in Expository Writing, and was also the Poet Laureate of her graduating class. When she is not writing, she is immersed in the world of tennis, and binge watching movies—mostly comedy as she loves to laugh.

For more information about **T.K. Richards**, visit her website at www.tkrichards.com and subscribe to her newsletter at: https://tkrichardsnewsletter.ck.page

Follow **T.K. RICHARDS** on the platforms listed below to interact with her personally:

- instagram.com/t.k.richards
- pinterest.com/TKWrites
- tiktok.com/@tkrwrites
- youtube.com/tkrichards
- goodreads.com/T.k.richards
- bookbub.com/authors/t-k-richards
- amazon.com/author/Tkrichards
- patreon.com/tkrichards
- bsky.app/profile/tkrichards

ACKNOWLEDGMENTS

Thank you to the readers on Kindle Vella for crowning The Vampiress in 2022 and 2023. Spreading the word about your love for this novel is greatly appreciated.

Special thank you to the following for your words of encouragement, support, and assistance in making the print version of The Vampiress exciting to produce, enticing to read, and visually aesthetic:

Racquel Henry
Kimani Lauren
Markeshia Kirksey
Ashley Coleman
Mia Lindler
Net Greene
Monica Manigault
Carolyn Taylor
Wakiza Hutchins
Jenn Lockwood Editing
Zack & Bria & Leon & Jagger & Lianna🤍

If I missed you, I still love you, and thank you for reading my work.